D<small>EATH</small>

At the luxurious Roarke Palace Hotel, a maid walks into suite 4602 for the nightly turndown—and steps into her worst nightmare. A killer leaves her dead, strangled by a thin, silver wire. He's Sly Yost, a virtuoso of music and murder. A hit man for the elite. Lieutenant Eve Dallas knows him well. But in this twisted case, knowing the killer doesn't help solve the crime. Because there's someone else involved. Someone with a more personal motive. And Eve must face a terrifying possibility—the real target may, in fact, be her husband, Roarke. . . .

"Sure to leave you hungering for more."
—*Publishers Weekly*

"The series [is] groundbreaking in its unique combination of futuristic setting, suspense, and romance."
—TheRomanceReader.com

Titles by J. D. Robb

Anthologies

SILENT NIGHT
(with Susan Plunkett, Dee Holmes, and Claire Cross)

OUT OF THIS WORLD
(with Laurell K. Hamilton, Susan Krinard, and Maggie Shayne)

REMEMBER WHEN
(with Nora Roberts)

BUMP IN THE NIGHT
(with Mary Blayney, Ruth Ryan Langan, and Mary Kay McComas)

DEAD OF NIGHT
(with Mary Blayney, Ruth Ryan Langan, and Mary Kay McComas)

THREE IN DEATH

SUITE 606
(with Mary Blayney, Ruth Ryan Langan, and Mary Kay McComas)

IN DEATH

THE LOST
(with Patricia Gaffney, Mary Blayney, and Ruth Ryan Langan)

THE OTHER SIDE
*(with Mary Blayney, Patricia Gaffney, Ruth Ryan Langan, and
Mary Kay McComas)*

TIME OF DEATH

THE UNQUIET
*(with Mary Blayney, Patricia Gaffney, Ruth Ryan Langan, and
Mary Kay McComas)*

MIRROR, MIRROR
*(with Mary Blayney, Elaine Fox, Mary Kay McComas, and
R. C. Ryan)*

DOWN THE RABBIT HOLE
*(with Mary Blayney, Elaine Fox, Mary Kay McComas, and
R. C. Ryan)*

BETRAYAL IN DEATH

J. D. Robb

BERKLEY
New York

BERKLEY
An imprint of Penguin Random House LLC
375 Hudson Street, New York, New York 10014

Copyright © 2001 by Nora Roberts

ISBN 9780425178577

First Edition: March 2001

Printed in the United States of America
23   25   27   29   31   30   28   26   24   22

Cover art by Oyster Pond Press
Cover design by G-Force Design

Carcasses bleed at the sight of the murderer.
—Robert Burton

Honour is sometimes found among thieves.
—Sir Walter Scott

BETRAYAL
IN
DEATH

prologue

A murder was taking place.

Outside the privacy-screened windows, and some forty-six floors below death, life—noisy, oblivious, irritable—rushed on.

New York was at its best on fine May evenings when flowers burst out of beautification troughs along the avenues and spilled from vendors' carts. The scent of them very nearly overpowered the stink of exhaust as street and air traffic clogged both road and skyways.

Pedestrians scurried, strolled, or hopped on people glides, depending on their frame of mind. But many did so in shirtsleeves or the neon-colored T-shirts that were the season's rage in this pretty slice of spring 2059.

Glide-carts sold fizzy drinks in those same violent hues, and the steam from grilling soy dogs rose merrily into the balmy evening air.

Taking advantage of the waning light, the young danced and leaped over the public sports' courts, working up a healthy sweat with balls and hoops and pegs. In Times Square, business in the video parlors was off as customers preferred the streets for their action. But the sex shops and venues held their own.

In spring, many a fancy still turned to porn.

Airbuses carted patrons to the Sky Mall, and ad blimps cruised with their endless stream of chatter, trying to herd yet more into the shopping arenas.

Buy and be happy. And tomorrow? Buy more.

Couples dined alfresco or lingered over predinner drinks, talking of plans, the lovely weather, or the minutiae of their everyday lives.

Life bustled, bloomed, and burgeoned in the city as one was taken above it.

He didn't know her name. It hardly mattered what label her mother had given her when she'd come squalling into the world. It mattered less, to him, what name she took with her when he sent her squalling out of it.

The point was, she was there. In the right place at the right time.

She'd come in to do the nightly turndown in Suite 4602. He'd waited, quite patiently, and she hadn't kept him long.

She wore the smart black uniform and fancy white apron of The Palace Hotel's housekeeping staff. Her hair was neat, as was expected of any employee of the finest hotel in the city. It was shiny brown and clipped at the nape with a simple black bar.

She was young and pretty, and that pleased him. Though he would have followed through in the intended manner if she'd been ninety and hag-faced.

But the fact that she was young, attractive enough with her dusty cheeks and dark eyes, would make the task at hand somewhat more enjoyable.

She'd rung first, of course. Twice, with a slight pause between as required. That had given him time to slip into the generous bedroom closet.

She called out as she opened the door with her passcode.

"Housekeeping," in that lilting, singsong voice people of her trade used to announce themselves to rooms most usually empty.

She moved through the bedroom into the bath first, carrying fresh towels to replace those the occupant, registered as James Priory, might have used since check-in.

She sang a little as she tidied the bath, some bouncy little tune to keep herself company. *Whistle while you work,* he thought from his station in the closet. He could get behind that.

He waited until she came back, had heaped the used towels on the floor for later. Waited until she'd walked to the bed and had finished folding down the royal blue spread.

Took pride in her work, he noted as she carefully formed a long triangle with the bed linens at the left corner.

Well, so did he.

He moved fast. She saw only a blur out of the corner of her eye before he was on her. She screamed, loud and long, but the rooms of The Palace were soundproofed.

He wanted her to scream. It would help get him in the mood for the job to be done.

She flailed out, her hand reaching down for the beeper in her apron pocket. He simply twisted her arm back, jerking it nastily until her scream became a whimper of agony.

"We can't have that, can we?" He plucked her beeper out, tossed it aside. "You're not going to like this," he told her. "But I am, and that's what counts, after all."

He hooked an arm around her throat, lifting her off the ground—she was a little thing, barely a hundred pounds—until the lack of oxygen had her going limp.

He had the pressure syringe of potent downers as a backup, but wouldn't need it with such a tiny woman.

When he released her, and she dropped to her knees, he rubbed his hands together, smiled brilliantly.

"Music on," he ordered, and the swelling sounds of the

aria from *Carmen* he'd already programmed into the entertainment system filled the room.

Gorgeous, he thought, drawing in breath deeply as if he could draw in the notes.

"Well now, let's get to work."

He whistled as he beat her. He hummed as he raped her. By the time he'd strangled her, he was singing.

chapter one

In death there were many layers. Violent death added more. It was her job to sift through those layers and find cause. In cause, to meet justice.

However the act of murder was committed, in cold blood or hot, she was sworn to pursue it to its root. And serve the dead.

For tonight, Lieutenant Eve Dallas of the New York City Police and Security Department wore no badge. It, along with her service weapon and communicator, was currently tucked in an elegant, palm-sized silk purse she considered embarrassingly frivolous.

She wasn't dressed like a cop, but wore a shimmering apricot-hued gown that skimmed down her long, slim body and was sliced in a dramatic V in the back. A slender chain of diamonds hung glittering around her neck. More sparkled at ears she recently, and in a weak moment, had been persuaded to have pierced.

Still more were scattered like raindrops through her short chop of brown hair and made her feel faintly ridiculous.

However glamorous the silk and diamonds made her appear, her eyes were all cop. Tawny brown and cool, they scanned the sumptuous ballroom, skimmed over faces, bodies, and considered security.

Cameras worked into the fancy plasterwork overhead were unobtrusive, powerful, and would provide full scope. Scanners would flag any guests or staff who happened to be carrying concealeds. And among the staff, weaving their way through the chatter to offer drinks, were a half-dozen trained security personnel.

The affair was invitation only, and those invitations carried a holographic seal that was scanned at the door.

The reason for these precautions, and others, was an estimated five hundred and seventy-eight million dollars' worth of jewelry, art, and memorabilia currently on dazzling display throughout the ballroom.

Each display was craftily arranged for impact and guarded by individual sensor fields that measured motion, heat, light, and weight. If any of the guests or staff had sticky fingers and attempted to remove so much as an earring from its proper place, all exits would close and lock, alarms would sound, and a second team of guards hand-selected from an elite NYPSD task force would be ordered to the scene to join the private security.

To her cynical frame of mind, the entire deal was a foolishly elaborate temptation for too many, in too large an area, in too public a venue. But it was tough to argue with the slick setup.

Then again, slick was just what she expected from Roarke.

"Well, Lieutenant?" The question, delivered with a whiff of amusement in a voice that carried the misty air of Ireland, drew her attention to the man.

Then again, everything about Roarke drew a woman's attention.

His eyes, sinfully blue, set off a face that had been sculpted on one of God's best days. As he watched her, his poet's mouth, one that often made her want to lean in for just one quick bite, curved, one dark brow lifted, and his long fingers skimmed possessively down her bare arm.

They'd been married nearly a year, and that sort of casually intimate stroke could still trip her pulse.

"Some party," she said and turned his smile into a fast, devastating grin.

"Yes, isn't it?" With his hand still lightly on her arm, he scanned the room.

His hair was black as midnight and fell nearly to his shoulders into what she thought of as his wild Irish warrior look. Add to that the tall, tautly muscled build in elegant black-tie, and you had a hell of a package. Obviously a number of other women in the room agreed. If Eve had been the jealous type, she'd have been forced to kick some major ass just for the hot and avaricious looks aimed in her husband's direction.

"Satisfied with the security?" he asked her.

"I still think holding this business in a hotel ballroom, even your hotel ballroom, is risky. You've got hundreds of millions of dollars' worth of junk sitting around in here."

He winced a little. "Junk is not quite the descriptive phrase we hope for in our publicity efforts. Magda Lane's collection of art, jewelry, and entertainment memorabilia is arguably one of the finest to ever go to auction."

"Yeah, and she'll rake in a mint for it."

"I certainly hope so, as for handling the arrangements for security, display, and auction Roarke Industries gets a nice piece of the pie."

He was scanning the room himself, and though he was anything but a cop, he studied, measured, and watched even as his wife had.

"Her name's enough to push the bidding far above actual value. I think we're safe in predicting that twice the actual value will make up that pie by the end of things."

Boggling, Eve thought. *Boggling.* "You're figuring people will choke out half a billion for somebody else's things?"

"Conservatively and before the sentiment factors in."

"Jesus Christ." She could only shake her head. "It's just stuff. Wait." She held up a hand. "I forgot who I was talking to. The king of stuff."

"Thank you, darling." He decided not to mention he had his eye on a few bits of that stuff for himself, and his wife.

He lifted a finger. Instantly a server bearing a tray of champagne in crystal flutes was at his side. Roarke removed two, handed one to Eve. "Now, if you've finished eyeballing my security arrangements, perhaps you could enjoy yourself."

"Who says I wasn't?" But she knew she was here not as a cop, but as the wife of Roarke. That meant mingling, rubbing shoulders. And the worst of human tortures in her estimation: small talk.

Because he knew her mind as thoroughly as he knew his own, he lifted her hand, kissed it. "You're so good to me."

"And don't you forget it. Okay." She took a bracing sip of champagne. "Who do I have to talk to?"

"I think we should start with the woman of the hour. Let me introduce you to Magda. You'll like her."

"Actors," Eve muttered.

"Biases are so unattractive. In any case," he began as he led her across the room, "Magda Lane is far more than an actor. She's a legend. This marks her fiftieth year in the business, one which often chews up and spits out those who dream of it. She's outlasted every trend, every style, every change in the movie industry. It takes more than talent to do that. It takes spine."

It was as close as Eve had ever seen him to having stars in his eyes. And that made her smile. "Stuck on her, are you?"

"Absolutely. When I was a boy in Dublin, there was a particular evening where I needed a bit of a dodge off the streets. Seeing as I had several lifted wallets and other pocket paraphernalia on my person and the garda on my heels."

The wide mouth she'd forgotten to dye for the evening sneered. "Boys will be boys."

"Well, be that as it may, I happened to duck into a theater. I was eight or thereabouts and resigned myself to sitting through some costume drama I imagined would bore me senseless. And there sitting in the dark, I had my first look at Magda Lane as Pamela in *Pride's Fall*."

He gestured toward the display of a sweeping white ballgown that shimmered under a firestorm of icy stones. The droid replica of the actor turned in graceful circles, dipped into delicate curtsies, fluttered a sparkling white fan.

"How the hell did she walk around in that?" Eve wondered. "Looks like it weighs a ton."

He had to laugh. It was so Eve to see the inconvenience rather than the glamour. "Nearly thirty pounds of costume, I'm told. I said she had spine. In any case, she was wearing that the first time I saw her on screen. And for an hour I forgot where I was, who I was, that I was hungry or that I'd likely get a fist in the face when I got home if the wallets weren't plump enough. She drew me out of myself. That's a powerful thing."

He avoided interruption by simply aiming a smile or wave in the direction of those who called him. "I went back and saw *Pride's Fall* four times that summer, and paid for it. Well, paid the fee once anyway. After, whenever I needed to be drawn out of myself, I went to the movies."

She was holding his hand now, well able to visualize the boy he'd been, sitting in the dark, transported away by the images flickering on screen.

At the age of eight he'd discovered another world outside the misery and violence of the one he lived in.

And at eight, she thought, *Eve Dallas had been born to a young girl too broken to remember anything that had come before.*

Wasn't it almost the same thing?

Eve recognized the actor. Roarke didn't really go to the movies these days—unless you counted his private theaters—but he had copies on disc of thousands of them. She'd watched more screen in the past year with him than she had in the previous thirty.

Magda Lane wore red. Screaming siren red that painted a stunning and voluptuous body like a work of art. At sixty-three she was just dipping into middle age. From what Eve could see, she was approaching it with a snarl. This was nobody's matron.

Her hair was the color of ripening wheat and tumbled to her bare shoulders in snaking spirals. Her lips, full and lush as her body, were painted the same bold red as her gown. Skin, pale as milk, was unlined and highlighted by a beauty mark just at the outer point of one slashing eyebrow.

Beneath those contrastingly dark brows were eyes of fierce and brilliant green. They landed on Eve coolly, a female to female measuring, then shifted to Roarke and warmed like suns.

She was surrounded by people, and simply shot them a careless smile, then stepped out of the circle, hands outstretched.

"My God, but you're gorgeous."

Roarke took her hands, kissed both. "I was about to say the same. You're stunning, Magda. As ever."

"Yes, but that's my job. You were just born that way. Lucky bastard. And this must be your wife."

"Yes. Eve, Magda Lane."

"Lieutenant Eve Dallas." Magda's voice was like fog, low and full of secrets. "I've been looking forward to meeting you. I was devastated I couldn't make the wedding last year."

"It seems to have stuck anyway."

Magda's brows rose, then the eyes beneath them began to glitter with appreciation. "Yes, it has. Go away, Roarke. I want to acquaint myself with your lovely and fascinating wife. And you're too much of a distraction."

Magda waved him away with one slim hand. Light shot off the diamond on her ring finger like the tail of a comet before she tucked her arm companionably through Eve's.

"Now, let's find someplace where a dozen people won't insist on speaking to us. Nothing more tedious than idle conversation, is there? Of course, you're thinking that's just what you're about to be trapped into with me, but I'll assure you I don't intend to make our conversation idle. Shall I start off by telling you one of my own regrets is that your ridiculously attractive husband is young enough to be my son?"

Eve found herself sitting at a table in the back corner of the ballroom. "I don't see why that would have stopped either of you."

Laughing delightedly Magda snagged fresh flutes of champagne, then shooed the server away. "My own fault. I made a rule never to take a lover more than twenty years older or younger. Stuck with it, too. More's the pity. But . . ." She paused to sip, studying Eve. "It isn't Roarke I want to talk about, but you. You're exactly what I thought he'd fall for when his time came around."

Eve choked on her wine, blinked. "You're the first person who's ever said *that*." She struggled with herself a moment, then gave up. "Why do you say it?"

"You're quite attractive, but he wouldn't have been blinded by your looks. You find that amusing," Magda noted, nodding in approval. "Good. A nice sense of humor's essential when dealing with any man, but particularly one of Roarke's nature."

They were solid looks though, Magda mused. Neither glamorous nor staggering, but solid with good bones, clear eyes, and an interesting dent in the center of a strong chin.

"Your looks might have attracted him, but they didn't snare him. I wondered about that as Roarke has an interest, and an affection, for beauty. So I, having some interest and affection of my own in the man, followed the media on you."

Eve angled her head, a kind of challenge. "Do I pass?"

Amused, Magda ran one scarlet-tipped finger around the rim of her flute, then lifted it to equally bold lips, and sipped. "You're a smart, determined woman who doesn't merely stand on her own feet but uses them to boot whatever asses need booting. You're a physical woman with brains, and a look in your eyes when you glance around an event like this that says: 'What a bunch of nonsense. Haven't we all got something better to do?' "

Intrigued, Eve studied Magda in turn. More here, she realized, than some fluff piece who liked to play make-believe. "Are you a shrink or an actor?"

"Either profession requires solid elements of both." She paused again, sipped again. "My guess is you didn't— don't—give a hang about his money. That would have intrigued him. I can't see you falling at his feet either. If you had, he'd likely have scooped you up and played with you awhile. But he wouldn't have kept you."

"I'm not one of his damn toys."

"No, you're not." This time Magda lifted her glass in a toast. "He's madly in love with you, and it's lovely to see. Now, tell me about being a policewoman. I've never played one. I have played women who go outside the law to protect what's theirs, but never one who works within it to protect others. Is it exciting?"

"It's a job. It has its ups and downs like any."

"I doubt like any. You solve murders. We . . . civilians, I

suppose you'd say, can't help but find the process, including the murder, fascinating."

"That's because you're not the one who's dead."

"Exactly." Magda threw back her magnificent head and roared with laughter. "Oh, I like you! I'm so glad. You don't want to talk about your work, I understand. People from outside think mine is exciting, glamorous. When what it is . . . is a job, with its ups and downs like any."

"I've seen a lot of your work. I think Roarke has everything you've done on disc. I like the one where you're a scheming conwoman who falls for her mark. It's fun."

"*Bait and Switch*. Yes, it was. Chase Conner was my leading man in that, and I fell for him, too. It was also fun, while it lasted. I'm auctioning off the costume I wore in the cocktail party scene."

She glanced around the ballroom, scanning her things, things that had once been vital to her, with amusement. "It should bring a good price, and help get The Magda Lane Foundation for the Performing Arts off the ground. So many bits and pieces of a career, of a life, going on the block before much longer."

She turned, studying a display arranged like a lady's boudoir, with a shimmering nightgown, an open jewelry case where chains and stones spilled gloriously onto a gleaming dressing table. "That's a lovely bit of female business, isn't it?"

"Yeah, if you're into that."

Magda swiveled back, smiling. "At one time I was desperately into that. But, a smart woman doesn't survive a fickle career like acting without regularly reinventing herself."

"What are you now?"

"Yes, yes," Magda murmured. "I like you very much. People ask me why I'm doing this, why I'm giving so much of it up. Do you know what I say?"

"No, what?"

"That I intend to live and to work for a great deal longer. Time enough to collect more." She gave that lusty laugh again, turned back to Eve. "That's true enough, but there's more. The Foundation's a dream of mine, a cherished one. Acting's been good to me. I want to pass it on, while I'm still around and young enough to enjoy it all. Grants, scholarships, facilities for all that new blood to swim in. It pleases me that a young actor or director might get his or her start from a break given in my name. That's vanity."

"I don't think so. I think it's wisdom."

"Oh. Now I like you even more. Ah, there's Vince, giving me the eye. My son," Magda explained. "He's handling the media and assisting in the security for this extravaganza. Such a demanding young man," she added, signaling across the room. "God knows where he got that particular trait. So that's my cue to get back to work." She rose. "I'm going to be in New York for the next several weeks. I hope we'll see each other again."

"That would be nice."

"Ah, Roarke, perfect timing." Magda turned to beam at him as he walked to the table. "I have to abandon your delightful wife as duty calls. I expect an invitation to dinner, very soon, so I can spend more time with both of you, and indulge in one of those spectacular meals your man arranges. What is his name?"

"Summerset," Eve said, lip curling.

"Yes, of course. Summerset. Soon," she said, and kissed both Roarke's cheeks before gliding off.

"You were right. I did like her."

"I was sure you would." As he spoke, he began to guide her smoothly toward the exit. "I'm sorry to interrupt your evening off, but we have some trouble."

"A problem with security? Somebody try to duck out with a pocketful of baubles?"

"No. It's nothing to do with theft, and everything to do with murder."

Her eyes changed. Woman to cop. "Who's dead?"

"One of the housekeeping staff, from what I'm told." He kept her arm, steered her toward a bank of elevators. "She's in the south tower, forty-sixth floor. I don't know the details," he said shortly before she could interrupt. "My head of hotel security just informed me."

"Have the police been contacted?"

"I've contacted you, haven't I?" Eyes grim, he waited while the elevator shot up to the south tower. "Security knew I was on site, and that you were with me. It was decided to inform me—and you—first."

"Okay, don't get testy. We don't even know if it's a homicide yet. People are always yelling murder at unattended deaths. Mostly they're accidents or natural causes."

The minute she stepped off the elevator, her eyes narrowed to slits. Too many people in the hallway, including one hysterical female in a housekeeper's uniform, lots of guys in suits, and several people who were obviously guests who'd popped out of their rooms to see what the commotion was.

She reached into her foolish little purse, pulled out her badge, and held it up as she strode forward.

"NYPSD, clear this area. You people go back in your rooms, anyone with hotel security stand by. And somebody deal with this woman here. Who's security chief?"

"That would be me." A tall lean man with a coffee-colored complexion and mirror-sheened bald head stepped forward. "John Brigham."

"Brigham, you're with me." Since she didn't have her master code, she gestured to the door.

When he opened it, she stepped through, scanned the parlor area.

Sumptuous, chock-full of fancy furniture, including a

full bar setup. And tidy as a church. The privacy screens on the generous windows were engaged, and the lights on full.

"Where is she?" Eve asked Brigham.

"Bedroom, to the left."

"Was the door open or closed as it is now when you arrived on scene?"

"It was closed when I got here. But I can't say it was that way before. Ms. Hilo from Housekeeping found her."

"That's the woman in the hall?"

"That's right."

"All right, let's see what we've got." She moved to the door, opened it.

Music poured out. The lights were on full here as well, and shone harshly on the body lying on the bed like a broken doll that had been tossed there by a spoiled child.

One arm was cocked at an impossible angle, her face was raw and blackened from a vicious beating, and her uniform skirt was hiked up to her waist. The thin silver wire used to strangle her cut deep into her throat like a slender and deadly necklace.

"I think you can rule out natural causes," Roarke murmured.

"Yeah. Brigham, who's been in this suite besides you and the housekeeper since the body was found?"

"No one."

"Did you approach the body, touch it or anything other than the doors in any way?"

"I know the drill, Lieutenant. I was on the job—Chicago PSD, Anti-Crime Division. Twelve years. Hilo alerted me. She was screaming into her communicator. I got here within two minutes. She'd run back to her base on the fortieth floor. I entered the suite, came to the doorway here, determined by visual that the victim was deceased. Aware that Roarke was on site, and accompanied by you, I contacted him immediately, then secured the suite, sent for Hilo, and waited for your arrival."

"I appreciate it, Brigham. Since you were on the job, you know how many times a crime scene's corrupted by helping hands. Did you know the victim?"

"No. Hilo called her Darlene. Little Darlene. That's all I could get out of her."

Eve was scanning the scene, keeping herself back from it, and calculating the steps that had led to murder. "You could do me a big favor and get Hilo somewhere quiet and private where she can't talk to anyone but you until I send for her. I'm going to call this in. I don't want to go into the room until I can seal up."

Brigham reached in his pocket, pulled out a minican of Seal-It. "I had one of my men bring this up. And a recorder," he added, handing her a collar clip. "Didn't figure you'd have a field kit with you."

"Good thinking. Do you mind sticking with Hilo for a while?"

"I'll take care of it. You can tag me when you want to talk to her. Meanwhile, I'll leave a couple of men at the door until your crime scene unit gets here."

"Thanks." Idly she shook the can. "Why'd you go off the job?"

For the first time Brigham smiled. "My current employer made me a hell of an offer."

"I bet you did," Eve said to Roarke when Brigham stepped out. "He's got a cool head, good eyes." She started to spray her shoes, then decided she'd do a hell of a lot better without them. After stepping out of them, she sprayed her feet, her hands, passed off the can, then the clip, to Roarke.

"I'll need you to record the scene." She pulled out her communicator and called it in.

"Her name's Darlene French." Roarke read off the data he'd called up from his PPC. "She's worked here for just over a year. She was twenty-two."

"I'm sorry." She touched his arm, waited until he shifted

those hot, angry eyes to hers. "I'm going to take care of her now. Record on, okay?"

"Yes, all right." He slipped the PPC back in his pocket, engaged the clip recorder.

"The victim is identified as Darlene French, female, age twenty-two, employed as housekeeper, The Roarke Palace Hotel. Apparent homicide, this location, Suite 4602. Present and acting as primary, Dallas, Lieutenant Eve. Also present and acting as temporary aide in recording this log, Roarke. Dispatch has been notified."

Now Eve approached the body. "The scene shows little sign of struggle, but the body shows bruising and lacerations consistent with a violent beating, particularly around the face. Blood spatter pattern indicates that beating was administered while the victim was on the bed."

She glanced around the room again, noted the beeper on the floor just outside the bath.

"The right arm is broken," she continued. "Other bruising on the victim's thighs and vaginal area indicates premortem rape."

Gently, Eve lifted one of the limp hands. Wishing for microgoggles, she examined it carefully. "Got a little skin here," she murmured. "Managed to get a swipe in, didn't you, Darlene? Good for you. We have skin, possibly hair and fiber under victim's fingernails."

Meticulous, she moved up the body. The uniform was still buttoned over the breasts. "He didn't bother with much foreplay. Didn't rip at her clothes or bother to take them off her. Just beat her, broke her, raped her. A thin wire, silver in appearance, has been used, garrote-style, to strangle the victim. The ends of the wire were crossed in front, then twisted into small loops, indicate the killer strangled her face-to-face, while he was ranged over her, and she was down. Have you got this from all angles?" she asked Roarke.

"Yes."

With a nod, she lifted the victim's head, tilting her own so that she could see the back of the wire. "Get this," she ordered. "It might shift a little when we turn her. The wire's unbroken in the back, and the bleeding's minimal. He didn't use it until he'd finished the beating, until he'd finished the rape. Straddling her," she said, narrowing her eyes to bring it into focus. "One knee on either side. She's not putting up much of a fight, if any, by this point. He just slips the wire over her head, crosses the ends in front, then pulls, opposite directions. It wouldn't have taken long."

But she'd have bucked, her body instinctively struggling to throw off the weight, her throat burning from the wire and the trapped screams of pain and terror. Her heart would have pounded, and that storm-at-sea sound would have exploded in her ears at the lack of oxygen.

Heels drumming, hands clawing for air. Until the blood begins to burst in the head, behind the eyes, and that frantic heart surrenders.

Eve stepped back. There was little more she could do without a field kit. "I need to know who this room is registered to. What the housekeeping routine is. I'll need to talk to Hilo," she added as she walked to the closet, glanced in. "And it would help for me to be able to interview anyone on staff who knew her well." She checked the dresser.

"No clothes. Not even a lint ball. A couple of used towels she might have dropped or simply set down on her way out of the bathroom. *Was* anyone registered to this room?"

"I'll find out. You'll want her next of kin."

"Yeah." Eve sighed. "Husband, if she had one. Boyfriends, lovers, exes. Nine times out of ten that's what you find in a sexual homicide. But I think this is number ten. Nothing personal about this, nothing intimate or passionate. He wasn't mad, wasn't particularly involved."

"There's nothing intimate about rape."

"There can be," Eve corrected. And she knew that, better than most. "When there's knowledge between the assailant and the victim, any sort of history—even just a fantasy on the part of the assailant, it lends intimacy. This was cold. Just ram it in and get off. I bet he spent more time beating her than he did with the rape. Some men enjoy the first more. It's their foreplay."

Roarke switched off the recorder. "Eve. Turn the case over to someone else."

"What?" She blinked herself back to the moment. "Why would I do that?"

"Don't put yourself through this." He touched her cheek. "It hurts you."

He was being careful, she noted, not to mention her father. The beatings, the rapes, the terror she'd lived with until she was eight.

"They all hurt if you let them," she said simply, and turned back to look at Darlene French. "I won't turn her over to someone else, Roarke. I can't. She's already mine."

chapter two

The suite was registered to one James Priory of Milwaukee. He'd checked in that afternoon at three-twenty, and had booked his accommodations three weeks in advance with a planned two-night stay.

Payment for the room, and any incidentals, was to be made through his debit card, which had been recorded and verified at check-in.

In the parlor of that suite while the crime scene unit and sweepers handled the crime scene, Eve watched the security disc Brigham had sent up to her.

The check-in recording showed Priory to be a mixed-race male, mid to late forties, dressed in the conservative dark suit of the successful businessman who could afford a high-priced suite in a high-priced hotel for a couple of nights. An expense account look, Eve noted.

But under the natty suit and well-styled hair, she saw thug.

He was burly, wide-chested, and easily weighed twice what his victim had. His hands were square, the fingers long and blunted. His eyes were the color of the scrim that forms on street puddles in January. A cold and dirty gray.

His face was square as well, with a blocky nose and a thin mouth. The dark brown hair, carefully styled and graying at the temples, struck her as an affectation. Or a disguise.

He made no attempt to conceal his face, even managed a brief smile for the desk clerk before he let the bellman lead him to the elevators.

He had a single suitcase.

With the next disc, she watched the bellman open the door to his suite and step back to let Priory enter first. According to the logs, he did not leave the suite again before the murder.

He used the AutoChef in the kitchenette for a meal—steak, rare, white potato, baked, sour dough roll, coffee, and cheesecake—rather than contact room service.

The service bar in the parlor had been lightly used, some macadamias and a soft drink.

No liquor, Eve noted. Clear head.

The next disc showed Darlene French wheeling her maid's cart to the door of 4602.

A pretty girl in a spiffy uniform and sensible shoes who had a dreamy look in big brown eyes. Delicate build. Small hands that played with the little gold heart on a thin gold chain she tugged from under her blouse.

She buzzed, idly rubbed the small of her back, then buzzed again. Slipped the heart and chain neatly under her blouse. Only then did she slide the passcode from her apron pocket into the slot, press her right thumb to the Identi-pad. She opened the door, called out cheerfully, then gathered fresh towels from her cart.

She closed the door behind her at 8:26 P.M.

At 8:58, Priory, suitcase and towels in hand, stepped out of the room. He closed the door behind him, neatly dropped the towels inside the cart before he skirted around it. Then strolled—like a man without a care in the world—to the door leading to the stairs.

It had taken him only thirty-two minutes to beat, rape, and murder Darlene French.

"A clear head," Eve said aloud. "A cold, clear head."

"Lieutenant?"

Eve shook her head, held up a hand to hold her aide off a moment longer.

Peabody zipped her lip, waited. She'd been working homicides with Eve for a year, and believed she had her lieutenant's rhythm.

Her eyes, nearly as dark as her straight chin-length hair, shifted to the screen where Eve continued to study the frozen image of a killer.

Looks mean, Peabody thought, but said nothing.

"What have you got for me?" Eve said at length.

"Priory, James, exec in sales at Alliance Insurance Company, based in Milwaukee. Deceased, January five of this year. Vehicular accident."

"Well, this guy's alive and kicking. Anything wonky about Milwaukee Priory's vehicular?"

"It doesn't appear so, sir. The report states a driver of a jet-truck nodded off at the wheel, took out Priory and another driver. We have a number of other Priorys in Milwaukee, but this is the only James that popped."

"Hold off running them. This guy's got a sheet somewhere. I know it. Tag Feeney at home. Shoot him this disc image and ask him to run it through IRCCA—the International Resource Center on Criminal Activity. That's an E-Division job, and IRCCA's his personal darling. He'll pop this guy out quicker than anyone else." She checked her wrist unit. "I want to talk to Hilo. She should be coherent by now. Where's Roarke?" she demanded, glancing around the parlor.

Peabody straightened her shoulders, looked directly at the opposite wall. "I couldn't say."

"Damn it." Eve strode out, pinned the guard at the door. "Hilo."

"She's in 4020, Lieutenant."

"Nobody goes in this room without a badge. Nobody." She walked to the elevator, jabbed the button. The fact that

Roarke had left the crime scene meant only one thing. He was up to something.

The good news was Hilo was indeed coherent. She was pale, red-eyed, but sat quietly in the parlor area of one of the hotel's smaller suites. There was a teapot on the table in front of her, and a cup in her hand, which she set down when Eve walked in.

"Ms. Hilo, I'm Lieutenant Dallas with the NYPSD."

"Yes, yes, I know. Roarke explained that you wanted me to wait for you here with Mr. Brigham."

Eve shot a look toward Brigham, who stood staring, with apparent fascination, at the painting on the far wall. "Roarke explained?" Eve repeated.

"Yes, he came down to sit with me awhile. Ordered this tea for me himself. It's just like him. He's a lovely man."

"Oh yeah, he's just peachy. Ms. Hilo, have you spoken with anyone but Mr. Brigham and Roarke since you've been waiting for me?"

"Oh no. I was told not to." She looked trustingly at Eve with swollen eyes the color of walnuts. "Mrs. Roarke—"

"Dallas." Eve didn't grit her teeth, but it was close. "Lieutenant Dallas."

"Oh, yes. Of course. Pardon me, Lieutenant Dallas, I want to apologize for causing such a scene before when . . . before," she finished, and drew in a shaky breath. "I couldn't seem to stop. When I found poor little Darlene . . . I couldn't seem to stop."

"It's all right."

"No, no." Hilo lifted her hands. She was a small woman, but solidly built. The kind of build, Eve always thought, that kept right on steadily marching after wimpy long-distance runners passed out on the field. "I just ran out and left her there, left her like that. I'm in charge, you see. From six to one, I'm in charge, and I just ran away from her. I didn't even touch her, or cover her up."

"Mrs. Hilo."

"Just Hilo." She managed a small smile that only made her weary face look sadder. "It's Natalie Hilo, but everyone just calls me Hilo."

"All right. Hilo." Eve sat, put off turning on the recorder. "You did exactly what was best. If you had touched her, if you had covered her up, you would have contaminated the crime scene. That would have made it more difficult for me to find the person who hurt her. To find him and make sure he pays."

"That's what Roarke said." Her eyes filled again, but she got a handkerchief from her pocket and briskly wiped the tears away. "He said just that, and that you *would* find the horrible person who did this to her. He said you wouldn't stop looking until you'd found him."

"That's right. You can help me, and Darlene. Brigham, could Hilo and I have some privacy?"

"Sure. You can reach me at ninety on the house 'link."

"I'm going to record what we talk about," Eve said when they were alone. "All right?"

"Yes." She sniffed, straightened. "I'm ready."

Eve set a recorder on the table. She recited the particulars. "Let's start with you telling me what happened. Why did you go to Suite 4602?"

"Darlene was behind schedule. When the evening routine's finished in each room or suite, the housekeeper presses Code Five on her beeper. This helps us keep track of the staff and the units completed. While it goes toward efficiency, it's also a security measure to protect the guests and the staff."

She sighed a little, and picked up her cup of tea. "Turndowns generally take between ten and twenty minutes, depending on the size of the unit and the pace of the particular housekeeper. We allow some leeway, of course. Quite often the state of a unit is such that it takes considerably longer. You'd be amazed, Lieutenant, really amazed, at how some people treat a hotel room. It makes you wonder how they live at home."

She shook her head. "Well, be that as it may. We're near full capacity right now, so we were hopping. I didn't notice that Darlene hadn't beeped in from Suite 4602. Forty minutes, give or take. That's long, but it's a large suite and Darlene was slow. Not that she wasn't a good worker, she was, but she tended to take her time."

Hilo began to wring her hands. "I shouldn't have said she was slow. I shouldn't have said that. I meant to say thorough. She was such a good girl. Such a sweet little thing. We all loved her. It's just that she took a bit more time than most to finish her units. She liked being in the bigger rooms, she liked tending to beautiful things."

"It's all right, Hilo. I understand. She was proud of her work, and she made sure she did it well."

"Yes." Hilo pressed a hand to her lips, nodded. "Yes, that's exactly so."

"What did you do when you noticed she hadn't checked in?"

"Oh." Hilo shook herself back. "I beeped her. The procedure is for the housekeeper to signal back or to contact base over a house 'link. Occasionally one of the other guests will detain or delay a housekeeper, asking for more towels or whatever. It's Palace policy to serve the guests, even if they just want to chat for a moment because they're away from home and lonely. This throws off the pace, but we're a service-first facility."

She set her cup down again. "I gave Darlene another five minutes, beeped her a second time. When she didn't respond to that, I was irritated. Lieutenant, I was annoyed with her, and now—"

"Hilo." Eve couldn't have counted the times she'd seen and heard this guilty misery in a survivor. "It was a natural reaction. Darlene would never have blamed you for it. You couldn't help her then, but you can help her now. Tell me what you can."

"Yes, all right. Yes." Hilo drew in a breath, let it out slowly.

"Yes. As I said, we were very busy. I went to the suite myself to move her along. I'd hoped her beeper was acting up. They don't very often, but it's been known to happen. Then I saw her cart outside the door, and was very annoyed."

She had to stop a moment, remembering how she'd planned to give Darlene a good piece of her mind. "I buzzed, used my passcode. I could see the parlor was fine. I marched straight to the bedroom, opened the door."

"The door was closed?"

"Yes, yes, I'm sure because I remember calling out as I pushed it open. And I saw her, poor little thing, I saw her on the bed. Her face was all swollen and battered, and there was blood around her neck and on the collar of her uniform, and drops of it on the spread she'd turned down. She'd been doing her job, you see."

"She'd turn down the bed," Eve interrupted. "Would that have been the first chore she'd have dealt with on entering the suite?"

"It depends. Everyone has their own routine, more or less. I believe Darlene liked to check the bath first, remove the used towels, and replace them. Then she'd check the bed. Some guests will demand a complete linen change at turndown if they'd had a nap or . . . made use of the bed in any way. If that was the case, she'd strip off the linens and take them and the towels to her cart, retrieve fresh linens, and so on. She would make a note of the use of inventory on her cart log. Efficiency, again. And it discourages staff pilfering. You see?"

"Yeah. From what you observed, she'd just gotten around to turning down the bed. There was music on. Would she have turned on the entertainment system?"

"Yes, perhaps. But never at that volume. If the guest isn't in the unit during evening turndown, the housekeeper programs the entertainment unit to the guest's requirements, or to a classical station if no requirements have been set. But always at a discreet volume."

"Maybe she intended to turn it down before she left."

"Darlene liked modern music." Hilo managed a smile. "Most of the young staff members do. She'd never have turned on—it was opera, wasn't it—that program for her own entertainment."

"Okay." *So he'd killed to opera,* Eve thought. *For his own entertainment.* "What then?"

"Then I froze, just froze. And I remember running out again, slamming that door behind me. I heard the crack of it through the screaming. I ran out the front, slammed that door, too. And I couldn't get my legs to move anymore, so I stood there, my back against the door, still screaming when I called Security."

She broke a bit, pressed her hands to her face. "People came out of rooms, ran down the hall. Everything was so confused. Mr. Brigham came, and he went inside. Everything got all muddled in my head, and he brought me down here and told me to lie down. But I couldn't. So I just sat right here and cried until Roarke came and got me tea. Who could have hurt that sweet little girl? Why?"

Eve waited, saying nothing to a question that could never be fully answered, while Hilo rocked herself steady again. "Did Darlene always do turndown on that particular suite?"

"No, but most usually. And traditionally each housekeeper is assigned two floors that remain theirs unless we have an unusual turnover. Darlene's had forty-five and forty-six since she finished her training."

"Do you know if she was involved with anyone? A boyfriend?"

"Yes, I think . . . Oh, there are so many young people on staff and they're forever having romances. I'm not sure I remember . . . Barry!" Blowing out a breath of relief, Hilo nearly smiled. "Yes, I'm sure she had a young man named Barry. He's on the bellstaff here. I remember because she was over the moon when he was able to switch to night shift. That way they had more time to spend with each other."

"Do you know his last name?"

"No, I'm sorry. She always lit up when she chattered about him."

"Any spats recently?"

"No, and believe me, I'd have heard about it. When one of them has a fight with a boyfriend or a girlfriend, we *all* hear about it. I'm sure . . . Oh. Oh!" The color that had crept into her face drained again. "You don't think he . . . Lieutenant, the way Darlene spoke of him, he seemed like such a nice young man."

"It's just a routine question, Hilo. I'll want to talk to him, you see. To find out if he has any idea who might have hurt her."

"I see. Of course."

Both women looked over when the door opened and Roarke stepped in. "I'm sorry. Am I interrupting?"

"No. We're finished for now. I may have to talk to you again," Eve told Hilo as she got to her feet. "But you're free to go now. I can arrange to have you taken home."

"I've already taken care of that." Roarke crossed the room, took Hilo's hand. "There's a driver just outside. He'll take you home. Your husband's waiting for you. I want you to go straight there, Hilo, take a soother and go to bed. Take all the time you need. I don't want you worrying about work until you feel up to it."

"Thank you. Thank you so much. But I think work might help."

"Do what's best for you," Roarke said as he took her to the door.

Hilo nodded, then looked back at Eve. "Lieutenant, she was a harmless little thing. Harmless. Whoever did this needs to be punished. It won't bring her back, but he needs to be punished. It's all we can do."

It was all, Eve thought, *and never quite enough.*

She waited until Rourke had finished a murmured conversation with what she assumed was the driver, then shut the door.

"Where'd you disappear to?"

"I had a number of things to see to, arrangements to make." He angled his head. "You don't care for civilians on your crime scenes in any case. There was little I could do there."

"And a lot to do elsewhere?"

"Do you want an accounting of my activities and where-abouts, Lieutenant?" Letting the question hang, he walked to the friggie bar and, opening it, selected a small bottle of white wine.

As he poured out a glassful, it occurred to her that the way she'd asked didn't sound very chummy. "I just wondered where you were, that's all."

"And what I was up to," he finished. "It's my hotel, Lieutenant."

"Okay, okay, let's step back." She raked a hand through her hair while he coolly sipped his wine. "It's the second time in a few weeks you've had an employee hit at one of your properties. That's hard. Of course, if you factor in that you own half of the city—"

"Only half?" he interrupted with a glimmer of a smile. "I'll have to speak to my accountant."

"Anyway, I could stand here and tell you it's not personal and you shouldn't take it personally, but that's pretty much bullshit because it is personal to you. I get that, and I'm sorry."

"So am I. For what happened here and for almost looking forward to taking it out on you. Now that that diversion's been avoided, I'll tell you again, I had a number of things to see to. The event downstairs being one."

He held out his glass of wine, but, as he'd expected, she shook her head. "The Palace and the upcoming auction are about to experience a media crisis," he continued. "Reporters salivate when a murder takes place in a well-known hotel, and you add all the star power downstairs and you have one hell of a story. It needs to be spun as quickly as we can manage. I also wanted to see that Hilo was taken care of."

"It made a difference," Eve said quietly. "It'll go easier for her because you took the time."

"She's worked for me for ten years." And for him, nothing else had to be said. "Word's already spread through the staff, and some panic needed to be avoided before it could set in. There's a young man on the bellstaff. Barry Collins."

"The boyfriend."

"Yes. He's taking it hard. I had him taken home. And before you slap at me for it," he said even as she wound up, "he was with two other of the bellstaff, dealing with luggage from an incoming medical convention during the time of the murder."

"And how do you know the time of the murder?"

"Brigham saw to it I was informed of the contents of the security discs. Did you think he wouldn't?"

"No, I didn't, but I still have to talk to the boyfriend."

"You wouldn't have gotten anything out of him tonight." His voice softened, the way it could that made it something like music. "He's twenty-two, Eve, and he was in love with her. He's broken to pieces. Christ," he murmured as pity stirred. "He wanted his mother. So that's where I sent him."

"Okay." She couldn't fight it. "I'd probably have done the same. I can talk to him later."

"I assume you've run James Priory."

"Yeah, and I assume you already know the results, so I'll just say I'm having him run through IRCCA. He'll be in the system. This isn't his first."

"I can get the data for you quicker."

He could, she thought, at home in the locked room that held his unregistered equipment. "Let's do it this way for now. He strolled out of here like a man who knew he had some place cozy to go. I'll find out where soon enough. The real question is why. He came here with a purpose. The fake ID, room booked well in advance, two nights. A time pad in case something didn't work out the first night. He settled down in his room and he waited for her. Darlene specifically? If so, that's another why. Any housekeeper? Why again. I might get some of that from his history."

But it troubled her. "He didn't care that we made him. That's a puzzler. Unless I'm way off and we don't find a sheet on him, it doesn't make sense he wouldn't have taken more precautions."

"Giving you, or possibly me, the finger."

"Yeah, sometimes it's just that simple. I have to go to New Jersey, notify next of kin before I go downtown to file my report. How about a lift?"

"You astonish me, Lieutenant," he said with surprise.

"Maybe I just want to keep my eye on you."

"Good enough." He set down his wine and, going to her, cupped her face in his hands. Pressed his lips to her forehead. "This one's going to be difficult for both of us. I'll apologize now for any hard words I might say before you close this."

"Okay." Marriage, she thought. It was some ride. She cupped his face in turn and gave him a long hard kiss on the mouth. "That's because I'll probably say meaner ones."

His arms slipped slyly around her. "Say something mean now, really mean. Then since we happen to be in a hotel room, you can make up for it on the spot."

"Pervert," she said, and with a laugh shoved him away.

"Ouch." He followed her to the door and out. "That'll cost you later."

Notification of next of kin was the most miserable part of being a homicide cop. With a few words you cut slices out of lives. No matter how they were put back together later, they were never the same. Once pieces were missing from the whole, the pattern was forever altered.

Eve tried not to think about it on the way back from New Jersey, where she'd left Darlene French's mother and younger sister devastated. Instead, she moved on to the steps that would bring them justice, if not comfort.

"If there were any like crimes in the city or other boroughs, I'd have heard about it." Still, she used the in-dash computer in Roarke's spiffy little 6000XXX to do a scan for them. "We got your strangulations, we got your rape, and we got your battery," she began.

"I love New York."

"Yeah, me, too. We're sick. Anyway, we have each of the basic elements here and there over the last six months, but none that include all three. And none with a silver wire used as a garrote. Nothing in a hotel either. But the fact that he used one means he could have hit other cities, countries, even off planet. I'll widen the scan when—"

She broke off as the communicator in her purse signaled. "Dallas."

"Can't you take one goddamn night off?"

She stared into Feeney's mournful eyes. "I was working on it."

"Well, work harder. You take one, maybe some of the rest of us get one. I was all kicked back with a bottle of brew, a bowl of cheese chips, and the Yankee game onscreen when Peabody tagged me."

"Sorry."

"Yeah, well, the sons of bitches lost, lost to the freaking Tijuana Tacos. Burns my ass." He blew out a breath, scratching his fingers in his wiry thatch of graying russet-colored hair. "Anyway, something about your guy rang some bells when Peabody shot the image through. Couldn't bring it together at first. Had to run him through IRCCA with disc image only. No prints. Sweepers say he musta sealed up. We'll get his DNA though, from the blood and skin under her nails, and the semen. Didn't seal up his dick."

"Yeah, I know how you guys hate putting a coat on your best friend."

He gave her a sour smile. "I don't figure he's worried about the DNA. Sealed up, I expect, to buy a little time to relocate. Take us a few hours to get the DNA results."

"Did you get a pop through IRCCA?"

"I'm getting to it. So I run him, image only. Get me some likelies with probable face-sculpting work. I fiddle around with them some on the morphing system, and I got a real pretty picture. Added in the murder weapon, and rang those bells. Name's Sylvester Yost. Sly Yost. Got him a shit pot load of aliases, but that's his birth name."

"Was Priory one of his a.k.a.s?"

"Not until now. I got it added into the mix. Anyhow, about fifteen years back I worked a case—serial strangulations, silver wire. Five victims scattered all over the damn planet. We had one in New York. Female. Licensed companion. Second-rate license. She had ties to the black market. So did the other four victims. Not the same organization. But every victim was a key player in something mucky. We got a line on Yost, but never tugged him in on it. The murders stopped, and the case sat there going stale."

"A hired hammer?"

"We figured, but who hired the bastard? He hit every major cartel. No bias there. He comes up most likely on no less than twenty strangulations before and since. And he did time in the thirties for assault with deadly."

"Yeah, I knew he'd seen what a cage looks like from the inside. Only one arrest?"

"Just the one. Records show he'd have been twenty when the Miami cops reeled him in. Looks like he's gotten better at his work over the years."

"I'm pulling into Central now. Send me everything you've got on him."

"Already did. I'm going to work it some more. Get you an update in the morning. I'd like a second shot at this guy."

"You've got it."

"Tomorrow, then. Hey, Dallas?"

"What?"

"What's that stuff in your hair?"

"What stuff?" She reached up, dragging fingers through, and felt the little raindrop diamonds. "It's just—I was out . . ." Mortified, she cleared her throat. "Never mind," she muttered and cut transmission.

The man who'd been born Sylvester Yost, who had strangled a young maid while under the name of James Priory and was currently carrying identification as Giorgio Masini, sipped his second glass of unblended scotch and watched the recording of the evening's Yankee game.

If he'd been the type to kill for personal reasons, he'd have hunted down the Yankee pitcher and gutted him like a fish. But since murder was a business, he merely sat, cursing quietly in a surprisingly feminine voice.

There had been some who'd made cracks about the thin, high pitch of his voice. If he was on a job, he ignored them. If he was on his own time, he beat the living hell out of them.

But even that was simply a matter of principle. He wasn't a passionate man, not about people or principles. The lack of passion made him an excellent killing machine.

The money for the night's work had already been deposited in an account under yet another name. He had no idea why the girl—because she'd been hardly more than that—had been targeted. He simply accepted the contract, fulfilled it, took the money.

This particular job had only just begun, and promised to reap him a considerable fee. As he was considering retirement, quite seriously considering it, it was a delightful little cushion.

Over the years, those fees had allowed him to develop, and indulge, a refined and cultured taste. He could afford the best, so he had studied and experienced and discovered just what the best entailed.

Food, drink, art, music, fashion. He'd traveled all over

the world, and off planet as well. At fifty-six he could speak three languages fluently, which was yet another sterling job tool, and could, when the mood struck, prepare a brilliant gourmet meal. What's more, he could play the piano like an angel.

He hadn't been born with a silver spoon in his mouth, but the silver wire had made up for it.

At twenty, he'd been the minor thug that Eve had seen beneath the polish. He'd killed because he could, and it paid.

Now he was a virtuoso of murder, a performer par excellence who had never disappointed his paying customers, and who left his own individual stamp on each target.

Pain—the beatings. Humiliation—the rape. The silver wire. Murder with class. For Sly, it was a tidy little three-act play, with only the set and the second lead as variables.

He was, always, the star of the show.

Sly enjoyed traveling, and had several scrapbooks filled with postcards he picked up as he did so. Occasionally he would page through them, sipping a drink, smiling over the reminders of places he'd been, and the trinkets he'd collected there.

The meal he had in Paris that summer after he'd dispatched the electronic's manufacturer, the view from his hotel window on a rainy evening in Prague before he'd strangled the American envoy.

Good memories.

He was confident that, though his current employment would keep him in New York for the run of the show, it would provide many more of those good memories.

chapter three

In the morning, Eve sat at her desk in Cop Central and reviewed all the data Feeney had sent her the night before. With a few hours' sleep, a fresh eye, and a third cup of coffee she let a picture form in her mind of one Sylvester Yost.

A career criminal. A stone killer, sired by a second-string gunrunner who'd disappeared, and was presumed dead, during the Urban Wars. Birthed by a diagnosed mental defective who'd had a penchant for boosting cars and slicing the unhappy owners with a switchblade. She'd died of a drug overdose in a recovery ward when her son had been thirteen.

Sly had apparently decided to carry on the family tradition, with his own style of mayhem.

She had his juvenile file now. He'd toyed with knives, cutting the ear off his caseworker two weeks after he'd been sucked into the system. He'd sampled rape, assaulting one of the girls in his group home and leaving her battered.

But he'd found his true calling with strangulation, and had apparently practiced on small dogs and big cats before graduating to the human species.

At fifteen, he'd escaped from the juvie facility. He was

now fifty-six. In those forty-one years, he'd spent only one in a cage, and was suspected of forty-three murders.

The information on him was sketchy, despite files compiled by the FBI, Interpol, the IRCCA, and the Global Bureau for Interplanetary Crimes.

The subject was a suspected killer-for-hire who had no living family, no known friends or associates, no known address. His habitual weapon of choice was wire of sterling silver. But victims attributed to him had also been strangled manually, with silk scarves and with gold rope.

In the early days, Eve noted as she read. *Before he settled on his signature style.*

Victims were both male and female, of all ages, races and financial groups. Bodily violence, including torture and rape, were often employed.

"Good at your work, aren't you, Sly? And I bet you don't come cheap." She sat back, studying the disc image of Yost at the check-in desk of The Roarke Palace Hotel. "Who the hell would hire you to kill a young maid who lived with her mother and sister in Hoboken?"

She rose, paced the crowded box of her office. There was a possibility he'd made a mistake, but that was slim.

You don't last forty-odd years in the assassin game by plucking at the wrong target.

Logically, Yost had done what he'd been paid to do.

So, who was Darlene French, and who was she linked with?

Roarke's connection was there, no question, but while the death would cause him personal unhappiness and some professional inconvenience, it just didn't make that much of a ripple in the big ocean of Roarke's holdings.

Back to the victim. Had Darlene heard or seen something, without even being aware she'd heard or seen it? Hotels were busy places, with a great deal of business being done.

But if the girl had brushed up against something, why

have her murdered in such an obvious and dramatic fashion? Take her out quietly and be done with it.

An accident, a botched mugging, everyone's shocked and sorry. The cops take a glance, offer their sympathies. And it all goes away.

Though the theory didn't gel for her, Eve decided she'd need to go back to the hotel and take a close look at who'd stayed in the rooms under Darlene's care for the last several weeks.

She stopped by her skinny window, watched the morning insanity. Sky and street traffic were vicious. An airbus lumbered by, jammed port to port with commuters who didn't have the luxury or the good sense to work out of their homes. A one-man traffic cam hovered with a scissor snap of blades as the rush hour was analyzed, reported, and broadcast to those already suffering through it.

The media needed to fill airtime with something, she supposed. She'd already ignored over a half dozen calls from reporters hoping for a comment or break on the murder. Until she was pushed into giving a statement by her commander, she was leaving the media spin to Roarke.

No one did it better.

She heard the unmistakable sound of cop shoes slapping against ancient linoleum, and continued to stare out her window.

"Sir?"

"There's a woman on this airtram out here with a lap full of flowers. Where the hell is she going with all those flowers?"

"It's coming up on Mother's Day, Lieutenant. Could be paying her duty call a little early."

"Hmmm. I want to run the boyfriend, Peabody. Barry Collins. If we swing with this being a hired job, somebody's footing the bill. I don't think a bellman's got the wherewithal for Yost's fee, but it could be he's the connection to someone who does."

"Yost?"

"Oh, sorry. You're not up-to-date." She corrected that oversight with her back to the room and her eyes on the sky.

"Captain Feeney's coming in on the investigation? Are you going to pull in McNab?"

Eve glanced over her shoulder. Peabody was working hard to look casual, but that square, earnest face wasn't fashioned for bluffing. "Not so long ago if I'd hinted about pulling McNab into an investigation, you'd have whined and bitched."

"No, sir. I'd have *started* to whine and bitch, then you'd have slapped me down. After that I'd have whined and bitched mentally." She broke into a grin. "Anyway, times change. McNab and I get along better now, mostly since we're having sex. Except . . ."

"Oh, don't. Don't tell me stuff about it."

"I was just going to say he's been acting a little weird."

"If you look up McNab in the dictionary, weird is the common definition."

"Different weird," Peabody corrected, but filed that little gem away to use on him at the first opportunity. "He's . . . nice. Really nice. Sort of sweet and attentive. He brings me flowers. I think he's stealing them out of the park, but still. And just a few days ago, he took me to the movies. A chick flick I'd made noises about wanting to see. He hated it, and made sure I knew it after, but he sprang for the admission and everything."

"Oh, man."

"So anyway, I think—" Peabody stopped, snorted out a laugh as her cool-eyed and courageous lieutenant let out a short shriek and stuck her fingers in her ears.

"I can't hear you. I don't want to hear you. I'm *not* going to hear you. Go do the run on Barry Collins. Now. That's an order."

Peabody simply moved her mouth.

"What?"

"I said, 'Yes, sir,'" Peabody explained when Eve unplugged her ears. She walked to the door, judged her timing. "I think he's setting me up for something," she said and fled.

"I'll set you up," Eve muttered and dropped behind her desk. "I'd like to set both of you up, then drop-kick your asses." Since she was in the mood to kick someone's, she called the lab and harassed the chief tech over verifying the DNA.

By the time she met with Feeney, she had conclusive DNA evidence that the man who had raped and murdered Darlene French was Sylvester Yost.

When she told him, he nodded, sat on her desk, and took his habitual bag of nuts from the sagging pocket of his wrinkled suit. "Never doubted it. I ran a scan for like crimes. Nothing in the past seven, eight months. He's been on vacation."

"Or somebody didn't want the bodies found. Any indication that he ever acts on his own? Personal reasons?"

"Nope." Feeney crunched on a nut. "Pattern's for profit. I've got McNab running the interplanetary and off planet scan. Might find something there."

"You're bringing McNab in?"

Her tone had him lifting his eyebrows. "Yeah. You got a problem with him?"

"No, no. He does good work." Even as she spoke she drummed her fingers on the desk. "It's just this thing with him and Peabody."

Feeney hunched his shoulders. "I don't want to think about that."

"Well, me neither." But if she was going to suffer, so was he. "He took her to a girl movie."

"What?" Feeney paled, and the nut currently in his mouth almost rolled off his tongue. "He went to a skirt movie? Took her?"

"That's what I said."

"Ah, Christ." He got off the desk, took a quick turn around the room on short, bandy legs. "That's it, you know. That's the finish. Boy's sunk. Next thing you know he'll be picking her flowers."

"Already done."

"Don't tell me this shit, Dallas." He turned back, basset hound eyes pleading. "Don't put this business in my brain. Isn't it bad enough I know they're, you know, getting naked together?"

"Nobody listens to me about this." She nodded, pleased to have found a like mind. "Roarke thinks it's sweet."

"He doesn't have to work with them, does he?" Feeney said, firing up. "He doesn't have to do the job knowing there's winking and tickling and Jesus Christ in heaven knows what going on. I thought she had her sights on that slick-faced LC, Monroe."

"She's juggling them."

Feeney peeled back his lips, sat again, offered Dallas the bag of nuts. "Women."

"Yeah, what is with them?" Feeling considerably better, she ate a handful. "So, I've got Peabody running the boyfriend. I don't think we're going to find anything, but once we have his data I'll swing over and interview him. Right now, I'm dodging the media. That's for Roarke to deal with. I'm going back to the crime scene, do some poking around the hotel. I expect the tox report on French within an hour. I figure it's going to be clean, but you never know about people."

"Especially female people," he muttered, still brooding.

"Yeah. French's parents divorced about eight years back. He's Harry D. French, currently living in the Bronx with his second wife. You got time to snip off that thread and take a look at his data? If it was a professional hit, maybe it was payback to him for something."

"I'll run him now. The mother?"

"Sherry Tides French. I ran her last night. Manages a damn candy store at the Newark Transpo Center. Whistle clean. I can't see it coming down through her."

She tossed him back his nuts, rose, and plucked her jacket from its hook. "Since you've got McNab, how about having him run the wire? Let's see if we can find out where he buys it. The lab analysis should be coming through before midday."

"Yeah, I'll put him on it, keep him busy. Keep his mind out of his pants."

"There you go." Eve shrugged into her jacket and headed out.

Eve's first stop was the hotel manager. She requested disc copies of guest records, records of current hotel personnel, and any employee who'd been terminated or had quit in the past year.

Before she could begin her song and dance about aiding the police in a homicide investigation, the possibility of a warrant, she was handed a sealed file containing everything she'd asked for.

She was told that the staff had been instructed by Roarke to give her full cooperation and any data she requested.

"That was easy," Peabody commented as they took the elevator to the forty-sixth floor.

"Yeah, he's been busy." Eve tapped the file on her open hand, then passed the file to Peabody.

She uncoded the police seal on the door, stepped in.

"How do you pass a few hours in a hotel while you're waiting to kill someone? Enjoy the view, watch a little screen, have some dinner. He doesn't make or receive any transmission from the room link or fax or computer. Maybe he does on his personal," she mused, wandering the parlor. "Checks in, verifies he's here."

She turned into the kitchen, studied the counter, grimy now with the sweepers' dust. In the sink was a neat stack of dishes.

"He uses the AutoChef at six. Plenty of time before turndown. A good hour before the earliest start. Probably he knows the routine, that this particular room gets done around eight most nights. He'd have checked the hotel events calendar, so he'd know a big deal party's going on, a convention's coming in, another's midswing. Hotel's near capacity, so housekeeping's not going to come by early. Hey, let's have a steak."

She moved closer to the sink. "He probably ate in front of the screen, on the sofa, or at the dining table. You wouldn't waste a hotshot place like this by eating standing up in the kitchen. Then he has dessert and coffee, pats his belly. He brings his dishes into the kitchen, puts them tidily into the sink. He's used to taking care of himself, picking up for himself. Doesn't like messy dishes in view."

She looked at the way the knife and fork were lined up beside the plate, how the dessert plate, the cup, and saucer were stacked on top. A little pyramid.

"He probably lives alone. Might not even go for a server droid. He doesn't live in hotels, not all the time. You live with maids around, you don't clear your plates from the table."

Peabody nodded. "I noticed something last night. Forgot to mention it."

"What?"

"You know all the goodies hotels like this have for guests. The bathroom stuff—fancy soaps and shampoos, creams, bath bubbles? He took them." She smiled at Eve's speculative look. "Lots of people do, but most of them aren't waiting to kill somebody, or haven't just finished killing somebody."

"Good eye. So he's either frugal or he likes souvenirs.

How about towels, the robes, those little slippers they put beside the bed at night?"

"They put slippers beside the bed at night? I've never stayed in a place that—the robes are there," she finished, catching herself before Eve could. "Two of them, bedroom closet, unused. I don't know how many towels you get in a place like this, but there's enough for a family of six in the bathroom. They're unused, too."

"He'd have used towels prior to turndown. A shower after his traveling day maybe." She started toward the bedroom as she spoke. "And a good boy who clears the table would certainly wash his hands after he pees. He didn't hold his bladder for five hours plus."

She paused at the parlor bath, a smaller version of the master with a blue glass shower stall, snowy white towels, and a gleaming john discreetly tucked behind blue glass doors. "Bath amenities are gone from here, too."

"I didn't catch that before. He cleaned the place out."

"Why spend money on soap and shampoo if you can get it free? Particularly when it's top-of-the-line stuff." She continued to the bedroom, scanning briefly before she walked into the bath.

This one was huge, with a pond-sized tub, a separate shower offering six jets at adjustable heights and speeds, and a drying tube. She'd spent time in a Roarke hotel before, and knew that the mile-long counter would have been artfully decorated with fancy bottles of creams and lotions. This one was bare.

Frowning, she walked over to the brass rack that held three thick and monogrammed hand towels. "He used this one. Let's have a bag."

"How do you know he used it?"

"The monogram's not centered like the others. He used it. Washed up after he'd finished with her, dried his hands, then, tidy guy that he is, hung it back up. She must've come in, walked straight in here to take the used towels, put in fresh. He's somewhere waiting for her, getting a look at her, figuring.

"Maybe the closet," she said. "She starts to walk through again, carrying the used towels, probably dumps them on the floor. She turns down the bed, doing her job, making it nice for the guests. Then he's on her. Snatches her beeper before she can press an alarm, tosses it over there where we found it."

The rest was done on the bed, Eve thought.

"He didn't give her time to try to run. There's no sign in the suite of a struggle, not that she could have managed much of one against a guy his size. The bed linens got soiled and tangled, but nothing else. Everything else is orderly, so he got her there, did it all there. To music."

"That's the creepy part," Peabody murmured. "The rest of it's nasty, but the music part's creepy."

"When he's done with her, he checks the time. Hey, didn't take so long. He washes his hands, probably *tsk-tsk*s about the little scratches she managed to dig into him, changes his clothes, packs up, scooping his amenities into his case. Then the son of a bitch picks up the towels she dropped and carries them out to her cart. Not going to change the sheets, of course, but we don't want to leave more of a mess than necessary."

"That's cold."

"Oh yeah, it's cold. An easy job. In and out of a plush hotel in a matter of hours, a good meal, a fresh supply of bath products and a big, fat fee. I can figure him, Peabody. I can figure him, but I can't figure who pointed him here, or why."

She stood silent a moment, bringing the image of Darlene French into her mind. And as she did, she heard the sound of the hall door opening. With one hand on her weapon, she signaled Peabody to the side with the other. She moved down the hall quickly, quietly, swung around the corner, weapon in hand.

"Damn it, Roarke! Damn it!" Disgusted, she shoved the

weapon back in her holster as he shut the door. "What are you doing?"

"Looking for you."

"This room is sealed. It's a crime scene and *sealed.*"

The seal, she imagined, would have taken him less time to uncode with his clever fingers than it had for her to do so with her master.

"Which is why, when informed you were on the premises, it was the first place I looked. Hello, Peabody."

"What do you want?" Eve snapped before her aide could answer. "I'm working."

"Yes, I'm aware of that. I assumed you'd want to follow through on some of the interviews you mentioned last night. Barry Collins is at home, but his supervisor's available at your convenience, as is another maid, Sheila Walker, who was a particular friend of the victim's. She came in to clear out Darlene's locker for the family."

"She can't touch—"

"And so I told her. Not until you clear it. But I've asked her to wait so that you can speak to her."

She sizzled, sparked, then cooled down to smolder. "I could tell you I don't need any help setting up interviews."

"You could," he agreed, so pleasantly she didn't know whether to snarl or laugh.

"But, you saved me some time, so thanks. I will say I don't want you, or anyone else in this room again until I've cleared it."

"Understood. When you're done you can reach me at zero-zero-one on any 'link."

"We're done, for now. Let's start with Sheila Walker."

"I have an office set up for you on the meeting room level."

"No, let me talk to her and the other one on their turf. Let's keep it informal, keep them comfortable."

"Whatever you prefer. She's in the domestic employees' lounge. I'll show you."

"Fine. You might as well hang around, too," Eve said as she walked through the door he opened. "You'll make her feel protected."

Less than three minutes into the interview, Eve saw she'd called it right. Sheila was a tall, thin black girl with enormous eyes. More times than Eve could count she looked toward Roarke for reassurance, direction, and comfort.

She had a beautiful accent, like island music, but between it and the muffled tears, Eve began to feel a headache brewing.

"She was so sweet. That girl was so sweet. You never heard a bad word out of her mouth about anybody. Had a sunny disposition. Usually, if a guest got to see her or talk to her when she was cleaning, they'd give her a big tip. 'Cause she made them feel good. Now, I'll never see her again."

"I know it's hard, Sheila, to lose a friend. Could you tell if there was anything on her mind, any worry?"

"Oh no, she was happy. In two days, we have off, and the two of us, we were going shopping for shoes. That girl, she loved to shop for shoes. Right before we went for turndowns we were saying how we'd go early and get ourselves one of those free makeovers at the beauty counter at the Sky Mall."

Her thin, exotic face crumpled. "Oh, Mr. Roarke, sir!"

At the fresh bout of weeping, he merely took her hand, held it.

Eve picked away for another half hour, and took away scattered pieces that formed an image of a carefree, cheerful young woman who liked to shop, go dancing, and was having her first serious love affair.

She'd had a regular breakfast date with her boyfriend every morning after shift. They ate in the employee lounge, except on payday, when they splurged on a meal in a coffee shop a few blocks away. Routinely, he walked her to her transpo station, waved her off.

But they'd been making tentative noises about getting a small apartment together, maybe in the fall.

She'd said nothing to her best friend, as Sheila claimed to be, about seeing, hearing, or finding anything unusual or concerning. And had wheeled away her cart that last evening with a smile on her face.

The bell captain, who she interviewed in a lounge for the bellstaff, gave her a similarly rosy picture of Barry. Young, eager, cheerful, and starry-eyed over a dark-haired house-keeper named Darlene.

He'd gotten a raise only the month before, and had shown anyone he could collar the little gold heart necklace he'd bought for his girl, for their six-month anniversary.

Eve remembered Darlene had been wearing just such a necklace, playing with it, as she'd waited to enter 4602.

"Peabody, girl question," she said as she walked between her aide and Roarke across the lobby.

"I'm quite a girl."

"Right. You have a fight with your boyfriend, or you're having second thoughts about the whole deal, anything like that, do you wear a present he's given you?"

"Absolutely not. If it's a big fight, you toss it back in his face. If you're considering dumping him, you shed a few tears over it, then stick it in a drawer until you work up to the break off. If it's a minor spat, you tuck it away until you see how things are going to shake down. You only wear something he's given you, at least in plain sight, when you want to show him and everybody else that he's your guy."

"How do you keep the rules straight? It's boggling. But that's sort of what I figured. Hey."

She slapped at Roarke's hand as he tugged the chain around her neck and popped the tear-shaped diamond he'd once given her from under her shirt.

"Just checking. Apparently, I'm still your guy."

"It wasn't in plain sight," she said with some satisfaction.

"Close enough."

And catching the gleam in his eye, she narrowed her own. "You try kissing me out here, and I'm going to knock you down. Let's go talk to Barry anyway, Peabody," she said, sliding the pendant under her shirt again. "Close off this angle. You," she continued, tapping a finger on Roarke's chest, "I need to talk to sometime later about the whole media business."

"I'll be at your disposal. Nothing I like better."

The smile he gave her faded, his eyes sharpened as he heard a voice softly crooning a verse of an old Irish ballad.

Before he could turn, an arm snaked around his neck, locked. He'd have countered, was shifting his weight to do so, when the laugh sounded in his ear, and sent him back, all the way back to the alleyways of Dublin.

Then his back was hard up against the wall, and he was looking into the laughing eyes of a dead man.

"Not as quick as once you were, are you now, mate?"

"Maybe not." In a lightning move, Eve had her weapon out and pressed to the man's throat. "But I am. Step back, asshole, or you're dead."

"Too late," Roarke murmured. "He already is. Mick Connelly, why aren't you in hell, and holding my place?"

Cheerfully ignoring the laser at his throat, Mick cackled. "Ah, you can't kill the devil, can you, till he's ready to go? Aren't you a sight, you bastard. Aren't you?"

And Eve watched, baffled, as the two of them grinned like morons.

"Easy, darling." Roarke lifted a hand, gently nudged Eve's, and her weapon, down. "This ugly son of a bitch is in the way of being an old friend."

"That I am. And isn't it just like you to hire yourself a female bodyguard?"

"Cop." Roarke's grin spread.

"Well, Jay-sus." Chuckling, Mick stepped back, tapped

Roarke playfully on the cheek. "You never used to be quite so chummy with a badge."

"I'm very chummy with this one. She's my wife."

Staring, Mick clutched his heart. "She needn't bother dropping me. I'm dying of the shock. I'd heard—oh, one hears all manner of things about Roarke. But I never believed it."

He bowed, rather charmingly, while Eve secured her weapon, then took her hand and kissed it before she could avoid it. "It's pleased I am to meet you, missus, pleased as I can be. Michael Connelly's my name, and Mick to my friends, which I hope you'll be. Your man here and I were lads together long ago. Very bad lads we were, too."

"Dallas. Lieutenant Dallas." But she warmed a bit because his eyes, green as summer leaves, were twinkling with such good humor. "Eve."

"You'll forgive the . . . exuberance of my greeting my old mate here, but the excitement got the better of me."

"It's his neck. I have to go," she said to Roarke, but held out a hand, in a manner that demanded a shake rather than a kiss on the knuckles. "Nice to meet you."

"Likewise for certain. And hope to see you again."

"Sure. Later," she said to Roarke, then signaled an avidly watching Peabody toward the door.

Mick watched her stride off. "She's not sure of me, is she, boyo? And why should she be? Christ, it's good to lay eyes on you, Roarke."

"And you. What are you doing in New York, and in my hotel?"

"Business. Always a little business. In fact, I'd hoped to run you to ground to discuss it with you. Deal and wheel, wheel and deal." He winked. "Have you any time for an old friend?"

chapter four

He looked damn good for a dead man. Mick Connelly wore a petal-green suit. Roarke remembered he'd always been one for color and flash. The cut and drape disguised most of the heft he'd added in the last years.

None of them had had any heft to speak of in their youth, as varying types of hunger had kept them bone lean.

His sand-colored hair was cut short and sharp around a face that had, like his body, filled out with age. He'd had the front teeth that had bucked out like a beaver's fixed somewhere along the way. He'd lost the pitiful excuse for a mustache he'd insisted on sporting, and had never come in at more than a smudge over his top lip.

But he still sported the Irish pug nose, the fast, crooked grin, and eyes of wicked and dancing green.

No one would have called him handsome as a boy. He'd been short and skinny and covered from top to bottom with ginger-colored freckles. But he'd had quick hands, and a quicker tongue. His voice was pure south Dublin, tough music suitable for choreographing flying fists.

When he stepped into Roarke's office in the old and elegant main house of the hotel, he planted his hands on his hips and grinned like a gargoyle. "So, you've done for yourself, haven't you, mate? I'd heard, of course, but seeing's a kick in the arse."

"Seeing you's the same." Roarke's voice was warm, but he'd had time to recover from that instant of surprise and pleasure. A part of him held back, calculating what this ghost from the dead past might want of him. "Have a seat, Mick, and catch me up."

"I'll do that."

The hotel office was designed to uplift its more pedestrian functions. And as anything Roarke designed, it was as much concerned with comfort as with efficiency. The top-flight communication center and equipment were blended into graceful furnishings and stylish wall panels. The ambiance was of an urban exec's fashionable pied-á-terre.

Mick took a seat in one of the deeply cushioned chairs, stretched out his legs, scanned the room—and Roarke imagined, the fenced value of its contents. Then he sighed and studied the view out the wide glass doors and the stone balcony beyond them.

"Yes, you've done for yourself." His eyes darted back to Roarke, the laughter in them impossible to resist. "If I give you my word not to lift any of your doodads here, will you stand an old friend to a pint?"

Roarke moved to a wall panel and, opening it, ordered two Guinnesses from the AutoChef inside. "It's programmed to draw them proper, so it'll take a minute."

"Been a while since we lifted one together. How long do you think? Fifteen years?"

"There or about." *And the fifteen before that,* he thought, *we had been as thick as, well, thieves.* Roarke leaned back against the table while the Guinnesses were built, but didn't fully relax his guard. "I'd been told you'd bought it in a Liverpool pub. Knife fight. My sources are usually reliable. So why is it, Mick, you're not making book in hell?"

"Well now, I'll tell you. You may recall my mother, God bless her cold, black heart, would often tell me that it was my fate to die with a knife in my belly. She claimed whenever she had a good snootful of the Irish to have the sight."

"Is she still living then?"

"Oh aye, last I heard. I left Dublin some time before you did, you'll remember. Traveling here and there, out to make my fortune however it could be made. Doing bits of business, mostly moving merchandise of one kind or another from one place to another place where it might cool off before moving it yet again. Which was what I was doing in Liverpool on that fateful night."

Idly, Mick opened a carved wooden box on the table beside him and arched his brows at the French cigarettes inside. They were vicious in price, and the use of them banned nearly everywhere a body could go.

"Mind?"

"Help yourself."

For friendship, Mick took only one rather than palming a half dozen as he would have otherwise. "Now where was I?" he said as he lit it with a slim gold perma-match out of his pocket. "Ah, yes. Well then, I had half the take in my pocket, and was to meet my . . . client for the rest of it. Something went wrong. Port Authority garda got wind, raided the warehouse. They were looking for me, as was the client who got it into his head I'd weaseled on the deal."

At Roarke's suspicious frown, Mick laughed and shook his head. "No indeed, I did not. I'd only half my take, so why would I? In any case, I ducked into the pub to think it through and see if I could arrange for some quick and quiet transpo. Getting out was the main thing, what with the cops and the thugs out for my blood. And wouldn't you know it, while I'm sitting there stewing about losing my fee, about going on the run, a fight breaks out."

"A fight in a waterfront pub in Liverpool," Roarke said

mildly as he slid two pints of dark, foamy Guinness from the AutoChef. "Who'd believe it?"

"A hell of a one it was, too." Mick took the beer, pausing in his story to raise his glass to Roarke. "To old friends then. *Slainté.*"

"*Slainté.*" Roarke took a seat, tasted the first thick sip.

"Well, I tell you, Roarke, fists and words were flying, and there I was just wanting to keep what you'd call a low profile for the time being. The barman, well, he's got himself a bat and he's banging it on the bar and the patrons are starting to whistle and take up sides. Then the two who started it—and I never heard what set them off—draw knives. I'd've slipped out at that point, but there was no getting past them without risking losing a slice of something off me person, which I wasn't willing to do. It seemed wiser to blend with the crowd, which was taking bets and circling. And some of the onlookers got into the spirit and began to punch each other for the fun of it."

It was easy to picture, and easy to remember how many times they'd started such an evening's entertainment themselves. "How many pockets did you pick during the show?"

"I lost count," Mick said with a grin, "but I made up a small portion of my lost fee. Chairs began to fly, and bodies with them. I couldn't help but get caught up in the thing. And damned if the two who'd started it didn't end up sticking each other. Mortal, too. I could see that right off by the blackness of the blood. And the smell of it. You know how that whiff of death hits the nose."

"Yes, I do."

"Well, most of the crowd backed off then quick enough, and began to disburse like rats leaving a ship. And the barman, he goes to call the cops. So it comes to me, like a flash of light, this one dead man here's my coloring and close to my build as well. So, it's fate, isn't it? Mick Connelly needs to vanish, and how better than to be dead on the floor of a Liverpool pub? I switched IDs with him and ran.

"So Michael Joseph Connelly died bleeding there, as his mother had predicted, and Bobby Pike took the next transpo for London. And that's my story." He drank deep, let out a breath of pleasure. "Christ, it's good to look at that face of yours. We had some times, didn't we? You and me and Brian and the rest."

"We did, yes."

"I heard about what happened to Jenny, and to Tommy and Shawn. It broke my heart knowing they died as they did. There's only you and me and Bri left from the old Dublin gang."

"Brian's in Dublin still. He owns The Penny Pig, and mans the bar himself half the time."

"I've heard it. I'll wind myself back to Dublin town again, and see for myself one day. Do you go back much?"

"No."

Mick nodded. "Not all the memories are good ones, after all. Still, you got well out, didn't you? Always said you would." He rose then, carrying his half-empty pint as he strolled to the glass doors. "Think of it. You own this whole bloody place, and Christ knows what besides. Last years, I've been over the world and off it, and nowhere I've been could I say I haven't heard the name of my old boyhood mate bandied about. Like a damn religion." He turned back and grinned. "Fuck me, Roarke, if I'm not proud of you."

It struck Roarke, oddly, that no one who had known the boy had ever said those words to the man. "What are you doing with yourself, Mick?"

"Oh, bits of business. Always bits of business. And when some of it brought me to New York City, I said to myself, 'Mick, you're going to get yourself a room in that fancy hotel of Roarke's and you're going to look him up.' I'm traveling under my own name again. Time enough's passed since Liverpool. And too much time's passed I'm after thinking since I had a pint with old friends."

"So you've looked me up, and we're having our pint. Now, why don't you tell me what's behind it all?"

Mick leaned back against the door, lifted the pint to his lips, and studied Roarke with those dancing eyes. "There never was any getting over on you. A natural radar you've always had for bullshit. But the fact is what I've told you is true as gold. It just so happens that it occurred to me that you might be interested in some of the business I'm here to conduct. It's a matter of stones. Pretty colorful stones just wasting away in some dark box."

"I don't do that sort of thing anymore."

Mick grinned, let out a short laugh, then blinked as Roarke merely sat watching him. "Oh come now, this is Mick. You're never going to tell me you've retired those magic hands of yours."

"Let's just say I've put them to different uses. Legal ones. I haven't needed to pick pockets or lift locks in some time."

"Need, who said anything about need?" Mick said with a bluster. "You've a God-given talent. And not just your hands, but your brain. Never in my life have I met anyone with a slick and cagey a brain as yours. And for larceny it was created." Smiling again, he walked back to sit. "Now you're not going to expect me to believe you run all of this fucking empire of yours on the up and up."

"I do." *Now.* "And that's a challenge in itself."

"My heart." Dramatically, Mick clutched his chest. "I'm not as young as once I was. I can't take this kind of shock to the system."

"You'll live through it, and you'll have to find another setting for your stones."

"A pity. A shame. A sin, really, but what is, is." Mick sighed. "Straight and narrow, is it? Well, I've got something straight as I like to mix things up to keep myself fresh. I've a little enterprise I've started with a couple of fellows. Small chickens compared to a big rooster like you.

Scents. Perfumes and the like, with the idea of packaging
the product with an old-fashioned spin. Romance, you
know. Would you be interested in an investment?"

"I might."

"Then we'll talk about it sometime while I'm in town."
Mick got to his feet. "For now I best see what sort of accommodations I've copped here, and let you get back to
whatever it is you do with yourself."

"You're not welcome at The Palace," Roarke said, rising. "But you are in my home."

"That's kind of you, but I'm not looking to put you out."

"I thought you were dead. Jenny and the others, save
Brian, are. I never had them in my home. I'll have your
luggage seen to."

There were already psychiatric, personality, and pattern
profiles generated on Yost through various law enforcement agencies around the globe. Still, Eve considered
sending them, and her notes on him, to Dr. Mira, the
NYPSD's top profiler, for a nutshell analysis.

But a professional killer was, in essence, only a tool.
However much she wanted him, she wanted his employer
more.

"The FBI estimates Yost's fee for a single hit to be in the
neighborhood of two million, USD. This doesn't include
expenses and escalates according to the target, and the difficulty of the job."

Eve inclined her head to the screen in the conference
room at Central where Darlene's image smiled out at her.
"What makes a twenty-two-year-old chambermaid worth
two million plus?"

"Information," McNab suggested. He'd been called in,
much to his delight, as consult from EDD. Now he sat, his
long blond hair meticulously looped through a trio of
round red clips, and his pretty, thin face sober.

"Possible. Going there we say the victim had, or was believed to have had, damaging information. If so, why not arrange, for a much lesser fee, a botched mugging? She had a regular routine coming and going to work, used public transportation, and walked, most usually alone, from the transpo stops to the hotel, and to her building. Stick her on the street, grab her purse, and she goes down as a mugging victim. Low profile."

"Yeah." And though he agreed, McNab felt he had to justify his addition to the team by playing devil's advocate. "But there's a real element of risk on the street. She gets lucky, gets away, some good samaritan comes to her rescue. You take her at work, in a room, and there's no mistake. She's out."

"And the murder gets priority, a big, fat investigative team, and Roarke," she added, though she didn't care for it. "Somebody's got enough wherewithal for a major hammer, he knows just what he's taking on by putting a murder into Roarke's lap."

"Could be he's stupid," McNab said with a glimmer of a grin.

"Could be you are," Peabody snapped back. "Whoever hired Yost wanted it high profile. Media, intense investigation. It's an attention grabber, so it follows he was looking for attention. Maybe paying for it, too."

"Okay, and maybe I agree with that." McNab, miffed, shifted to Peabody. "But why? The hammer and the victim get the attention. He doesn't. So what's his point? We've got no real motive for French. Fact is, we can't say for sure if she was a specific target or just a handy one."

"She's the dead one," Peabody shot back.

"And if she'd switched rooms with another maid that shift, she'd be alive, and they'd be dead."

"McNab, you surprise me." Eve kept her voice mild, and just faintly sarcastic. "That's almost real detective thinking. According to hotel records, James Priory, a.k.a. Sylvester Yost, didn't specify that particular room, or even that particular floor when he booked. This tells me, and is corroborated by the probability scan that I, just for the hell of it, ran before this meeting—just one of those pesky investigative chores we use over here in Homicide. This tells me," she continued as both McNab and Peabody winced, "that Darlene French was not a particular target. Which in turns tells me that it's unlikely she had any particular purpose or meaning other than being alive and in that room."

"Lieutenant, why does anyone pay a couple million to have someone killed at random?"

"Let's add to that," Eve said with a nod toward McNab. "Why does anyone choose a hammer who's known to every law enforcement agency on or off planet, a hammer who will be identified within hours, to do the job? Why is it arranged that the job takes place in a landmark facility that will stir the scent for the media until drool forms?"

When there was silence, Feeney finally sighed. "I don't know, Dallas, you try to raise them right, give them the benefit of your experience, and they sit like idiots. Roarke," he said. "Roarke's the target."

It was the *why* that worried her. Why was someone going to this trouble and expense to signal Roarke? Here's what I can do, here's what I can dump right at your front door.

What was the point?

The media would buzz, and he would spin the swarm around. The hotel itself might take a few cancellations and would receive twice that much in new reservations due to the morbid curiosity and sick excitement factors.

Some employees might resign. Others would scramble to fill the slots.

In the end it would cost him nothing, and in the short-term only garner him publicity he knew exactly how to turn to his advantage.

Unless, whoever hired Yost knew the way Roarke worked. Inside. Unless they knew how having an innocent young girl killed on his property, under his employ would work on him.

The price Roarke would pay was personal. And if the motive had been personal as well . . . Yes, that worried her.

Her motivation for bringing Yost to justice was twofold now. Justice for Darlene French. Answers for Roarke.

At her desk she studied Yost's file again. No family. No known associates. No known address. *No nothing,* she thought in disgust. For the first time in her career she knew the identity of the killer, had a solid case of physical evidence, every *i* dotted toward conviction, all within twenty-four hours of the crime.

And had not a single string with which to tug him closer to hand.

No leads. No avenues.

"Where do you sleep, you son of a bitch? Where do you eat? What do you do with yourself when you're off the clock?"

She pushed away, leaned her head back, and closed her eyes.

Low-key, she thought, letting the image of his face, his eyes, his mouth, form in her head. Nothing to grab attention. *You're a loner. Nice quiet homes in nice neighborhoods. Gotta have more than one. You're a traveling man. Personal transpo? Probably, probably. But nothing flashy. Solid, dependable, discreet. Classic. Like the music you kill by.*

But if you drove into New York, you didn't use the garage facilities at the hotel.

Meat and potatoes, she thought, remembering his hotel meal. Basic, expensive. The clothes he'd worn, in and out, had met the same criteria. As had his luggage.

Luggage.

She sat up, ordered the file disc that contained his check-in.

"Yeah, yeah, one business traveler's wheel-on. Basic

and expensive. And new. Looks brand-spanking-new to me. Computer, enlarge sector twelve through twenty-eight, magnify twenty percent."

WORKING . . .

The portion of the image that showed the suitcase standing tidily at Yost's feet popped. She could see no sign of wear on the heavy-duty black leather, none of the flaws that showed after even minimal trips through the rigors of handling or security checks.

"Enlarge sector six through ten, this image."

WORKING . . .

And when the image popped this time, she read clearly the fancy brass tag of the manufacturer. "Cachet. Okay, what does that give us? Computer, identify model of baggage on screen, manufactured through Cachet."

WORKING . . . UNIT IDENTIFIED AS MODEL NUMBER 345/92-C, MARKETED AS BUSINESS ELITE AND AVAILABLE IN LEATHER OR CLOTH. UNIT MEASURES FOURTEEN BY EIGHT BY SIX AND PASSES FAA AND PAA CARRY-ON REQUIREMENTS FOR ALL AIR AND SPACE TRANSPORTATION. 345/92-C IS A NEW MODEL, AVAILABLE SINCE JANUARY OF THE CURRENT YEAR. CACHET IS THE TRADENAME OF A DIVISION OF SOLAR LIGHTS, A ROARKE INDUSTRIES CORPORATION.

"Who didn't know that," Eve muttered. "Out since January. There's a nice little break. Computer . . . No, never mind." She shifted to her interdepartment 'link and snagged McNab.

"Cachet, luggage. Their model 345/92-C, called Business Elite. Get me a list of where that model was sold, in black leather, since its intro in January of this year. I want locations, and from those locations, I want names. Who bought the bag?"

"That's going to take—"

"Time," she finished. "Did you run out of that substance?"

"No, sir. I'm on it."

"So am I," she murmured, then rose. She grabbed her jacket, her files, then strode out to Peabody's cubicle in the bull pen. "I'm heading home to run some data. I want you to check on the hair."

"Hair, sir?"

"Yost's hair. No way that was his. Just doesn't fit his face, and it's too damn fussy for his style. So it's a rug, a good one. And my hunch is he has a collection. Start off with the one he's wearing on the security tapes, check salons and beauty suppliers, top-level ones, major cities. He doesn't fool around with second line. And start with stuff that's natural fiber and nonallergic or whatever it's called. He likes things clean. He carries a leather suitcase rather than the lighter, manmade cloth."

Peabody opened her mouth, but Eve was already striding away so she didn't get to ask what a leather suitcase had to do with a wig.

Eve walked in the front door of the house just as Roarke came down the stairs. She blew her bangs out of her eyes and frowned at him.

"What are you doing here?" she asked.

"I live here."

"You know what I mean."

"Yes, and I might ask the same. You're not off-shift as yet."

"I've got stuff I want to run here instead of at Central."

"Ah."

"Yeah, ah. And since you're here, I should be able to cut some time. I've got some questions you could—"

She started up as she spoke, breaking off when he laid a hand on her arm. "I was just upstairs, settling Mick into one of the guest rooms."

"Mick? Oh." She paused. "Oh."

"Do you have a problem with him staying here for a few days?"

"No." *The timing sucks,* she thought. *Seriously sucks.* "Like you said, you live here."

"As do you. I realize he comes from a time in my life that isn't entirely comfortable for you." He ran a finger over the strap of her shoulder harness. "Lieutenant. But it is, in fact, a time in my life."

"I met a few of your friends from Dublin before. I like Brian."

"I know." He laid his hands on her shoulders now, ran them down her back, moving closer until his brow rested on hers. "Mick was important to me, Eve. As close, likely closer than a brother might have been through some very ugly times, and some good ones. I thought he was dead, and I'd adjusted to that."

"And now you know he isn't." She understood friendship, its pulls and tugs and its puzzles. "Would you mind asking him not to do anything I'd have to arrest him for while he's staying in one of the guest rooms?"

He shifted just enough to press his lips to hers. "I think you'll like him."

"Yeah." And they both knew he hadn't agreed to her request. "You Irish guys are pretty likable. Listen, I just want to say you don't need any trouble right now, with the way this homicide investigation is heading."

He nodded. "It was never her, was it? That poor little maid."

"I don't think so. We need to sit down and figure who would go after you this way, and why."

"All right, when I can. I've some arrangements to put into motion just now. We're having some people over for dinner."

"Tonight? Roarke—"

"I can make your excuses if it's not convenient for you. Magda and her son, and a few key people will be here. It's important to smooth out feathers ruffled by the incident last night, and to reassure everyone involved in the upcoming auction that security and publicity are under control."

"No point in asking you to postpone the whole deal."

"None at all," he said cheerfully. "I can hardly put the hotel, or any of my projects or my life for that matter, on hold because it's believed that someone's hoping to upset me."

"The next move might be on you."

His smile never dimmed. In fact, it sharpened. "I'd prefer it. I don't want another innocent life on my conscience. In any case, I have the most reliable of bodyguards very close at hand."

And she intended to be closer. "What time's the dinner thing?"

"Eight."

"Then I'd better get some work done. I guess I have to put on some fancy deal."

"Leave that to me." He took her hand, kissed it. "Thank you."

"Yeah, yeah, save it. I want some of your time before tomorrow," she added, jogging up the stairs.

"Darling Eve, I want a great deal of yours."

She snorted, kept going, and when she reached the second floor paused as Mick came out of one of the countless guest rooms. He'd removed his suit jacket and looked, to her eye, casual and at home.

He gave her a quick, crooked smile. "Ah, Lieutenant. Nothing more annoying than an unexpected houseguest, is there? And add on to that an old boyhood friend of your husband's who's a stranger to you, and you have tedium on top of it. I hope you're not too inconvenienced by my staying."

"It's a big house," she said, then realized that was probably not the most polite of responses. But he received it with such a huge, rollicking laugh she had to grin back at him. "Sorry, I'm a little distracted. Roarke wants you here, so that's fine with me."

"Thanks for that. I'll try not to bore the ears off your head with stories of our youthful escapades."

"Actually, I like hearing that kind of thing."

"Well now, that's opening the worm can." He winked at her. "Some house," he said, letting his gaze wander the generous hall and stairs. "House isn't the word, I suppose, not near to grand enough for this palace. How do you find your way about?"

"I don't always." She noticed his gaze shifting again, resting contemplatively on her weapon harness. "Problem?" she said, coolly now.

"No, indeed, though I'm not shamed to say I'm not one to care for that sort of weapon."

"Really." Idly, she laid her hand on it. "What kind of weapon do you prefer?"

He lifted his arm, cocked it at the elbow, and bunched his fist. "This always did fine enough for me. But in your line of work, well . . . And speaking of that, I was just thinking this is one of the rare pleasant conversations I've experienced with a person in your profession. Roarke and a cop. Begging your pardon, Lieutenant, there's a brain rattler. Maybe you'd sit and tell me the story of how that came to be one of these days. God knows I'd love to hear it."

"Ask Roarke. He's better at stories than I am."

"I'd like your version all the same." He hesitated, then

appeared to come to a decision as he approached her. "Roarke wouldn't have settled for less than smart, so I figure you for a smart cop, Lieutenant. And as one, you'd know the likes of me when you look. But maybe you don't know that Roarke's my oldest friend in this world. I hope I can work a truce, if nothing better than that, with the woman my friend married."

When he held out a hand, Eve came to a decision of her own. "I'll take a truce with a friend of the man I married." She clasped his hand. "Keep it clean in New York, Mick. I don't want any trouble for him."

"Nor do I." He gave her hand a squeeze. "Or for meself for that matter. You work in the homicide part of things, don't you?"

"That's right."

"I can say, looking you in the eye, that I've never had occasion to kill anyone, and have no plans to begin. That might help things along here."

"It doesn't hurt."

chapter five

Leaving the houseguest for Roarke and Summerset to deal with, Eve buried herself in her home office to study the case files on the long list of murders tagging Yost as the primary suspect.

She picked them apart, put them back together, searching for holes in the investigative process, for pieces that had been mislaid or ignored.

Whenever she found something she set it aside in what she began to think of as her Screwup File. There'd been a number of definite screwups, to her way of thinking. Witnesses who hadn't been thoroughly interviewed, or pushed during an interview. Trace evidence that had been logged, but not tracked down to its root source.

In a smattering of the cases she found there had been some small, personal item taken from the body of the victim. A ring, a hair ribbon, a wrist unit. All inexpensive items that held consistent with the lack of robbery as motive.

But that didn't, Eve felt, hold consistent with pattern.

"If he took something from one, he took something from all," she muttered.

He was anal, tidy, habitual.

Souvenirs, she thought. *He takes a token. What had he taken from Darlene French?*

She brought up the security video, keyed it into the section where Darlene had wheeled her cart to the door of 4602, froze the image, magnified it.

"Earrings." In the image Darlene wore tiny gold hoops at her ears, all but hidden by her dark, curling hair. Though Eve was certain no such jewelry had been on the body, she checked the record, split-screening images so that she could examine Darlene, battered and broken on the bed. "He took your little earrings."

A collector, she decided, sitting back. *Because he enjoys the work?* she wondered. *Wants to be able to look back on various jobs, remember them, revisit them.*

So it wasn't just the money. No, not just the money. Are they thrill kills after all?

Her desk 'link signaled, and still studying the two images of Darlene, she answered.

"Dallas."

"Got a line on the wire," McNab began. "It's sold by length or by weight, primarily to jewelers—professional and hobbyists—or artists. You can get it retail but it's a hell of a lot pricier that way than going to a wholesale source. Most of the retail suppliers sell small lengths, and my information is most of that's to consumers who buy it for hairdos or a quick wrap around the wrist or ankle. Impulse stuff."

"Wholesalers," Eve said. "He's not an impulse guy, and he doesn't like to overpay," she added, thinking of the hotel amenities.

"Figured. We got way over a hundred wholesalers globally, and another twenty or so off planet. You need an artist or craftsman license, or a retail ID number to purchase at wholesale level. You got that, you can get it from the source or order electronically."

"Okay, run them all." She brought up her evidence list as she spoke, checked the length of the wire removed from the crime scene. "He used a two-foot length, exactly two feet, on French." She made a quick scan of other case files, nodded. "Yeah, he likes that length. Check on orders of that length, and lengths with two-foot multiples." She shut her eyes a minute. "Silver tarnishes, doesn't it? Gets spotty or something with age."

"You gotta keep it polished unless it's coated. Lab said this was uncoated sterling. I got the report right here, and there's no mention of any chemical, any polish on the metal. He could've wiped it pretty clean, I guess. I don't know how much might stay on, or what the hell it does to the metal."

"Highlight the two-foot purchases," Eve decided. "List them chronologically, going back from the date of the murder. My guess is he'd want a nice, shiny new tool for each job."

She cut transmission, pondered a bit over the properties of sterling silver, then picked through the files yet again, following the wire.

Other investigators had followed it as well, but in less than half the cases they had done full scans on specific lengths. And in half of those, the primary had focused on suppliers in the city and environs of the murder only.

Sloppy. Goddamn sloppy.

She glanced up, still scowling, as Roarke came in. "What happens to silver when you polish it?"

"It gets shiny."

"Ha-ha. I mean, does the polish stuff leave a coat on it, or what?"

He sat on the edge of her desk, smiled at her. "Why, I wonder, would you suppose I'd know the answer to that?"

"You know every damn thing."

"That's flattering, Lieutenant, but domestic activities

such as silver polishing are just slightly out of my aegis. Ask Summerset."

"I don't want to. That would require speaking to him on a voluntary basis. I'll tag somebody in the lab."

But when she started to reach for her 'link, Roarke simply waved her away, and contacted his majordomo on the house 'link. "Summerset, does silver polish leave a coating of any sort on the metal?"

Thin-faced, pale of complexion, and dark of eye, Summerset filled the 'link screen. "On the contrary, if properly done the polish is buffed away or the silver would be cloudy, and the process removes a minute layer of the metal."

"Thank you. Helpful?" he asked Eve when he'd ended transmission.

"Just plugging holes. Do you sell silver wire?"

"Oh, I imagine."

"Yeah, so did I."

"If you'd like help tracing the murder weapon—"

"McNab's on it. We'll see how far we can fumble without you in that area."

"Of course. But you did want to discuss something with me."

"Yeah. Where's your pal?"

"Mick's enjoying the pool. And we've a couple of hours before our guests begin to arrive."

"Okay." But she rose, walked across the room, and closed her office door. And standing there, looked back, studying the man she loved, had married, and lived with. "The hit, if we accept the theory that this was a hired job, cost two million plus expenses, at the minimum. Who would spend that much to inconvenience or embarrass or upset you?"

"I can't tell you. There are certainly a number of competitors, professional rivals, or foes, those who have a personal dislike for me who have the financial resources to invest that much money to disturb me."

"How many of that number wouldn't see murder as too high a price?"

"In business?" He lifted his hands. "I've made a lot of enemies, certainly, but the battles are generally waged in meeting rooms, over ledgers. While it's not unthinkable that one of them might reach flash point and decide eliminating me is a worthwhile business move, I can't think of a reason, logically, why killing a maid in one of my hotels would answer."

"Not all your battles used to be waged in meeting rooms, or over ledgers."

"No. But even they were direct. If we're dealing with an old grudge, it would still be me or mine targeted. I didn't even know that girl."

"There." She stepped forward now, moving in on him, her eyes on his face. "That's the point I keep circling back to. It hurts you, it preys on your mind. And it pisses you off."

"There are other ways to accomplish all of that without killing an innocent girl."

"Who wouldn't care?" she insisted. "Past or present. What major deals do you have going on right now where the balance could be shifted if you're not focused, not on top of it. Olympus? When we took those few days last week you spent a lot of time fixing stuff."

"The sort of thing that's expected to arise in a project of that size and scope. It's under control."

"Would it be if you weren't at the helm?"

He considered. "There might be some added delays, costs, some complications, but, yes, I have a strong team in every area of that project. As I do on all major holdings. I'm not indispensable, Eve."

"Bullshit." She said it with such force, it startled him. "You have your finger on every button in every deal or organization. The whole damn mess you've built would spin without you, fine, but it wouldn't spin the same way. There's only one you. Who've you bumped up against who doesn't want to play it your way?"

"No one in particular. In any case, if someone wanted to yank my attention away from a project, cause me to neglect it, the most certain way of doing that would have been to try for you."

"And have you hound them until they're no more than husks you can kick into dust? I don't think so."

He skimmed a finger down the shallow dent in her chin. "You have a point."

"If it's nothing from now, then you have to think back. The past can circle back on us no matter what kind of maze we build. We both know that. Part of yours is splashing around in your swimming pool right now."

"True enough."

"Roarke." She hesitated, then leaped. "You haven't seen him for a long time. You don't know who he is now, or what he's done in the years between. He shows up, right in the lobby of the hotel, hours, really, after the murder."

"You're looking at Mick in this?" He was able to smile again, shake his head. "He's a thief, a grifter, a liar, certainly, and not one you'd trust farther than a good boot in the ass would send him, but murder isn't in him. This kind," he continued before she could argue, "this cold and calculated kind is either in a man or isn't, Eve. We both know that."

"Maybe. But people change. And paying for murder can add a nice, cozy buffer for some."

"For some. Not Mick." On that point, at least, he hadn't a doubt. "You're right that he may have changed. But never on that most elemental level. He'd cheerfully cheat a grandmother, even his own, out of her life's savings, but he wouldn't kill a mongrel dog, or order it done, for rubies. He was the softest of us when it came to bloodshed."

"Okay." But she'd keep an eye on Mick Connelly nonetheless. "Someone else from back then. You need to put your mind to it. To deals from before, to deals right now. Something I can work with."

"I'll set my mind on it, I promise you."

"Good. And you'll increase your personal security."

"Will I?"

She'd hoped to sneak that one in, but hadn't really counted on it. "You're the target. It's possible Darlene French was just a warning shot. 'Look how close I can get without really trying.' The next step might be to go after you directly."

"Or you," he countered. "Are you increasing your personal security?"

"I don't have any personal security."

"Exactly."

"I'm a cop."

"And I sleep with one." He snuck an arm around her waist. "Aren't I lucky?"

"Cut it out. This isn't a joke."

"No, indeed it isn't. But that crack about increasing my personal security I'll take as one so I don't become annoyed with my wife right before we have guests for dinner. Shut up," he suggested as she opened her mouth, then insured she did so.

The kiss was long, and it was hard, and not particularly playful. So when she surfaced from it, her eyes narrowed.

"I can hang cops all over you."

"You could," he agreed. "And I could shake them right off again, as you well know. You're the only cop I want hanging all over me, Lieutenant. In fact . . ." His clever fingers had her shirt half-unbuttoned before she slapped them away.

"Cut it out. I don't have time for this."

He grinned. "Then I'll be quick."

"I said—" But his teeth sunk lightly into her throat,

shooting the thrill straight down the center of her body, right through the toes. Her eyes might have crossed, but she gave him a decent elbow jab. "Stop it."

"I can't. I have to hurry." And he was laughing as he unfastened the hook of her trousers. Laughing when his mouth came back to cover hers.

She might have kicked him if her feet hadn't gotten tangled, but her heart wouldn't have been in it. Even her yelp as he plopped her onto her own desk didn't register much of a protest.

Half-naked, already breathless, she levered herself on her elbows. "All right, just get it over with."

He leaned over her, nipped her chin. "I heard that snicker."

"That was the sound of a sneer."

"Was it?" Amused, aroused, he distracted her with a nibble on her bottom lip. "I can never tell the difference. And what sound is this?"

"What sound?"

He drove himself into her, one powerful and deep thrust that ripped a shocked cry from her throat.

"That one." He lowered his head, tasting the heat that rose to her flesh even as her hips arched to meet him. "And that one."

She struggled to get her breath back. "Tolerance," she managed.

"Oh, well, if that's the best we can do." He started to move back. She reared up, wrapped around him.

"I need to practice my tolerance." She skimmed the hair away from his face with her fingers, then fisted her hands. Her lips curved, met his.

When the in-house 'link signaled, he simply reached over and manually switched it to standby.

It turned out he wasn't as quick as he was thorough. When she was reasonably certain her legs would hold her again, she pushed off the desk and stood, wearing her boots, an open shirt, and her shoulder harness.

Absurdly sexy, he thought, his cop.

"I don't suppose you'd wait just a moment while I get a camera."

Not quite steady, she glanced down, got a reasonably clear picture of herself, and curled her lip at him. "Play time's over." She reached down for her trousers, then had to simply stay bent over. "Man, you fuzz up my brain."

"Thank you, darling. It wasn't my best effort, but I was under considerable time restraint."

With her hands on her knees she looked up. His hair was tousled from her fingers, his eyes deep blue and sleepy with satisfaction. "Maybe I'll let you try again later."

"You're too good to me." He walked by, patting her affectionately on the ass. "We'd better tidy ourselves up for dinner."

The thing about dinner parties, Eve had discovered, was that you couldn't just sit down at the table and ask your neighbor to pass the potatoes. There was a whole ritual to be observed, which included proper attire and body adornments, an exchange of pleasantries, even if you weren't feeling particularly pleasant, and the premeal consumption of alcohol and tiny bits of food in a room other than the one fashioned for serious dining.

This, by her estimation, added about an hour to the event, and didn't begin to include the after-meal section of the interlude.

She thought she'd become reasonably adept at handling the ceremony—not as smoothly as Roarke, but then who could? Still it didn't take that much brain power to act as host to a bunch of people in your own house, even if her mind did tend to wander now and again toward activities she'd rather have been involved in.

If she could get a solid line on the luggage and on the

silver wire, she could begin to put together a geographic pattern on Yost. Where he shopped, how he shopped. Which could lead to the area of where and how he lived.

The man liked steak, medium rare. Slabs of prime beef didn't come cheap. Did he buy his own meat, or go out to restaurants?

Top of the line, whichever it was.

Did he treat himself to the best when he was working, or was it a daily habit?

What else did he spend his money on? He had plenty of it. How did he access his funds? If she could—

"You seem to be somewhere else entirely."

"What?" Eve focused on Magda, struggled to clear her head. "Sorry."

"No, don't apologize." They were sitting on the silky cushions of one of the antique sofas in the formal parlor. Diamonds, bright and round as planets, flashed at Magda's ears and at the hollow of her throat. She sipped at a frothy and pale pink drink in a small flute. "What's on your mind is, I'm sure, a great deal more important than the foolishness on ours. You were thinking about that poor girl who was murdered. Do you know my suite's directly below where she was killed?"

"No." Eve let that play around in her mind a bit. "I didn't know."

"Horrible. She was hardly more than a child, wasn't she? I believe I saw her, just the night before it happened, in the hall as I was leaving my room. She said good evening to me, and called me by name. I gave her no more than an absent smile because I was in a hurry. Little regrets," Magda murmured, "that make no difference at all."

"Was she alone? Did you see anyone with her? Do you remember the time?" Even as Magda blinked, Eve was shaking her head. "Sorry. Sorry. Occupational hazard."

"It's perfectly all right. I didn't notice anyone, but I do know it was seven-forty-five, because I was to meet people

in the bar at seven-thirty, and I was annoyed with myself
for being late. So divalike. I'd been on the 'link with my
agent about a new project I'm considering."

Put it away, Eve ordered herself. "A new movie?"

"It's sweet of you to ask when you couldn't be the least
bit interested. Yes, a good, solid part. But I can't give the
decision the attention it deserves until after the auction.
Now, should I tell you about your guests tonight, or has
Roarke already briefed you?"

"There wasn't a lot of time for that," Eve said and
thought about the fast, impulsive sex on her desk. Nearly
grinned.

"Good, it gives me a chance for quick gossip. My son."
She glanced over with affection at the golden-haired man
standing by the fireplace, his face handsome and serious.
"My one and only. He's becoming quite the sober and
steady businessman," she said with pride shining. "I don't
know what I'd do without him. He's not yet settled down to
give me the grandchildren I've begun to crave, but I have
hope. Not," she said with some spirit, "that I see Liza Trent
in the role of my daughter-in-law. She's gorgeous, of
course."

Magda leaned back and studied the curvy blonde who
stood with her hand on Vince's arm and appeared to hang
on his every word. "Ambitious, and a reasonably good
actor. Not Vince's type for the long haul. Not very bright,
all in all. But so good for the ego. See how she looks at
him as though the words fall from his mouth like gold
coins."

"You don't like her."

"I don't dislike her. It's the mother in me, I suppose, becoming impatient for Vince to move on."

It didn't look like it would happen anytime soon, Eve
mused. Vince Lane might have been his mother's apple,
but to her he looked a bit weak around the chin.

Fashion-wise, he went for the trendy and expensive, and

looked, in her opinion, elaborate and overdressed next to Roarke's understated elegance.

But then, what did she know about fashion?

"Then there's Carlton Mince," Magda went on. "Looks a bit like a mole, doesn't he? Bless him. He's managed my finances for more years than I care to count. He's helped me tremendously with the ins and outs of the foundation. Steady as a rock, that's Carlton, and I'm afraid just as interesting to most people. His wife, the woman in the remarkably ugly and unsuitable gown, is Minnie. Minnie Mince, can you imagine? She's walking proof that you can indeed be too thin and too addicted to body sculpting."

Eve felt herself smirk before she could stop it. The fact was, the woman looked like an overdressed, overpolished stick with a tower of gaudy red hair.

"Twenty years ago she was his bookkeeper," Magda continued, "with bad hair and an eye on the goal. The last twelve she's been his wife. She got the goal, Carlton, and still has bad hair."

Eve laughed. "That's probably mean."

"Oh, probably. But where's the fun in talking about people if you only say nice things? You look at Minnie and are assured money can't buy taste, but at the same time she suits Carlton to the ground. She makes him happy, and since I'm enormously fond of him, I like her for that alone. Last, we have Roarke's charming friend from Ireland. What can you tell me about him?"

"Not a lot. They were boys together in Dublin, and haven't seen each other for a number of years."

"And you watch him with a calculating eye."

"Do I?" Eve moved her shoulders. It paid to remember that actors were the observant sort. At least the good ones were. "I probably watch everyone that way. Another occupational hazard."

"You don't look at this one with a cop's eye," Magda commented as Roarke crossed the room toward them.

"Ladies." In a gesture both absent and intimate, he trailed his fingers over Eve's shoulder. On cue, Summerset came to the door to announce dinner.

During the meal Eve confirmed that Magda was, for the most part, a keen observer of human nature. Liza Trent either giggled or knit her brows in rapt concentration whenever Vince spoke. The fact that she could put on a good show of fascination with his tedious remarks earned her points, in Eve's mind, as an actor.

Carlton Mince was as quiet as the mole Magda had compared him to, speaking in polite and modulated tones when called on to do so, and otherwise steadily burrowing his way through each course. As for his wife, Eve caught her surreptitiously examining the silverware for the maker's mark.

Conversation wound its way around to the auction, and there, at least, Vince appeared to know his business. "Magda Lane's collection of theater memorabilia, particularly costume, is unrivaled." He cut delicately into his pressed duck. "In fact, I tried to persuade her to limit the auction to that alone."

"One fell swoop," Magda said with a laugh. "I never could do anything in pieces."

"Truer words." Her son sent her a warm, if exasperated look. "Still, saving the ball gown from *Pride's Fall* until last will end the event on a high note."

"Ah, I remember it well." Mick let out a wistful, lover-like sigh. "The spoiled and headstrong Pamela sweeps into the ballroom at Carlyle Hall in her simmering gown of the ice goddess, daring any man to resist her. The dreams I had that night, after seeing you in that dress, Miss Lane, why they'd bring a blush to your cheek."

Obviously delighted, she leaned toward him. "I don't blush easily, Mr. Connelly."

He chuckled. "I do. Does it hurt your heart, a little, to part with your memories?"

"I'll never part with them, just the visual aides. And what the foundation will do with the proceeds will keep me very warm at night."

"It costs the earth to keep all those costumes protected and stored," Minnie put in, and earned the faintest of sneers from Magda.

"As a former bookkeeper, I'm sure you'll agree, at the end of the day, the investment's been well worth it."

"Unquestionably." Though he kept his attention focused on his duck, Carlton nodded his head. "The tax benefits alone from—"

"Oh, not taxes, Carlton." Magda held up her hands in surrender. "Not at such a lovely meal. Even the thought gives me indigestion. Roarke, this wine is sinful. One of yours?"

"Mmmm. The Montcart '49. Elegant," he said, lifting his glass to the light. "Polished with just a hint of bite. I thought it suited you."

She all but purred. "Eve, I'll have to confess to being desperately in love with your husband. I hope you don't arrest me for it."

"If that was a crime in this state, I'd have three-quarters of the female population of New York in cages."

"Darling." Roarke looked down the table, met her eyes. "You flatter me."

"That wasn't flattery."

Liza giggled, as if she didn't know what else to do. "It's so hard not to be jealous when you've got a handsome, powerful man." She gave Vince's arm a quick squeeze. "I just want to scratch their eyes out when they come on to my Vinnie."

"Yeah?" Eve sipped the elegant '49, enjoyed the little bite. "Me, I just punch them in the face."

While Liza tried to decide whether to look shocked or impressed, Mick smothered a laugh behind his napkin. "From what I've seen, and heard, Roarke's stopped collecting women. He found the jewel of the lot, one with numerous facets and who shines in the setting he had waiting. Now when we were lads, he could barely walk for all the girls throwing themselves at his feet."

"You must have stories." Magda danced her fingertips on the back of Mick's hand. "Fascinating ones. Roarke's always so mysterious about his past accomplishments. It only whets the curiosity."

"I've stories in bushels and more. The pretty redhead with the rich father visiting Dublin from Paris, France. Or the little brunette with the lovely shape on her who baked scones twice weekly to curry his favor. I think her name was Bridgett. Do I have the right of that, Roarke?"

"You do. And she married Tim Farrell, the baker's son, which seemed to suit everyone." He recalled, just as clearly, that they'd plucked the Parisian redhead's—whatever her name might have been—deep purse to the bottom while he'd seduced her.

No one had been dissatisfied with the end results.

"Those were the days." Mick sighed. "But being a friend, and a gentleman, I'll tell no tales on my old mate. No more collecting women for the likes of Roarke, but a collector he always was. Rumors are you've an impressive one of weapons."

"I've picked up a few here and there over the years."

"Guns?" Vince brightened up, and his mother rolled her eyes.

"Vince has been fascinated by guns all his life. Drove the property masters wild whenever I was in a period piece and he came on set."

"I have a number of guns in my collection. Perhaps you'd like to see it."

"I'd love it."

It was a room that echoed with violence, and the tools men devised to wield against men. Pikes and lances, muskets, the Colts they'd called Peacemakers, and the auto-blasters that had made life among the cheapest commodities during the Urban Wars.

The tasteful setting with its soaring ceiling and sparkling glass didn't disguise the grim purpose of each display. Nor did it dim the elemental and human fascination for the art of self-destruction.

"Lord." Vince circled the room. "I haven't seen anything like this outside of the Smithsonian. It must have taken you years to put your collection together."

"A number of them." He noticed Vince's avaricious glance at a pair of nineteenth-century dueling pistols. Obligingly, Roarke used the palm plate and his code to release the lock on the reinforced glass case. He drew a pistol from its slot, passed it to Magda's son.

"Beautiful."

"Oooh." Liza gave a little shudder, but Eve caught the bright lust in her eyes. "Isn't it dangerous?"

"Not in its present state." Roarke spared her a smile and showed her another case. "The little one there, the one with the jeweled grip. Designed for a lady's hand and her purse. It once belonged to a wealthy widow who, in the unsettled days of the early part of the century, carried it with her whenever she took her morning walk with her Pomeranian. She's reputed to have shot an unlucky mugger, two looters, a discourteous doorman, and a Lhasa apso with carnal intentions regarding her Pom."

"Goodness." Gilt lashes fluttered over Liza's violet eyes. "She shot a dog?"

"So they say."

"A far different time." Mick studied a semiautomatic in gleaming chrome. "Amazing, isn't it," he said to Eve, "that anyone with the price in his pocket and the desire in his heart could pick up one of these over the counter, or under it, before the Gun Ban?"

"I always thought more stupid than amazing."

"You aren't a defender of the right to bear arms, Lieutenant?" Vince asked, turning the dueling pistol in his hand. He imagined himself looking very dashing.

She glanced back at the mean little automatic. "That's not designed to defend. It's designed to kill."

"Still." With some reluctance, he replaced the pistol in its slot and wandered over to where she stood with Mick. "People continue to find a way. If they didn't, you'd be out of a job."

"Vincent, that's rude."

"No, it's not." Eve nodded. "You're right, people find a way. But it's been some years since we've had disturbed children slaughtering other children in school hallways, or half-asleep spouses shooting their partners when they stumble in the dark, or neighborhoods under siege from gangs who carelessly shoot bystanders while they try to shoot each other. I think the old slogan was, Guns Don't Kill People, People Kill People. And it's true enough. But a gun gives them a hell of a lot of help."

"I can't argue with that," Mick put in. "Never did like the ugly, noisy things myself. Now a good sticker—" He strolled away a bit to a display of knives. "At least a man's got to get close enough to look you in the eye before he tries you with one of these. Takes more courage to stand toe-to-toe and stick a man than it does to blast away at him from a distance. But me, I'll stick with my fists."

He turned away, grinned. "A good, sweaty brawl solves most disputes, and mostly everyone can limp away from it and have a pint. We broke some noses in our day, didn't we, Roarke?"

"Probably more than our share." He relocked the case. "Coffee?" he said smoothly.

chapter six

Eve strapped on her weapon and eyed her husband. He was enjoying a light breakfast in the sitting area of their bedroom. The morning news was playing on the wall screen and the stock reports skimmed by in a puzzling series of codes and figures on the tabletop unit.

The cat, Galahad, lounged beside him, with one of his dual-colored eyes aimed hopefully at a slice of Irish bacon neglected on Roarke's plate.

"How can you look like you've just come home from a week's vacation in some pamper spa?" she demanded.

"Clean living?"

"My ass. I know you were up till after three, drinking whiskey and telling lies with your pal. I heard his looney laugh as the pair of you stumbled upstairs."

"He might have been a bit unsteady at the end of it." He turned to her, his eyes blue and clear and rested. "A few fingers of whiskey's never been known to set me under. I'm sorry we woke you."

"It couldn't have been for long. I never heard you come to bed."

"I needed to pour Mick into his first."

"What are you going to do with him today?"

"He has business of his own, and will make his way about well enough. Summerset can tell him where I'll be if he wants to know."

"I thought you'd probably work from here today."

"No." He watched her over his coffee cup. "Not today. Stop worrying about me, Lieutenant. You have enough on your plate."

"You're the main course."

He laughed at that and rose to kiss her. "I'm very touched."

"Don't be touched." She gripped his arms once, firmly, to make her point. "Be careful."

"I'll be both."

"Will you at least use a driver? And the limo." The limo, she knew, was reinforced and could withstand a hailstorm of boomers.

"Yes, to set your mind at ease."

"Thanks. I've got to get going."

"Lieutenant?"

"What?"

He cupped her face in his hands, gently touched his lips to her forehead, her cheeks, her mouth. "I love you."

Everything inside her shifted, shimmered, settled. "I know. Even though I'm not a French redhead with a rich daddy. How much did you take her for?"

"In what area?"

She laughed, shook her head. "Never mind." But at the door she stopped, looked back at him. "I love you, too. Oh, and Galahad just copped your bacon."

She strode down the hall, but caught the mild exasperation in Roarke's voice. "Haven't we discussed that sort of behavior?" It made her smirk a little as she took the steps in a jog.

At the bottom, lurking as she thought of it, was Summerset. He held her leather jacket between one long thumb and one bony finger. "I will assume you'll be home for the evening meal unless I hear to the contrary."

"Assume all you want." She took the jacket, but glanced back up the stairs as she shrugged into it. "I need you a minute."

"I beg your pardon?"

"Stuff the attitude back up your pointy nose," she suggested, but she kept her voice lowered. She aimed a finger at the front door, then swung it open. "Come on."

"I have several tasks on this morning's schedule," he began.

"Quiet." She shut the door behind him, drew in a breath of sweet spring air. "You've been with him for a long time, and you know all there is to know. First give me your take on Mick Connelly."

"I'm not in the habit of gossiping about houseguests."

"Goddamn it." She rapped a fist on his chest, an impatient gesture that caused Summerset to show his teeth. "Do I look like I want a cozy gossip here? Somebody wants to shake Roarke. I don't know why, I don't know the bottom line, but someone's looking to cause him trouble. Give me your take on Connelly."

Summerset's eyes, which had gone black as onyx at the fist to his chest, narrowed. Considered her. "He was wild as they all were. They were wild times. My understanding was he had a difficult home life, but then all of them did. Some worse than others. He came around when Roarke settled in with me. Polite enough, if rough around the edges. Hungry, but they were all hungry."

"Did he ever square off with Roarke?"

"There were words and fists at one time or another between all of them. Mick would have cut off his fingers for Roarke. Any of them would. Mick looked up to him. Roarke took a beating for him once, from the cops," Summerset added with a sneer. "When Mick fumbled a pass off after a pocket dip."

"Okay. All right." She relaxed a little.

"This is about the chambermaid."

"Yeah. I want you to use that yard-long nose of yours for something other than looking down at inferiors. Sniff around, past and present. If you catch a whiff of anything, *anything* that's off, contact me. You can monitor Roarke without putting his back up. He expects you to know where he is. Make sure you do."

Summerset put a hand on her arm to stop her from turning away. "Is he in any sort of physical jeopardy?"

"If I thought he was, he wouldn't get out of the house even if I had to drug him and put him in restraints."

Forced to be satisfied with that, Summerset watched her go down the steps to where her increasingly dilapidated city-issue vehicle was parked.

Eve imagined the steam gushing out of her ears as she marched through the detective's bull pen and on to her office. Her 'link light was blinking busily from messages and her computer was beeping from fresh incoming data.

She ignored both and began riffling through her drawers.

"Sir? McNab—"

"I want a riot laser," Eve snapped at Peabody. "Full body armor." She yanked a six-inch combat knife from its leather sheath and watched, with glee, as its wicked serrated edge caught the sunlight through her little window.

Peabody's eyes popped. "Sir?"

"I'm going down to Maintenance, and I'm going locked and loaded. I'm taking those piss-brain sons of bitches out, one by one. Then I'm going to haul what's left of the bodies into my vehicle and set it on fire."

"Jesus, Dallas, I thought we had a red flag."

"I've got a red flag. I've got one." Her eyes wheeled to Peabody. "I've got under fifty miles on my ride since those lying, cheating, sniveling shitheads said it was road ready. Road ready? Do you want me to tell you about road ready?"

"I would like that very much, Lieutenant. If you'd sheathe that knife first."

With one last oath of disgust, Eve rammed the blade home. "It starts bucking on me while I'm sitting at a light. Just sitting and it's kicking like a . . ."

"Mule?"

"Probably. I run the diagnostic, and you know what it does? It brings up the dash map with directions to the morgue. Is that some sick joke?"

Peabody's lips quivered. She bit down hard on the inside of her cheek. "I couldn't say, sir."

"Then it coughs and stalls, and I get it going again. Two blocks and it's lurching. You know, lurching like . . ."

"Frankenstein's monster?"

Out of steam now, Eve dropped into her chair. "I'm a lieutenant. A ranked officer. Why can't I get a decent vehicle?"

"It's a sad state of affairs. Sir, if I might suggest, rather than going down with a riot laser, you could try a case of beer. Get on the good side of a couple of the crew down there. Make nice."

"Make . . . *nice*? I'd rather swallow a live snake. You call down. Tell them I need my vehicle up and running within the hour."

"Me?" Peabody's eyes pricked with what might have been tears. "Oh, man. Before I go off to debase myself, I should tell you that we tightened the line on the wire, and the luggage."

"Why the hell didn't you say so?" Instantly Eve swung to her computer.

"I don't know what got into me, Lieutenant. Standing here like a chatterbox." When that didn't get a rise, Peabody huffed out a sigh and went back to her cubicle to bargain with Maintenance.

"Okay, okay, what have we got." Eve ordered the data on-screen. There were numerous sources for and purchases of the silver wire that matched the murder weapon. But when you filtered it down to two-foot lengths and two-foot multiples, that number narrowed to eighteen globally and six nationwide. With one single purchase of four lengths of two, cash payment, from a wholesaler right in Manhattan.

"Right here, what do we bet you bought it right here. Twenty blocks from the murder scene."

As she read the data on the luggage, a grim smile tightened her lips. There were thousands of purchases of the black leather carry-on since January, but focusing on the last four weeks, she found less than a hundred. And of the dozen or so purchased in New York City, there were only two selected on the same day the wire had been bought. And only one paid for with cash.

"There are no coincidences," she murmured. "You got your supplies right here. Now why would a man buy a transpo carry-on if he'd already done the trip? There was no trip. You were already here."

Wigs, she thought, and switched to Peabody's search and scan. "Jesus, why don't people just grow their own hair?" Literally millions of wigs, hairpieces, extensions, fillers, and fluffers had walked out of salons and stores and suppliers over the last six months.

She more than tripled that amount if she included rentals.

Patient as a cat at a mouse hole now, she pulled up the image of Yost outside the door of the suite, highlighted head and shoulders, erased the face, ordered a computer image of three hundred and sixty degrees, then dumped the result into the data bank.

"Computer, list cash-only purchases of human hair wig matching current image."

WORKING . . . FIVE-HUNDRED-TWENTY-SIX PURCHASES, CASH, OF IMAGED PRODUCT IN REQUESTED PERIOD. LISTING . . .

While her computer spewed out the supplier locations and dates of purchase, Eve followed on-screen.

PARADISE SALON, RETAIL, FIFTH AVENUE, NEW YORK, MAY THREE.

"Hold. And we have a winner. Busy boy that day, weren't you, shopping all over town. Computer, list any other purchases on this receipt."

WORKING . . . IN ADDITION TO HUMAN HAIR WIG MODEL DISTINGUISHED GENTLEMAN, RECEIPT INCLUDES PURCHASE OF HUMAN HAIR WIG MODEL CAPTAIN STUD; TWO TWELVE-OUNCE BOTTLES OF WIG GROOMING PRODUCT, BRAND NAME SAMPSON; ONE SIX-OUNCE BOTTLE OF COLLAGEN ELIXIR FOR FACE, BRAND NAME YOUTH; ONE EACH OF TEMPORARY EYE TINT, BRAND NAME WINK, IN VIKING BLUE, SEA MIST, AND CARAMEL CREAM; ONE DIETARY PRODUCT, BRAND NAME FAT-ZAP FOR MEN; AND TWO THREE-BY-SIX-INCH SCENTED CANDLES, SANDLEWOOD. PURCHASES TOTAL EIGHT THOUSAND, FOUR HUNDRED AND TWENTY-SIX DOLLARS AND FIFTY-EIGHT CENTS, INCLUDING ALL APPLICABLE TAXES.

"A lot of cash," Eve mused, "but why leave a paper trail, even a false one, if you don't have to? Computer, add image of Captain Stud brand wig to file. Copy addresses of luggage store, salon, and jewelry supplier, my PPC."

While her computer completed the tasks, Eve turned to her 'link. Thirty-two calls, she noted, since she'd logged out the day before. Odds were the bulk of them were from reporters hoping for a statement or sound bite.

It was tempting just to dump them, but until Peabody reported her vehicle was a go, she could spare a little time.

She started through them, automatically transferring the usual media pleas to NYPSD Media Relations. Until she was told differently, directly from her commander, she wasn't talking to the press.

She paused on the transmission from Nadine Furst, the

star of Channel 75, and a personal friend. "Not yet, pal," she murmured, but answered the message with a time delay. That way, she'd be in the field before Nadine received it.

"No point in nagging me," Eve said. "I don't have anything you can use at this point. The investigation is ongoing, all leads are being pursued with diligence, and blah, blah. You know the routine. When and if I have something for you, I'll be in touch. You tie up my 'link, I'm not going to feel very friendly."

Satisfied with that, Eve programmed the message to transmit in sixty minutes. She took twenty of them to write an updated report, then transmitted it to her commander.

She'd no more than pushed away from her desk and reached for her jacket when the summons from Commander Whitney came through.

As a matter of course, she snagged Peabody on the way up. "Maintenance?"

"Well, you know they have the whole how-backed-up-and-put-upon-they-are routine down pretty pat."

Eve stepped onto the people glide, scowled. "Did you mention riot weapons?"

"I thought it best to hold that possibility in reserve, sir." Just as she thought it best not to mention the snide comments made about a certain lieutenant's track record with city vehicles and equipment. "But I made the priority of your current investigation clear, and indicated that Commander Whitney frowned on having his ranked officers going out into the field in a piece of junk."

"That was good thinking."

"As long as nobody down there calls him for verification. You know, Dallas, you could request that the commander put the arm on them."

"I'm not whining to my superior, or pulling rank."

"You don't mind having me do it," Peabody muttered.

"That's right." Slightly more cheerful, Eve switched from glide to elevator. "You'll get your update on where we are in the case when I give the oral to Whitney. I think our man has a homey little hole right here in New York."

"Here?"

"Yeah." Geared up, Eve stepped off the elevator on Whitney's level.

Since she was waved directly through, Eve knocked briefly on Whitney's door, then stepped in.

He was seated behind his desk, and didn't rise. He was a big man with dark, wide face and beefy shoulders, hair rapidly going gray and eyes that remained street-sharp.

There were two other people in the room, male and female. Neither of them rose either, but both studied her closely. As she did them.

The dull and boxy black suits with ties ruthlessly knotted at the neck, the good shoes with their military shine, and the cold survey tipped her off.

Feds. Shit.

"Lieutenant, Officer." Whitney inclined his head and kept his big hands folded on his desk. "Special Agents James Jacoby and Karen Stowe. FBI. Lieutenant Dallas is primary on the Darlene French homicide investigation. Officer Peabody is her aide. The FBI has some interest in your case, Lieutenant."

Eve said nothing, and stayed on her feet.

"The Bureau, in cooperation with other law enforcement agencies, has been pursuing the individual Sylvester Yost for several years in connection with various crimes, including murder."

Eve met Jacoby's eyes. "I'm aware of that from my research."

"The Bureau expects the cooperation of the NYPSD in this pursuit. Agent Stowe and myself will run the case from the New York field office."

"Agent Stowe and yourself are certainly free to run your case wherever it suits you best. You will not run my case from anywhere."

Jacoby had brown eyes, dark and smug. "Yost's activities come under the federal net."

"Yost is not the exclusive property of the FBI, Agent Jacoby, nor of Global or Interpol, or the NYPSD. But the investigation into the murder of Darlene French is mine, and it's going to stay mine."

"You want to stay connected to this, Lieutenant, you'd better dump the attitude."

"If you want to stay in this office," Whitney cut in, "you'd be wise to dump yours, Agent Jacoby. The NYPSD is prepared to cooperate with the FBI as regards suspect Yost. It is not prepared to remove or replace Lieutenant Dallas as primary of the Darlene French homicide. Your jurisdiction has limits. You'd be smart to remember what they are."

Jacoby angled himself toward Whitney, his posture aggressive, his eyes going hot. "Your primary's connection to the individual Roarke, who may or may not be tied to this homicide and has long been under the federal eye as a suspect in various illegal activities, makes her a poor choice to head this investigation."

"If you're going to make accusations, Jacoby, put something behind them." It took all Eve's control to keep her voice level. "Would you like to produce the individual Roarke's criminal record at this time?"

"You know damn well he doesn't have one." He got to his feet now. "You want to sleep with a man who's run every dirty game in the book and still wear a badge, that's on you. But—"

"Jacoby." Stowe rose as well, neatly positioning herself between her partner and Eve. "For God's sake. Let's keep personalities out of this."

"An excellent suggestion." Whitney pushed back from his desk, stood. "Agent Jacoby, I will ignore that inappropriate attack on my officer. Once. If it's repeated, in any way, in any shape, in any form, I will report your conduct to your superiors. Your request for cooperation and for inclusion in any data generated on the Darlene French matter by my lieutenant and her investigation team will be considered, after said request is submitted formally, in writing, from your command. This meeting is over."

"The Bureau has the weight to take over this case."

"That's debatable," Whitney returned. "But you're free to submit the appropriate paperwork to that end. Until that time, let me suggest that you refrain from coming onto my turf and insulting this office and my officers."

"I apologize, Commander Whitney." Stowe shot Jacoby a look that warned him to keep silent. "And we appreciate your time, and your consideration." She gave her partner a not-so-subtle nudge to get him moving out of the room.

"Take a minute," Whitney advised when the door closed behind them, "before you say something you may regret."

"I assure you, Commander, I couldn't regret anything I might say at the moment." But she took a breath. "I appreciate your support."

"Jacoby was out of line. He was heading over the line when he strutted in here thinking he could rattle his federal balls at me. He asks for cooperation properly, he'll get it. He will not take over your case. It may come down to you working in tandem with Jacoby and Stowe. Is that a problem?"

"It won't be my problem. Sir."

A smile flickered around his mouth before he nodded, sat again. "Fill me in."

She did so, as thoroughly and concisely as her written report. And as she did so, she watched Whitney's lips purse, his eyebrows raise. Those were the only reactions.

"In all these years the Feebs haven't put Yost in New York?"

"They may have, sir, but not as indicated by any data I've been able to access. They have followed the wire, but not, as far as it shows, the specific length to specific outlets. I fail to understand how something that basic could have been neglected. The luggage, the hairpiece, those apply directly to French. But it's likely he's repeated that pattern, or a slight variation at other times. The FBI profile on the suspect is intricate and thorough, which is why I have yet to request one from Doctor Mira. I intend to do so, as corroboration, and with the additional data I've accumulated."

"Cover that, and make certain you have documentation and paperwork on every step. Jacoby may be the type to try to hang you up on technicalities. Media-wise, I want you low profile. The tone of the case shades toward Roarke, which shades toward you. I don't want you to give any statements until you're cleared to do so."

"Yes, sir."

"Don't look so smug about it. You'll be tossed to the media hounds before it's finished. No leads, I take it, on who might be pulling the strings here, or why?"

"No, sir."

"Then keep your focus on Yost. Smoke him out. Dismissed."

"Yes, sir." She turned to the door, one step behind Peabody.

"Dallas?"

"Yes, Commander?"

"I believe you can tell Roarke to expect a little federal pressure."

"Understood." She strode to the elevator, resisted kicking the wall. "She's nothing but a tool to him. Darlene French to Jacoby," she muttered. "No more human to him than she was to Yost. The son of a bitch."

"She's got you, Dallas."

"That's right. And she's going to keep me." Eve started to step into the elevator, then spotted Stowe inside. "Stay out of my face."

Stowe raised a hand in a gesture of truce. "Jacoby's gone back to the field office. I just want a minute. I'll ride down with you."

"Your partner's an asshole."

"Only about half the time." Stowe tried a smile. She was a trim woman in her middle thirties who did her best to spruce up the federal dress code with a pretty swing of honey brown hair. Her eyes were shades darker, and direct. "Listen, I want to apologize for Jacoby's remarks, and his attitude." She let out a sigh. "And my apology doesn't mean squat, however sincere."

"Maybe it means squat, even if it doesn't mean diddly."

"Fair enough. Look, when you cut out the red tape, we're all cops and all after the same thing."

"Are we?"

"Yost. You want him, we want him. Does it matter to you who turns the key in his cage?"

"I don't know. You guys have had a lot of years to turn that key. About as many years as Darlene French got to live."

"True enough. Personally, however, I've had three months, and of the three probably one in pure man hours to assimilate data on Sylvester Yost. If it gets us closer to stopping him, I'll hand you the key."

When the doors opened on the garage level, Stowe glanced out. She'd have to ride back up to the main lobby level. "I'm just asking you not to let Jacoby's temperament get in the way of the goal. I think we can help each other."

Eve stepped out, but turned and laid her hand on the door to keep it open. "Keep your partner on a leash, and I'll consider it."

She let the doors close and walked to her parking slot. Her pea-green unit sat, dented, scarred, and with a bright yellow smiley face some joker in Maintenance had painted beaming out from the rear window.

It was probably a very good thing Eve didn't have that riot laser.

chapter seven

Eve hit the salon first and was pleasantly surprised when her vehicle made the trip without embarrassing her.

She'd walked through the doors of Paradise before, tracking another murderer, another sexual homicide. Another case that had involved Roarke. *The first one,* she thought, *that had connected us.*

It had been more than a year, but the opulent decor of the salon hadn't changed. Soft, soothing music played, harmonizing with the splashing waterfalls and drifting through the air delicately scented by the long sweeps and tall spires of fresh flowers.

Patrons sat or lounged amid the splendor of the waiting area, sipping tiny cups of genuine coffee or spring-hued glasses of fruit juice or fizzy water. The receptionist was the same bountifully breasted woman in snug, short red who had greeted Eve before.

The hair was different, Eve noted. This time around it was Easter egg pink and styled in a streaming fountain of curls that burst out of a high cone on the crown of her head.

Recognition didn't register in her eyes, but dismay and

annoyance did the moment she spotted Eve's worn jacket, scarred boots, and shaggily styled hair.

"I'm sorry, we serve by previous appointment only in Paradise. I'm afraid all our consultants are fully booked for the next eight months. May I suggest an alternate salon?"

Eve leaned on the high counter, crossed her boots at the ankles. "You don't remember me, Denise? Gee, I'm really hurt. Wait a minute! I bet you'll remember this." Smiling cheerfully, Eve pulled out her badge and pushed it under the receptionist's expensively sculpted nose.

"Oh. Oh. Not again." Even as the words tripped out of her mouth, Denise remembered just who the cop had married since last they'd met. "I mean, I do beg your pardon, miss, I—"

"That's Lieutenant Miss."

"Of course." Denise tried out a lilting laugh. "I'm afraid I was distracted. We're so busy today. But never too busy to make room for you. What can we do for you?"

"Where's your retail section?"

"I'd be delighted to show you. Is there a particular product you have in mind, or are you just browsing? Our consultants will—"

"Just show me what you've got, Denise, and get me the manager of the area."

"Right away. If you'd just come with me. Can I get you and your associate any refreshment?"

Peabody spoke fast, knowing Eve would cut off any hope given half a chance. "I'd like one of those pink fizzy drinks. Nonalcoholic," she added when Eve gave her a baleful stare.

"I'll have it brought right in to you."

Retail was up a level, a short ride on a silver glide, and beyond a small oasis complete with pool and palms. Wide glass doors parted with a fluid little tinkle at their approach. On the other side, the retail area spread in an artful fan, with each spoke dedicated to a different form of beautification.

Staff here wore flowing red coats over snowy white skinsuits. And those were worn over perfect bodies.

Each display counter held its own miniscreen where simultaneous demonstrations were being shown on skin care, body toning, relaxation techniques, and emergency hairstyling.

All with lavish use, of course, of products sold on site.

"Please, feel free to look around while I fetch Martin. He oversees our retail service."

"Man, look at all this great *stuff*." Peabody edged toward a display of skin care with a dazzling arrangement of frosted glass bottles, gold tubes, and red-capped pots. "Fancy places like this give out great free samples."

"Keep your hands in your pockets and your mind on the job."

"But if it's free—"

"They'll just talk you into spending six months' pay on gunk to go with the giveaways." *The place smells like a jungle,* was all Eve could think. Hot, oversweet, and eerily sexual. "It's got to be the oldest con in the books."

"I won't buy anything." She spotted one of the enhancement displays with all those fascinating colors. *Girl toys,* she thought. And yearned.

But all the color and flash was nothing compared to Martin.

Denise hurried out in front of him, clicking her three-inch red heels over the white floor, like a handmaiden before royalty. She didn't bow, but Eve was certain she thought about it before scurrying away and out the glass doors again.

Martin swept up, his long trailing cloak of sapphire brushing the floor, the skinsuit of silver beneath it sparkling over a long, muscled body. His pecs rippled, his biceps strained, his privates bulged.

His hair, as silver as his suit, was swept up from a sharply planed face in a complex arrangement of twists that were caught in sapphire cord and left to dangle down his back.

He smiled, held out a hand crowded with rings.

"Lieutenant Dallas." His voice was seductively French, and before she could stop him, he'd taken her hand and kissed the air an inch above her knuckles. "We're honored to welcome you to Paradise. How may we be of service to you?"

"I'm looking for a man."

"*Cherie*, aren't we all?"

"Ha. This particular man," she said, amused despite herself. She drew a hard-copy image of Yost out of her file bag.

"Well." Martin studied the photo. "Handsome in a brute fashion. The Distinguished Gentleman does not, in my opinion, suit his facial features nor his style. He should have been gently dissuaded from that purchase."

"You recognize the wig?"

"Hair alternative." And his eyes twinkled as he said it. "Yes. It's not one of the more popular styles as the gray is something most looking for alternatives wish to avoid. May I ask why you're seeking this man here in Paradise?"

"He bought the hair alternative here, along with a number of other products. May third. Cash. I'd like to talk to whoever waited on him."

"Hmmm, do you have a list of the products he purchased?"

Eve pulled it out, handed it over.

"Quite a lot for a cash purchase. As for the Captain Stud, much more appropriate for him, don't you agree? Just one moment."

He strolled off, showed the list and photograph to a brunette at the near skin-care section. She frowned, studied the papers, then with a nod, hurried away.

"We think we may know the consultant who tended to this customer. Would you prefer to use a privacy area?"

"No, this is fine. You didn't recognize him?"

"No, but I don't interact with customers unless there's a problem of some sort. Or unless the customers are, such as yourself, VIPs. Ah, here's Letta now. Letta, *ma coeur*, I hope you'll give Lieutenant Dallas your assistance."

"I'm sure." And there was just enough Midwestern twang in the voice to make Martin wince.

"You waited on the man in this photograph?" Eve asked, tapping a finger on the picture Letta held.

"Yes. I'm almost sure it's him. He's had a little sculpting around the eyes and mouth in the picture, but it's the same basic facial structure. And this product list fits."

"Was this the first time you'd seen him?"

"Well . . . I think he's been in before. But he wears different wigs—hair alternatives," she corrected, sliding an apologetic glance toward Martin. "And he varies his skin tones, eyes. He likes a lot of different looks. A number of customers—clients," she amended, shaking her head at herself, "do. It's one of the services we provide at Paradise. Varying your looks can vary your mood and improve—"

"Save the sales pitch, Letta. Tell me about the day he bought those items."

"Okay. I mean, yes, madam. I think it was early afternoon, because we still had some of the lunch crush. I'd spent a lot of time with a woman who had to look at everything we had in blonde. I mean everything, and then she ended up doing the 'I'll think about it' routine."

She rolled her purple eyes, caught Martin's, then after a jolt, relaxed when she saw his smile of sympathy. "So when this client approached asking to see the Distinguished Gentleman, true black and gray, it was a relief. He knew just what he wanted, even if it wasn't what I thought of as right for him."

"Why wasn't it right for him?"

"He was a big, beefy guy—gentleman—with a square-shaped head. Just a look about him that made me think he worked with his hands, like a trade. The DG was just too fussy elegant for him. But he was set on it. He put it on himself, seemed to know just how to fit it."

"What kind of hair did he have? His hair, not the alternative."

"Oh, he's bald as a baby's . . . He's a natural scalp. Totally. Very healthy scalp, too. Good tone and polish to it. I don't know why he'd cover it. He saw the Captain Stud on display and asked for that, too. It was a better look. Sort of made him look like a general, I thought, and when I said so he looked very pleased. Smiled. He has a really nice smile. He was very polite and courteous, too. He called me Miss Letta, and said please and thank you. You don't get that sort of thing all the time in retail service."

She paused a moment, frowned up at the ceiling. "Then he told me he wanted to buy some Youth. He laughed a little, because you know how that sounds—buy some youth—and I laughed a little and we went over to skin care. We're trained to assist clients in all areas of our product line, to streamline their Paradise experience and all. I took him from department to department that way. With him telling me exactly what he wanted, and with him, very courteously again, turning off my suggestions for add-ons. We finished with the dietary product, and I said that he certainly didn't need it. And he said that he was afraid he enjoyed his food a little too much. When he was done, he indicated that he would take the purchases rather than take advantage of our free messenger service, so I totaled and made him a carryout parcel. Then he handed over that huge wad of cash, and my eyes about fell out on my shoes."

"It's not usual for a client to pay cash?"

"Oh, we do a lot of cash transactions, but I've never personally done one over two thousand dollars, and this was more than four times that. I guess he saw I was goggling, because he smiled at me again and said that he preferred to pay as he went."

"You spent a lot of time with him then."

"More than an hour."

"Tell me about his speech pattern. Did he have an accent?"

"Sort of. Not really anything I could place. He had a kind of high voice. Almost like a woman's. But very nice, soft and well, cultured, I guess. Come to think of it, his voice fit the DG more than it fit him, if you know what I mean."

"Did he mention his name, anything about where he lived, where he worked?"

"No. Early on, I tried to coax his name out by saying something like: I'd be happy to show you other styles, Mr. . . . But he just smiled and shook his head. So I called him "sir" the whole time. I suppose I thought he lived in New York because he took away rather than having sent or shipped, but I suppose he could have been from anywhere."

"You said you thought you'd seen him in here before."

"I'm pretty sure. Not long after I started working here, in the early part of the Christmas rush. Late October, maybe early November. At the skin counter again. He was wearing a coat and hat, but I really think it was the same man."

"Did you wait on him?"

"No, it was Nina. But I remember, sure, I remember now because we bumped into each other behind the counter getting products for our clients and she said how this guy was buying the whole Artistry skin-care line—that's who makes Youth. That's a couple thousand, and a really good commission, so I took a peek thinking how I wished I'd snagged him instead of Nina."

"But you hadn't noticed him before or since."

"No, ma'am."

Eve took her through a few more questions, then asked to see Nina.

Nina's memory wasn't as keen as Letta's. But when Eve moved from her to other clerks, she picked up just enough to be certain Yost dropped into Paradise once or twice a year.

"He'll have other places, other cities," she told Peabody when they were back in the car. "But on this same level. He won't settle for less. Always cash, and he'll know what he wants when he walks in. He pays attention to advertising, researches his products."

"Watches a lot of screen."

"Likely, but I'd bet this guy runs the product data on his computer. He wants a handle on the ingredients, the manufacturer's record, the consumer endorsements. Let's see what EDD can do about tracing that skin line backwards from last October when he made that purchase. He bought the whole ball of wax so that could mean he'd seen the ad, done the research, then decided to try it out. Artistry's bound to have a site for consumer information and questions."

She tried the luggage store next. None of the clerks recalled a man meeting Yost's description buying the carry-on. But downtown, she hit gold, so to speak, with the silver wire.

The clerk had an excellent visual memory. Eve clued into this the moment she stepped up to the small display counter with its riot of loose stones, silver coils, and empty settings under the glass. The clerk's eyes wheeled, his lips began to tremble. She heard his breath heave and initially feared a cardiac incident.

"Mrs. Roarke! Mrs. Roarke!"

His voice was heavily accented with what she thought might have been East Indian, but she was too busy wincing to worry about his origin.

"Dallas." She slapped her badge on the countertop. "Lieutenant Dallas."

"We are honored. We are unworthy." He began to shout something unintelligible to one of his associates. "Please,

please. You will select anything you want in our humble establishment. As a gift. You like necklace? Bracelet? You like maybe earrings."

"Information. Only information."

"We take a picture. Yes? We see you many times on-screen, and hope for the day you might come into our unworthy shop." He piped something else to the young man who scrambled over with a miniature holo-camera.

"Hold it, hold it. Just hold it!"

"Your famous husband is not with you today? You are shopping, yes, with your companion. We will give also a gift to your companion."

"Yeah?" Delighted, Peabody edged closer.

"Shut up, Peabody. No, I am *not* shopping. This is police business. *Police* business."

"We did not call for the police." He turned to the younger man busily taking holo-shots, let out a series of quick high sounds. The response was rapid, and accompanied by a fierce head shake.

"No, we did not call for the police. We have no trouble here. You would like this necklace." He pulled one out of a long shallow drawer under the counter. "Our gift to you. We design, we make. You will honor us to wear it."

Under other circumstances, Eve would have been tempted to just punch him to shut him up. But his dark eyes were shining with hope, and his smile was as sweet as a cocker spaniel's. "That's very nice of you, but I'm not allowed to accept. I'm here on police business. If I accept your gift, it would cause trouble."

"Trouble for you? No, no, we want to give you no trouble. Just a gift."

"Thanks very much. Some other time. You could help me by looking at this picture. Do you recognize this man?"

Confusion and disappointment drenched his eyes. He continued to hold the necklace up as he looked at the photograph. "Yes, this is Mr. John Smith."

"John Smith?"

"Yes, Mr. Smith, he is a hobby—*has* a hobby," he corrected. "To make the wearable art. But he buys no stones that we suggest. Only the silver wire. Two feet in length. Very specific."

"How often does he buy his wire?"

"Oh, he comes in two of the times. First it was cold outside. Before the Christmastime. Then in the last week, he comes again. But he does not have this hair on his head. I welcome him back to our store and ask if he would like now to look at stones or glass, but again he wants only the silver."

"And he pays in cash?"

"Yes, both of the times in cash money."

"How do you know his name?"

"I ask him name. Please to give me your name, sir, and will you tell me how you have heard of our humble establishment."

"What was his answer?"

"He is John Smith and he has seen our business page on the Internet. Is this helpful to you, Mrs. Lieutenant Dallas Roarke?"

"Just Lieutenant, and yes, it's helpful. What else can you tell me about him? Did he talk about his hobby?"

"He did not care to talk. He did not . . ." He closed his eyes, searching for a word. "Linger," he said, beaming. "I say to my young brother that I do not see how Mr. Smith can have success with his hobby as he does not have interest in stones or glass or other metals. He does not look at the many designs we have on display. He does not wish to speak about his work. He is instead . . . very strict business ways. Business . . . like. That is correct?"

"Yeah."

"He is polite. Once the 'link in his pocket rings, but he does not answer while he is doing business. I ask if the wire he purchased in the winter worked well for him, if he was satisfied. He tells me only that it did the job. Then he smiles, and I hope he is not your friend, because I do not like his smile at that time. I sell him the wire and am glad he leaves. I have offended you."

"No. You interest me. Peabody, do we have a card?"

"Yes, sir." Peabody rooted one of Eve's cards out of her own pocket.

"I'd appreciate you contacting me if he comes in again. I don't want you to alert or alarm him in any way, or tell him anyone's asked about him. If he comes in, you or your brother should go into the back, away from him, and contact me."

The clerk nodded. "He is a bad man?"

"A very bad man."

"This is my thinking when he smiles. I tell my cousin of it, and he agrees."

Eve shot a look at the young man still wielding the camera. "I thought he was your brother."

"My cousin in London where we have another humble shop. He is agreeing with me when we discover that Mr. John Smith has purchased silver from him also."

"In London?" Eve laid a hand on his wrist. "How does your cousin know it's the same man?"

"Silver wire, three lengths of two feet. But Mr. Smith has hair on his head there the color of sand. And hair also on his lip, but we think it is the same man."

Eve pulled out her memo book. "Give me the name and address of the shop in London. Your cousin's name." She noted it down. "Do you have any other humble shops?"

"We have ten humble shops."

"I'm going to ask you to do me a favor."

His eyes lit up like jewels. "This would be my very great honor."

"I'll want the locations of all of your shops. I'd appreciate it if you would contact your relatives in each and ask if there have been other purchases of silver wire in two-foot lengths. I'm going to send each shop a picture of this man. I want to be contacted if he should go into any of the shops."

"This I can arrange for you, Mrs. Lieutenant Dallas Roarke." He turned to his brother, had a brief exchange. "My brother will get this information for you, and I will personally call my cousins."

"Tell them either I or my aide will contact them."

"They will stand beside themselves with pleasure at this." He took the disc his brother brought out, handed it to Eve with some ceremony. "Will you please also take our business card for your famous husband? Perhaps he will consider visiting our humble establishment."

"Sure. Thanks for the help."

He walked her to the door, opened it for her, bowed her out, watched her, with eyes shining with delight, cross the sidewalk to her car.

"Tag Feeney," Eve ordered when she was behind the wheel. "Have him run like crimes in and around London."

"It would be my honor, Mrs. Lieutenant Dallas Roarke." At Eve's burning look, Peabody only grinned. "Sorry. I just had to do it once. I'm over it."

"If we've finished laughing uproariously, tell Feeney if no like crimes pop to take a hard look at missing persons. I don't think all the bodies have turned up. He does the job," she said half to herself as Peabody called into EDD. "If his client wants someone to disappear, permanently, he disappears them. But the murder itself would still follow pattern. He's a creature of habit. We follow the pattern."

"Feeney's on it," Peabody announced. "What's the next step?"

"Yours is to contact the cousins. I'm going to track down Mira. I want an NYPSD profile on this guy. The Feebs aren't the only ones who can generate paperwork."

• • •

"You've already done most of my work."

Dr. Mira lowered her computer screen and turned to where Eve stood, hands in back pockets, eyes on the view beyond the window. "You seem to know this man very well, on very short acquaintance. And the FBI profilers are very thorough."

"You can give me more."

"I'm flattered you think so." Mira rose, programmed her AutoChef for tea, then wandered away from it. She wore a simple suit of dusky blue, and her rich brown hair waved back to flatter her soft and pretty face. Her fingers twisted the long gold chain around her neck.

"He's a sociopath, and is probably intelligent and self-aware enough to know it. It may be a point of pride. Pride is one of the engines that drives him. He considers himself a businessman, the top in his chosen field. And choose it, he did. He enjoys fine things. He may not be aware that the rape adds to his satisfaction. It's just another way of erasing his victim. Male or female matters not at all. It isn't sex, of course, it's debasement."

Mira glanced at her wrist unit, her 'link, then into space. "More efficient would be the simple garroting, but he most often beats and rapes. These are part of the whole to him, like a man testing the color and bouquet of a good wine before drinking."

"He enjoys his work."

"Oh, yes," Mira confirmed. "Very much. But it is, in his mind, very much work. It's unlikely he ever kills indiscriminately or for personal motives. He's a professional, and expects to be paid and paid well. The silver wire is his calling card, an advertisement if you will to potential customers."

"He hides nothing. The wire, his face, makes no attempt to conceal DNA. Yet he does wear moderate disguises."

"My belief would be he wears those disguises to amuse himself. To add a bit of adventure. Partly vanity." She wandered the office, her movements restless and out of character.

"He would enjoy fussing with himself, viewing the results before heading out to work. The way another man might select a new shirt for a day at the office. You, the law, don't worry him in the least. He's evaded the legal system for years. I would say, at most, you amuse him."

"He won't be laughing for long."

Eve glanced back over her shoulder, saw Mira look down at her wrist unit yet again, frown. She'd forgotten the tea, too, and that was a first as far as Eve knew. "Everything okay?"

"Hmm. Oh, yes, everything's fine."

"You seem a little distracted."

"I suppose I am. My daughter-in-law's in labor. I'm waiting for word. Baby's tend to take their own sweet time while the rest of us wait."

"I guess." Because Mira gave her desk 'link a worried look, Eve went to the AutoChef, retrieved the tea.

"Thank you. That's the second time in an hour I've forgotten I've made tea. I'll write your profile, Eve. It'll help keep my mind occupied. But I don't think it'll add much to what you already know."

"Why Roarke? Can you tell me that?"

Her own concerns, Mira realized, had blinded her to the fact that Eve was worried on a personal level. Now Mira sat, waited for Eve to do the same. "Not beyond what I imagine you already suspect. He's rich, powerful, has enemies. Professional and personal rivals. He has a background with a great many holes, officially. There may be people hiding in those holes who wish to cause him difficulties. I'm sure you've discussed it with him."

"Yeah, but it's not getting me anywhere. If someone had tried a frame, tried to set up a murder so he'd look like a suspect, or have some direct involvement, I could see it. Go after one of his business rivals, somebody high profile.

Hit someone who's given him grief or causing him trouble. But a chambermaid at one of his hotels? What's the damn point?"

Mira laid a hand over Eve's. "It has both of you concerned and troubled. Perhaps that was point enough."

"To take a life for it? Yost, all right. To him it's a job. But there has to be more in it for the client. Yost bought four lengths. That's too many for backup on Darlene French, Dr. Mira. He's still on the clock."

"I'll continue to study the data. Run an analysis. I wish I could do more."

Her desk 'link beeped, and she was out of the chair like a woman on springs. "Excuse me."

Eve was surprised to see the dignified Mira scramble around the desk.

"Yes? Oh, Anthony, is—"

"It's a boy. Eight pounds, five ounces, twenty-one perfect inches."

"Oh. Oh." Mira's eyes swam as she lowered herself into a chair. "Deborah?"

"She's great. She's fine. They're beautiful. Have a look."

Eve shifted, angling her head enough so that she could see a dark-haired man hold up a wriggling, red, squalling baby.

"Say hello to Matthew James Mira, Grandma."

"Hello, Matthew. He has your nose, Anthony. He's gorgeous. I'll come by to see you all as soon as I can. I can't wait to hold him. Have you called your father?"

"He's next."

"We'll be over tonight." She ran a finger over the screen as if stroking the baby's head. "Tell Deborah we love her. And we're so proud of her."

"Hey, how about me?"

"And you." She kissed her fingertips, laid them on the screen. "I'll see you all soon."

"I'll call Dad. You have a good cry."

"I will." She dug out a handkerchief even as she ended transmission. "Sorry. A new grandchild."

"Congratulations, he looked . . ." *Like a red, wrinkled fish with limbs*, Eve thought, but figured that wasn't the thing people wanted to hear at such moments. ". . . healthy."

"Yes." Mira sighed, dabbed at her eyes. "There's nothing like a new life coming into the world to remind us why we're here. The hope and the possibilities."

Eight pounds, was all Eve could think. It must be like passing an arena ball with limbs. She got to her feet. "You'll want to get out of here. I'll just—"

Her communicator signaled. "Dallas."

"Sir." Peabody's face, sober and stern, filled the little screen. "We have another homicide, same MO. Private residence in this case. Upper East Side."

"Meet me in the garage. I'm on my way."

"Yes, sir. I ran the address through. The residence is owned by Elite Real Estate, a Roarke Industries division."

chapter eight

It was a lovely brownstone in a neighborhood known for its high rents, swank restaurants, and fancy, specialized markets. Sumptuous white flowers shimmered on long pink stems in a trio of slim stone pots on the front steps.

A few blocks south, and those pots would have been lucky to stay put and intact overnight.

But here, people lived comfortably, privately, and didn't stoop to vandalizing their neighbors' homes. Security was ensured by the addition, at residents' expense, of private droids who patrolled on foot in snappy navy blue uniforms. This precaution tended to keep the riff and raff from outside the area from sneaking in and soiling the sidewalks.

Jonah Talbot had enjoyed that comfortable security in his two-story home where he had lived alone. And there he had died, but it hadn't been comfortable.

Eve stood over him. He'd been a well-built male in his early thirties. He'd been beaten, as had Darlene French, primarily around the face. There was additional bruising around the kidney area and the ribs. He wore only a gray T-shirt. The matching athletic shorts were tossed into a corner. He'd been sodomized.

His killer had left him facedown, with the silver wire crossed at the back of his neck, curled up into loops at the edges.

"Looks like he was working at home. Did you run his data yet?"

"Yes, sir, it's coming through now."

Eve took the gauge out of her field kit to establish time of death.

"Jonah Talbot," Peabody read off. "Male, single, age thirty-three. Vice president and deputy publisher, Starline Incorporated. Residing this address since November 2057. Parents divorced, one sibling, one half-sibling through mother, no children."

"Hold the rest of the personal. What's Starline?"

Peabody keyed in the request for data. "They publish discs, books too, e-mags, holo-journals, the whole shot of written and electronic material." Peabody read on, then cleared her throat and lowered her PPC. "They were established in 2015, then purchased in 2051 by Roarke Industries."

"Closer," Eve murmured and felt the chill dance up her spine. "Taking a step closer. He took him in here. This guy's no hundred-pound girl, but he still didn't put up much of a fight."

Gently, she lifted one of Talbot's hands, saw the raw and broken skin of his knuckles. "Got a few hits in. Why not more? He's not as big as Yost, but he's in good shape. We've got one table turned over. Two guys like this square off, they'd tear up the room."

She had reason to know, as not long before she'd had the experience of watching two furious and well-toned men try to pound each other into meat in her home office.

"We've got enough on record from this angle. Let's turn him."

She sat back on her heels as Peabody bent down to help with the job. As they turned him, Eve felt the jags and swelling of broken ribs.

"He waited awhile to kill him," she said when she lifted the shirt and examined the vicious discolorations over the torso. "And he fights dirty, the son of a bitch. Goggles."

Peabody handed over the microgoggles. Through their powerful lenses, Eve studied the body. "Just here, just under the left armpit. Pressure syringe. He pulled a tranq when he got too much resistance. When Talbot went down, he wailed on him awhile. Did he wait until he was coming out of it to rape him? I bet he did. What's the point in rape if the victim doesn't know the violation, the humiliation?"

Her father had done that, she remembered. If he'd hit her just a little too hard and knocked her out, he'd waited. He'd always waited until she knew, until she could feel, until she broke enough to beg.

"Yeah, wake up," she whispered. "Wake up. How's a guy supposed to get off if you just lie there, little bitch?"

"Sir?"

"He waited," she said, shaking it off. "Kept him alive long enough for the blood to gather into bruises, long enough for him to struggle with whatever energy he had left. Then he slips the wire over the head, finishes the job."

She pushed the goggles back. "I'll take over the record. Check with Feeney and McNab. See what they've got off the security cameras."

"Yes, sir."

"You got some hits in," she murmured, carefully sealing the injured hand.

So had Darlene French, she remembered. *And the others? Was that cut or bruise Yost took away from the job another kind of souvenir? A war wound? Something to admire later?*

What little trinket did he take from Jonah Talbot?

With the microgoggles back in place, she examined the

body for any sign of piercing. She found what she was looking for on the left scrotum.

She shuddered, remembering the quick shocking sting of her recent ear piercing. "Jesus, what's up with people? For the record, piercing mark in left scrotum indicates victim wore or had worn some body ornamentation in this area."

She took off the goggles, rose, and standing over the dead began to slowly scan the room.

When she heard the footsteps, she spoke with her back to the door. "Peabody, tell the sweepers to keep an eye out for a small body ornament. The kind guys hook on their balls, for reasons I don't care to explore. Our guy likes souvenirs, and the victim's missing his genital bauble."

"I can't help you with that, Lieutenant."

She turned, looked at Roarke. Instinctively she moved forward, stepping between him and the body. "I don't want you in here."

"You can't always have what you want."

They both stepped forward, and she lifted a hand, pressed it firmly to his chest. "This is my crime scene."

"I'm fully aware of what it is. Move aside, I won't go any farther."

The tone of his voice answered the question she'd yet to ask. With a little jerk around her heart she stepped to the side. "You knew him."

"Yes." Anger stirred with pity as he studied the body. "You have his data by now, but I'll tell you he was a smart, ambitious man who moved up the publishing ranks quickly. He liked books. Real books. The kind you hold in your hand so you can turn the pages."

She said nothing, but knew Roarke also liked real books. That would have been a link between him and the dead. That enjoyment of turning the page.

"He would have been editing today," Roarke told her, and now guilt, sneaky and slick, slid in with the anger and pity. "He took one day a week at home for editing, though he could easily have passed that job on to his admin or any number of editors. As I recall, he liked to sail, and kept a small boat in a marina on Long Island. He talked of buying a weekend place there. He was seeing someone recently."

"The girlfriend found him. I have her in another room with a uniform."

"None of the things I've just told you have anything to do with why he's dead. He's dead because he worked for me."

His eyes shifted back to Eve's, and the heat in them was brutal. "That's a line of inquiry I intend to pursue." Below the range of the recorder, she put a hand on his. And under her fingers she could feel the vibration of violence, ruthlessly restrained.

"I need you to wait outside. I need you to let me take care of him."

There was a moment, a bad one, where she feared he would do something, say something she would have to expunge from the record. Then his eyes cooled, a change so abrupt it brought a chill. He stepped back.

"I'll wait" was all he said, and left her.

It was a relief that Talbot's current girlfriend, Dana, had apparently cried herself out by the time Eve sat down to get her statement. Her eyes were red, and she continually sipped water as if the bout of tears had dehydrated her. But she was steady enough, and she was clear.

"We were supposed to have a late lunch date. He said he'd be ready for a break about two. It was Jonah's turn to pay."

Her lips quivered, and she bit down on the bottom one hard. "We took turns with who paid for lunch. There's a restaurant, Polo's, just over on Eighty-second, we both like. I don't live far from there, and we both take Wednesdays to work at home. I'm a literary agent with Creative Outlet. That's how we met, at an industry function a few months ago. I was late. Didn't get there until about twenty after."

She paused, sipped, closed her eyes briefly. She had a

strong face, with more character than beauty. "Long 'link call from a client who needed some stroking. Jonah always jokes about me being late for everything. He calls it Dana time. So when I got there, and he hadn't shown up, I was feeling pretty smug. Planned to rib him about it. Oh, God, just a minute, okay?"

"Take your time."

This time she pressed the glass to her forehead, rolled it slowly back and forth. "About two-thirty, I thought I should give him a call, see what was going on. He didn't answer, so I waited another fifteen minutes. He could walk from here to there in five. I was half-pissed off and half-worried. Do you know what I mean?"

"Yeah, yeah, I do."

"I decided to walk over to his place. Kept thinking we'd run into each other on the way, and he'd be running, have all these excuses. I was deciding whether I'd be mad or let him weasel out. Then when I got here . . ."

"Did you have a key to the door?"

"What?"

Her swollen eyes had glazed. Now they focused again. *Good*, Eve thought. *You're doing good. You'll get through.*

"Did you have a key or code to the door?"

"No. No, I didn't have his key or code. We hadn't taken it quite that far yet. We both wanted to keep it loose. The modern American dating couple, each cautiously guarding his own space."

A tear leaked out now, and she ignored it, let it trail down her cheek. "The door wasn't closed, not all the way. That's when I was more worried than pissed. I pushed the door open and called out. I kept telling myself he'd gotten involved in the book he was editing and lost track, but I started feeling scared. I nearly turned around and walked out, but I couldn't seem to do it. I kept calling, kept going back toward his office. Then I was at the door, and I saw him. Saw Jonah. I saw him on the floor, and the blood around his head. Sorry," she said, and quickly lowered her own between her knees.

As the dizziness passed, she saw the book on the floor. With a choked sound she picked up the battered paperback, and straightening again, smoothed the covers.

"Jonah was a story junkie. Any form. Books, discs, audio, visual. You'd find them all over his house and office, even on his boat. Can I . . . do you think I could keep this?"

"We're going to need to keep everything on the premises, for now. When we're done, I'll see that it gets to you."

"Thanks. Thanks for that. Okay." She took a breath, and held onto the book as if it steadied her. "After I found him, I ran outside. I think I was going to keep running, but I saw one of the patrol droids, and I called it. I sat down on the steps and started to cry."

"Did Jonah always take Wednesdays off to work at home?"

"Yes, except when he was traveling or there was a meeting scheduled he couldn't miss."

"Did you routinely have lunch with him on Wednesdays?"

"In the last two, two and a half months, we tried for a late afternoon lunch. I guess it was a routine. We both pretended we weren't in any sort of routine. Keeping it loose," she said again, and pressed tears out of her eyes.

"You were intimate?"

"We had sex, routinely." She nearly managed a smile. "We shied away from words like intimate. But neither one of us was seeing anyone else. Not for weeks now."

"I know it's very personal, but could you tell me if Mr. Talbot was in the habit of wearing body ornamentation?"

"A little silver hoop, left ball. Very silly, very sexy."

At the end of the interview, Dana had drained a second glass of water. When she got to her feet, she swayed, and Eve reached out to take her arm. "Why don't you sit down until you're steadier?"

"I'm all right. I really want to go home. I just want to go home."

"A uniformed officer will take you."

"I'd rather walk, if it's allowed. It's only a few blocks, and I . . . I need to walk."

"That's fine. We may have to talk to you again."

"Just no more today. Please." She walked to the door, stopped. "I think I might have been falling in love with him. I'll never know. I'll just never know now. That makes me so sad. Over this horrible wrench of what happened to Jonah, that makes me so sad."

Eve sat for a moment, just sat. There was too much going on inside her head, and she needed to streamline. She had a body on its way to the morgue, a killer methodically working his way through a job, two FBI agents who wanted to snag her case. A houseguest she couldn't quite trust and a husband who could very well be in severe jeopardy and was certainly going to cause her considerable trouble.

When Feeney walked in she was still sitting, her eyes half-closed, and her mouth in a grim line. Judging her mood, he pursed his lips, then walked over to sit on the low table in front of her. He pulled out a bag of nuts, offered it.

"You want the good news or the bad news?"

"Start with the bad. Why change the rhythm now?"

"Bad is he walked right in the front door. Guy's got himself a master and that ain't good."

"A police master?"

"That, or a good simulation. We can enhance that sector of the disc back at EDD, see if we can clean it up enough to tell for sure. Point is, Dallas, he walked right up to the door like he belonged here. Slid in a master code, and strolled inside. No question it was Yost, even without the DNA the sweepers'll pick up. Dressed spiffy—new wig, dark hair long enough to tie back in a stub at the nape. Sort of an arty look. Guess it fits in with the neighborhood."

"He knows how to blend."

"Carried a briefcase. Took the time to put the master into an outside pocket, secure it. Knew the house, too, walked right back to the office."

Eve leaned forward. "Feeney, are you telling me the house cams were activated?"

"Yeah, that's my good news." He gave her a fierce smile. "Either Yost didn't consider that or didn't give a rat's ass, but the house cams were up. I gotta figure the victim didn't remember to shut them down when he got up this morning. We got a lot of him poking around doing usual morning stuff before he settled down to work. Audio, too. It's a solid system."

She got to her feet. "He didn't think of it. Nobody keeps inside security on when they're working at home. Who wants their every fart and scratch on record? Yost missed a step, Feeney."

"Yeah, could be he did. We got the murder on disc, Dallas. All of it."

"Where are you set up? I want to—" She broke off, remembering Roarke. She made some sound that might have been frustration, might have been pity, or a combination of both. "I'll look at it at Central. Can you set us up in a conference room? I got something to take care of before I head in."

"Yeah, he's outside." Feeney shifted his feet, rattled the bag of nuts, stuffed it in his pocket. "I don't like to poke my nose in."

"I know. I like that about you, Feeney."

"Yeah, well. I just want to say, he's going to be feeling some weight. Got to. You can tell him he shouldn't, but it won't matter. After a bit, he's going to find his mad. Probably be pretty hot at first, then he's the type to chill it down. Seems to me that's not such a bad thing all around. We might be able to use Roarke in a cold temper."

"You're a regular philosopher today, Feeney."

"I'm just saying, is all. Maybe you're thinking it'd be better to keep him out of the loop." He nodded, seeing those exact thoughts mirrored in her eyes. "That would be from the gut, and not the head. You use your head you're going to figure out sometimes the target's the best weapon. You can try to stand in front of this particular target, Dallas, but this one'll knock you out of the way anyhow."

"Is this your roundabout way of suggesting I bring him in on this? Officially?"

"It's your case. Maybe I'm saying you should think about using all the resources available. That's all I'm saying."

Deciding that was more than enough, Feeney gave a little shrug and left her alone.

She started out, selecting uniforms to do a neighborhood canvass and knock on doors. Out of the corner of her eye, she watched Roarke. He leaned against the rear fender of a sharp-looking sedan. *Watching me,* she thought. *Waiting.* But there was nothing of patience in the stance.

"Give me a minute here," Eve murmured to Peabody, then crossed to him.

"I thought you were going to use the limo and driver."

"I was. Have been. I didn't choose to wait for them when I got the call about Jonah."

"Who informed you?"

"I have sources. Are we going into Interview, Lieutenant?" When she said nothing, he swore softly, viciously, under his breath. "Sorry."

"Do yourself a favor and go home for a while. Kick something down in the gym."

He nearly smiled. "That's your way."

"It usually works."

"I need to go into the office. I have a meeting. Will you be informing next of kin?"

"Yes."

He looked away from her, toward the lovely little

brownstone. And thought about what had been done inside. "I want to talk to his family myself."

"I'll make sure you're contacted after the official notification."

His eyes shifted back to hers. Feeney had been right, she thought. He was carrying the weight, but he was also finding his mad. She could see both in his eyes.

"Tell me what you know of this, Eve. Don't make me go around you for it."

"I'm going into Central. After notification of next of kin and my prelim report, I will, together with my team, study and analyze all available evidence. Meanwhile, the ME and the lab will do their jobs. Dr. Mira is working up a profile. Other leads, which I'm not prepared to stand here outside a crime scene and talk about, are being actively pursued. While all this is going on, I'm fending off an FBI takeover attempt and will no doubt be ordered to release a statement to the media."

"What leads?"

He would, she thought, *latch onto that one statement.* "I said I'm not prepared to discuss them at this time. Give me some space here. Give me time to think. I'm not as good as you are at balancing worry over somebody I love and the work."

"Then I'll answer that with something that should sound very familiar to you as it's forever coming out of your mouth. I can take care of myself."

She expected to feel anger, resentment, or at the least, impatience. Instead, there was only concern. He, a man who rarely lost control, was on the edge of rage. And mired in grief.

She did something she had never done in public, never done while on the job with other cops looking on. She put her arms around him, drew him close, and held him with her cheek pressed gently to his.

"I'm sorry." She murmured it, wishing she knew more of the art of comforting. "I'm so damn sorry."

The rage that had been spitting into his throat, the burn scorching the rim of his heart eased. He closed his eyes and let himself lean.

Through all the other miseries in his life there'd been no one to offer him the simple soothing of understanding. It swamped him, washed away the worst edge of grief, and left him steadier for it.

"I can't get a handle on it," he said quietly. "And I can't see through the murk of it to any answers."

"You will." She eased back, skimmed her fingers through his hair. "Try to put it aside for a little while, and you will."

"I need you with me tonight."

"I'll be with you tonight."

He took her hand, pressed his lips to her knuckles. And let her go. "Thanks."

She waited until he'd gotten into his car, until he'd pulled away from the curb. She was tempted to send a black-and-white out to follow him back to midtown. But he'd make a tail, and be just annoyed enough to lose it.

Instead, she let him go as well.

When she turned around, she noted a number of cops get very busy looking in other directions. She refused to waste time being embarrassed. She signaled to Peabody.

"Let's get to work."

In his midtown base, Roarke rode the private elevator to his suite of offices. He could feel the anger building inside of him again. He couldn't permit it, not until he had time alone, time to find an outlet.

He knew how to strap it down. It was a hard-learned skill that had kept him alive during the bad years, and the building years. A skill that had helped him create what he had now, and who he was now.

And what was he now? he wondered as he ordered the elevator to stop so he could have another moment to find a grip on that fine skill. A man who could buy whatever he chose to buy so he could fill his world with all the things he'd once starved for.

Beauty, decency, comfort, style.

A man who could command what he chose to command so that he would never, by God never again, feel helpless. Power. The power to amuse himself, to challenge himself, to indulge himself.

One who reigned over what some called an empire and had countless people dependent on him for their livelihoods. Livelihoods. Lives.

Now two had lost theirs.

There was nothing he could do to change it, to fix it. Nothing he could do but hunt down the one who had done it, and the one who had paid for it to be done. And balance the scales.

Rage, he thought, *clouded the mind*. He would keep his clear, and see it through.

He ordered the elevator to resume, and when he stepped off his eyes were grim but cool. His receptionist popped up from her console immediately, but still wasn't quite quick enough to ward off Mick, who strolled over from the waiting area.

"Well now, boyo, it's a hell of a place you've got here, isn't it?"

"It does me. Hold my calls for a bit, would you?" Roarke ordered the receptionist. "Unless it's from my wife. Come on back, Mick."

"That I will. I'm hoping for the grand tour, though from the size of this place of yours that might take the next several weeks."

"You'll have to make due with my office for now. I'm between meetings."

"Busy boy." As he followed Roarke down a glass

breezeway snaking over Manhattan and through a wide
art-filled corridor, he looked around, his eyes bright and
scanning. "Jesus, man, is any of this stuff real?"

Roarke paused at the black double doors that led to his
personal domain, managed a half-smile. "Not still dealing
in art that finds its way into your hands, are you?"

Mick grinned. "I deal with whatever comes, but I'm not
looking toward yours. Christ, do you remember that time
we hit the National Museum in Dublin?"

"Perfectly. But I'd as soon members of my staff aren't
entertained with the story." He opened the door, stepped
back so Mick could precede him.

"I'm forgetting you're a law-abiding soul these days.
Holy Mother of God." Just over the threshold, Mick
stopped.

He had heard, of course, and had seen enough for himself already to know the reports and rumors of just what
Roarke had accomplished weren't exaggerated. He'd been
dazzled by the home, but unprepared, he realized, for the
sleek and rich lushness of the workspace.

It was huge, and the view out the three-sided window
was as grand as the art chosen to enhance the atmosphere.
The equipment alone, and he knew his electronics, was
worth a fortune. And all of it—from the ocean of carpet,
the acres of real wood, the glint of glass new and antique to
the streamlined efficiency of the communication and information centers—belonged to the childhood friend he'd
once run with down the stinking alleyways of Dublin.

"Want a drink? Coffee?"

Mick blew out a breath. "Coffee, my ass."

"For me, then, as I'm working. But I'll stand you to a
glass of Irish." Roarke moved to a polished cabinet, and
opened it to reveal a full bar. He poured Mick a drink before programming the AutoChef for a single cup of coffee,
strong and black.

"To larceny." Mick lifted his glass. "It may not be what

keeps you here these days, but by Christ, it's what got you here."

"True enough. What've you been up to today?"

"Oh, this and that. Seeing a bit of the town." Mick wandered as he answered, poked his head through a doorway and whistled at the enormous bathroom. "All this is missing is a naked woman. Don't suppose you could be ordering one of those up for an old friend."

"I never dealt in the sex trade." Roarke sat, sipped his coffee. "Even I had my standards."

"That you did. 'Course, you never needed to buy a night of affection either, as us mortals did from time to time." Mick came back, made himself at home in the chair across from Roarke's.

It came to him, fully came, that there was much more than years and miles between them. The man who could command all Roarke commanded was far away from the boy who'd plotted thievery with him.

"You don't mind me dropping in this way, do you?"

"No."

"It occurs to me that it's a bit like having a poor relation land on your threshold. An annoying embarrassment a man hopes to sweep outside and away again at the first opportunity."

Roarke thought he heard a faint edge of bitterness in the tone. "I have no relations, Mick, poor or otherwise. I'm pleased to find an old friend."

Mick nodded. "Good. And I'm sorry for thinking it might be otherwise. I'm dazzled, and in truth, not a little envious of what you've managed here."

"You could say I've had a good run of luck. If you really want a tour, I can arrange one while I'm taking the meeting, give you a lift home after."

"I wouldn't mind, but I have to say you look more like you could use a couple pints in a pub. You've got trouble on you."

"I lost a friend today. He was killed this afternoon."

"I'm sorry to hear that. It's a violent city. A violent world come to that. Why don't you cancel your meeting, and we'll find a pub and wake him proper."

"I can't. But thanks for the thought."

Mick nodded, and sensing it wasn't the time for old stories, drained his glass. "Tell you what, I'll have that tour if you don't mind. Then I've business of me own I've been neglecting. I'm going to try to swing it into a dinner meeting, if that doesn't inconvenience you any."

"Whatever works for you."

"Then I'll plan on that, and likely not be back to your place till late. Will that be a problem with your security?"

"Summerset will see to it."

"The man's a wonder." Mick got to his feet. "I'll stop by St. Pat's in my travels today, and light a candle for your friend."

chapter nine

Eve sat in the conference room and watched Jonah Talbot die. She watched, and she listened, to every detail again and again.

The concentration of an attractive young man at his desk, reading a story on his screen, making notes with the quick fingers of one hand on a spiffy little PC unit while something classical played on the speakers.

He'd played the music loud. He'd never heard his killer come in the house, walk through it, step into the home office.

She watched yet again, saw yet again the instant Talbot had sensed something, someone. That instinctive brace of the body, that quick whip of the head. His eyes had widened. There had been fear in them. Not full panic, but alarm, shock.

Nothing on Yost's face. His eyes were dead as a doll's, his movements precise as a droid's as he'd set his briefcase aside.

"Who the hell are you? What do you want?"

Knee-jerk, Eve thought as she listened to Talbot's angry

demand. People so often asked the name and business of an attacker, when the first hardly mattered and the second was all too obvious.

Yost hadn't bothered to respond. He'd simply started across the room. Graceful for a man with his bulk. *As if,* she thought, *he'd had dancing lessons along the way.*

Talbot had come around the desk, and come around fast. Not to flee, but to fight. And there, in that little blip of time, Eve saw those dead eyes light. The dawn of pleasure in the job.

He'd let Talbot strike the first blow, spill first blood. And with the corner of his lip spurting, Yost moved in.

Grunts, the crunch of bone on bone played under the soaring music. But only briefly. Yost was too efficient to toy with his target for long, to indulge himself by taking more time than he'd allowed. He'd let Talbot take him down, knocking over the table, letting him think, just for one heady instant, that he might win.

Then the pressure syringe was out of Yost's pocket, into his hand, and its rounded tip pressed just under Talbot's armpit.

Still Talbot had struggled, even with his eyes rolling back he'd tried to land a disabling blow. The drug would have blurred his vision, clouded his brain, slowed his reflexes until he was limp, helpless, then unconscious.

That's when Yost had beaten him. Slowly, methodically. No wasted motions or energy. His mouth moved a bit as he worked. After the music was cleaned out of the disc, she would know that he'd been humming.

When he finished with the face, he stood and began to kick in the ribs. The sound was vile.

"He's not even winded," Eve murmured. "But he's excited. He enjoyed it. He likes his work."

Now, leaving Talbot broken and bleeding on the floor, he wandered over, ordered a glass of mineral water from the AutoChef. He checked his wrist unit before sitting down and sipping the glass dry. Checked it again when he rose to go to his briefcase. He took the silver wire out of it, tested its strength by snapping it between his hands, once, twice.

When he smiled, as now he smiled, she understood why the clerk in the jewelry store had trembled. He looped the wire around his own throat, crossed the ends to hold it in place, snugly. She could see that while it wasn't tight enough to bring blood, it was secure enough to cut down on the flow of oxygen.

On the floor, Talbot stirred, moaned.

On his feet, Yost removed his suit jacket, folded it neatly on a chair. Removed his shoes, then tucked his socks into them. He stepped out of his trousers, aligning the center pleats precisely before he laid them aside.

He went to Talbot, stripped off the man's shorts, nodded in approval as he squeezed as if checking muscle tone.

He wasn't yet fully aroused. He tightened the wire around his neck slightly, using the autoerotic method to enhance his mood as he stroked himself hard.

Then he knelt between Talbot's legs, leaned over, tapping the battered cheek lightly.

"Are you in there, Jonah? You don't want to miss this. Come on out now. I've got a lovely parting gift for you."

Talbot's bloody eye fluttered open, blind with confusion and pain.

"That's the way. Do you know the movement that's playing? Mozart, from his Symphony Number 31 in D Major. Allegro assai. It's one of my favorites. I'm so pleased we can share it."

"Take what you want," Talbot managed between broken teeth. "Just take what you want."

"Oh, that's very kind of you. I intend to. Up you go." He lifted Talbot's hips in his big hands.

The rape was long and brutal. Eve made herself watch, as she had made herself watch each time, despite her stomach wanting to heave, despite the whimpered pleas that struggled to rise into her own throat.

She watched, and she saw the moment that Yost lost himself, when he threw his big head back so the wire around his throat glinted in the light. He cried out, a roar of triumph that smothered the music, smothered Talbot's helpless weeping.

The orgasm bucked through him. His face gleamed with it, his eyes shone. He shuddered, shuddered, sucked in air. Then braced himself with a hand between Talbot's shoulder blades until he came back to himself.

His eyes were as bright now as the wire he slid from around his own neck and looped around Talbot's. They stayed bright, dark and bright as a bird's as he crossed the ends and pulled. Talbot's body jerked, his fingers scrabbled at the wire, his feet drummed the floor.

But it was quickly done. At least it was quick.

And when it was done, the killer's eyes were as dead as his victim's. He calmly turned Talbot over, examined the body, then with some delicacy removed the tiny body ornament. With it cupped in his palm, he used his foot to shove the body facedown again.

Naked, gleaming with sweat, he turned away, gathered his clothes and briefcase.

He would walk into the first-floor bath where the house cams didn't reach. In precisely eight minutes, he would come out again, scrubbed, neatly dressed, the briefcase in his hand. He would leave the house without looking back.

"End disc." As Eve gave the order and rose, she heard Peabody's sigh, a broken sound that was relief and pity.

"He checked his wrist unit a number of times," Eve began. "He was on a timetable. Since it appears from his movements he knew the house, either from a previous break-in or through blueprints, I believe he knew about Talbot's usual lunch date. According to the time print on the disc, he entered the premises at thirteen hundred, almost on the dot. He left the scene fifty minutes later. Ten minutes before the lunch date and well before anyone expecting the victim would bother to check on him. He left the door unlatched so Talbot could be found quickly. There's no reason for him to wish to postpone the knowledge of the crime. Whoever hired him wants it out as soon as possible."

She walked over to the board used for the investigation, and where stills of Darlene French and now Jonah Talbot held prominence. "More than forty known or suspected hits in his career, but Talbot gives us the first visual of the act. This break-in pattern indicates Yost was unaware the house cams were activated. Even so, he could and should have checked."

"He's getting sloppy," McNab put in. "Sooner or later, they get sloppy."

"Sloppy maybe, but factor in his profile. Arrogance. He didn't bother to check, didn't put it on his to-do list. He isn't worried about us. He pinches us off like fleas before we ever get the first bite. He bought four lengths of wire. Four potential victims. This is the biggest job, done separately, for a single client we can find in Yost's case history. He's flirting with exposure, almost daring it. I say he feels protected. Maybe invulnerable."

"His take from this job would be, at his suspected minimal fee, ten to twelve million." Feeney scratched his chin. "He's moving through them fast, and at this pace would finish the contract in a week or so. That's a hefty paycheck."

"None of his data indicates a previous with this number at this speed," Eve confirmed.

"Maybe he's planning on retiring after this one, or at least taking himself a long vacation. He can get himself a new face and live the high life somewhere."

"A vacation." Eve considered it as she studied Yost's image posted on the board. "He's never hit four in close geographic proximity before, never spread out connected hits in the same area over different dates and locations."

She let it filter through. "He's been at this twenty-five years or more. Thinks of it as a job. Twenty-five, thirty years, then retirement. Could play. Certainly a vacation after a big important job is something a lot of execs go for. The arrangements would have already been made. He's a planner."

"Where would Roarke go?"

Eve turned her head to frown at Peabody. "What do you mean?"

"Well, the profile indicates he sees himself as a highly successful businessman, one of impeccable taste. He likes fine things, and he can afford the best. The only person I know who falls in that slot is Roarke. So if he were going to take a break after a big job, where would he go?"

"That's good thinking." Eve nodded, tried to focus on her husband's pattern. "He owns places all over hell and back. It would depend on whether he wanted to be alone, solitude and a couple house droids. Not a city, because he wants relaxation at first, not stimulation. From the profile and pattern, Yost is more of a loner than Roarke. He's booked or bought himself an estate somewhere, with a good wine cellar and all the trimmings. Finding that on the data we have would be like looking for a ripple in a pool."

Then her scowl began to turn into a slow smile. "But I think that's a damn good lead to feed the feds. One for us is music. He knew the Mozart thing playing. Called it by name, hummed along with it. Peabody, I want you to start checking out the high-dollar season tickets to the symphony, the ballet, the opera, all the highbrow stuff. Single ticket holders. He'd go alone. McNab, you concentrate on purchases, cash purchases of recorded discs for the same kind of music. He's a collector."

She paced the room as she spoke because the steps and the thoughts were lining up for her now. "We need the lab results. I'll hound Dickhead there. I want to see what the sweepers got out of the bathroom drain. He took a shower, but the guest soap was dry. Our fastidious sociopath probably carries his own soap, shampoo, and so on in his briefcase when he's on a job like this one. It won't be an ordinary brand, so we could have another line to tug there. Feeney, can you go back to following the wire, talk to those cousins, while I kick at Dickhead?"

"Can do." Even as he agreed, his communicator beeped. "Hold on." He rose, pulling it out, and stepped away as he answered.

"Lieutenant?" McNab called for her attention. "I was thinking about the . . . can't be delicate about this. I was thinking how Yost used the wire to help him get off during the rape. So even if the guy goes for Mozart and fine wine, he's got some experience with porn or licensed companions who'll skirt the sexually deviant line. If he's a loner, it's most likely he gets into it at home with VR or video or holo. You gotta have programs or discs. You can get some through legitimate sources, and the darker versions—right down to snuff porn, which it strikes me he'd go for— through the black market."

"You sure seem to know a lot about it," Peabody commented.

"I worked in Vice awhile and stuff." Still he squirmed a little under her stare and gave his attention to Eve. "I could start hunting in that venue. Like you said, he's a collector. They even got some of this stuff that leans toward the art film side. I could start with that."

"McNab, sometimes you surprise me. Do it."

"Want to watch some dirty discs, She-Body?" he whispered, and Eve pretended, mostly for her own sake, she didn't hear.

"Son of a bitch." Feeney pocketed his communicator. "We got a break. I've been running the like crimes, couldn't find any in London or England for the time frame you wanted. I put a man on it to run variations of the pattern, just in case. He got a hit."

"Where?"

"It's a place in Cornwall, along the coast. Cops found some bodies out in the moor. They were in pretty bad shape—exposure and they've still got, you know, wild life around there. Thing was, they were garroted, but there was no wire, so I didn't get the pop. Plus the locals there hadn't hooked it into the network until two months after the crime."

"Why do you tag it as Yost?"

"Timing fits, once they were able to determine time of death. Kill pattern fits. Both victims, male and female, were beaten badly, especially around the face. Both tranqued. Both raped. My man brought up the dead shots and compared the neck wounds, what could be made of them, and that fits. Hiker who called it in didn't hang around for the cops. Could be he took the wires."

"Did they ID the victims?"

"They did. Couple of badass smugglers who kept a base in a cottage up there. I can follow up on this, get more data, talk to the primary."

"Yeah, and pass it all through to my home unit. I'm going to feed this one to the feds, too. It might get them off my back, and better yet, off my turf for a while. With that in mind, let's pick this up at eight hundred tomorrow, my home office. Anybody gets anything between now and then, contact me."

She hit Dickie, the chief lab tech, and hit him hard. He whined, but it was almost casually. She threatened him, then bribed him with a bottle of Jamaican rum, which completed their relationship dynamic. He agreed to put her bathroom drains on top of his workload.

Next she reported to Whitney, got his go-ahead to feed her selected data to Jacoby and Stowe. And as expected,

was told she would be needed at a press conference scheduled for fourteen-thirty the following afternoon.

She brooded about that all the way back down to her office where she settled down and contacted Stowe.

The agent came on screen, her attractive face showing
annoyance. "Lieutenant, why did I have to hear on a public
news report of a murder that most certainly appears to be
perpetrated by Sylvester Yost?"

"Because news travels, Agent Stowe, and I've been
busy. I'm contacting you now to bring you up-to-date on
this latest incident. But if you'd rather break my balls,
you're just wasting my time."

"You should have informed me or my partner before you
left the scene and had it sealed."

"I don't recall seeing that directive written down anywhere. This is a courtesy call, and I'm starting to feel
pretty discourteous."

"Cooperation—"

"You want cooperation, then shut up and listen."

Eve paused, saw Stowe simmer, then swallow her wrath.
"I have some data that might be of help to your investigation, and to mine, and which I believe your agency can
track more quickly than mine. You want to deal, let's deal.
I'm going to be at a downtown club, the Down and Dirty,
in twenty minutes. Bring something to trade."

She cut transmission before Stowe could respond.

And she made certain she got to the D and D in fifteen,
just in case.

An enormous black man with tattoos and feathers and a
head as bald and shiny as a bowling ball grinned wide
enough to split his remarkably ugly face when she walked
in.

"Hey there, white girl."

"Hey back, black boy."

It was too early for the bulk of the clientele an all-nude
club like the Down and Dirty appealed to. Still, there was a

scatter of customers hulking at tables and a single bored dancer working up just enough energy to shake her impressive breasts to the beat of recorded music.

Crack, all seven feet of him, ran the club, but would concentrate on bouncing the more irritating of the customers out on their heads when the action heated up. He'd gotten his name for the sounds those heads made as they met concrete.

For now, he loitered behind the bar, and came up with a nasty-looking cup of black coffee.

He slid it over to Eve. "Don't see your skinny ass in here awhile, I get to missing it."

"Golly, Crack, you're making me all misty." One sip of the coffee took care of that. She hoped her throat lining would regenerate eventually. "I got a couple of federal types meeting me here."

He looked so pained even the grinning skull tattooed on his cheek drooped. "Now why you wanna do that thing, sweet lips? You bring federal heat to my place."

"I wanted to show them a highlight of our wonderful city." She laughed. "And I wanted to make their clean-cut, East Washington selves see what it's like in the real world. The female half of the team may be all right under it all, but the guy's a butt pain squared."

"You want me to maybe give them some grief?"

"No, maybe just one of your hard looks, the kind they'll remember long after they're safe back in their little field office. Oh, and you could make sure they get this coffee."

His teeth gleamed like marble columns. "You got you a mean streak."

"A mile wide, pal. Anything in here you don't want the feds sniffing?"

"We clean . . . right now." His eyes skimmed past her. "Mmm-mmm. More white meat. Whiter than white. They ever hire color in the effing-bee of eye?"

"Sure, but working federal probably turns them white.

Give me a little room here, Crack," she murmured, then shifted on her stool. "Agents."

"You sure pick the nicest places, Lieutenant." With a wrinkle of the nose, Jacoby inspected a stool before gingerly sliding on.

"This is my little home away from home. Want some coffee? My treat."

"I guess that's as safe a bet as you'd get in a dump like this."

"You calling my place a dump." Crack leaned over the bar, stuck his huge face into Jacoby's.

"He's just being a moron." Karen Stowe stepped gamely between them. "It's genetic, so he can't help it. I'd love some coffee, thank you."

"Then you're welcome." With surprising dignity, Crack stepped back and worked on the coffee under the bar. His gaze slid up briefly, met Eve's, gleamed good humor.

"You got a trade?" Eve demanded.

"The Bureau is not in the habit of bartering with the locals."

"Jacoby, for God's sake, fall in or shut up." Stowe turned to Eve. "Can we get a table?"

"Sure." Eve picked up her coffee, waited until they had theirs, then strolled away to a table in the far corner.

Stowe led off. "I picked up some information on a hit that looks like Yost. A Supreme Court judge, went down two years ago."

"A Supreme Court justice gets raped and garroted, it makes the media wild. I don't remember hearing anything on this. And none of my searches picked it up."

"Politics. They covered it because the justice wasn't alone. He was with an underage female."

"Dead?"

"No. I'm still picking out the pieces but what I get is the kid was drugged, then bound, and locked in an adjoining room. I can't get a name on her, can't get past the seals, but it looks as if she was whisked away by the government. I'm guessing Witness Protection. They don't want her talking about the judge's bad habit of boinking youngsters. Official word is he died of a heart attack, and was beyond resuscitation by the time medical aid arrived."

"That's not bad."

"Your turn."

Eve nodded and managed to conceal a smile of satisfaction when Jacoby took a gulp of coffee and turned nearly the same pea-green tone as her city vehicle. While his eyes watered and he gasped, she gave Stowe the appropriate data.

"I can get the files from the Brits within the hour," Stowe said. "We should be able to track down the hiker. The vacation or retirement property's a good line. My data runs with yours. He's never hit more than two at a time in the same location. If he's planning on four here, he might want a break. I'll put some drones on that to start, and we'll see what they come up with. I'm going to want to talk to your husband."

"I already gave you two for one. Don't push it."

Marginally recovered, Jacoby leaned forward. "We can pull him in, Dallas. We don't need your permission."

"Try it. He'll eat you for lunch. Listen to me," she said, turning to Stowe. "If he had any answers, if he had a goddamn clue what's driving this, he'd tell me. He knew Jonah Talbot, he liked him, and he feels responsible. You get in Roarke's face on this, you'll just make it worse for him and get nothing for yourself. I've got personal reasons for wanting this guy. So does Roarke. He'll work with me on this, he'll work with the NYPSD, but he won't work with you."

"He would if you asked him to."

"Maybe. But I won't. Take what I've given you and see where it takes you. It's more than you had when you came in here."

She pushed away from the table, got to her feet. Then

she took a good, hard look at both of them. "Let me make this clear. You make a move toward him, you'll have to get through me. If by some miracle you get through me in one piece, he'll slice you in half without breaking a sweat, and you'll spend the rest of your life wondering what the hell happened to your promising career. Work with me, and we'll take this murdering son of a bitch down. You can have the credit, I don't give a shit about that. You try an end run around me toward Roarke, I'll burn you."

She turned on her heel, strode to the bar, and slapped down credits for the coffee.

"Kicking ass, white girl," Crack said with a wink.

"I haven't even started."

Stowe blew out a breath when Eve stalked out. "Well, didn't that go well?"

"Local heat," Jacoby said in disgust. "Who the hell does she think she is, dicking with us?"

"A good cop," Stowe snapped back. Christ, she was tired of playing with Jacoby. But he was her ticket to the Yost investigation. "One who'll protect her personal and professional territory."

"Good cops don't marry criminals."

For one long moment Stowe just stared at him. "You really are an idiot. Ignoring that supercilious and ridiculous statement, whatever the suspicions are about Roarke's former activities, nobody, *nobody* in any law enforcement agency on or off planet has any documentation, any proof, not even any they could cook up out of steam, that links him to any crime. And the point here, Jacoby, is in this matter he's a victim. He knows it, she knows it, and we know it. So cut the crap."

He was annoyed enough to take another gulp of coffee before he remembered. "Whose side are you on?"

"I'm trying to remember. I'm pretty sure it was law and order. I don't think that local heat has any trouble remembering that."

"Like hell. She was holding out on us. She's got more."

"Well, gee, Jacoby, you think?" Sarcasm dripped, frigid as icicles. "Of course she was holding out on us. In her place we'd do exactly the same thing. But the point is, she told the truth. She gave us straight leads, as far as they went. And when she said she didn't care who got the credit for taking Yost down, she meant it."

She shoved her untouched coffee aside and got to her feet. "I wish I could say the same. I wish I knew I could say I didn't care, and mean it."

chapter ten

Eve's intention was to go straight to her home office, run more data, gather whatever fresh information the rest of her team had shot over, then follow up on the nibble the feds had passed her way.

Plans changed the minute she was through the front door. She wasn't surprised to see Summerset in the foyer. The fact was it no longer seemed her day was complete if she didn't exchange a few pithy words with him every evening.

But even as she opened her mouth for the first serve, he was cutting her off.

"Roarke's upstairs."

"So? He lives here."

"He's disturbed."

Her stomach sank. Neither of them noticed that when she started to strip off her jacket, Summerset not only helped her out of it, but laid it neatly over his arm.

"What about Mick?"

"He's out for the evening."

"Okay. No help with a distraction there then. How long has he been home?"

"Nearly half an hour. He's made calls, but has yet to go into his office. He's in the master bedroom."

She nodded, started up the stairs. "I'll take care of it."

"I believe you will," Summerset murmured.

She found him in the bedroom. He was taking a call on his headset rather than the 'link, and stood looking out one of the tall windows to the gardens that were wild with spring.

"If there's anything I can do to help you with the arrangements, or anything at all . . ."

As he listened, he threw up the window, leaned out as if, Eve thought, desperate for air.

"We'll all miss him, and very much, Mrs. Talbot. I hope it's some comfort to you to know how much Jonah was liked and respected. No," he said after a moment. "There are no answers to the why. That's true, yes. Will you let me do that for you and your family?"

He said nothing for quite some time, and Eve had been on this side of enough victim survivor calls to know how much grief and confusion were pouring out of Talbot's mother.

And into Roarke.

"Yes, of course," he said at length. "Please contact me if there's anything else I can do for you. No. No, it's not. I will. Good-bye, Mrs. Talbot."

He drew the headset off, but stayed at the window, his back to the room. Saying nothing, Eve crossed to him, slipped her arms around his waist, pressed her cheek to his back.

She felt his body, already tensed, brace.

"Jonah's mother."

"Yeah." She held on. "I heard."

"She's grateful to me for offering to help. For taking the

time to offer my personal condolences." His voice was quiet, too quiet, and violent with sarcasm. "Of course, I didn't mention he'd be alive if he hadn't worked for me."

"Maybe you're right, but—"

"Fuck maybe." He snapped the headset in two, heaved it out the window. The abrupt movement knocked Eve back a step, but she had her feet planted and was ready to face him when he whirled.

"He'd done *nothing*. Nothing but be mine. Just like that young maid. And for that alone they're beaten and raped, and their lives ended. I'm responsible for those who work for me. How many more? How many will be betrayed to death simply because they're mine?"

"This is what he wants. You questioning yourself, blaming yourself."

The mad that Feeney had predicted was there now. Ripened to bursting. "Well, he can have it. I'll take a bloody ad out."

"Give him what he wants," she said evenly. "Let him know he got to you, he'll want more."

"Then what?" He lifted his hands, and they were fists. "I can fight what comes at me. One way or the other I can take it on. But how do I fight this? Do you know how many work for me?"

"No."

"Neither did I. But I ran figures today. I'm a wonder with figures. There are millions. I've given him millions to pluck from."

"No." She moved forward, wrapped her fingers firmly around his forearms. "You know better. You've given him nothing. He takes. Your mistake will be to give him part of you. To let him know he has it."

"If I let him know, maybe he'll come at me."

"Maybe. I've thought of that, and it worries me. But . . ." She ran her hands up his arms, down again in an unconscious effort to soothe. "That's mostly when I'm thinking with my heart. When I use my head, it doesn't play. He doesn't want you dead. He wants you wounded. Do you understand what I mean? He wants you broken or in turmoil or . . . he wants you like this."

"For what purpose?"

"That's for us to figure out. We will figure it out. Sit down."

"I don't want to sit down."

"Sit," she repeated, using the cool, unbending tone he often used with her. When his eyes flashed, she turned away to pour out a snifter of brandy.

Briefly, she considered slipping a soother into it, but he'd know. She could attempt to pour it down his throat as he'd done to her, but she didn't think she could pull it off.

Then they'd both be mad.

"Have you eaten?"

Too distracted to be amused by the sudden role reversal, he let out an impatient breath. "No. Why don't you go to work?"

"Why don't you stop being so stubborn?" She set the brandy on the low table in the sitting area, put her hands on her hips. "Now, you can sit down or I can take you down. A little hand to hand might make you feel better, so I'm up for that."

"I'm not in the mood for a fight." And because he wasn't, but in the mood to brood, he walked over and sat. "Screen on," he ordered.

"Screen off," she countermanded. "No media."

Now his eyes glinted. "Screen on. If you don't want to watch, go away."

"Screen off."

"Lieutenant, you're treading a thin line."

Temper rerouted outward, toward her. Just as she'd intended. *It wasn't iced yet, no, not yet,* she thought. But that would come.

"I have good balance, pal."

"Then put it to use elsewhere. I don't want your brandy or your company or your professional advice right at the moment."

"Fine, I'll drink the brandy." She hated brandy. "I'll stow the professional advice. But," she said as she sat and curled herself into his lap. "I'm not going anywhere."

He took her by the shoulders to set her aside. "Then I will."

She simply locked her arms around his neck. "No, you won't. Am I this much trouble when I'm in a mood?"

He let out a sigh, then defeated, lowered his forehead to hers. "You're a constant annoyance to me. I don't know why I keep you."

"Me either. Except." She brushed her lips over his. "This maybe. This is pretty good." And skimming her fingers through his hair, tipping his head back, kissed him long and slow and deep.

"Eve." He murmured it, mouth against mouth.

"Let me." Her lips traced over his cheeks, soft. Tender. "Just let me. I love you."

And couldn't bear to see him hurt. Couldn't bear to see him weary. They would work, and work together. They would fight, and fight together. But for now she only wanted to give him peace.

He was so strong, that strength both appealed to her and challenged her. Now those muscles were taut and knotted with a tension that so rarely showed. She stroked, letting her hands soothe while her mouth seduced.

So controlled, she thought, shifting to scrape her teeth lightly over his jaw. She found both frustration and security in his control. Now it wavered, and she would exploit the weakness, channel anger into lust.

Her busy hands moved to his shirt, slowly opened buttons. Her lips followed down the trail of exposed flesh to his heart where the beat was strong, but still too steady.

"I love the taste of you." She ran her hands up his chest, over his shoulders, flicked her tongue over that warming skin. "Everywhere."

Again she shifted, straddling him now. And when she saw his eyes, the dark smoke of need over the wild blue, the beat of her own blood quickened.

She'd been wrong, she realized. The rage in him wasn't ready to cool, and wouldn't be quenched with gentle strokes and quiet sighs. It was heat that would smother heat.

Watching him, she hit the release on her weapon harness, let it slide to the floor behind her. Watching him, she unbuttoned her shirt, shrugged it off. Beneath she wore a thin cotton tank, dipping low. She saw his gaze shift down, felt her nipples throb as if his mouth had already claimed them.

But he didn't touch her. Knew the moment he did, the chain would break and he'd ravish. Devour, he thought, furious with himself, when she was offering him comfort. He gathered himself, touched a hand lightly to her cheek.

"Let me take you to bed."

She smiled, and there was nothing comforting about it. "Let's take each other." She stretched up, stripping the tank over her head and tossing it aside. "Right here."

She fisted her hands in his hair, curved her body to his, sliding flesh to flesh. "Put your hands on me," she demanded, then crushed her mouth to his.

His control snapped. In one violent move she was under him, pinned. He fed on her, filling himself, swallowing each ragged breath. He put his hands on her, taking greedily, recklessly driving her to that first frantic peak.

And when she cried out, he took more.

His mouth closed over her breast, teeth nipping tiny, delicious pains into sensitive flesh. The thrill of it drummed through her so that she arched up, urging him on, digging her nails into his back. She twisted under him, her hands searching, her mouth seeking. Their needs matched, desperation for desperation. And their limbs tangled as they fought with clothes.

Sweat-sleeked flesh.

With that savage rage whipping through him, he could think of nothing but her. Of mate. The long, agile length of her. The curves and dips of her that miraculously fit against him. The pale, beautifully delicate skin that rode so smoothly over hard muscle. The taste of that skin when the heat of passion bloomed over it.

More. All, was all he could think while his blood burned.

She was hot, so hot and wet when his fingers stroked into her. Smooth and tight as her hips pumped. He wanted, needed, to see her come, needed to feel it, to know when her system exploded, everything she was, was his.

Her body arched, a tight little bridge of sensation. Her breath tore out into a sob. She poured into his hand.

Still, he couldn't stop, gave her no chance to slide gently down again. Instead he drove her ruthlessly, rushing up her body with teeth and tongue.

When his mouth was on hers, when he could feel her about to shatter yet again, he plunged into her, knocking her over the edge with that first rough stroke.

And still he thought: *More.*

Even as she shuddered, he shoved her knees up and went deeper inside her. His vision blurred, but through the red haze of lust he could see her eyes. Deep, dark, glazed like glass to throw his own reflection back at him.

"I'm inside you." He panted it out as he pushed them both to madness. "Everything I am. Body, heart, mind."

She struggled through layers of pleasure to say the one thing he needed. Her hands wrapped around his wrists to hold the beat of his blood. "Let go. I'll stay with you."

He pressed his face to her hair, let both heart and mind go, and let body rule them both.

• • •

Eve wasn't sure how much time had passed before her brain cleared enough to allow a clear thought through. But when she managed to remember her name, Roarke was still pinning her to the cushions. His heart continued to gallop against hers, but his body was very still.

She stroked her hand down his back, gave him an affectionate pat on the butt. "I think I'm probably going to need to breathe sometime within the next ten or fifteen minutes."

He lifted his head, then considerately propped himself on his elbows. Her face was flushed, her lips slightly curved, her eyes half-closed. "You look pretty pleased with yourself."

"Why shouldn't I? I'm pretty pleased with you, too."

He leaned down just enough to touch his lips to the dent in her chin. "Thank you."

"You don't have to thank me for sex. We're married."

"Not for the sex, though that was worthy of a few cheers. For understanding me. For, let's say, tending to me."

"I've had a lot of practice on the other side of it." She reached up, brushed the hair from his brow. "Feeling better?"

"Yes." He shifted, and as he sat up drew her with him. "Let me just hold this for a minute," he murmured, nuzzling her in his lap.

"Keep that up, we'll end up horizontal and sweaty again."

"Mmm. And it's tempting." The rage was still inside him, but chilled now. Calculated. "But there's work. Do I have to argue with you, Lieutenant, about letting me work with you on this, and spoil the nice place we're in?"

She said nothing a moment. "I don't want you to. No, don't start. Let me finish." She turned her face into the curve of his throat. "The part that doesn't want you to is personal. That part's afraid for you, and worried about you. The professional part knows the more involved you are, the more help you can be, the quicker we close this thing. The personal side doesn't have a chance against the cop and you pushing together."

"Would it help if I tell you I'll handle all this better if I'm involved in the work? It won't eat at me in the same way."

"Yeah." She held on another moment, then drew back. "Yeah, I guess I know that, too. Let's get a shower, some fuel, then I'll lay out the ground rules."

"I've never liked that phrase," he said as she rose. "Ground rules."

She let out a short laugh. "There's something else I know."

When they were dressed and sharing a meal of seafood pasta, she set out her stipulations.

"With Whitney's approval, you'll come onboard this investigation officially, as an expert consultant, civilian. With this appointment there are privileges and limitations, and a moderate fee."

"How moderate?"

She speared a scallop with her fork. "Less," she said as she popped it in her mouth, "then I imagine you paid for any one pair of your six hundred shoes. You will be issued ID—"

"A badge?"

She spared him a withering look. "Don't be ridiculous. Standard photo and print ID. You will *not* be issued a weapon."

"That's all right. I've plenty of my own."

"Shut up. You will be privy to data relating to this investigation at the discretion of the primary. That happens to be me."

"Handy."

"You will be expected to obey orders, or this appointment can and will be terminated. Again, at the discretion of the primary. We run this by the book."

"I've always wondered. How many pages are in that book of yours?"

"And smart mouthing to the primary can result in disciplinary action."

"Darling. You know how that excites me."

She sneered, even though she wanted to celebrate that he was himself again. "During the course of the investigation, the primary and investigative team will require access to some of your files."

"That's understood."

"Okay." She scooped up one last forkful of pasta. "Let's go to work."

"That's it, for ground rules?"

"We'll hit them as we go. My office. I want to bring you up to date."

The advantage of working with Roarke was that he understood cop. The fact that this had more to do, she suspected, with him spending most of his life outwitting them than it did with being married to one was irrelevant.

She didn't have to spell things out for him, and that saved time.

"You didn't give the FBI everything you've put together, but they'll know that."

"Right. And they'll live with it."

"They'll also suspect, or at least wonder, if you've put more salient data together on Yost in less than a week than they have in years. That won't sit well."

"Yeah, and that just breaks my heart."

"Your competitive streak's showing, Lieutenant."

"Maybe. When it comes down to it, the Feebs can have the glory. Yost will know who brought him down. That does the job for me. They didn't pay enough attention to the wire, the exactness of it. Their profile gives a strong indication of pattern, his obsessiveness with detail, and still they missed subtleties."

"Don't they, you think, as a Bureau, tend to concentrate more on the overview, and depend too heavily on pure data, rather than instinct and possibilities?" He smiled easily when she frowned at him. "Not that I've had any personal dealing with them that I'd want to take up your time discussing just now."

"Is that so? Well, we'll have to make time later."

"Mmm. But my point is, while you're one to use your data, to see the overview and quite clearly, you trust your gut and you never forget possibilities."

"Maybe. Then again, most Feebs aren't hooked to a guy who can buy a case of fancy shampoo at five thousand a pop, so they don't look at that angle. At the rich, self-indulgent guy angle."

"I never buy shampoo by the case for personal use, and you'd have looked there in any event. You don't miss details. Still, I know more about high-end products than you, which is why I'm an expert consultant."

"Civilian," she added. "And you're not, until tomorrow after Whitney's approval."

"In anticipation of that, I need to see the security disc run from Jonah's murder."

"No."

"I need to see what Yost was wearing, how he wore it. I've reviewed the hotel disc. In that he prefers British designers."

"How the hell do you recognize a designer from looking at somebody's suit jacket on a disc run?"

"Darling Eve." With a faint smile he skimmed a finger over the shoulder of her ancient and faded NYPSD T-shirt. "Fashion is more a priority for some of us than it is for others."

"You think that's a dig, but it doesn't hit the mark with me, ace. Anyway, I should've figured one clothes snob would recognize another." She pulled the disc out of her file bag. "You get a good look at him as he's coming to the door. That should do it for you."

And that, she thought as she loaded it into her desk unit, was as much as she intended to show Roarke. "Computer, run current disc file, point mark zero to point mark fifteen. On wall screen."

WORKING . . . BEGIN SEGMENT RUN.

They both looked on-screen, both watched Yost stroll casually up the steps to Jonah Talbot's door. And there the image froze.

"Definitely British," Roarke confirmed. "As are the shoes. I need a closer look at the briefcase."

"Okay. Computer, enhance segment twelve through twenty-two, ten power."

WORKING . . .

The image shifted with the hand and the briefcase it held separating and magnifying.

"So he sticks with the Brits. That's a Whitford bag, made exclusively in London. I own the bloody factory."

"This is good. We concentrate on sales in London. British designers."

"The conservative ones," Roarke added.

Her forehead knitted. "I thought it was more the arty type of look."

"He's added the wig and scarf for that, but under it, it's straight arrow. The suit looks like a Marley, but Smythe and Wexville make that same sharply angular style. The shoes are Canterbury's, almost certainly."

She frowned at them. They looked like shoes to her, simple black slip-onto-the-feet shoes. "Okay, we'll follow it up. Eject disc."

"Computer, disregard. I'll see the rest."

"No. There's no point in it."

"I'll see the rest," he said. "Would you prefer I access it and view at another time and place?"

"I'm telling you there's no point in putting yourself through that."

"I spoke to his mother. I listened to her weep. Computer, continue run."

Eve cursed under her breath and stalked away. She did her best to get her temper under control, and poured out two glasses of wine. He hadn't touched the brandy earlier.

She didn't need to watch the tape to live it again. She could close her eyes and see every movement, every horror. And she feared when she closed her eyes that night to sleep, she would see it again. Or worse, see herself, as a child, bleeding and broken in a filthy room where a red light blinked over and over and over again.

She bore down, and with Mozart soaring, walked back to finish the nasty job of watching it again beside her husband.

"Freeze image," Roarke ordered and his voice cut like sharpened ice. He stared at the screen, where Jonah Talbot lay unconscious and the man who would kill him stood in the act of unbuttoning his shirt.

"Enhance image, segment thirty to forty-two." And when the computer complied, Roarke nodded. "The little design on the cuff. The shirt's handmade, on Bond Street, London. Finwyck's. Computer, resume."

He saw it through, saying nothing, showing nothing. If Eve had been a fanciful woman she'd have said she could feel the heat pumping off him, the rage of it. And how that rage cooled, chilled, iced until the air in the room crackled with it.

When it was done, he walked to the computer, ejected the disc, laid it on her desk. He took a moment, a moment only, to gather himself in again.

"I'm sorry I insisted on viewing that now, so that you

felt obliged to watch it again. I'll never fully understand how you stand it, how you cope with it, day after day. Death after death."

"By telling myself I'll stop him, that I'll see to it he's put somewhere so that he can never do it again."

"It can't be enough. It never could be." He sipped the wine now, burying his grief and pity deep so that the cold fury held control. "His wrist unit was Swiss, which is to be expected. A multitask Rolex. I have one myself, as do thousands of others who insist on dependable accuracy in such matters. I can help you with that, as—"

"You own the factory."

"And several of the major outlets that sell that model," he finished. "And with the briefcase, and the shoes. The rest of the wardrobe will take more time, I assume, as they'll insist on proper paperwork and warrants and what have you to release any customer data. London's closed at this hour."

"I'll get on that in the morning. Get me what you can on the rest. I'm going to see what I can dig out on the Supreme Court judge."

He nodded but stayed where he was, drinking his wine. "You have McNab checking on season tickets for the symphony and so on. If he runs into any snags, I can have that for you, and through proper channels, with a simple 'link call."

"I'll let you know."

"As far as the black market on the porn and snuff discs, I still have contacts in that murky arena. Meaning I know people who know people and so on."

"No. It gets out you're looking in that muck, it could alert whoever's supplying him that I'm looking."

"I can cover that easily enough, but we'll see how Ian does if you'd rather. My other equipment could cut through a great many layers without anyone being aware," he reminded her.

"Not this round, Roarke. I use unregistered here, even to

tickle out some data, and I've got no way to justify it to myself, no way to explain to the rest of the team how I came by it. By the book."

"You're the boss." So saying, he carried his wine through the doorway into his own office.

Several blocks south, in his crowded, disordered downtown apartment, McNab huddled over his computer. Beside him, Peabody, down to her shirt and uniform pants, worked on one of his mini-units.

The man, she often thought, *collects computers the way some men collect sport holos*.

Working her way through the porn sites for names had begun to give her a headache, but she continued doggedly, concentrating on the titles and come-on, and the screen names of potential customers who took advantage of the thirty-second preview.

McNab's theory was that Yost might cruise the labyrinth of sex sites available online, make his selections through previews. It was possible he ordered them on-screen and that would be the luckiest of breaks as he'd have to use an ID and credit number to do so. But even if he simply scanned the previews, he'd have logged on under a screen name.

Most were laughable and obvious. Bigkok, Cumlvr, Hornydog. She didn't think Sylvester Yost would go for the crude or the foolish.

She sat back, rubbed her gritty eyes then began to root through her bag for a pain blocker.

Absently McNab reached over and rubbed her neck. "Want to take a break?"

"I just need to ditch the headache. Maybe stretch my legs."

She rose, rolling her shoulders as she went to the kitchen for water.

He knew she'd broken a date with Charles Monroe to work with him that night. McNab was darkly pleased that the suave LC had gotten the boot, even if it was for work. What he really wanted was to plant his own boot right in Monroe's pretty face, and one of these days . . .

The action on the screen scrambled his thoughts. He goggled as two men and two women began to roll and writhe on the floor in a mass of naked bodies and impossibly flexible limbs.

"Holy Jesus."

"What? What? Did you hit on something?" Peabody rushed back, leaned down to the screen, then with an oath rapped McNab over the head with the flat of her hand. "Damn it, stop jerking off. I thought you'd found . . ." She trailed off, stupefied. "Wow" was the best she could do.

Following the action both of them tilted their heads to the side.

"She must be double-jointed."

"Triple," McNab decided. "And it's obvious nobody in this group has a spine, otherwise they couldn't get in that position."

They turned their heads again, this time toward each other, and their eyes met with identical gleams of lust and challenge.

"We can't let a bunch of porn actors outdo us." McNab was already pulling at the hook of her trousers.

"Damn right we can't. But it's probably going to hurt."

"Cops feel no pain."

"Oh yeah? Try this." She was laughing as she pulled him to the floor.

In another part of town, Sylvester Yost finished his after-dinner brandy and cigar. He'd activated his single server droid for precisely twelve minutes, to deal with the disarray of his kitchen and dining room.

Of course, he would check on the job himself. Even well-programmed droids usually failed to see that all was in the perfect order Yost demanded.

He'd prepared himself a delightful veal picatta for dinner. Often after a job he liked to putter around his kitchen, enjoying the scents and textures of cooking, sipping an appropriate wine as his sauces thickened.

But an indulgence like that dirtied pots and pans and so on. The droid came in handy there, as Yost preferred to relax with his brandy and cigar rather than loading the dishwasher.

With his eyes half-closed and his big, muscular body draped in a long robe of black silk, he listened to the swelling strains of Beethoven.

Such moments, he believed, were a man's right after a successful day's work.

And soon, very soon, such moments would stretch to days, and days to weeks as he moved into quiet retirement. Oh, he would miss the work, he supposed. Now and then. Of course, if he missed it enough he could certainly take the occasional contract.

Interesting ones, just to slay any dragons of tedium.

But for the most part he was certain he would be quite content with his music and his art, his leisure and his solitude.

When this contract had been offered, Yost had taken it as a sign. It was the perfect end to his career. Never before had he had occasion to come so close to a man of Roarke's stature or capabilities. Because of that, he'd been able to demand, and receive, three times his usual fee for three targets.

The fourth was to be acted on only at his discretion. If he saw his way clear to assassinating Roarke himself within two months after the initial contract was fulfilled, he would receive a lovely bonus of twenty-five million dollars.

Such a pretty retirement nest, Yost thought.

He had no doubt he would see his way clear, quite clear.

It would be the most brilliant act of his career. And one he looked forward to with relish.

chapter eleven

Eve methodically picked her way through the first reel of red tape to access personal data on Justice Thomas Werner. According to official data, Werner had suffered a fatal heart attack and died at his home in an exclusive suburb of East Washington.

It had taken a little time to identify the judge from the scanty data she'd been given, but she'd run through the archives of the screen news bulletins for the previous winter and had finally hit on Werner's death.

Now, it was a matter of winding her way around and through the Privacy Act that shielded a man of Werner's standing from curiosity seekers. And, even with proper identification, hampered an official inquiry.

"You stupid son of a bitch," she muttered. "I'm a cop. You've got my badge number, my case file code, my voice print. What do you want now, blood?"

"Problem, Lieutenant?"

She didn't bother to glance over at Roarke's question. "East Washington bureaucracy bullshit. It wants me to submit my request again during working hours. Well, I'm working, aren't I?"

"Perhaps I could—"

She snarled at him, hunched protectively over her unit. "You just want to show off."

"Would I be that small?"

"To cut me down on this, you'd shrink to microscopic."

"Just to show how big I really am, I'm going to overlook that insult. Why don't you take a look at the purchase list I've printed out for you, and I'll see if I can unravel some of your red tape."

YOUR REQUEST, THE COMPUTER ANNOUNCED IN DULCET TONES, FOR PERSONAL AND MEDICAL RECORDS CONCERN-ING JUSTICE THOMAS WERNER CANNOT BE PROCESSED AT THIS TIME. PLEASE SUBMIT REQUEST THROUGH THIS AGENCY BETWEEN THE HOURS OF EIGHT A.M., AND THREE P.M. EST, MONDAY THROUGH FRIDAY. REQUESTS OF THIS NATURE MUST BE SUBMITTED IN TRIPLICATE AND ACCOM-PANIED BY THE ATTACHED FORM, WITH ALL QUESTIONS ANSWERED THEREON. AN INCOMPLETE OR MISSING FORM WILL DELAY PROCESSING. NO REQUESTS WILL BE CONSID-ERED OTHER THAN THOSE MADE BY PROPERLY AUTHOR-IZED PERSONS. IDENTIFICATION MUST BE INCLUDED AND VERIFIED. NORMAL PROCESSING TIME FOR RECORD RE-QUESTS IS THREE WORKING DAYS.

WARNING!!! ANY ATTEMPTS MADE TO ACCESS RECORDS WITHOUT PROPER REQUEST, PROPER IDENTIFICATION AND VERIFICATION OF SAME IS A FEDERAL VIOLATION AND WILL RESULT IN ARREST, A FINE NO LESS THAN FIVE THOU-SAND U.S. DOLLARS, AND POSSIBLE IMPRISONMENT.

"Not very friendly, is it?" Roarke murmured.

She said nothing, merely pushed to her feet, stalked around the desk, and picked up the hard copy he'd brought with him. Deliberately, she took it with her to the kitchen on the pretext of getting coffee when he took her place.

Damned if she'd watch how easily he cut through the tape.

She stood, scanning the lists as she reached in the AutoChef for her mug of coffee. He'd already done the work there, she noted, highlighting the range of cash purchases made on a single date in February.

It fits Yost's style, she thought. Another little shopping spree. New briefcase, new shoes—six pairs—new wallet, four leather belts, several pairs of socks—silk or cashmere. He'd ordered two shirts, tailored to his measurements, from the fancy shop Roarke had identified from the Talbot disc.

In only two stores, two stops, he'd dropped over thirty thousand Euro dollars.

Roarke had added the data from the jeweler in London. The New York clerk's cooperative cousin had confirmed that Yost had purchased, for cash, two two-foot lengths of silver wire.

No backup tool, she thought. That was his arrogance again. He was confident in his skill.

And according to the best estimate on time of death of the smugglers in Cornwall, he'd done his shopping two days, three at most, before he'd headed north and killed two people.

He'd had to get north, she thought. Did he keep a car in London? A house? Did he stay at some swank hotel, then rent transpo, take the train, fly?

Since it was a good bet he hadn't walked, she might be able to track his movements.

"Question," Eve said as she stepped back into her office. "Do you have a house in London?"

"Yes, though I rarely use it. I generally prefer my suite at The New Savoy. The service is impeccable."

"Got a car there?"

"Two. Garaged."

"How long a drive to Cornwall?"

"I've never done it, so I'd have to check." He spared her a glance now, turning in the chair and looking, she thought, entirely too comfortable at her work station. "If I were going that far north, I'd likely save time and take the jet-copter from one of my offices. Unless I was in the mood to see the countryside."

"If you wanted to keep a low profile?"

"I'd probably rent a discreet, well-built vehicle."

"That's what I think, because if you took the train or an air shuttle, you'd have to arrange for transpo on the other end. That adds an unnecessary step. He doesn't like unnecessary steps. The New Savoy's the top digs in London?"

"I like to think so."

"Yours?"

"Mmmm. Do you want to see this data?"

"Are we going to be arrested, fined, and imprisoned?"

"We can insist on adjoining cells."

"Gee, that's real funny." She walked to the desk, leaned over his shoulder, and scanned the data. "This just confirms the heart attack. If the Feebie's info was right, there's got to be something under it."

"Accessing private hospital records." He clucked his tongue. And since it was there, he turned his head a fraction to nip her jaw. "I'm quite sure there's a law against it."

"If it's good enough for the feds, it's good enough for me. Dig them out."

"I love when you say that." He simply executed one keystroke, and had the files he'd already accessed popping on-screen.

"You did that before I told you to."

"I don't know what you're talking about. I merely followed the orders of the primary investigator, in my capacity as expert consultant, civilian. But if you feel you must discipline me—"

She leaned over just a little more, and bit his ear. "Oh, thank you, Lieutenant."

She stifled the laugh, but stayed where she was. "Broken nose, fractured jaw, separated eye socket, four broken ribs, two broken fingers. Subdural this and hemorrhaging that. A lot of damage for a bad heart."

"Sodomized as well."

"But alive through it. Cause of death's the strangulation. The feds fed me straight on this. While we're in here, let's see if they brought the girl in for exam and treatment. Look on this date, same time frame, for a female, under eighteen. Probably examined for sexual molestation, for shock. Maybe minor bruises and lacerations, possible illegals consumption."

He set the scan, then picked up her coffee. "What does finding her matter? You know who killed Werner."

"It ties an end. And there's a possibility she helped set him up for the hit."

"There she is," Roarke murmured when the data popped. "Mollie Newman, female, age sixteen. You hit it down the line, even to the traces of Exotica and Zoner in her system."

"She's the only one we know of who's seen Yost on the job, and lived."

Zoner, she thought. *That wouldn't have come from Werner. Why screw around with a kid who's zoned?* That would have been Yost's addition to the mix.

"I want to find Mollie. She should have parents or guardians listed here . . . Freda Newman, mother. We'll run her, see what we get."

"Lieutenant? Your federal friends already have this data, and in all likelihood know where she is. They tossed you this to bog you down."

"I know it. But I still want to run it down. And I want to find where he bought the wire in East Washington. Habitually, he buys it near the hit. Let's see where—" She broke off, turned to the signaling 'link. "Yeah, Dallas."

"Lieutenant, I think we've got something from the porn sites."

"Peabody, what the hell are you wearing?"

Her aide flushed, looked down at herself and the wildly flowered ankle-skimmer she'd installed in McNab's closet for convenience. "Um, it's a robe type thing."

"And quite fetching," Roarke put in.

Peabody's flush turned into a glow as she fiddled with the bright pink lapels. "Oh, well, thanks. It's just for comfort, really. I—"

"Save it," Eve ordered. "What have you got?"

"I've run through the sites, pulling screen names and hits until my eyes fell out. You wouldn't believe some of the handles these jerks use. Anyhow, going by profile, I figured this guy would use something classier. I started picking up hits on Sterling. Just Sterling. You know, like—"

"Silver. I get it. Did you trace source location?"

"Well, we—"

She was bumped rudely aside as McNab came onscreen. He wasn't wearing a robe. Or, Eve noticed with a scowl, a shirt either.

"That's when the excitement started. Now, some of these pervs use some cloaking, especially the ones with families or high-powered jobs. Don't want people to know they're getting off watching sex discs. But when I started running Sterling, the beam bounces all over hell and back. Nobody goes to that much trouble, especially on legal sites. I got him zipping transmission from Hong Kong to Prague, from Prague to Chicago, from there to Vegas II, and on."

"Give me bottom line here, McNab."

"I can't even come close to true source, especially on my home units. I'm going to take it into EDD. Better toys there. I might be able to smoke him out. I can't tell you how long, but I'll head in now and get started."

"No, you've already put in fifteen, sixteen hours today." Though it was a good bet some of the activities hadn't been of a professional nature. "I'll do it from here."

"Ah, no offense, Lieutenant, but you need pretty sharp tech skills to get through the primary layers, and after that, you gotta have magic."

Roarke simply shifted again, so that he came on-screen. "McNab" was all he said.

"Oh. Well, if you're doing it, frigid. I'll shoot what I've got going over. Like I said, the hits we got with this Sterling are on legal sites. A couple of them are on the edge, but hold up. Nothing's popped on the real nasty stuff yet, but we've got a long way to go."

"Good work. Take a break."

"We already did." He couldn't help but grin. "We're pretty recharged now."

"Thank you for sharing," Eve said dryly. "Send the data to Roarke's home office unit."

She broke transmission, wandered away to let her mind clear.

"I'll leave the tracking to you. You can pass it, at whatever stage you might be in, to Feeney and McNab in the morning. I know you've got other stuff going on."

"I'll deal with it."

"I should have told you, I have a press conference tomorrow. You might want to squeeze in one of your own."

"Already scheduled. Don't worry about me, Eve."

"Who said I was?" She heard the beep from his office. "That's your data coming in."

She tracked the wire. Now that she knew where and how to look it was remarkably simple. One length, cash purchase, the day before Werner had his "heart attack." The store, Silverworks, carried a Georgetown address. Its ad page boasted of seventy-five years in business, serving the discerning.

She imagined she would find that Yost had dropped in on several other shops that day, treating himself to a few gifts.

She did a travel search, requesting the top five hotels in the East Washington area, then switched to transpo, picking out companies who offered rentals on high-end vehicles.

She ordered her computer to cross-reference, and list any names that appeared on both scans.

While it processed, she got more coffee and decided to give her overworked eyes a rest. She didn't know how the drones in EDD managed it. She kicked back in her sleep chair, closed her eyes, and went through her mental list of priorities for the morning.

Contact the silver shops, the hotels, and vehicle rentals in East Washington and London. Request proper authority to locate Freda and Mollie Newman. Won't get it, but ask anyway. Prep for stupid damn press conference. Check Mira's progress on profile and Feeney's on the wire.

Real estate holdings. Private estates. She'd ask Roarke about that.

The lab. Pound Dickhead. The morgue. Check if remains of Jonah Talbot are ready to be released to next of kin.

Better see how Roarke's doing now. Check on that in just a minute, she thought. And it was her last thought before she dropped into sleep.

Into the dark.

Shivering in the dark, but not from the cold. Fear was like a skin of ice over her small and fragile bones, rattling them together so she could almost hear the helpless, hollow sound of them.

No place to hide. There was never anywhere to hide. Not from him. He was coming. She could hear the heavy, deliberate footsteps growing louder outside her door. She glanced toward the window and wondered what it would be like if she just leaped from the bed, threw herself through the glass, and let herself fall. Fall free.

Freedom in death.

But she was too afraid, even with what would walk into her room, she was more afraid of the leap.

She was only eight.

The door opened, nightmare within nightmare, dark against dark with only the faintest of light washing behind the shadow of him, giving her his shape without a face.

Daddy's home. And he sees you, little girl.

Please, don't. Please, don't.

The plea was a scream in her head, but she didn't say it. Saying it wouldn't stop him, could make it worse. If it could be worse.

His hands were on her now, creeping under the blanket like spiders, skittering along her icy skin. It was worse, horribly worse, when he took time to touch her before . . .

She closed her eyes tight, tried to go somewhere else in her mind. Anywhere else in her mind. But that he wouldn't allow. It wasn't enough just to defile, just to abuse.

So he hurt her. He knew how. Fingers squeezing, invading, until she began to weep. When she wept, his breath thickened, the filthy excitement of it clogging the air in the room.

Such a bad little girl.

She tried to push him away, tried to make her body somehow smaller, small enough that even he couldn't get inside it. And now she begged, too desperate, too terrified to stop herself. And she screamed, a long, broken cry of pain, of despair when he pushed himself into her and began to plunge.

Her eyes, swollen with tears, opened. She couldn't stop them. And she watched, frozen with horror, as her father's face changed, as the features melted and re-formed.

It was Yost who raped her now, Yost who slipped a silver

wire around her throat. And though she was no longer a child but a woman, a cop, she couldn't stop him.

No air. No breath. The cold trickle of blood on her skin where the shining wire cut into fragile flesh. A roar in her head, a torrent of sound like the world screaming.

She flailed out, using her fists, her nails, her teeth, and was pinned.

"Eve, come back. Eve."

It was Roarke who held her now, but she was trapped in the dream. He could see her eyes, wild and blind, feel the frantic thunder of her heart. And she was cold, so cold.

He said her name, over and over, pressing her close as if that alone would bring the warmth back to her body. Her fear had him by the throat, like a mad dog that refused to release either of them.

She fought him, gasping for air like a woman drowning, until in desperation he pressed his mouth to hers as if to give her breath.

She went limp.

"You're all right, you're safe." He rocked, comforting them both. "You're home. Baby, you're so cold." But he could not bear to leave her, even to get a blanket. "Hold onto me."

"I'm okay. I'm all right." But she wasn't, not yet.

"Hold onto me anyway. I need it."

She wrapped her still unsteady arms around him, let her face burrow into his shoulder. "I smelled you. Then I heard you. But I couldn't find you."

"I'm right here." It ripped at him; he couldn't begin to tell her what it did inside him every time she went back to the horrors of her childhood in dreams. "Right here," he murmured, pressing his lips to her hair. "It was a bad one."

"Yeah, as bad as they get. It's over now." She drew back, as far as he would allow, and tipped her face up to his. His eyes were dark, emotions burning in them. "Bad for you, too."

"As bad as it gets. Eve." He pulled her against him again, heart against heart until the worst of it ebbed. "I'll get you some water."

"Thanks."

When he walked to the kitchen, she let her head fall into her hands. She'd get past it, she told herself. She could always get past it. She'd swallow back the bitter dregs of the fear and get on with things. She'd remember who she was now, and not what she'd been.

A victim. Always a victim.

Work. She drew a deep breath and lifted her head. She'd get back to work where she had control. And power. And direction.

She was steadier when he came back with the water and crouched at her feet.

Steady enough for suspicion to worm its way through relief and gratitude. "Did you put a soother in this?"

"Drink it."

"Damn it, Roarke."

"Damn it, Eve," he said mildly, and drank half the glass himself. "Drink the rest."

She frowned, and sipping slowly, studied him over the rim. He looked a little frazzled, which was a rare thing for him. A little weary, which was even more rare.

It wasn't work he needed, she realized, but rest. Rest he wouldn't take, even if she put the work aside for the night. He'd just wait until she'd run down, until she slept, then he'd keep going.

But he wasn't the only one who knew how to press the right buttons. She set the empty glass aside. "Satisfied?"

"More or less. You should leave this until morning and get some sleep."

Perfect, she thought, but made sure her nod was reluctant. "I guess. I can't keep my mind focused anyway, but . . ."

"But what?"

"Would you stay here with me?" She reached for his hand. "I know it's stupid, but . . ."

"No, it's not." He got into the sleep chair with her, stroking her hair as her arms came tightly around him. "Just turn it off until morning."

"I will." Just as she'd keep her arms around him to make sure he did the same. "Don't go away, okay?"

"I won't."

And knowing he wouldn't leave her, would rest, she closed her eyes, and let herself drift into dreamless sleep.

After a while, a long while, so did he.

She woke first, still wrapped around him, when the dark began to soften and thin. She stayed very still so as not to lose the rare opportunity to watch him sleep.

Love struck her, as it did often and without warning. Not the steady day-to-day feeling she'd grown used to, but the hot, wild spurt of it that geysered up and filled her with so many feelings they couldn't be separated.

Delight, confusion, possessiveness, lust, and a kind of smugness that butted right up against wonder.

He was so ridiculously beautiful, she doubted she'd ever fully comprehend how he could be hers.

He'd wanted her. Out of all the women in the world, he'd wanted her. Wanted, hell, she thought, grinning now. Pursued, demanded. Taken. And while she could admit all of that was exciting, he'd gone one step further.

He cherished.

She'd never believed anyone would, or could. And had never believed there was enough inside her to give all of those things back.

So here they were, the cop and the billionaire, squished

together in an office sleep chair like a couple of over-worked drones.

It was just fucking great.

She was still grinning when those fabulous eyes of his opened. Clear as blue crystal, alert, and ever so mildly amused. "Good morning, Lieutenant."

"I never get how you can come awake like that, from sleep to full alert, and without coffee."

"Annoying, isn't it?"

"Yeah." He was warm, he was beautiful, he was hers. She could have lapped him up like cream. *And why not,* she thought. *Why the hell not?*

"But since you're awake." She slid her hand down his body, found him hard and ready. "All the way awake. I've got a little job for you."

"Do you?" Her mouth was already roaming over his face, just missing his lips in teasing little bites. To his considerable surprise, and considerable pleasure, her fingers got very busy. They closed around him, not teasing at all, as her tongue laved thirstily along his throat.

"Well then," he managed. "Anything for the NYPSD. Christ!" He could all but feel his eyes roll back in his head. "Am I on the clock?"

Sometime later, feeling loose and limber, she came out of the kitchen with two mugs of coffee. It surprised her that Roarke still sat in the half-dark. The cat was on his lap now, and with the faintest of smiles on his face, Roarke stroked Galahad's back.

"I think, for an expert consultant, civilian, you've loafed long enough."

"Mmm-hmm." He took the coffee she offered. "Shutting down early to sleep, morning sex, bringing me coffee. You're very wifely these days. Are you taking care of me, Eve?"

"Hey, if you don't want the coffee, I'll drink it myself.

And so what if I am? *And* don't call me wifely. It pisses me off."

"I do want the coffee, thank you very much. I'm touched and grateful you'd take care of me. And pissing you off by calling you wifely is one of my small pleasures."

"Great. Now that we've got all that settled, get your ass up so we can do some work."

chapter twelve

She made the first calls and reached the detective sergeant working the homicides in Cornwall. During their fifteen-minute conversation, she was given the facts of the case in a broad North Country accent, the names of the two victims who had been identified by fingerprint, and DNA matches through Feeney's love child, IRCCA.

DS Fortique was cheerful and forthcoming and told her that after considerable tracking and backtracking they had finally tagged the identity of the hiker who had allegedly found the bodies and made the emergency call.

Fortique was perfectly willing to save Eve time and trouble by hauling the witness in and grilling him over a pair of two-foot silver wires.

Eve decided the British police were a great deal more cooperative than her own federal agents. She gave him back in kind by passing along the data on Yost's shopping adventures in London. They ended transmission on good terms.

Her call to the silver shop netted her a full description of Sylvester Yost, who was fondly remembered for his discriminating taste, impeccable manners, and extensive cash purchases.

Another knot tied off, Eve thought, and shifted her search to hotels.

The New Savoy wasn't quite as cooperative as the police or the merchants in London. She was passed from desk clerk to supervisor, from supervisor to hotel manager. And it seemed there she would stall.

The manager was a woman in her mid- to late fifties with hair the color of polished steel pulled ruthlessly away from a scrawny face that ended on a pointed chin. Her eyes were a surprising baby blue, and her voice, while remaining scrupulously polite, droned on and on over the same notes.

"I'm afraid I can't accommodate you, Lieutenant Dallas. It is the policy, the firm policy of The New Savoy, to ensure its guests' privacy as well as their comfort."

"When your guests start raping and murdering they lose some of that privacy, don't you think?"

"Be that as it may, I'm unable to give you any information on a guest. It's entirely possible you're mistaken, and I would have breached the code of The New Savoy and insulted a guest. Until you have the proper documentation, as well as international authorization that requires I make information available to you, my hands are tied."

I'd like to tie your hands, Eve thought, *then kick your skinny butt out the window of the top floor of your stupid hotel.*

"Ms. Clydesboro, if I'm forced to wake up my commanding officer and an international liaison advocate at five-fifty in the morning they're going to be very displeased."

"I'm afraid that's a difficulty you'll have to surmount. Please feel free to contact me if you—"

"Now, listen, sister—"

"One moment." Roarke, who'd stood in the adjoining

doorway and had listened to the last thirty seconds of the exchange, crossed the room and took over the 'link. "Ms. Clydesboro."

At least Eve had the satisfaction of watching the woman's pruney face go pale and those milky blue eyes bulge. "Sir!"

"Give Lieutenant Dallas any and all data she requires."

"Yes, sir. Of course, sir. I beg your pardon. I had no idea that you had authorized the release of this information."

"How could you?" he said pleasantly. "But now that you do, get it done."

"I'll see to it personally. Lieutenant Dallas, if you would forward the description of the man you believe stayed at our hotel, I will instruct the staff to confirm or deny."

"I'm sending you a visual image, the dates we believe the individual was in London, and a written description. Instruct the staff that this man may have been wearing a disguise. Hair and eye color and some facial features may vary. He would have booked one of your best suites, would have been traveling alone, and would likely have had private transportation."

"I'll have an answer for you within an hour of receiving your transmission."

"Good."

She cut transmission, scowled. "Tight-assed bat."

"She's only doing her job. You'll find the same policy will hold true for any of the top hotels in London. Would you like me to smooth the way?"

She gave a bad-tempered shrug and got up. "Why the hell not? Getting anywhere on the location search?"

"Yes, I believe I am. I believe we're going to find they were sent and received from here in the city. The rest is shadows, echoes."

"How close can you pinpoint?"

"Given a bit more time I can take you to his doorstep."

"How much time?"

"Until it's done."

"Yeah, but how long until—"

"Lieutenant, impatience won't speed the process." He glanced over as Mick came to the doorway.

"Sorry. Interrupting?"

"Not at all." But Eve noticed Roarke saved data and blanked her screen manually. "Your . . . business must have gone well if you're just getting in."

Mick grinned. "I can say with truth it went better than any man has a right to expect. Is that coffee I smell?"

"It is, yes." Though he could almost hear Eve grinding her teeth in frustration, Roarke got to his feet. "Would you like some?"

"I like it fine, especially if a good drop of Irish found its way into it."

"I think that can be arranged."

Mick smiled at Eve as Roarke walked back to the kitchen, with the cat—sensing the possibility of break-fast—jogging behind him.

"The man sleeps less than is human. He must be pleased to have found a woman who can start the day before dawn as he does himself."

"You look pretty perky for a guy who's been up all night yourself."

"Certain activities energize a man. So you work here at home from time to time, do you?"

"From time to time."

He nodded. "And anxious, I imagine, to get back to what you were doing. I'll be out of your way in just a moment. I hope you'll pardon me for saying so, but it's an odd sight to see the man working hip to hip with a cop."

"Odd all around." She looked over her shoulder as Roarke came back with a thick, working man's mug steaming with coffee and whiskey.

"The answer to a prayer, thanks. I'll just take it off to my room and let it lull me off to sleep."

"A moment first. Eve, do you have the name of the couple in Cornwall?"

"What I have or don't have is police business."

"Mick might know them." He shifted his eyes to Eve's face. "And their competitors."

It was a good point. A potential weasel was a useful tool, even when he was a houseguest. "Britt and Joseph Hague."

"Hmm, well." Mick gave his attention to his laced coffee. "It's possible, of course, that I may have heard the names somewhere in my travels. I couldn't say." He gave Roarke a hard, meaningful look. "I couldn't say," he repeated.

"Because you've done business with them?" Eve shot back. "The kind Customs frowns on?"

"I do business with a great many people." He spoke coolly, evenly. "And I'm not in the habit of discussing them or their affairs with cops. I'm surprised you would ask me to," he said to Roarke. "Surprised and disappointed that you'd expect me to roll on friends and associates."

"Your friends and associates are dead," Eve said flatly. "Murdered."

"Britt and Joe?" His green eyes widened, clouded, and he slowly lowered himself into a chair. "I hadn't heard that. I never heard that."

"Their bodies were found in Cornwall," Roarke told him. "Apparently they weren't found for some time, and it took longer yet to identify them."

"Good Christ. God rest their souls. A lovely couple they were. How did it happen?"

"Who would have wanted them dead?" Eve countered. "Who would have paid a great deal of money to take them out of the equation?"

"I don't know for sure. They'd been having considerable luck running prime liquor and high-grade illegals into London, and dispersing them from there into Paris, Athens, Rome. Stepped on some toes, I imagine, along the way.

They'd only been in business, in a serious way, for a couple years. God, I'm sick about this."

He drank from the mug, made an obvious effort to settle himself. "You wouldn't have known them," he said to Roarke. "As I said, they'd only been exporting for a few years, and stuck to Europe. They had a little cottage on the Moors. Liked the country life, Christ knows why."

"Whose profits were they cutting into?" Roarke asked him.

"Oh, a little here, a little there, I'd say. Always room for another smuggler, isn't there, with all the goods in the world to be moved? Francolini, maybe. Aye, he's a vicious bastard, and they'd have cut into him a bit. He wouldn't think twice about sending one of his men up to cut them out, permanently."

"He doesn't use a paid assassin." Roarke remembered Francolini well. "He has enough men to let blood when blood needs to be let. He wouldn't go outside his own family."

"Paid assassin? No, not Francolini then. Lafarge, maybe. Or Hornbecker. Hornbecker's more likely to pay for blood. But he'd need good reason for it, enough to balance his ledgers."

"Franz Hornbecker, Frankfort," Roarke told Eve. "He was small-time when I was exporting."

"He's had a good run of luck in the last few years." Mick sighed. "I don't know what else to tell you. Britt and Joe. I can't imagine it. Why, can I ask, should a New York City cop be interested in the fate of two up and coming smugglers out of England?"

"It may tie to a case here."

"If it does, I hope you catch the murdering bastard who did them." He rose. "I don't know what sort of work they might have been up to at the end of it, but I can do some asking. On the quiet."

"I'd appreciate any information you can give me."

"Well, we'll see what we see." He bent down and picked up the cat, who was rubbing against his legs. "I'm for bed. Oh, Roarke," he said when he reached the door, "if you've time later I'd like to discuss the business I mentioned to you before."

"I'll have my admin work it in."

"God, listen to the man. Admin working it in," he said to Galahad as he carried cat and coffee away. "Did you ever hear the like of it?"

"Other business?"

"Perfume," Roarke said. "And legal. Whatever else he might be up to, I've told him I'm not interested as it would displease my cop. I'll make those calls for you."

"Why is your unit beeping in there?"

"Is it?" He shifted his thoughts, heard the signal. Grinned. "I think I'm about to land you on Yost's doorstep."

She was on his heels as he walked into his office, then leaning over his shoulder as he studied the data, skimming over the monitor.

"Hmmm. On wall screen," he ordered, and shifting his stance studied the run of numbers and slashing lines.

"What are they? Coordinates?"

"Yes, exactly. This is very interesting. Computer, display New York City street map, screen two. He did a bit of bouncing right here in the city as well. A good cloak, a smart move because it tends to skew the directional search when it becomes that finite."

"What do you mean, East Side to West Side, that kind of thing?" She tried to decipher the numbers, and ended up frustrated.

"More or less. But he shoots back and forth, up and down, a little side trip to Long Island and back. It gives us a couple of possibilities, but the most likely . . . Computer, enhance grid, Upper West Side. Ah, yes. Now decode directional formula to street location, and match. Do you see?" Roarke asked Eve, laying a hand on her neck as the computer screens flashed and changed. "It appears Yost is a neighbor."

"That's four blocks away. Four fucking blocks."

"Yes. Obviously you and I don't stroll through the neighborhood often enough."

"We never stroll through the neighborhood. How sure are you?"

"Ninety percent."

"Sure enough. Okay, I need a description of that building, the layout, the tenant list, security setup."

"That should be simple enough. Actually, I think I own that building."

"Think?"

"One does lose track occasionally. Computer, who owns the property currently displayed on screen two?"

WORKING . . . PROPERTY IS OWNED AND MAINTAINED BY
ROARKE INDUSTRIES.

"Ah, there we are. Just let me take a look at my real estate files. I'll have the data for you in a moment."

"Lose track occasionally?" she repeated, staring at him. "Of an entire building?"

"I do a bit of buying and selling of property, particularly in my own backyard." He smiled at her. "Everyone needs a hobby."

He sat down, settled in, and brought up the tenant list first. "That's lovely, isn't it? Fully occupied. I do hate seeing nice apartments vacant."

"Cut out the families, the couples, those with roommates, and all single women."

The computer acknowledged her directive, making her jolt a bit before she realized Roarke had it programmed to accept her voice commands.

The list narrowed to ten.

"Bring up application for rent data."

She skimmed down the new information, mentally discarding men over sixty or under forty. And now there were two.

"Jacob Hawthorne, computer analyst, age fifty-three. Single. Estimated annual income two point six million. He has the penthouse, right? Yost would want the best digs."

"Agreed."

"Several years shaved off the age, but I like Hawthorne. Do a run on both these single males. Let's be sure. Damn sure. I'm calling it in."

Within two hours, Eve had her team assembled in her home office. Added to the investigative team were twenty Special Tactics officers and ten hand-selected uniforms. Some might call it overkill, but she wasn't going to risk Yost slipping through a hole.

While she waited for the warrant for search and seize to come through, she ran over the plan yet again.

"There are fifty-six units in the building. They are all occupied. Civilian safety remains a priority."

The building's blueprints were up on-screen. Eve used a laser pointer to highlight each section as she spoke. "Our information indicates that the subject occupies the top floor. There are no other units on that floor. All elevators and glides will be inoperable. Stair access will be blocked off. We don't want him getting off that floor and taking any hostages. This unit has four exits. Two men from Team B will be stationed at each exit. Team A will handle building exits. On command, black-and-whites will move in here, and here, closing off the street to all outgoing and incoming traffic. Subject is not to be terminated. All weapons on stun, medium setting."

She glanced away from the screen to scan faces, to judge and measure. "This is a professional assassin, and he's managed to elude and evade authorities for more than forty years. Confirmed and suspected kills top forty during that time period. He's smart, and he's fast, and he's dangerous. Containing and capturing him within the building is our top objective. If those efforts fail, the second line will take him down. Full-body armor is required for all team members."

She turned back, used a remote to split the screen and bring up Yost's face. "This is our man. You all have printouts of this image. Be aware that he uses disguises. Captain Feeney will explain EDD's function in this operation."

Feeney sniffed, pulled on his nose, got to his feet. "Security cams on that floor will be adjusted to relay direct to Base One. We have verified the subject is in target area as of thirty minutes ago. We will reverify before moving in.

"All the subject will see if he checks his monitor is an empty hallway. We can't stop him from scratching his ass and looking out his windows, so all team members and uniformed backups will keep to their stations until ordered otherwise. I'll run Base One, and with Lieutenant Dallas will coordinate all movements. Communicators are to be set on Channel Three for straight interteam communications. There's to be no chatter and bullshit during the operation. Let's get it done and put this guy away."

Eve nodded. "Detective McNab and Officer Peabody, along with Lieutenant Marks and myself, will move in on the subject, using this entrance. All movements will be transmitted to Base One, and to each team leader. Any questions?"

She waited, again watching faces. These were hard men and hard women. They knew their job.

"Go down to your units and suit up. We'll begin the op as soon as the warrant comes through."

And what the hell was taking it so long? she wondered as the room emptied. She'd called in the data and request nearly two hours before. She'd need to tag the judge again, give him a goose.

Then she looked at Feeney. He outranked her, and had considerably more tact. It was likely the judge would respond to him more quickly.

"Feeney, they're dicking with this warrant. Want to see what you can do to expedite?"

"Politics." He might have grumbled, but he walked to her desk 'link to make the call. While he worked, she moved over to Roarke.

"We appreciate your help with the security cams and the layout. This should go off fast and smooth."

Should, he thought, *was a disturbing word.* "As owner of the building, I can insist on accompanying you to the penthouse."

"That's bullshit, and you know it. Keep it up, and I'll change my mind about letting you hang with Feeney at Base One. I know how to apprehend a suspect, Roarke, so don't distract me."

"Where's your body armor?"

"Peabody's got it. It's hot and it's heavy, so I'm not suiting up until I have to." She glanced back, her brow creasing as she heard Feeney's squawk. "Something's up," she muttered, and had just started across the room when Commander Whitney walked in.

"Lieutenant. Your operation is aborted."

"Aborted? What the hell is this? We've got his hole. We can have him in custody within the hour."

Feeney was on his feet now, cursing at the 'link. "Goddamn double cross. Fucking political double fucking cross."

"That's right." Whitney's voice was clipped and cold, but his dark eyes burned with fury. "That's exactly right." His own outrage and frustration were why he was there in person instead of informing Eve of the abort order over communications. "The feds got wind of the operation."

"I don't care if they got wind of the Second Coming," Eve began, then with a vicious effort yanked herself back.

"This operation is a result of my investigation, Commander, of data I accessed. The suspect killed two people on my turf. I'm primary."

"Do you think I didn't argue those very points, Lieutenant? I've just spent the last half hour exchanging insults with Assistant Director Sooner, FBI, bitching to two judges, and threatening anyone I could tag. The Feebs managed to get your warrant delayed and slip one of their own through ahead of it. When I find out who leaked your request to them, I'll happily kick someone's ass. But the fact is we're out, they're in."

Eve's hands were fisted at her sides. Deliberately, she relaxed them. *Later,* she promised herself. Later, she'd beat the hell out of something. "They didn't pull this off by sticking with chain of command or going through channels. When this is over, I want to file an official protest."

"Get in line," Whitney told her. "Politics is a dirty business, Dallas, but it's *my* turf. Believe me, I'll deal with this. Agents Jacoby and Stowe might think this bust will make their careers. They're in for a hell of a surprise."

"Respectfully, sir, I don't give a rat's red ass about Jacoby and Stowe. As long as they bring Yost in. I want to interview him on the French and Talbot homicides. I want to talk to him before the feds make him any deals."

"I'm already working on that. I have some powerful connections, and Chief Tibble has even more. You'll get your interview, Dallas."

She didn't quite trust herself to speak, at least not reasonably, so only nodded, then walked to the window. There were cops down there waiting to do their job. Now they had no job to do.

"I'll tell the team," Feeney said.

"No. It was my command. I'll tell them."

"Feeney," Whitney said when Eve strode from the room. "I want you to put the best man you can spare to work on plugging that leak. Someone in Communications on our end, or on Judge Beesley's end, notified Jacoby of the warrant request. I want to know who it is."

"I'll get started on it." He slid his eyes to Roarke, lifted his eyebrow in question. Roarke inclined his head.

Oh yes, he thought, *I'd be delighted to assist EDD in plugging this particular leak.*

"Roarke." If he'd seen the exchange, Whitney pretended not to. "Regardless of how this particular event has panned out, the NYPSD would like to offer its official appreciation for your help and cooperation in this investigation."

"Then you're officially welcome. May I ask how much you know about these two agents?"

"Not as much as I will know, very shortly. They have no idea, no possible idea who they've pissed off."

"I recall you can get down and dirty when you're riled, Jack."

Whitney turned to give Roarke a thin and fierce smile. "That's true, and I will. But I was talking about Dallas. She'll skin them, and I intend to do whatever I can to provide her with the room to do so."

When his communicator signaled, he stepped out of the room before slipping it out of his pocket.

"This was her collar." Feeney paced around the room, a wiry-haired rooster defending his favorite chick. "The feds knew it. She got within blocks of Yost inside a week. One goddamn week and she's on top of him. They had years and never got close. I bet that burns their spongy federal butts. I bet that's why they pulled this stinking stunt."

"Undoubtedly. Feeney, would certain classified data on Agents Stowe and Jacoby be of any use to you, should it fall into your hands unexpectedly and from an anonymous source?"

Feeney stopped pacing to eye Roarke speculatively.

"Might be useful. Of course, doing an unofficial run on federal agents is a dicey business. Federal offense."

"Really? As a law-abiding citizen I'm glad to know such matters are treated seriously."

Now he walked to the window, looked down. "This is hard for her," Roarke murmured. "Facing her team, telling them, basically, that all her work, all theirs gets them nothing. That cops have just been kicked aside and told to stand down so the federals can have the glory."

"She's never worn a badge for the glory."

Roarke looked back over his shoulder. *This is the man who'd taught her,* he thought. *The one who had helped mold her into the kind of cop she was.* "You're right, of course. The satisfaction then, of knowing you've done your job, seen it through, and made what justice you can for the dead. You know how difficult sexual homicides of this nature are for her."

"Yeah." Feeney looked down at his shoes. "Yeah, I guess I know that."

"I woke her from a nightmare last night, brought on by this. A vicious and violent nightmare," he said as Feeney lifted his head again. "Yet we both watched her stand here this morning, in command of herself and her team. Prepared to do what needed to be done. You understand what that takes, and I've come to. There's one thing those two fucking federals will never understand. Her courage."

He looked back out the window again, watching her walk back toward the house. "Her absolute and unwavering courage. The dead don't matter a damn to them. They're names and data, statistics on discs. For her, they're faces. They're people. No, they'll never understand the guts, and the heart, in her that make her what she is."

"You're right." Feeney blew out a breath. "You're right and that's something to think about. There's something else that can be said, and will be, because I'll say it to her myself, and to everyone else who'll listen. The feds may bring him in, but she's the one who brought him down."

"Nobody's bringing him in." His face set like rock, Whitney stepped back into the room. "He's gone."

chapter thirteen

Feeney erupted. It was a vicious, feral, and inventive tirade that was peculiarly Irish in tone. It was that brilliant and blue rant Eve heard as she walked back up the stairs, down the hall, and into the room.

And she knew they were screwed.

"Not bad enough they're bastards," Feeney continued. "But they're fucking stupid turnip-brained bastards with it. Tipped him. Tipped the bloody murdering son of a bitch off with their greedy, glory-hunting federal maneuvering so now he's gone rabbit and none of us have a flaming thing to show for it."

"We can't be certain he got wind of the bust," Whitney began, and Feeney, forgetting rank, seared his commander with one violent look.

"Bullocks. That's bullocks, Jack, and you know it. They've a leak, and screwing with our op gave it time to spring. We'd have him now, we'd by Christ have him now if they hadn't wagged their government-issue cocks around."

"He's gone." Eve didn't feel rage. Oddly, Feeney's ripe temper kept her own in check. She simply felt hollow.

"The government bust was a wash." Whatever bitter rage bubbled inside Whitney didn't show. "They moved on Yost minutes ago. He wasn't there."

"Did they check the security cams? Confirm with the doorman or building guards if he was in residence?"

"I don't have the details. The word is the suspect has fled. The apprehension operation failed."

She only nodded. "I would like to confirm, personally, sir."

"So would I." Whitney scanned her face, then Feeney's. "Let's move."

The federals weren't particularly friendly. There was an air of gloom and resentment that spilled through the elegant lobby and glossy hallways of the target building. The looks shot toward local badges dripped with both.

Eve imagined she'd have engaged in a few pissing contests, but Whitney's rank, his bulk, and his cold control cleared the way.

Knowing Feeney was still simmering, she gestured to McNab. "See if you can use some boyish charm to pry some information from the federal E-guys. They'll have checked or will be checking the security discs. I want to know when Yost left the premises, which exit he used, and what he had with him."

"You got it." He sauntered off, hands in the pockets of his strawberry-colored slacks.

"Peabody, see if you can knock on some doors without alerting any federals. Let's see what his neighbors have to say. If you can manage to dig up a maintenance or guard droid, all the better."

Eve stepped into the elevator with Whitney and Feeney, and rode up in silence. She wanted to think. The timing had been close and slick. Yost had solid connections. Through the FBI? Through the NYPSD? Probably both.

He moved fast, and he moved well. But he wasn't finished in New York. Fast and well, but not far then. A hotel? Possibly. She was more inclined to believe he, or his current employer, had a private hole for him to burrow in. Until the job was done.

With this much heat, how long would he wait to make the next target?

Because she was focused on Yost and his pattern, she stepped off the elevator ahead of her commander. And found herself face-to-face with Jacoby.

His eyes went instantly hot, and he shifted to the balls of his feet like a boxer prepping for the next round. "This is an FBI operation."

"This," Whitney said, moving in before Eve could speak, "is an FBI screwup of major proportions. You want to explain to me, Agent, how you and your team managed to lose the suspect my officers had located?"

Jacoby knew just where the ax was going to fall. He intended to do everything in his power to deflect it onto locals' necks and save his own. "This operation, this *federal* operation has been ongoing for a considerable length of time. I don't have to explain—"

"That's right," Whitney interrupted. "You've been trying to catch a whiff of Yost for years. My lieutenant managed to pin him down in a matter of days. You not only took advantage of the careful, *successful* investigation through my house, but then botched it. If you don't think you're going to have to explain that, Agent Jacoby, to me, to my chief, to my lieutenant, and to your own superiors, you're sadly mistaken. Now . . ."

He shifted his bulk, subtly signaling Eve to move on. "Why don't you start with me?"

There were a half-dozen men and women milling

around, all still in riot gear with the initials of their agency emblazoned on the back in bright yellow. Eve walked through them and into the penthouse.

It was already being picked apart by sweepers, by other agents. But there was enough to give her what she'd wanted. A chance to see, for herself, how Yost lived.

Richly, she thought, with deep carpets and thick cushions. A wall of glass opened onto the city and boasted a wide stone terrace where artfully arranged plants spilled lavishly out of glossy pots.

Tastefully, she noted, with blending pastels that soothed the eye and carefully arranged paintings in sleek gold frames. The furniture was wood, and old. She knew how to recognize the quiet extravagance of antiques now.

And he lived efficiently. The disarray was minimal in the living area, and was the result, she was sure, of the sweepers. Polish gleamed under the dust already spread.

On a low table with carved and curved feet there was an arrangement of fresh flowers in cut crystal. On a pedestal stand stood a single nude in white marble, all long lines and flowing hair.

There were entertainment and communications centers built into paneled cabinets and already being dismantled.

He wouldn't have worked here, she thought. *No, not in his living space. Amused himself here, perhaps, but not serious work.* Still she turned a slow circle, recording the room on her mini-unit.

She imagined Roarke would be able to make the paintings, maybe the sculptures and the furniture as well.

The busy on-scene unit took no notice of her as she wandered through. A wide archway led her to a formal dining area with a multitiered crystal chandelier and heavy, somehow masculine furniture.

More flowers here, a low spill of color and shape in the center of the dining table. Candlesticks of silver with long white tapers.

The kitchen was directly off to the right, and polished to a gleam. She pursed her lips as she poked into the tank-sized refrigerator and found it fully stocked, as was the AutoChef. Both ran to expensive food, heavy on the red meat.

There were cooking utensils in the drawers, neatly filed in slots. Jars and bottles of oils and spices and the various ingredients needed if someone made a habit of actually cooking.

Interesting, she thought, and imagined Yost standing over the huge stove, delicately sautéing something. Listening to music, classical music or opera, as he worked. Wearing the snow-white butcher's apron she found hanging, pressed and pristine, in a narrow closet.

He'd cook for himself, an efficient and self-sufficient man. Or order up one of his choices on the AutoChef. He'd set his table with the fancy china in his cupboard, light his candles, and savor his solitary meal.

A man of refined tastes, who liked to kill.

She backtracked, moved into the room he'd remodeled into a high-tech gym. The walls were mirrored, the ceiling high, the floor a gleaming solid wood.

Here was a treadmill with VR capabilities, a personal aqua tank, a resistance center, gravity bench and boots, and a wall of mirrors with a viewer to record workout. Roarke's at-home gym was better equipped, she thought, but what was here was top of the line.

Yost kept himself in shape, and liked to watch himself doing so.

She found his bedroom next, and here he'd indulged himself. Slick materials, sensual colors, a gel bed the size of a lake flowing under a canopy of blue satin. A mirrored canopy, she noted, another viewer.

Yost liked to watch himself doing more than working out.

The master bath followed the scheme of efficient indulgence, and there she found his horde of soaps and lotions and oils from exclusive hotels around the world and off it. *Travel-size*, she mused. *Tuck them into your job bag, do you, Yost, so you can clean up after work?*

Rape and murder were a messy business. But with these handy containers of the best hygiene products around, you can be fresh as a daisy in no time.

The containers were arranged in a tall cupboard, according to purpose. The gaps between told her he'd taken some with him.

Waste not, want not.

The walk-in closet, if a room that size and complex could be called a closet, was sheer genius.

She imagined he'd left in somewhat of a hurry. And yet there was no untidiness. Several slots were empty in the revolving cabinet, a number of the stone gray wig stands were now bald, but every inch was ruthlessly organized.

There were a lot of inches.

Forests of suits ranging from blue to gray to black, a parade of shirts in tones of white or the most delicate pastels, hung in precise order on a two-level set of bars.

More casual wear. Skinsuits, workout apparel, lounging robes, were meticulously arranged across the wide room.

A waterfall of ties, scarves, belts hung ruler-straight in their individual areas. Shoes, mountains of them, were displayed in clear boxes that were not only stacked but numbered.

She counted six missing pairs.

A long and spotless white counter was nestled between the wardrobe bars and build-ins. Over it spread a wide triple mirror ringed by fancy round lights. There was a padded seat, and kneehole room in the cabinet below. It boasted two dozen drawers. She opened them at random and saw enhancements that would have made her friend Mavis's heart swell with joy.

She scanned labels even as she recorded. She knew less about enhancements than she did about paintings.

She walked out, over carpet, through archways, and found what she was looking for. The hub of activity, Yost's workspace, where Karen Stowe and two other Feebs were currently running discs on Yost's desk unit.

"He was in a hurry," Stowe said as she stood, hands on hips, staring at the scrolling data. "He couldn't have gotten everything."

"He got everything he wanted to get," Eve said from the doorway, and Stowe's head snapped up as if she'd taken an uppercut to the jaw. Her mouth thinned.

"Let me know if anything clicks," she ordered, then moved to the doorway, through. She gave a come-with-me signal to Eve. And was ignored.

"He packed his bags," Eve continued, "tucked in whatever he felt most necessary, went through his data discs, his files. Wouldn't take a lot of time if you're as anal and organized as he is. He'd have a notebook, a portable, a number of nice, convenient, travel-sized units. They'd have gone with him, too. All in all, I'd say he was out the door in thirty minutes, on the outside, after his source tipped him about your operation."

"I don't want to discuss this here."

"Too bad. My team ran him down while yours was racing in circles. You wouldn't be standing this close to him if it hadn't been for the work my team put into this."

"If you'd cooperated—"

"Like you did?" Eve shot back. "Yeah, you're full of co-operation. Who'd you pay off to get the information on my warrant? What favors did you call in to get yours bumped in front of it so you could screw this up?"

"Federal takes precedence."

"Bullshit, Stowe. Justice takes precedence, and if I'd gotten my warrant in a timely fashion Sylvester Yost would be in a cage now instead of setting up shop somewhere else."

She knew it. Goddamn it, she knew it. "You can't be sure of that."

"I can be sure of one thing, and so can you: He's gone. You fucked up and he's gone. How's that going to sit with you when we stand over the next body?"

Stowe closed her eyes a moment, drew in a breath. "Can we go somewhere private and discuss—"

"No."

"Fine." On a snap of temper, Stowe pulled the door closed so the agents inside were deprived of the gossip. "Look, you're steamed, and you've got a right to be. But I did my job. Jacoby came to me with the data on the warrant, and he'd already done the dance. I had a chance to bring Yost down, to bring him in, and I took it. You'd have done the same."

"You don't know me, pal. I don't play games and I don't try to rack up points on someone else's work. You wanted a big bust, and you didn't care how you got it. Now we're both empty, and odds are someone else is going to die."

Eve paused, seeing the quick wince in Stowe's eyes. "Yeah, you've figured that much out, haven't you? As much as I'll enjoy seeing you and your partner's butts fry over this foul up, it doesn't make up for another hit. Nothing does."

"All right," Stowe said as Eve turned away. She reached out, grabbed Eve's arm. Her voice was low, her eyes miserable. "You're right. You're right, straight down the line."

"Being right doesn't mean shit just now, does it? Keep away from me, Stowe. You and that moron you work with keep away from me, my team, and my investigation. Otherwise, neither of you will have enough ass left to fry when I'm finished with you."

She strode, out, heading for the door. Before she could pass through, Jacoby stepped in front of her. "Did you have that recorder on?" he demanded.

"Get out of my way."

"You aren't authorized to record this scene," he began and made a grab for her lapel unit. Fast and vicious as a snake, she snatched his wrist, pushing her thumb into the pulse point and twisting.

"Keep your hand off me. You don't, I'll snap it off at the wrist and make you eat it."

Pain radiated up his arm, paralyzing him. But his other hand bunched into a fist, lifted. "You're assaulting and threatening a federal officer."

"Funny, I thought I was assaulting and threatening a federal asshole. You want to take a shot at me, Jacoby"—she tilted her chin up in invitation—"go ahead, right here in front of all your friends and associates. Let's see which one of us walks out on two feet."

"Lieutenant."

"Sir." She acknowledged Whitney, but kept her eyes on Jacoby's. His were starting to water.

"Your presence is required at Central to finalize the formal complaint against Agents Jacoby and Stowe. Let that idiot go," he said mildly. "He's not worth it."

"Affirmative," Eve murmured, then released Jacoby's wrist and stepped back.

Perhaps it was embarrassment, or perhaps he was simply a moron. But he lunged at her. She didn't think; she didn't hesitate. With a half-pivot, she shot her elbow up, caught him just under the chin. She heard his teeth snap together an instant before he went down.

She had a moment to hope he'd bitten off a chunk of his tongue before he scrambled to his feet, eyes dazed. She finished the pivot, planted her feet. And supposed it was probably for the best when Whitney stepped between them.

"I'm filing charges." Blood trickled out of Jacoby's mouth as he fumbled for his communicator.

"I wouldn't advise that, Agent. You came at my officer, a violent action, when her back was turned. She defended herself. That's on record." With a fierce grin, he patted his own lapel recorder. "Make that call and I'll have you up before your own disciplinary committee before your tongue stops bleeding. You're not just taking on my officer, you're taking me on, and my whole goddamn department. So back off before I see that what's left of your career is flushed down the toilet."

He held Jacoby's eyes another testing moment, signaled to Eve to go, then followed.

As they walked toward the elevator, Feeney examined his fingernails. "Shoulda followed through with a knee to the balls."

"I would have, but he doesn't have any." Then she sobered, straightened. "Commander, I apologize for—"

"Don't spoil it." He stepped into the elevator, rolled his shoulders. "I have to get out in the field more often. I forgot how much fun it could be. I want your observations and analysis of the scene on disc as soon as possible, Lieutenant. Run a probability on his still being in or near the city, and if that comes through positive, run one on where he might hole up. Contact—"

He broke off, looked down into her face. "You show admirable restraint, Dallas, in not telling me you know how to do your job."

"The thought never crossed my mind, sir." Since decking Jacoby had brightened her mood, she worked up a smile. "Hardly."

"Since you do know I'll let you get on with it." He walked off the elevator. "I have a number of calls to make. A number of ears to burn."

"He's revved up," Feeney murmured when Whitney left them.

"Is he?"

"Yeah. You didn't know him when he worked the streets. Got cold blood, Jack does. Heads'll be rolling by end of shift, and he won't have broken a sweat." Feeney pulled his bag of nuts from his pocket. "I'll gather up McNab. You taking this into Central?"

"For now." She pulled out her communicator, intending

to tag Peabody when her aide stepped off the elevator across the wide lobby. "You're with me."

Eve waited until they were out the doors and inside her unit. "Report?"

"Kept to himself. Very polite, if aloof. Always perfectly dressed. Always alone. I talked to a dozen neighbors, and two guards, none had ever seen him with anyone. But, he had a server droid. One of the guards told me the Feebs carried out what was left of it. He claimed it looked like a self-destruct."

"Covered his ass there."

"A woman on the fifteenth floor, one of those society-type matrons, said she'd spoken to him occasionally in the lobby, and a number of times at the ballet and opera. You hit that one. She said he had season tickets to both, box seat, stage right. He always went solo."

"We'll put some men on that, but he's not going to risk it now, no matter how much he gets into that stuff. He'll know we've blown his cover in this building, talked to neighbors. He'll bypass his usual haunts, at least for the time being."

"I've gone to the opera with Charles a few times. I've been trying to pull it in, get a visual on that box. But it's not clicking. I could ask him. He goes a lot. Could have noticed."

Eve drummed her fingers on the wheel, weighed, considered and ruthlessly cut off a Rapid Cab. "Run it by him, but don't fill him in. We've got too many fingers in this pie already without adding another civilian."

"Speaking of pie," Peabody said, and looked longingly toward a corner glide-cart.

"It's not even noon. You can't be hungry."

"Can, too. I bet you didn't have breakfast. Missing the most essential meal of the day can make you cranky, and logy, and seriously affect your mental and emotional well-being. Studies—"

"Oh Christ!" Eve whipped to the curb, cut off yet another cab, then gave Peabody a steely glare. "You've got sixty seconds."

"Watch me rock."

She was out of the car like a laser flash, whipping out her badge to clear her path toward the scoop of soy fries her stomach was yearning for.

She popped back in the car, seconds to spare, and offered Eve a beaming smile and a second scoop of fries. The smile wobbled only slightly when Eve took the scoop and tucked it between her thighs.

"I didn't think you were hungry."

"Then why'd you buy me a scoop?"

"Just to be nice," Peabody said with some dignity as her hopes for two scoops—after all she wouldn't have felt right about letting them go to waste—were dashed. "I guess you want this, too."

"Yeah, thanks." Eve snagged the tube of Pepsi, plucked out some fries, and shot back into traffic. "Record on my collar." Eve gestured to it with her chin. "Upload onto hard drive and disc. Get me your knock-on-doors report within the hour, and contact Charles Monroe."

Peabody plucked off the recorder, slipped it onto her own jacket. "Yes, sir."

"You know more about girl stuff than I do. Scan the record, the segment in Yost's dressing room deal. Give me a rundown on the enhancements. If it's out of your scope, I'm going to pass it to Mavis. She knows everything."

"Anything above discount counter is out of my scope, enhancement-wise. I might recognize some of the brands though."

"Make another copy of that segment. I'll tag Mavis."

She finished the fries on the way up to her office, pitched the empty container, then closed herself in her office. She had one step to take before she hunkered down to paperwork, and she wanted to take it in private.

As an extra precaution, she used her personal palm-link.

Roarke answered on the second beep. "Hello, Lieutenant. How did it go?"

"It went. I got to deck Jacoby with no official flak coming down on me, so that's something."

"I hope you got it on record. I'd love to watch."

"Har. Actually I did, which is why I had to deck him, and why I'm calling. I got . . ." She trailed off as she managed to look beyond his face and recognized the room.

"What are you doing in there?" she demanded. "I told you I didn't want any data accessed on your unregistered."

"Who said I was accessing data for you?"

"Listen—"

"I do have other business. I have no intention of passing you data accessed in other than official and legal means."

He'd simply filter it through Feeney first.

"By the way, you've had the return transmission from The New Savoy. Confirmation of Yost's stay there. I've sent the pertinents to you. Now, what else can I do for you?"

She studied him through narrowed and suspicious eyes. "Are you lying?"

"About Yost's stay in London?"

"Don't be a wiseass. About what you're doing in that room right now."

"If I were, I'd simply compound it by lying again. I suppose you'll just have to trust me, won't you?" He smiled at her. "Now as much as I'd love to while away the day chatting with you, darling, I do have work. What do you want?"

"All right." She hissed out a breath. "I got Yost's place on record. Fancy stuff. You'd like most of it. I can run it down, or try to piece by piece, but I figured if you took a look, you might be able to tag it faster. Paintings, sculptures, antiques. You'd know if they're the real thing by looking at a disc?"

"I would, most likely. I can't guarantee, as good copies need to be examined in person."

"I don't peg him as the good copy kind of guy. He's vain about that stuff, like somebody else I know."

"You're insulting your expert consultant, civilian."

"Gotta get the digs in where I can. Anyway, maybe you can narrow down the sources for the artwork and the jazzy furniture."

"Shoot it over. I'll take a look."

"Appreciate it."

"See that you do. Good-bye, Lieutenant."

He disconnected, leaned back, and examined the data on his wall screen.

Jacoby, Special Agent James.

The date and place of birth, the family data weren't of particular interest. But he noted Jacoby hadn't precisely excelled in his studies. He'd gotten through by staying nearly dead average, with minute peaks and valleys. His social skills were the deepest valleys, his analytical talents the highest peaks.

He'd barely skimmed by the minimal requirements for FBI training, but had excelled in the areas of weapons training, electronics, and tactics.

His sealed profile indicated a difficulty with authority and coworkers, a tendency to ignore or circumvent procedure, and a marginal ability for teamwork.

He'd been cited three times for insubordination and had faced an internal investigation for suspicion of tampering with evidence.

He was single, heterosexual, and appeared to prefer the company and services of licensed companions to a personal relationship with a woman.

He had no criminal record, even as a juvenile, no questionable vices. That made Roarke shake his head. He didn't doubt the FBI file. They were usually every bit as thorough and covert as he could be himself. A man with-

out vices was either a dangerous man or a terminally tedious one.

He bought his clothes off the rack, lived in a small, mod-
est apartment, and had no particular friends.

Small wonder, Roarke mused, and since he'd gone that
far, set his computer to work picking through Jacoby's case
files.

As it searched, he switched the screen to Karen Stowe's
data.

She was the stronger of the team, Roarke thought, and
the smarter. Graduated cum laude, American University,
where she'd double-majored in criminal justice and electronics. She'd been recruited straight out of college and
had completed her training precisely on schedule and in
the top five of her class.

The personality profile on her found her driven, focused,
intense, with a tendency to overwork and take personal and
physical risks. She followed the rules, but could find ways
to bend them to her needs. Her weakness was a difficulty
with objectivity. She often became too involved in a case,
projecting personalities rather than law.

She was, Roarke thought, so much like Eve in this area
he was surprised the two of them had yet to come to blows.

Ambition, skill, and tenacity were pushing her steadily
up the ranks. And interestingly, he noted, she had requested and campaigned for her current assignment.

On a personal level, she'd had four lovers, all at different
times, all male. The first had been in high school. The second her third year of college. She'd spaced them out meticulously, with only one relationship, during her first year in
training, lasting more than six months.

She had a close circle of friends, liked to paint in her
spare time, and had no reprimands or cautions on file.

He ran a search on her cases as well, then began to skim
through Jacoby's.

An hour later, he broke for coffee, noted his incoming data light blinking. *The lieutenant,* he thought, *had transmitted her visual.* He nearly postponed Stowe's case files, just for a change of pace, but even as he began to issue the command to save and close, something caught his eye.

Not one of her cases, but a request to review, a request made nearly six months before she'd been assigned to the Yost investigation.

Just why, he wondered, *had Special Agent Karen Stowe wanted to read and study the details of a murder in Paris?* Yost was the prime suspect, but nothing had been proven. No motive established for the rape and strangulation of one Winifred C. Cates, age twenty-six, employed as a speech writer and special assistant to the American ambassador in Paris. It was the method, not the motive, nor any ties to the victim that had popped Yost's name onto the top of the suspect list.

"Maybe you weren't looking so hard at him then," Roarke murmured. "But at the victim. Computer, search for personal data on victim, Cates, Winifred C."

WORKING . . .

He sipped his coffee, listened to the machine hum.

CATES, WINIFRED CAROLE, FEMALE, MIXED RACE, DOB FEBRUARY 5, 2029, SAVANNAH, GEORGIA. PARENTS MARLO BARRONS AND JOHN CATES, DIVORCED. NO SIB-LINGS. VISUAL ON-SCREEN. IS PHYSICAL DESCRIPTION DESIRED?

"No, move on."

AFFIRMATIVE. EDUCATIONAL BACKGROUND AS FOL-LOWS. ELEMENTARY EDUCATION: HOME STUDY PRO-GRAM. FULL SCHOLARSHIP TO MOSS-RILEY SECONDARY

EDUCATION FACILITY, HONORS PROGRAM IN LANGUAGE
AND IN POLITICAL SCIENCE. FULL SCHOLARSHIP TO
AMERICAN UNIVERSITY —

"Hold. Cross-reference files, Cates and Stowe, educational data. Any and all matches on screen."

WORKING . . . SHIFTING TASK FUNCTION . . . SUBJECTS
CATES AND STOWE ATTENDED AMERICAN UNIVERSITY
SAME DATES. CATES GRADUATED MAGNA CUM LAUDE,
STOWE SIGMA CUM LAUDE, SAME GRADUATING CLASS.
RANKED FIRST AND SECOND RESPECTIVELY.

"Hold. Knew her, didn't you?" Roarke murmured. "This isn't just a case. It's personal."

chapter fourteen

Peabody hustled off the glide, rounded the corner toward her squad room, and ran straight into McNab.

"There you are." He beamed at her like a boy who'd just found his lost puppy after a long, whistling search.

"No, there you are. I was looking for you. I just got word the FBI's going to hold a media conference. They're pushing to have Dallas attend and fall into the spin."

"Oh, yeah, that'll happen. Have you heard the one about the Easter Bunny, too?" There was a door beside him. Never one to miss an opportunity, McNab bumped the handle.

"So far I haven't heard if Whitney's going to toss her in, but if he does, I think we should all be there. The one our guys had on for this afternoon's on hold."

As he nudged her into the narrow empty maintenance room he nodded. "Just tag me and let me know when and where if it comes down. Meanwhile . . ." He already had her up against the wall so he could chew on her neck.

"Jeez, McNab." But she wasn't putting up much of a struggle. "Get a grip."

"Gonna." With one hand he fumbled down, engaged the lock. With the other, he began disengaging the buttons on her uniform jacket. "Mmm, She-Body, you are so *female*. What's a guy supposed to do?"

His teeth were nibbling their way down . . . over . . . Oh yeah. "I think you're doing it."

She flipped open the hook of his trousers. After all, if she couldn't spare a few minutes for a fellow officer, what kind of cop was she?

He was hard as rock.

"How do you guys walk around with this thing kicking between your thighs?"

"Practice." The smell of her, the *feel* of her was driving him crazy. When her firm, capable hand wrapped around him, he decided he was the happiest madman on or off planet. "Jesus, Peabody." His mouth found hers, all but gulped her down. "I need—"

Her pocket-link rang, shrill and insistent.

"Don't answer it." He tugged at her trousers, in a rage to get inside her. "Don't."

"Have to." She couldn't breathe, and her knees were trembling, but duty was duty. "Just . . . wait." She wiggled away, sucked in air then blew it out explosively. Her cheeks were flushed, her breasts achy and exposed. She had the wit to block video as she opened transmission.

"Peabody."

"Delia. You sound so official and out of breath. Very sexy."

"Charles." She willed away the fog over her brain and didn't notice McNab go rigid and slit-eyed beside her. "Thanks for getting back to me."

"One of my favorite things to do is getting back to you."

That made her smile, a little foolishly. He always said the sweetest things. "I know you're busy, but I thought you might be able to help me out on a detail in an investigation."

"Never too busy for you. What can I do?"

Furious, McNab turned to stare at a line of industrial-sized cleaners and disinfectants. Couldn't she *hear* the snake oil in his voice? Didn't she *know* if he'd been busy it was because he'd been collecting a fat fee after doing the naked tango with some rich and bored society chick?

"I'm trying to confirm an identification," Peabody went on. "A man, mixed race, middle fifties. Opera buff. He takes the front box seat, stage right, at the Met."

"Front box, stage right . . . Sure, I know who you mean. Never misses an opening performance, comes alone."

"That's him. Can you describe him?"

"Other than what you've already said, he's big. More like an Arena Ball tackle than an opera fan. Clean-shaven, head and face. Designer black-tie. Always perfectly groomed. Doesn't mingle during intermission. I had a client recognize him once."

"Recognize him?"

"Yeah. She pointed him out, mentioned that he was an entrepreneur, which could mean anything."

"Did she tell you his name?"

"Probably. Give me a second. Roles. Martin K. Roles. I'm nearly positive."

"Can I have her name?"

"Delia." His voice was pained now. "You know how awkward that is for me."

"Okay, how about this. Could you contact her, casually ask how she knows this man? That might be enough."

"That I can do. Why don't I relay whatever information I get to you over drinks later? I have a ten o'clock appointment, but that leaves plenty of time. I could meet you at The Palace Hotel, The Royal Bar, say about eight?"

The Royal Bar, she thought. It was so lush and gorgeous, and they served olives the size of dove's eggs in pretty silver dishes when you sat down for a drink.

Plus, you never knew which celebrity might drop in for a glass of champagne.

She could wear her blue dress with the long skirt that slimmed down her hips, or . . .

"I'd really like that. I just don't know if I'll be working or not."

"A cop's life. I miss seeing you."

"Really?" Pleasure shimmered through her, and had her smiling again. "Me, too."

"Why don't we do this? I'll leave the early evening open. If you can spare time for a drink any time between six and nine, we'll get together. Otherwise, I'll take a rain check and just pass on what I find out."

"Great. I'll let you know as soon as I can. Thanks, Charles."

"Always my pleasure. Later, Beautiful."

She disengaged, glowing a bit. Beautiful wasn't a term she heard applied to herself often. "That might be a break," she began briskly, and after pocketing her 'link began to hook her bra and button her shirt. "If he can—"

"What the hell do you take me for?"

She blinked. That raw and dangerous edge in McNab's voice was something else rarely heard. And when she focused on his face she saw his eyes were glittering, sharp as shards of green glass. "Huh?"

"What do you take yourself for?" he tossed out. "You let me put my hands on you one minute, and I'd have been inside you in another. Then you're flirting on the 'link and making a goddamn date with a goddamn LC."

She nearly said "Huh?" again, because her mind wasn't quite computing the words. But the tone, the basic and nasty meaning of them, rang through loud and clear. "I wasn't flirting, you idiot." *Or hardly,* she thought, despising the quick, vicious tug of guilt. "I was doing a follow-up, as ordered by my lieutenant. And it's none of your business."

"It isn't?" He had her by the shoulders, had her shoved back against the wall again. But there was nothing sexual now, nothing playful.

Nerves jittered up to dance with guilt. "What's the matter with you? Let go or I'll knock you down." Normally, she would have been sure she could do just that. But this wasn't normally and her belly was quivering.

"The matter with me? You want to know what's the matter with me?" Fury exploded out of him. "I'm sick and tired of having you roll out of my bed and prance on over to roll in Monroe's, that's what's the matter with me."

"What?" She goggled. "What?"

"You think I'm going to keep playing backup fuck to some hired dick, you're wrong, Peabody. You are way wrong."

Her color flashed, then faded. It was nothing like that. *Nothing* like that, as her relationship with Charles was purely platonic. But she'd be damned if she'd say so now.

"That's a stupid and a horrible thing to say. Get off me, you son of a bitch."

She shoved, and was as angry as she was uneasy when she didn't budge him. "Yeah? Well, that's what I'm saying. How would you feel if I'd taken a call from some skirt while my hands were still on you? How the hell would you take that?"

She didn't know. It had never occurred to her. So she swung back hard to anger. It seemed to be her only defense. "Look, McNab, you can talk to anybody, *skirts* included, any time you damn well want. And you better crawl back out of my throat over who I talk to and what I do. We work together, we have sex together, but we're not exclusive, and you've got no right taking pops at me for talking to a source. And if I want to dance naked on Charles's tabletop while I do it, it's none of your damn business."

Not that she ever had. She'd never *been* naked with Charles. But that was beside the point.

"That's the way you want it?" Hurt was fighting to slice through temper. He couldn't allow it. So he nodded, stepped back. "That flows with me just fine."

"Well, good."

"Yeah, great." He yanked at the door, cursed because he'd forgotten to unlock it and had spoiled his exit. He sent her one last fulminating look and got out, closing the door smartly behind him.

She snarled, hastily buttoned her uniform jacket, smoothed it. Sniffled. Heard herself. *Oh no,* she thought, straightening her shoulders. She was not going to cry in the maintenance closet. And she was certainly not going to waste perfectly good tears over a moron like Ian McNab.

Eve was adding the results of her probability scans to her updated report when Nadine Furst walked into her office.

The first thing Eve did was swear. The second was to save and dump on-screen data before the slick reporter could get a look at it over her shoulder.

"What?" was Eve's greeting.

"Nice to see you, too. Looking good. Why, yes, I'd love some coffee." At home, Nadine strolled to the AutoChef, programmed for two cups.

She was a lovely woman, with perfectly styled dark blonde hair that flattered her somewhat foxy face. Her suit was poppy red and tailored to flatter a curvy figure and really good legs.

All of that was part of the requirement for being one of the top on-air reporters in the city. Added to it, Nadine had a few more advantages. A sharp and clever brain, and a sensitive nose that could sniff out a story even when it was buried under two tons of bullshit.

"Busy here, Nadine. See you later."

"Yes, I imagine so." Unmoved, unoffended, Nadine set a fresh cup of coffee on Eve's desk and settled down in the creaky and uncomfortable chair beside it. "Media conference in about an hour with the FBI on that botched bust uptown."

"So why aren't you prepping for it?"

"Oh." With a feline smile, Nadine sipped her coffee. "I am. I get word about the conference, then get a whiff that you're to be involved. Even as I begin to ponder on that, I get word you're out. And, the previously scheduled media conference with the NYPSD is now washed. So . . . comments, Lieutenant Dallas?"

"None." She'd spent twenty minutes strategizing with Whitney over just that. "It was a federal operation, not mine or my department's."

"But you were there, after the fact. I got a whiff of that, too. Why were you there?"

"I was in the neighborhood."

"Come on, Dallas." Nadine leaned forward. "It's just you and me. No camera, no recorder. Give me an edge."

"You're edgy enough all by yourself. I'm swamped here, Nadine."

"Yeah, swamped in homicides. Two. Same method, which points to one killer. If you're so swamped with them and the social obligation of the upcoming Magda Lane auction, why are you poking into a failed federal bust?"

"I don't poke."

"That's right, Dallas, you don't." Pleased, Nadine sat back again. "What's the connection between your homicides and the FBI operation?"

Now Eve smiled, kicked back, sipped coffee. "Why don't you ask Special Agent Jacoby that question? Why don't you ask him, and/or Special Agent Stowe why they took an entire team, at taxpayers' expense, into a privately owned building without first assuring that their target was in residence? And you might ask how they feel about the fact that tromping their FBI asses into that building without first pinpointing their target has now alerted that target, who remains at large."

"Well, well. I might not be getting answers, but I'm getting some very nice questions. Did they screw with you?"

"Off the record? They undermined my investigation, jumped over my bust, then mucked it up."

"And yet they live. You disappoint me."

Eve merely showed her teeth. "I think they'll be bleeding after the media conference. I doubt you'll disappoint me."

"Ah, I'm being used. I feel so satisfied." Nadine finished off her coffee, toyed with the empty cup. "Since I'm being so nice and cooperative, how about a favor?"

"I've given you all you're going to get."

"On another topic. On the auction. My media pass will get me in, but if I use it, I'm not allowed to bid. I really want to bid. Dallas, I'm a huge fan. How about finding me an extra ticket?"

"That's it?" Eve shrugged. "Sure, I should be able to lay my hands on one."

Tilting her head, putting a pretty plea in her eye, Nadine slowly held up two fingers.

"Two?"

"It would be more fun if I could bring a date. Be a pal."

"Being a pal can be a real pain in the butt. I'll see what I can do."

"Thanks." She hopped up. "I have to get over to the federal field office, stake out my turf. Tune in, and watch them bleed."

"I just might."

"Hey, Peabody." Distracted, Nadine flipped her a wave as she dashed out.

"Peabody, I may not be able to catch the screen for the media conference. See that it's recorded."

"Yes, sir. Then you won't be required to attend?"

"No. The Feebs are on their own." She brought her report back on-screen. "I want a briefing with the team. Let's make it for sixteen hundred if that suits Feeney and McNab. Book a conference room."

Inwardly, Peabody winced, but she simply nodded. "Yes, sir. I spoke with Charles Monroe."

Though her mind was elsewhere, the crackle of ice in Peabody's voice had Eve glancing over. "Problem?"

"No, sir. He tagged Yost, and confirms he's a regular patron at the opera. Prefers opening night of a new performance. A client pointed Yost out to Charles and stated he was an entrepreneur named Roles, Martin K."

"That's a fresh alias. Good. I'll run it now. What's the client's name?"

"Charles was hesitant to give me that information. He's agreed to contact the client and ask how she knows Roles. If . . ." She cleared her throat because something was burning inside it. "If that information isn't complete or satisfactory, I'll press."

"That works for now." Eve's stomach began to clench and jitter. There were tears swimming in her aide's eyes. Peabody's lips were quivering. "What are you doing?" she demanded.

"Nothing. Sir."

"How come you're going to cry? You *know* how I feel about crying on the job."

"I'm not crying." And it appalled her that she was on the edge of it. "I just don't feel very well, that's all. I wonder, sir, if I could be excused from the briefing at sixteen hundred."

"Too many soy fries," Eve said, relieved. "If you're sick, go by the infirmary and get them to fix you up. Get horizontal for thirty." She glanced at her wrist unit to check the time, and heard a soft and muffled sob.

Her head snapped up. Relief vanished and comprehension hammered through. "Damn it. Damn it. Damn it. You went a round with McNab, didn't you?"

"I'd appreciate if you wouldn't mention that name in my presence," Peabody said with watery dignity.

"I knew this was going to happen. Knew it. Knew it." She sprang to her feet and kicked her desk.

"He said I was—"

"No!" Eve threw up her arms as if warding off an incoming meteorite. "No, uh-uh, forget it. You are not dumping it on me. I don't want to hear about it, don't want to know about it, don't want to think about it. This is a cop shop! A cop shop and you are a cop." She said it fast, and she said it clear, terrified as those tears shimmered in Peabody's dark eyes.

"Yes, sir."

"Oh, man." Eve pressed the heels of her hands to the sides of her head so her brain would stay in place. "Okay, here's what I want you to do. Go to the infirmary and take something. Lie down. Then you pull yourself together and get your butt to that briefing. I'll set it up and you behave like a cop. You save personal business for after shift."

"Yes, sir." With another sniffle, Peabody turned.

"Officer? Do you want him to see you all blubbery?"

That stopped her. Peabody's shoulders stiffened, straightened. "No." She swiped a hand under her nose. "No," she said again and marched out.

"Wasn't that just perfect?" Eve muttered, then sat down to do her aide's job.

In another section of Cop Central, the corridors were wide and the floors scrupulously clean. Cubicles were jammed with the best equipment the budget could bear and manned by cops in snazzy suits or in casual chic.

The hums and buzzes and beeps were constant, like music. Wall screens flashed with images and data in never-ending reels.

There were three holo-rooms designed for simulations and reenactments. They were used for these purposes and, nearly as often, for personal fantasies, romantic interludes, and naps.

The Electronic Detectives Division was never quiet, always crowded and painted a brain-stimulating red.

When Roarke stepped in, he scanned the room. The

equipment, he noted with an expert's eye, was reasonably good, and would be outmoded within six months. He happened to know this as one of his research and development companies had just finished a new prototype laser computer that would outpace and outperform everything currently on the market.

He made a note to himself to have one of his marketing directors contact the NYPSD's acquisitions liaison. He imagined he could make his wife's home away from home a very good deal.

He spotted McNab in one of those clear, three-sided cubes and made his way through the forest of them. A number of the E-detectives paced the room wearing headsets while calling out data and punching codes into palm PCs, but McNab sprawled at his desk with a brooding look in his eye.

"Ian."

McNab jumped, rapped his knee on the underside of his desk. After the obligatory oath, he looked at Roarke. "Hey. What're you doing here?"

"I'd hoped to see Feeney for a moment."

"Sure, he's back in his office. Through there," he said, pointing at an opening in the wall. "And to the right. His door's usually open."

"Fine. Something wrong?"

McNab jerked his bony shoulders. "Women."

"Ah. What else can be said?"

"They're not worth it. That can be said."

"Trouble with Peabody?"

"Not anymore. It's time I got back to spreading out my talents. I've got a date with a redhead tonight with the best manmade breasts money can buy and an affection for black leather."

"I see." And because he did, very well, Roarke gave McNab's shoulder a pat. "I'm sorry."

"Hey." McNab brushed it off and pretended his belly

wasn't full of lead weights. "I'll get by. The redhead's got a sister. We're going to see if we can make it a trio." His 'link beeped. "Got work."

"Then I'll let you get to it."

Roarke passed the cubicles and the pacers and slipped into the short corridor that led to Feeney's office. The door was indeed open, and Feeney sat at his desk, his hair standing on end, his eyes blurry as they scanned data flashing like lightning on three wall screens.

He held up a hand as he caught the movement at the door, eyes still tracking. Then he blinked. "Save, compile, and cross-reference current data with file AB-286. Hold results until command."

Now he sat back, focused on Roarke. "Didn't expect to see you."

"Sorry to interrupt."

"Need a minute to process anyway."

Roarke smiled. "You or your equipment?"

"Both. I'm doing search and scans looking for probables and likelies on Yost's employers on various hits. Maybe we find one to pigeonhole and we can get enough data to crawl up his back again."

He reached into his bowl of nuts. "Hard on the eyes, hours of this. Going to need them fixed again."

Roarke tipped his head so he could study Feeney's equipment. "That's a nice unit."

"Took me six weeks to hound them to budget it in for me. Captain of EDD, and I gotta beg for the top of the line. It's pitiful."

"Your top of the line's going to be a poor second in a few months."

Feeney sniffed. "I know about your 60 T and M, and the upgrade on the 75,000TMS. Not that I've seen them anywhere but your and Dallas's in-home offices. Guess it's taken you so long to get them on the market, you've run into a few snags."

"I wouldn't call them snags. What would you think of a Track and Monitoring Unit, running on a 100,000 system, boosting up to five hundred simultaneous functions."

"There is no 100,000 system. There isn't a chip or combo of chips that can sustain that many functions, no laser power that can reach that speed."

Roarke merely smiled. "There is now."

Feeney went pale, laid a hand over his heart. "Don't toy with me, lad. Jokes like that could bring a man to tears."

"How would you like to test one of the prototypes for me? Put it through its paces, give me your opinion?"

"My firstborn son is as old as you are yourself, so I don't think you'd have much use for him. What do you want?"

"Your weight, when it comes to negotiating a contract for Roarke Industries to provide electronic equipment, including this new model, to the NYPSD and after them, as many other police and security departments nationwide, to start, as can be managed."

"I'll use every ounce of weight that's in me if she does what you say. When can I have her?"

"Within the week. I'll let you know." He started toward the door.

"That's what you came in for?"

"That, and to see my wife before I go. I've some appointments." He turned back, met Feeney's eyes. "Good hunting."

With a shake of his head and a sigh of lust at the thought of a 100,000 T and M System, Feeney turned back to his own unit.

And saw the disc beside it. *The one,* he mused as he lifted it, *that hadn't been there before Roarke had come in.*

His eyes might have been tired, Feeney admitted, but they were still sharp enough. Damned if he'd seen the boy plant the disc.

Slick as they came.

He turned the disc over, then with a chuckle loaded it.

They'd just see what one slick Irishman had slipped to another on the sly.

In a lovely detached town house of three stories, Sylvester Yost enjoyed the soaring final aria from *Aida* while he finished a light lunch of veggie pasta in tarragon vinaigrette, topped off with a glass of excellent Fume Blanc.

He rarely indulged in wine at lunch, but felt he had earned it. He had passed the FBI's bumbling tactical team on their way to his building, had smiled at them through the privacy-tinted glass of the long black limo minutes, literally minutes before they'd arrived at his building.

He didn't care for such close calls, but they did add some stimulation to routine.

Still, he was not pleased. The wine had helped mellow him.

He ordered the music lower by several notches, then made his call. Both he and the receiver kept video blocked, and voices electronically altered, as agreed.

Even fully secured and encoded palm units could be hacked, if one knew where to start.

"I've settled in," Yost said.

"Good. I hope you have everything you need."

"I'm comfortable enough, for the moment. I lost a great deal this morning. The art alone was worth several million, and I'll have to replace a considerable amount of wardrobe and enhancements."

"I'm aware of that. I believe we can retrieve most, if not all of your possessions, given time. If not, I'll agree to pay half your losses. I cannot and will not assume full responsibility."

Yost might have argued, but he considered himself a fair man in business. The detection, and the resulting losses, were partially his fault. Though he had yet to determine where and when he'd made mistakes.

"Agreed. Since your transmission this morning was

timely, and your pied-à-terre quite adequate for my temporary needs. Do I proceed on schedule?"

"You do. Hit the next target tomorrow."

"That's your decision." Yost sipped his after-lunch coffee. "At this point, however, I feel obliged to tell you I intend to dispose of Lieutenant Dallas in my own time and fashion. She's inconvenienced me, and beyond that, she's come too close."

"I'm not paying you for Dallas."

"Oh no, this is a bonus."

"I told you from the beginning why she wasn't chosen for this project. Hit her, and Roarke will never stop hunting. Just keep her busy otherwise until the job is completed."

"As I said, Dallas is for me. In my time and in my way. You aren't contracting for her, therefore you aren't involved and have no say in the matter. I'll complete your contract."

On the table, over the spotless white linen, Yost's fist bunched and began to pound, softly, rhythmically. "She owes me, and she will pay. Consider this: With her death, Roarke will only be more distracted and make your job that much easier."

"She is *not* your target."

"I know my target." The pounding increased until he caught himself, flexed his big hand. No, he realized with some annoyance, he wasn't as mellow as he'd believed. There was a terrible anger inside him. And something he hadn't felt in so long he'd forgotten the taste of it.

Fear.

"He'll be terminated tomorrow, on schedule. And there won't be any cause for concern about Roarke hunting either of us after I deal with the cop. I intend to eliminate him. For that, you will pay."

"You succeed with deleting Roarke within the time agreed upon in our addendum, you'll collect your fee. When have I ever failed to pay off a contract?"

"Then, were I you, I'd begin making arrangements to transfer funds."

He cut transmission abruptly, pushed from the table, paced. When he felt the worst of the rage ebbing, he made himself go upstairs, into the attractive office where he'd set up his portables.

Sitting, ordering his mind to clear, he brought up the public data on Eve. And for some time he sat, studying her image and her information.

chapter fifteen

Roarke didn't quite make it to Eve's office. He found her down the corridor, in front of one of the vending machines. She and the machine appeared to be in the middle of a vicious argument.

"I put the proper credits in, you blood-sucking, money-grubbing son of a bitch." Eve punctuated this by slamming her fist where the machine's heart would be, if it had one.

ANY ATTEMPT TO VANDALIZE, DEFACE, OR DAMAGE THIS
UNIT IS A CRIMINAL OFFENSE.

The machine spoke in a prissy, singsong voice Roarke was certain was sending his wife's blood pressure through the roof.

THIS UNIT IS EQUIPPED WITH SCANEYE, AND HAS
RECORDED YOUR BADGE NUMBER. DALLAS, LIEU-
TENANT EVE. PLEASE INSERT PROPER CREDIT, IN COIN
OR CREDIT CODE, FOR YOUR SELECTION. AND REFRAIN

FROM ATTEMPTING TO VANDALIZE, DEFACE, OR DAMAGE
THIS UNIT.

"Okay, I'll stop attempting to vandalize, deface, or damage you, you electronic street thief. I'll just do it."

She swung back her right foot, which Roarke had cause to know could deliver a paralyzing kick from a standing position. But before she could follow through he stepped up and nudged her off balance.

"Please, allow me, Lieutenant."

"Don't put any more credits in that thieving bastard," she began, then hissed when Roarke did just that.

"Candy bar, I assume. Did you have any lunch?"

"Yeah, yeah, yeah. You know it's just going to keep stealing if people like you pander to it."

"Eve, darling, it's a machine. It does not think."

"Ever hear of artificial intelligence, ace?"

"Not in a vending machine that dispenses chocolate bars."

He made the selection for her.

YOU HAVE SELECTED THE EIGHT-OUNCE ROYAL CHOCO-
LATE DREAM BAR. THIS FOOD PRODUCE CONTAINS
SIXTY-EIGHT CALORIES AND TWO POINT ONE GRAMS OF
FAT. ITS INGREDIENTS INCLUDE SOY AND SOY BYPROD-
UCTS, NONDAIRY MILK SUBSTITUTE, THE CHEMICAL
SWEETNER TRADEMARKED AS SWEET-T, AND THE
TRADEMARKED CHOCOLATE SUBSTITUTE CHOC-O-LIKE.

"Sounds just yummy," Roarke said and retrieved the bar.

THIS PRODUCT HAS NO KNOWN NUTRITIONAL VALUE
AND MAY CAUSE IRRITABILITY OR WAKEFULNESS IN
SOME INDIVIDUALS. PLEASE ENJOY YOUR SELECTION
AND YOUR DAY.

"Up yours" was Eve's suggestion as she ripped off the wrapper. "They stole my candy again. I taped it on the back of my AutoChef. Two bars of the real stuff, not this chemi-mix crapola. They tagged it. I'm going to catch them sooner or later and peel the skin off their face. Slowly."

Still, the first bite perked her up. "What are you doing here?"

"Adoring you. Absolutely." Unable to help himself, he took her face in his hands and kissed her hard. "My God, what did I ever do before you were there?"

"Jeez, cut it out." Even as the thrill whipped through her, she scanned the corridor for eavesdroppers and Peeping Toms. She'd be razzed for a week if anyone had spotted them. "My office."

"Happy to."

He walked with her, moved through the door just behind her, then yanked her back to indulge in a deeper, longer kiss.

"I'm on duty." She murmured it against his mouth as her brain went to fizzle.

"I know. Just a minute." One day, he thought, he might actually get used to the way the love for her, the need for her, could leap up and grab him by the throat. But in the meantime, he'd just enjoy the ride.

"Okay." He drew back, ran his hands from her shoulders to her wrists. "That should hold me."

"You blow the top of my head off." She shook it clear. "Pow. A lot better than fake chocolate."

"Darling Eve, I'm touched."

"Yeah, and this was fun, but I've got a briefing coming up. Why are you here?"

"I wanted to buy you a candy bar. By the way, did you know Peabody and McNab have had a spat?"

"I hate that word. They've had something, just like I told

you they would, and it's your fault for giving McNab advice. I sent Peabody off to take a soother or something and lie down."

"Did you talk to her about it?"

"No. No, I didn't, and I'm not going to."

"Eve."

The way he said it, with just a hint of censure, put her back up. "We're working here. You know murder and mayhem, law and order, little stuff like that. What am I supposed to do when she comes moping in here all teary-eyed?"

"Listen," he said simply, and took the wind out of her sails.

"Oh, man."

"In any case," he continued, amused. "I came by to let you know I have a dinner meeting with Magda and her people. She wanted you to come, but I've explained you're booked. I shouldn't be late."

She choked back a little sigh. "If you let me know where the meeting is, and when, I'll try to swing by if I get loose."

"I don't expect you to squeeze it in."

"I know. I guess that's why I'll try to swing by."

"Top of New York, eight-thirty. Thank you."

"If I'm not there by nine-fifteen, I'm not going to make it."

"That's fine. Is there any progress I should know about in my capacity as consultant?"

"Not much, but you can sit in on the briefing."

"I can't. I'm due in midtown shortly. You can give me a private briefing tonight." He lifted her hand, kissed the knuckles she'd bruised punching the vending machine. "Try to get through the rest of the day without fighting with another inanimate object."

"Ha-ha," she said when he walked out.

Then, because she could, she moved to the door and

watched him go. *The man has a great ass,* she thought as she nibbled on her candy bar. *A truly great ass.*

She pulled herself back, gathered the files and discs she needed for the briefing, and headed off to the reserved conference room to set up.

She'd barely begun when Peabody came in. "I'll do that, Lieutenant."

Her eyes were dry, Eve noted with relief, her voice steady, and her spine straight.

Eve opened her mouth, nearly asked Peabody if she felt better before she realized the danger of that. Like quicksand, that sort of comment or inquiry would suck you right down into the muck of dialogue about a subject you prefer to pretend didn't exist in the first place.

So she stood back and kept her mouth shut, firmly, while Peabody loaded discs and stacked hard copies of the updates on chairs.

"I also have the record of the media conference, Lieutenant. Do you want me to load it?"

"No, that goes home with me, for my personal viewing pleasure. Did you catch it?"

"Yeah, they danced and they dodged, then Nadine pinned them with a question on operational procedure. Like, duh, you moved on the building without verifying the target was in place? So, Jacoby juggled around with that, trying to pull 'We can't comment on operational procedure' and blah, blah, then she pinned them again with the fact that the target, a known professional assassin, slipped through their fingers and is now at large even after a complex and expensive operation was put into effect, and why did he think that happened?"

"Good old Nadine."

"Yeah, she asked it really polite, too, with a sympathetic expression and everything. Before he could recover, other reporters had picked up the hammer. They smashed right through and all the spinning in the known universe couldn't get them back on rhythm. They called the conference ten minutes ahead of schedule."

"Media, one. Feebs, zero."

"Subzero. I guess it's not fair to blame the whole Bureau over the idiocy of two agents."

"Maybe not, but it's working for me right now."

She glanced over as Feeney burst in. He was showing his teeth in what might have been a grin and waving a disc. "Got some data here." He all but sang it. "Primo data. Let's see the Feebs try to muscle us off our own turf again. We got the arm now. Special Agent Stowe knew one of the victims. Personally."

"How?"

"Went to college together, took some of the same classes, belonged to the same clubs. *And* roomed together for three months before the victim went overseas."

"They were pals? How'd I miss that in the profiles?"

"Because Stowe didn't mention the connection in her profiles. She buried it."

Eve felt the comfortable warmth of a fresh weapon in her hand, then stopped, backtracked, eyed the disc Feeney was busy loading. "Where did you get the data?"

He knew she'd ask, which was one reason he'd copied the disc onto one out of his own stash. "Anonymous source."

Her eyes narrowed. Roarke. "You've suddenly got a weasel who can access FBI files and personal data on its agents?"

"Looks like," he said cheerfully. "It's a mystery to me. The disc just showed up on my desk. Nothing to stop us from using data accessed from an anonymous source. For all I know, it came from a mole in the FBI."

She could have argued, she could have pressed. But the fact was, even if he knew the data had come from Roarke, Feeney would never admit it. "Let's have a look. You're late," she said when McNab strolled in.

"Sorry, Lieutenant, unavoidably detained." He sauntered over, took a chair, and made it clear to everyone in the room that he wasn't so much as looking at Peabody.

She made it equally clear she wasn't so much as looking at him.

The result was the temperature in the room plummeted, the air went frosty, and Eve and Feeney exchanged pained glances.

"You have the hard copy of my updated report. We have a fresh alias to hang on Sylvester Yost." She gestured toward the board where Yost's various images and names were posted, alongside his known victims, the location of each murder, and the physical evidence found on scene.

"I did a run," she continued. "Computer, data on Roles, Martin K., on-screen. You'll note he developed this alter ego carefully. He has full identification, credit line, residence, but the address is bogus. He filed taxes under this name, maintained a health card, carried a passport. We have some of these activities under other aliases, but none that we have verified to date maintain and employ all these activities. This, at my guess, is his retirement identity, the one he's keeping clean and normal so it sends up no flags via CompuGuard or any security agency."

"If he's a skilled hacker, he may have adjusted the data here and there to suit," McNab put in.

"Agreed. He is unaware that we've made this match. This is the identity we focus on, and we make sure we don't send up flags. All search and scan on this individual will be Level Three. He'll own property under this name. Find it."

"I'll start the search right after the briefing," said McNab. "I've been trying a scattershot scan on known victims, getting probabilities on who might have contracted the hits. I've got a couple of possibles, but nothing solid enough to move on yet."

"Taking a page out of the book ignored by our pals in

the FBI, we don't move until we know. A man as experienced and as efficient as this has solid backup ID. We spook him, he could ditch Roles and go with something we don't have a tag on. Let's keep him confident. Now, for Captain Feeney's big surprise."

She gestured and turned the briefing over. Feeney rubbed his hands together, got to his feet, and ran through the data Roarke had passed on to him.

McNab nearly bounced in his seat. "This is hot stuff."

Peabody spared a look for McNab now, a withering one. "Like you'd know hot."

He was so pleased she'd been the first to break, the insult barely registered. "I was born hot. How'd you get into the files?"

Feeney looked down his pug nose. "Accessing official data or the attempt to access is illegal. This data was given to me by an anonymous source. As it's gone deep into confidentials without sending flags, I have to assume the source is federal."

"And pigs fly," Eve said under her breath. "However the information came into our hands, we have it. It's a tool. Not a hammer," she said, scanning faces and watching disappointment form. "A pry bar. Feeney, I'd like to arrange a private meet with Stowe—use this. Her record's spotless, and if this data proving she lied and/or falsified her official documents got back to the Bureau drones, she'd have a big ugly mark on it, along with a reprimand. She'd be kicked off this investigation and likely assigned, at least temporarily, to some field office in Bumfuck. She doesn't want that. I say she doesn't want it bad enough to trade."

"As long as you squeeze till it stings, that'll do for me. You'll note, our dear friend Special Agent Jacoby, while not exactly a birdbrain, does not go to the head of the class. His profile shows average intelligence, offset by arrogance, ambition, and a resentment for authority. You add that all up, spit it out, and you got a dangerous individual. If anybody's going to fuck this up, it's going to be him. I wouldn't mind asking Mira to take a look at him, give us her take."

"The data came to you," Eve told him. "Your call. Now probability results." She ordered them on-screen. "You can see we've got a ninety-eight point eight percent that he'll attempt to complete the job. He has a rep; he won't want it marred. He'll go for the next target, and he'll try to stay on schedule. The first two came close together. I believe the third attempt will be within the next twenty-four. Probability, again, goes to ninety-three point six that subject is in the city or within easy transpo distance. But that's qualified by the assumption his target is also in the city or its environs. There's no way we can be sure of that single fact, and due to it, no way we can begin to protect whoever he intends to hit next."

She looked back at the screen. "So we work on it. And we wait on it."

She closed the briefing, detailing assignments, scheduling a morning briefing for eight. "We've got an hour till end of shift. If nothing pops by then, we'll call it for the night. Get some sleep, and we'll start pushing tomorrow."

"Works for me, but I might have to pass on the sleep. I've got a date." McNab had waited through the briefing just for the chance to say it. And he resisted, through enormous will, looking around for Peabody's reaction.

But Eve saw it. The jerk of shock, the initial hurt that burned cleanly toward fury, then iced into dismissal. *Iced,* she thought, *if you didn't know her well enough to see through the shield to the wound.*

Damn it.

"I'm sure we're all thrilled for you, McNab," Eve said coolly. "Eight hundred, this conference room. Dismissed." She kept her eyes on his as she spoke, had the nasty pleasure of seeing him shrink a little.

Then he was up and swaggering out the door. Feeney

rolled his eyes and followed. Followed just close enough to smack his detective smartly on the side of the head with the flat of his hand.

"Ow! What the hell?"

"You know what the hell."

"Oh, fine. Great. She can rumba off with some sex-for-hire sleazebag, and nobody says a thing. I have a date and I get blindsided."

Because he recognized misery when it was staring him in the face, Feeney scowled, drilled a finger into McNab's skinny chest. "I'm not talking about it."

"Neither am I." McNab hunched his shoulders and steamed off in a sulk.

"Peabody." Eve jumped in before her aide had the chance to speak. "Unload and file all discs, book this room for the scheduled time."

"Yes, sir." She had to swallow, hated the fact that the simple act was audible and painful.

"Check in with Monroe, see if he has any more information on Roles. Then stand by in your work area until I contact you."

"Yes, sir."

Eve waited until Peabody had finished gathering what she needed and had moved out of the room like a droid. "This is really going to suck," she decided. "Just listen, he says. A lot he knows about it."

Doing her best to push Peabody out of her mind, Eve sat down and made the call to the federal building.

"Stowe."

"Dallas. I need a meet. Just you and me. Tonight."

"I'm busy, and have no interest in meeting you tonight or anytime. Do you think I'm an idiot? Do you think I couldn't figure out who fed that reporter?"

"She eats just fine on her own." Eve waited a beat. "Winifred C. Cates" was all she said, and watched Stowe go pale.

"What about her?" she returned, with admirable composure. "She's one of Yost's likelies."

"Tonight, Stowe, unless you want me to go into detail over the 'link."

"I can't get away until seven."

"Nineteen-thirty hours, the Blue Squirrel. I'm sure a smart federal agent can find the address."

Stowe lowered her voice, moved closer to the screen. "Just you?"

"That's right. For the moment. Seven-thirty, Agent Stowe. Don't keep me waiting."

She broke transmission, checked her wrist unit and did her best to gauge her time. Feeling slightly less apprehensive than she might have if going in to face a team of chemi-heads armed with laser scalpels, she walked down to the squad room, detoured into her office for her jacket, then out to Peabody's cubicle.

"You tag Charles?"

"Yes, sir. His client met the man purporting to be Roles at a Sotheby's auction last winter. He outbid her on a painting. A Masterfield landscape, circa 2021. She believes it went for two million four."

"Sotheby's. It's after five. They'd be closed. Okay, you're with me." She started out, waited for Peabody to fall in step. "Did she have impressions?"

"Charles said she found Roles impeccably mannered, knowledgeable about art, and elegantly aloof. She admitted she'd tried to wrangle an invitation to see the painting once he had his displayed, but he didn't even nibble. Charles says she's a stunner, a real babe, mid-thirties, and falling-down rich. Since most men would have jumped at the chance, she figured he was into men. But when she tried out the chatter—you know, who they might know, what club he patronized, and all that—he evaded and slipped away from her."

"If she's such a babe, why does she need to hire an LC?"

"I guess because Charles is a babe, and there isn't any danger of strings. He'll do whatever she wants during the scheduled time." Peabody sighed as they stepped out into the garage. "People hire or hang with LCs for a lot of reasons. It isn't always about sex."

"Okay, okay. We'll see what we can dig up in Sotheby's tomorrow." *That*, she thought, *might be something to tap Roarke about*.

"Yes, sir. Where are we going now?"

"Up to you." Eve opened her car door, stood looking at Peabody over the roof. "Want to go get drunk?"

"Sir?"

"I had a big mess-up with Roarke not that long ago. That was my choice. It's a pretty good temporary cure."

Peabody's eyes filled, not just with tears but with gratitude. "I'd rather have ice cream."

"Yeah, most of the time, given the choice, so would I. Let's go get some ice cream."

Eve stared down at the hot fudge supreme in the dish in front of her with a combination of greed and nausea. She would no doubt eat it all. She would no doubt be ill after.

The things you had to do for a pal.

She dug in for the first spoonful. "Okay, spill it."

"Sir?"

"Let's hear what happened."

Peabody stared, more dazzled now by Eve's statement than by her own banana boat surprise. "You *want* me to tell you about it?"

"No, I don't want you to tell me about it. I'm telling you to tell me about it because that's how this friendship thing is supposed to work. I hear. So." She dug for more ice cream with one hand, waved a go-ahead with the other.

"That's so nice of you." Peabody got misty again, and

soothed herself with nondairy whipped topping. "We were in one of the maintenance closets, sort of fooling around, and—"

Mouth full, Eve held up a hand, swallowed. "Excuse me, you and Detective McNab were engaged in some sexual activity on departmental property, while on duty?"

Peabody pokered up. "I'm not going to tell you if you're going to start citing regulations. Anyway, we hadn't gotten to the actual sex part yet. We were fooling around."

"Oh, well then. That's different. Cops are always fooling around in maintenance closets. Jesus, Peabody." She shut her eyes, shoveled in more fudge, breathed out. "Okay, I'm over it. Move on."

"I don't know what it is. There's this thing, this primal sort of thing."

"Oh. Ick."

Maybe it was having kick-ass Dallas say "ick," maybe it was the pained way it was said, but the response made Peabody grin and didn't bruise her feelings a bit. "I would've thought so myself until we did it. The first time was in an elevator."

"Peabody, I'm trying here. But do we have to go back that far and discuss you and McNab doing it? It puts really weird pictures in my head."

"Well, it all sort of goes together. Anyway, it's not like I'm thinking about sex with him all the time, or even the fooling around part, but then something happens and we're just, you know, doing it again. So we were fooling around . . ." she continued quickly, afraid of losing her audience.

"In the maintenance closet."

"Right, and Charles called on my 'link. About the case. I was getting the information from him and stuff, and when I was finished, McNab got really ugly." She filled her mouth with banana and cream and gooey caramel sauce. "He yelled at me and was like, 'What do you take me for?'

And he said nasty things about Charles, who was just doing me a favor, and in an official capacity. Then he grabbed me."

"He got physical with you?"

"Yes. Well, no, not really. But he looked like he wanted to punch me. And you know what he said?" She wagged her spoon, heating up again. "You know what he said?"

"I wasn't there, remember?"

"He said he was sick and tired of playing backup fuck to a hired dick." She stabbed her spoon back into the rapidly dwindling banana boat surprise. "He said that to my face. And how I wasn't going to be popping out of his bed and into Charles's."

"I thought you weren't having sex with Charles."

"I'm not. That's beside the point."

Actually, Eve thought it was the point, then remembered her role. "McNab's an asshole."

"Damn straight."

"I don't suppose you told him you and Charles weren't doing it?"

"Hell no."

Eve nodded. "I don't guess I would have either. I'd have been too pissed off. What did you say?"

"I said how we weren't exclusive and I could see anybody I wanted, and so could he. Then, *then*, the bastard makes a date with some bimbo."

Since that seemed perfectly reasonable, Eve dug deep for something supportive to say. "Pig."

"I'm never speaking to him again."

"You work together."

"Okay, I'm never speaking to him again except in an official capacity. I hope he gets a suspicious rash on his gonads."

"That's a happy thought."

They pondered it and ate more ice cream.

"Peabody." Eve had a feeling she was going to hate this

part of the whole support thing the most. "I'm not good at this relationship business."

"How can you say that? You and Roarke are like, perfect."

"No, nobody's perfect. We're making it work. Actually, he's done most of the work on that, but I'm sort of catching up. He's the only man I've ever had a real relationship with."

Peabody's eyes popped. "No kidding?"

Yep, Eve thought. *Quicksand.* "Okay, we're not getting into all that, I'm just saying this isn't my field. But if I stand back and look at this like a case, we've got three players. You, McNab, Charles." She outlined a triangle with her spoon in what was left of her sundae. "You're the connection, so each of the other point's reaction to each other springs out of their relationship with you. McNab's jealous."

"Nuh-uh, he was just being a pig."

"His classification as pig is verified. However . . . Peabody, you're dating Charles, right?"

"Sort of."

"You're having sex with McNab."

"Was."

"McNab assumes you're having sex with Charles." She held up her finger before Peabody could speak. "It's a wrong assumption, and it's probably stupid of him not to just ask you what's up. And even if you were sleeping with Charles you're a free agent, but, this is his assumption. You." She tapped the tip of her spoon on one point of the triangle. "Sex. Both guys. So there you are playing where's the soy sausage in the closet, then you break it off with one guy to talk on the 'link with the other."

"It was police business."

"I bet you weren't in full uniform, but regardless, McNab's there, all hot and worked up and suddenly you're talking to his competition. Knowing Charles, he didn't stick to just giving you data. He flirted. So while you're talking to Charles, McNab's growing fangs. I'm not saying he's not a moron. Obviously, he's a moron. But, well, even moronic pigs have feelings. Probably."

Peabody sat back. "You think it's my fault."

"No, I think it's Roarke's fault." At Peabody's blank look, Eve shook her head. "Never mind that. It's not a fault thing. Look, you start a personal deal with a guy you work with, there's going to be trouble. I don't think he's got any right to tell you who you can see or sleep with or whatever. But I don't think it's real smart to push his face in it either. I figure you both screwed up."

Peabody considered. "But he screwed up more."

"Absolutely."

"Okay. Okay," she repeated after a moment's thought. "I guess you're right about the triangle stuff and the reaction business. But, he's the one who jumped right on some redhead, so if McNab thinks I'm going to get whacked out because he managed to talk some stupid female into going out with him, he's more stupid than he looks."

"That's the spirit."

"Thanks, Dallas. I feel a lot better."

Eve stared into her empty dish, put a hand on her uneasy and overfull stomach. "Glad one of us does."

chapter sixteen

The one good thing about setting the meet at the Blue Squirrel after an ice-cream binge was Eve wouldn't be tempted to actually eat or drink anything in the club.

Club was a lofty word for a joint like the Squirrel, where the best thing that could be said about the music was that it was there and it was loud. As far as the menu, the only positive recommendation Eve could make was that, as far as she knew, no one had died from eating the food.

There was no reliable data on hospitalizations.

Still, even this early in the evening, the place was jammed. Spool-sized tables were crowded with orders from the after-office crowd who liked to live dangerously. The band consisted of two men wearing neon body paint and towering blue hair who appeared to be howling about bleeding for love while they pounded with long rubber sticks on dueling keyboards.

The crowd howled right back.

That was one of the things Eve loved about the Squirrel. Since she wanted a table in the back, she pushed her way through, doing a room scan in case Stowe had beat her there. The table she staked out was currently occupied by a couple who were busy seeing who could stick whose tongue farther down whose throat. Eve broke up the contest by slapping her badge down on the table and jerking her thumb.

Out of the corner of her eye she saw the group at the table to the left hurriedly stuff their party packs of illegals into all available pockets. Everyone slunk off.

The power of the badge, she thought, and sat down, got comfortable.

In her single days she'd dropped into the club on and off, most often when Mavis had been performing. But her friend had moved on to bigger and better gigs and was now one of the hottest rising singers in the business.

"Hey, hot lips, wanna get down?"

Eve glanced up, eyed the gangly club cruiser with his smirky grin and optimistically bulging crotch. When he saw where her gaze landed, he patted his pride and joy.

"Big Sammy wants to come out and play."

Big Sammy was probably fifty percent padding, minimum, and assisted by a strong dose of Stay-Up. Eve simply took her badge out again, laid it on the table, and said, "Blow."

He blew, and with the badge in full view, she was left alone to enjoy the howling and the color until Stowe came in.

"You're late."

"Couldn't be helped." Stowe squeezed around the table and sat. She nodded toward Eve's badge. "Do you have to advertise?"

"Pays to in here. Keeps the scum from surfacing."

Stowe glanced around. She'd ditched the tie, Eve noted, and had even gone crazy and unbuttoned the collar of her shirt. The federal government's employee's version of casual wear.

"You sure pick interesting spots. Is it safe to drink in here?"

"Alcohol kills off the germs. Their Zoners aren't half-bad."

Stowe ordered one from the automated menu bolted to the side of the table. "How did you find out about Winifred?"

"I'm not here to answer questions, Stowe. You are. You can start by telling me why I shouldn't take your connection to your superiors and get you, and possibly Jacoby, out of my hair."

"Why haven't you done that already?"

"You're asking questions again."

Stowe bit back what Eve imagined was a sarcastic remark. She had to admire the control. "I have to assume you're looking to deal."

"Assume anything you want. We won't get past point one until you convince me I shouldn't make a call to East Washington and the assistant director of the Bureau."

Stowe said nothing, but reached for the glass of pale blue liquid that slid through the serving slot. She studied it, but didn't drink. "I'm an overachiever. Compulsive/competitive. When I went into college I had one specific goal. To graduate first in my class. Winifred Cates was the obstacle. I studied her as hard as I studied anything else, looking for flaws, weak spots, vulnerabilities. She was pretty, friendly, popular, and brilliant. I hated her guts."

She paused, sipped, then let out an explosive breath. "Holy Jesus Christ!" Shocked, she stared at the drink in her hand. "Is this legal?"

"Just."

Cautious, she set it down again. "She made overtures to me, friendly ones. I rebuffed them. I wasn't going to fraternize with the enemy. We pulled through the first semester, then the second, neck-in-neck. I spent the summer buried in data, studying as if my life depended on it. I learned later she'd spent hers hanging out at the beach and working part-time as an interpreter for her state senator. She was a hell of a linguist. Of course that burned my ass. Anyway, we got through half the semester that way, then one of the professors assigned us both to the same project. A team deal. Now I wasn't just competing with her, I had to work with her. Steamed me."

Something crashed behind them as a table was bumped. Stowe didn't look around, but she began to slide her drink around the table at geometric angles. "I don't know how to explain it. She was irresistible, and everything I wasn't. Warm, open, funny. Oh, God."

Grief, horribly fresh still, spurted through her. Stowe closed her eyes tight, grabbed for control. She took her time now, sipped the potent liquor in her glass. "She made me her friend. I still don't think I had a damn thing to say about it. She just . . . was. It changed me. She changed me. Opened me up to things. Fun and foolishness. I could talk to her about anything, or not talk at all. She was the turning point in my life, and so much more than that. She was my best friend."

Finally, Stowe lifted her gaze, met Eve's eyes. "My best friend. Do you understand what that means?"

"Yeah, I understand what it means."

Stowe nodded, closed her eyes again, steadied herself. "After graduation, she moved to Paris to work. She wanted to make a difference, and she wanted to experience while she was at it. I visited her there a few times. She had this pretty flat in the city and knew everyone in the building. She had a little goofy-looking dog she called Jacques and a dozen men in love with her. She lived huge, and she worked hard. She loved her job, the glamour, and the politics. Whenever her work brought her to East Washington, we'd get together. We could go months without seeing each other, then when we did, it was like we'd never been apart. Just that easy. We were both doing what we wanted, both moving up in our careers. It was perfect.

"About a week before . . . before it ended, she called me. I was on a field assignment, and didn't get the message for a few days. She didn't say a lot, just that something was going on. Something odd, and she needed to talk to me. She looked and sounded angry, with a little worry at the edges. Told me not to contact her at work, and not on her home 'link. She gave me a portable number, a new one. I thought that was weird, but I wasn't really concerned. It was late when I got in, so I decided to get back to her the next day, and went to bed. I just went to bed and slept like a goddamn baby. Fuck."

She lifted her glass again, drank deeper this time. "I got an early buzz in the morning, some complication with the case I was handling. I had to go in, and I didn't take the time to get in touch with Winnie before I left. It wasn't until the next day I even remembered about it. I took a minute to call the number she'd given me, but I didn't get a response. And I didn't follow through. I was busy, so I shrugged it off and told myself I'd try later. I never got the chance."

"She was already dead," Eve filled in.

"Yeah. She was already dead. They found her beaten and raped and strangled and dumped on the side of a road outside the city. She died two days after I got her message. Two days when I might have helped her. I never called her back. She would have gotten back to me, no matter what. She would never have been too busy to help me."

"So you accessed her case file and buried your connection to her."

"The Bureau frowns on personal involvement. They'd never have put me on Yost if they'd known why I wanted him."

"Does your partner know?"

"Jacoby's the last person I'd tell. What are you going to do?"

Eve studied Stowe's face. "I have a friend. Met her when I busted her for grifting. I never had a friend before her. If anyone hurt her, I'd hunt them down if it took the rest of my life."

Stowe drew in a shaky breath, had to look away. "Okay," she managed. "Okay."

"But understanding where you're coming from doesn't mean you get off free. Your partner's a jerk and a fuck-up, I'm betting you're not. And I'm betting you're smart enough to have thought it through now and admit that if you hadn't gotten in the way, that son of a bitch Yost would be in a cage now."

It was hard, almost painful to look back and face it. "I know it. And that's on me as much as Jacoby. I wanted to be the one to take him, and I wanted it enough to risk losing him. I won't make the same mistake again."

"Then show me your cards. Your friend worked at the Embassy. What did you find out there?"

"Next to nothing. It's hard enough to dig under the walls of politics and protocol in your own country. Try it as a foreigner. Initially, the French authorities put her death on a lover's quarrel. Like I said, she had a lot of men. But that was a wash. I looked into that myself. When they ran for like crimes, they hit on Yost. But after they looked around, they put it down to copycat."

"Why?"

"First place, she was clean. Squeaky. No connections with anything that would have drawn down a contract on her. And none of the men she'd been involved with could have afforded his fee, and if they could have, they just weren't the type. She didn't leave lovers bleeding, it wasn't Winnie's style. She was upset when she called, and didn't want me contacting her at work, so I tried poking around there."

"And?"

"The best lead I got was that Winnie'd been assigned to

interpret for the ambassador's son in some diplomatic deal with the Germans and the Americans on a multinational off planet project. New communications station. It involved a lot of meetings, a lot of travel, and was virtually all she'd been doing for three weeks before she died. I got the names of the main players, but when I tried to slide through and do a deep search I sent up a million flags. These are important, rich, and protected individuals. I had to back off. I push there too hard and I've got no chance to work on the Yost investigation."

"Give me the names."

"I'm telling you, you can't dig there."

"Just give me the names, I'll worry about when and how I dig."

Shrugging, Stowe dug a memo out of her bag and coded the names in. "Jacoby's fixated on you," she said as she handed the e-memo to Eve. "He has been since before we got here. If he can give you a few professional bruises while he brings Yost down, it'll make his life complete."

"Now, you're scaring me," Eve said with a wide smile as she pocketed the memo.

"He's got contacts, he's got sources. Deep ones. You ought to take him seriously."

"I take parasites very seriously. Now, here's the way it's going to be. Whatever data you've got, whatever leads, whatever angles, you send to my home unit. Tonight."

"For Christ's sake—"

"All of it," Eve said, edging forward. "Hold out on me, and I'll bury you before it's done. You keep me fully apprised of every move made, every source tapped, every thread tied."

"You know, I was actually starting to believe you just wanted him stopped. But it's the kick, isn't it? It's the glory at the end of the bust."

"I haven't finished," Eve said mildly. "You play that straight with me, and if I get to him first, I'll tag you. I'll do everything I can to make sure you're in on the takedown, and that you're the one to bring him in."

Stowe's lips trembled open, then firmed. "Winnie would have liked you." She stretched her arm across the little table, offered her hand. "Deal."

Eve got back in her vehicle, checked the time. It was nearly nine, which meant she couldn't manage to get all the way uptown, change into appropriate clothes for a fancy dinner, get back to midtown, and join Roarke's party by the dead-line she'd given herself.

That left her two choices. She could do what she really wanted to do, ditch it, go home, take a hot shower, and wait for whatever data Stowe sent her to come through.

Or she could go to the Top of New York with its silver tables and staggering view of the city in her work clothes, sit with a bunch of people she had nothing much in common with, get home late, potentially cranky, and work until her eyes fell out of her head.

She struggled between desire and guilt, heaved a sigh, and headed to midtown.

At least she could do something with the lag time. She put through a call to Mavis's palm-link.

Noise erupted, floods and spikes of it that had Eve's ears ringing even before she saw Mavis's face on-screen. There was a new temp tattoo decorating Mavis's left cheekbone. It might have been a green cockroach.

"Hey, Dallas! Wait, wait. You in your car? Hold on, and check this out."

"Mavis—"

But the in-dash screen went blank. A few seconds later, her friend popped onto, or partially into, the passenger's seat.

"Jesus Christ!"

"Iced, huh? I'm in the holo-room at the recording stu-dio. We use it for video effects and stuff." Mavis looked down at herself, noticed her butt was in the seat rather than on it and hooted with laughter. "Hey, I lost my ass."

"And most of your clothes from the looks of it."

Mavis Freestone was a tiny woman, and her designer lover had obviously spared the material when he'd decked her out in what appeared to be three hot pink starbursts. They were placed precisely where the law demanded, and connected with thin silver chains.

"It really rocks, huh? There's another on my ass, but you can't see it since I'm sitting down. You caught me between sets at the studio. What's up? Where are we going?"

"I've got one of Roarke's dinner things midtown. I need a favor."

"Sure."

"I've got video of a large collection of enhancements. Top of the line junk. Can you take a look at it and put me onto the retail sources and possibly wholesale, too, most likely? They're going to need to be replaced."

"Is it like for a case? I just love doing detective stuff."

"I just need the sources."

"No problem, but you should really ask Trina. She knows everything about beauty products, and since she's in the business she'd know retail and wholesale right off."

Eve winced. She'd thought of Trina, but, well . . . "Look, this is hard for me to admit, and if it goes outside of this vehicle, I'll have to kill you but . . . she scares me."

"Oh, get off planet."

"If I tag her, she'll get that look in her eye, and tell me I have to have my hair cut, then she'll start glopping stuff on my face and start on that breast cream she's always pushing."

"It comes in kiwi now."

"Whoopee."

"And you really need a trim. You're starting to go

shaggy again. And I bet you haven't had your nails done since the last time we tied you down."

"Give me a break. Be a pal."

Mavis heaved a long-suffering sigh. "Tell you what, send the video over, and I'll take a look. I'll get Trina over to my place to, like, what-do-you-call-it, collaborate. Or corroborate."

"Either works. Thanks."

"Solid." She glanced over her shoulder, waved toward the empty rear seat. "Gotcha. Two minutes. I gotta go," she said to Eve. "They're ready with the next setup."

"I'll send the image to you tonight. The sooner you can get back to me, the better."

"I'll catch you tomorrow. What are friends for?"

Eve thought of Stowe and Winnie, and wished she could reach over and touch Mavis. Just make that genuine contact. "Mavis . . ."

"Yeah."

"Um. I love you."

Mavis's eyes widened, sparkled, grinned. "Wow, frigid. I love you back. See you."

And she was gone.

Roarke had decided against the private dining room at the Top. He preferred the less formal atmosphere of the main restaurant. Their table was beside the glass wall that circled the room, and as the night was warm and clear, the roof had been opened to provide that alfresco feeling.

Occasionally tourist trams crept just a little closer than the city ordinances allowed. Close enough so you could see the recorders and cams busily capturing a scene of glamour and privilege. But when and if they became too much of a nuisance, air security whipped out in their one-man copters and buzzed them firmly back.

Otherwise, such matters were easily ignored.

The restaurant revolved slowly, offering panoramic views of the city from seventy stories up while a two-man orchestra played silky background music from the stationary central core.

Roarke had chosen that venue to entertain his guests because he hadn't expected Eve to join them.

She disliked heights.

It was the same group who'd dined at his home a few nights earlier, including Mick. His friend was enjoying himself, and keeping the rest of the party lively with stories and lies. If he drank a bit more of the wine than Roarke considered wise, no one could accuse Michael Connelly of not having a good head for spirits.

"Oh, you can't make me believe you jumped overboard and swam the rest of the way across the Channel." Laughing, Magda shook a finger at Mick. "You said it was February. You'd have frozen."

"It's true as your born, darling. Fear that my associates would realize I'd jumped ship and harpoon me in the ass kept me warm so that I arrived safe, if a bit waterlogged, on the other shore. Do you remember, Roarke, when we were barely old enough to shave and we relieved that vessel on its way out of Dublin of its cargo of illegal whiskey?"

"Your memory's considerably more flexible than mine." Though he did remember, and well.

"Ah, I'm forgetting himself's a solid citizen these days." He winked across the table at Magda. "And will you look at this. Here's one of the reasons why."

Eve strode across the circling room—boots, leather, and badge—with the tuxedo-clad maître d' scurrying after her and wringing his hands. "Madam," he continued to say. "If you please, madam."

"Lieutenant," she snapped back, struggling to ignore both height and movement. The ground, for her peace of mind, was entirely too far away. She stopped just long enough to turn and drill her finger into the maître d's chest. "And I do please, so go away before I arrest you for being a public nuisance."

"Good Lord, Roarke." Magda watched the show in awe. "She's magnificent."

"Yes, isn't she?" He got to his feet. "Anton." He spoke softly, but his voice carried and the maître d' snapped to attention. "Would you see we have another chair and place setting for my wife?"

"Wife?" Anton nearly turned white, which wasn't an easy process with his dark olive complexion. "Yes, sir. Immediately."

He began snapping his fingers as Eve stepped to the table. Deliberately, she looked at faces, any faces, and ignored the view. "Sorry I'm late."

After some necessary shuffling, and her waving away the waiter by saying she'd just have some of Roarke's dinner, she was able to sit as far away from the glass shield as possible. This put her between Magda's son, Vince, and Carlton Mince, so she resigned herself to being bored brainless for the rest of the evening.

"I assume you've been on a case." Vince went back to his appetizer as he spoke. "I've always been fascinated with the criminal mind. What can you tell us about your current quarry?"

"He's good at his work."

"But then, so are you, or you wouldn't be where you are. Do you have . . ." He waggled his fingers as if trying to pluck the word out of the air. "Leads?"

"Vince." Magda smiled across the table. "I'm sure Eve doesn't want to talk about her work over dinner."

"Sorry. I've always been interested in crime, from a safe distance. Since I've been somewhat involved with the security arrangements for the display and auction I've become more curious how the whole process works."

Eve picked up the wine one of the waiters had, with

some ceremony, put in front of her. "You go after the bad guy until you catch him, then you put him in a cage and hope the courts keep him there."

"Ah." Carlton scooped up some creamy seafood dish and nodded. "That would be frustrating, I'd think. Having done your job, then having the next phase circumvent it. It would feel like failure, wouldn't it?" He studied her kindly. "Does it happen often?"

"It happens." Yet another waiter slid a plate under her nose. On it was a lovely little pinwheel of grilled prawns. One of her favorites. She glanced at Roarke, caught his smile.

He had a way of making such small miracles happen.

"You have solid security," she said. "As tight as it gets under the circumstances. I'd prefer you'd selected a more private venue, one with less access."

Carlton nodded enthusiastically. "I tried to argue for that, Lieutenant. And my arguments fell on deaf ears." He sent Magda an affectionate look. "I can't bear to think just now of the costs of security and insurance, or I'd spoil my appetite."

"Old fogey." Magda winked at him. "The venue is part of the package. The elegant Palace Hotel—the very fact that the display can be viewed by the public before the auction just adds to the buzz. We've generated invaluable media attention, not only for the auction itself but for the Foundation."

"And an impressive display it is," Mick commented. "I wandered over there today and had a look at it."

"Oh, I wish you'd told me you wanted to see it. I'd have taken you through personally."

"I wouldn't want to impose on your time."

"Nonsense." Magda waved that away as the first course was cleared. "I do hope you plan to be in town for the auction."

"I hadn't been, to tell you the truth, but after meeting you and seeing it all myself, I'm determined to go and to bid."

While his guests chatted, Roarke signaled to the sommelier. As he shifted to order another bottle of wine, he felt a bare foot—a small, narrow bare foot—slide suggestively up his calf. Without a flicker, he finished his request, shifted back.

He knew Eve's foot, it was narrow but long, and she was just a bit too far away to be able to play with him under the table. One casual glance gave him the angle, and his lifted eyebrow was his only reaction as he noted the secret, cat-like smile on Liza Trent's face as she began to nibble on her second course.

He debated ignoring the overture or being amused by it. Before he could decide, she looked up. The gleam in her gaze wasn't for him, but for Mick. She had, Roarke realized, simply missed her mark.

Interesting, he thought, as those bare toes tried to work their way under his cuff. And complicated.

"Liza," he said and had the pleasure of feeling her foot jerk like a spring. When he looked at her, coolly, he could see understanding and a faint embarrassment cross her features. Her foot slid away. "How is everything?" he asked pleasantly.

"Lovely, thanks."

Roarke waited until the meal was done, the dessert champagne consumed, and he was driving home with Mick.

He took out a cigarette, offered the case. For a moment, they smoked in companionable silence.

"Do you remember when we boosted that lorryload of smokes? Christ, what were we, ten?" Pleased with the memory, Mick stretched out his legs. "We went through near a carton between us that same afternoon—you, me, Brian Kelly, and Jack Bodine, and Jack, bless him, got sick as six dogs from it. And the rest we sold to Six-Fingers Logan for the prettiest of profits."

"I remember it. And that a few years later Logan was found floating in the Liffey missing all his digits, including the extra one."

"Ah well."

"Mick, what are you thinking of, fucking Vince Lane's woman?"

Mick acted shocked. "What are you talking about? Why I barely know . . ." He trailed off, shook his head, and laughed. "Christ, trying to lie to you's a waste of energy. You never bought a con in your bloody life. How'd you figure it?"

"She gave me a lovely little leg massage on her way to you. She has good feet, but poor aim."

"Women, not a discretionary bone in their beautiful little bodies. Well now, the fact of it is, I bumped into her today in your palatial hotel when I went to see the display. One thing led to another, and the another eventually led up to her suite. What's a man to do, after all?"

"You're poaching."

Mick only grinned. "And your point would be, lad?"

"Try to keep it inbounds until my business with them is finished."

"First time I've ever heard you make a fuss about a little side of sex. But I'll do that for you, for old time's sake."

"I'm grateful."

"It's not so much of a thing. A woman's just a woman, after all. Surprises me you haven't taken a nibble of Liza yourself. She's a tasty one."

"I have a woman. A wife."

Mick gave a careless burst of laughter. "Well, when has that ever stopped a man from taking a sample here and there. Hurts no one, does it?"

Roarke watched the gates of his home open, a graceful, silent motion. "Once, I recall the lot of us, you and Bri and

Jack, Tommy, and Shawn as well—got half-pissed on home brew. And as we sat around the question came up as to what the one thing in the world would be we'd want and need most. The one thing we would give up anything else to keep. Do you remember that, Mick?"

"Aye. The brew put us in a philosophical state of mind on that occasion. I said I'd be more than satisfied by a great sea of money. For then I could buy all the rest, couldn't I? It seems to me Shawn, being Shawn, wanted a dick big as an elephant's, but he was more pissed than the rest of us, and wasn't considering the logistics of it."

He turned his head, studied his friend. "Now that I'm thinking of it, I don't recall you said anything, made that selection of the one thing."

"I didn't, no. Because I couldn't see what it might be. Freedom, money, power, going one bloody week without having the old man pound on me. I couldn't decide, so I didn't say. But I know it now. Eve. She's my one thing."

chapter seventeen

Since Eve arrived home first, she made up what she could of lost time by heading straight to her office and sending the transmission to Mavis.

Her incoming data light was on. She booted it up, and began to scan the files, standing behind her desk with her palms pressed on its top.

Stowe matched her profile, Eve mused. The woman was thorough and she was efficient. The official data was less than she'd hoped for, but the agent's side notations were illuminating.

Been copying the files for personal use all along, haven't you? Eve decided. *I'd have done the same.*

It appeared that Stowe had begun to take Feeney's tact of cross-referencing the victims by friends, family, business associates. All of those individuals had been questioned, a select few had been taken into an official interview as suspects.

Nobody played out.

Eve shifted documents, read on, then smiled thinly. It looked as though the FBI had run into some of the same tangled tape with Interpol as she had with the Bureau. Nobody wanted to share.

"One of the many reasons he keeps sliding through."

She sat back, considered. *He knows something about law enforcement,* she thought. *Knows about the bumps and the ruts and the paperwork, the politics and the grandstanding.*

He counted on it.

Do a job in one place, bounce to another, and work there or take a nice holiday until things chilled out again. Hit Paris, zip back to New York, take in the opera, do some shopping, contemplate the view from your penthouse terrace while the French cops are chasing their own tails.

A quick trip to Vegas II, a little gambling to amuse yourself, hit your target, and take a luxury shuttle back home before Interplanetary gets the data up.

She glanced up as Roarke walked in. "Maybe he can pilot."

"Hmmm?"

"You can't always depend on public transpo, even premier class. You got delays, equipment failures, cancellations, rerouting. Why risk it? Private plane or private shuttle. Maybe both. Yeah, I can put McNab on that. Be like picking a needle out of a . . . a hill of needles, but we could get lucky. How come the cat didn't follow you in?"

"Deserted me for Mick. They're fast mates now."

He wrapped his arm around her from behind, nuzzled her neck. "Shall I tell you how you looked striding across that restaurant tonight?"

"Like a cop. Sorry. I didn't have time to change."

"A very sexy cop. Long legs and lots of attitude. I appreciate you taking the time."

"Yeah?" She turned. "I guess you owe me one."

"At the very least."

"I might have a way for you to pay up."

"Darling." His hands began to roam. "Happy to."

"Not that way. You're always good for sex."

"Why . . . thank you."

"So . . ." She nudged him back before his hands got too busy, then sat on the desk. "I had a couple of meets after the briefing. First was with Peabody."

"That was good of you."

"No, it wasn't. I can't count on her to focus if she's moping around, can I? Don't grin at me. It'll piss me off." She blew out a breath. "McNab gave her a hard shot by talking about his hot date tonight."

"A standard and unimaginative ploy."

"I don't know anything about ploys. It hit the mark. Left her all sad and shaky. So I fed her ice cream, and let her dump on me. Now you get to hear it."

"Do I get ice cream?"

"I don't want to see anything from the ice-cream food group for at least two weeks."

She filled him in, mostly because she wanted assurance she'd made the right moves, said the right things. He knew more about the lending a shoulder deal than she did.

"He's jealous of Monroe. Understandably."

"Jealousy is a small, ugly emotion."

"And a human one. At this point, I'd say that his feelings for her are stronger, or at least clearer, than hers for him. It would be frustrating. Is frustrating," he corrected, skimming his fingers along her jaw. "As I remember very well."

"You got your way, didn't you? Anyway, I'm hoping it blows over and they go back to sniping at each other like they used to, instead of groping in maintenance closets."

"You really should try to rein in that wild romantic streak."

"I'm not going to say I told you so."

He laughed at her, at both of them. "Yes, you are."

"Okay, I did tell you. We're in the middle of a messy investigation and they're trying to score off each other, and sulking. They're cops, damn it."

"That's right. But they're not droids."

"Okay, okay." She threw up her hands. "But they better table it until we close this. Moving on, Whitney used his arm and got me some additional data on Mollie Newman."

"Ah, the justice's minor entertainment."

"Entertainment for him maybe. Upshot is she was his niece through marriage. A nice, impressionable kid who did well in her classes and wanted to be a lawyer. The justice was going to help her out there, and apparently just helped himself. I'm leaving her out of it, at least for now."

"You might get closer after a little chat with her."

"I might, but it's not worth it." She'd worked those angles everywhere they would fit and had decided they simply didn't fit at all. "Yost doesn't worry about ID, so her seeing him means nothing. I don't think he touched her, not his style."

"He wasn't being paid to."

"Exactly. And her medical indicates illegals and sexual molestation. I'd hang Exotica and the molestation on the judge, the Zoner on Yost to put her down while he did the job. I don't need her to build a case, so unless it looks like there was some connection through her or her mother to Yost, I'm leaving her alone. She's got enough to get over."

No one would understand better, Roarke thought. "Then we'll leave her be."

"Meanwhile, Feeney popped into the briefing with some very interesting data, right out of Jacoby's and Stowe's sealed profiles."

If they'd been playing poker, his mildly interested expression would have pulled in the pot with a hand full of trash. "Is that so?"

"Don't give me that. It had your fingerprints all over it."

"Lieutenant. I've told you before, I never leave fingerprints."

"I told you before I didn't want you veering off the regulations to get me information."

"And I haven't."

"No, you just used Feeney as a bridge."

"Did he say that?" When she hissed, he smiled. "Apparently not. I can only assume this data received from some unidentified source proved useful."

She scowled at him, pushed off the desk to pace away. Paced back. Then gave up and told him about her meeting with Karen Stowe.

"Losing a friend is never easy," he murmured. "Losing one when you feel you might have done something to stop it leaves a hole."

Because she knew he lived with that, she laid her hands on his shoulders. "And going back to what you might have done helps no one."

"But you're helping her close it, just as you helped me close mine. What do you want me to do?"

"She gave me the names of three men. I want to know about these men, without sending up flags. It's not illegal to look at them. Looking from an angle that won't alert their personal security is a trickier area. But it's not against the law unless you break sealeds. I don't want that. I just want a discreet search. If you generate it, the Feebs aren't likely to hit on it. If I do, they will."

"And if you take more than a standard scan, officially, on Winifred's case file, Jacoby might clue in, might look at it closer himself. That potentially exposes Stowe."

"Exactly. Can you do it without breaking the law?"

"Yes, but I might have to bruise it slightly. Nothing that would generate more than a knuckle rap and a small fine if I were the clumsy type and got caught at it."

"I can't risk asking for a warrant again to keep it all aboveboard. We haven't plugged the leak."

"What are the names?"

She took out the memo, handed it over.

"Well now, as it happens I know these men, and we may be able to avoid too much hacking."

"You know them?"

"I know Hinrick, the German, and know of Naples, the American. I believe he's set up a more or less permanent residence in London. Gerade, the ambassador's son, is also known by reputation. On the surface he's a diplomat, a devoted husband and father, and a spotless civil servant. His father's paid a considerable amount of money to maintain that veneer."

"What's under it?"

"A spoiled, rather nasty young man, from what I've heard, with a demanding temperament, a taste for group sex, and a distressing illegals addiction. He's been through private rehab a few times, at his father's insistence. Doesn't seem to stick."

"How do you know all this?"

"He lives high when he can manage it, and that addiction and sex are expensive. He's been known to arrange for certain valuable articles, in certain households to which he had access, to change hands, let's say."

"He arranged for you to steal property?"

"No, indeed. I always arranged that quite well on my own, when I was into such regrettable activities. I simply assisted another associate with the transportation. A number of years ago, Lieutenant. I wouldn't be surprised if the statute of limitations is in effect."

"Then I'll sleep easy tonight. Before she was killed, Winifred Cates was acting as interpreter for these men on what was supposed to be a multinational communications station."

"No." He frowned, considering. "No, I'd have known if that had been in the works and certainly if it had gone through with those players. I might be out of certain areas of activities, but communications isn't one of them."

"Is that ego or fact?"

"Darling Eve, my ego is fact." He patted her arm when she snorted. "You can trust me on this. It was a cover.

Naples is successful in communications, but at the base he's a smuggler. Illegals, contraband, and people in particular. Hinrick diversifies, but smuggling is one of his favored pastimes."

"And you say Naples lives in England now. Those smugglers hit in the countryside—the Hagues. Might have been on him."

He said nothing for a moment. "Yes," he murmured. "Quite possibly."

"It's not much of a stretch to draw the scenario that Winifred heard or witnessed something she shouldn't have. Something that rang enough bells with her that she contacted her pal in the FBI. For help. She needs to be taken out of the mix, Yost is hired. When a couple of independent-minded smugglers get a little too big for their britches, Yost is hired. If we can tie one or all of these men into either hit, I'm one step closer to Yost."

She paused, frowned. "Why didn't any of their criminal activities pop for the feds?"

Roarke nearly smiled. "Some of us, Lieutenant, know how to be careful."

"Are they as good as you? Delete that," she said before he could answer. "No one is. Okay, which one of the three is most likely to have hired Yost to off a civil servant?"

"I don't know enough about Gerade. If it's between Naples and Hinrick, Naples. Hinrick is a gentleman. He'd have found another way to deal with her. Killing her? Well, he'd have considered that rude."

"Nice to know I may be dealing with a polite criminal."

While Roarke used his office to dig for data, Eve settled down in her own. She correlated Stowe's files with her own, ran probables, and studied all possible matches.

Yost wasn't going to wait much longer. She had no clue as to his target, and was still several layers away from shaking off his current cover.

Someone is going to die, she thought, *probably within hours.* And she couldn't stop it.

She pulled up her victim files again. Darlene French. An ordinary young woman with a simple life, who should have had a long, uncomplicated future.

Site of murder: The Palace Hotel.

Connection: Roarke.

Jonah Talbot. A bright, successful man. Upwardly mobile, who should have continued to rise.

Site of murder: rented home.

Connection: Roarke.

Both had worked for him. Both had died while on property he owned.

French had been a stranger to Roarke. A faceless employee. But Talbot had been a friend of sorts.

The third would be closer yet.

Would he come after her? She would have preferred that, but thought it was too large a leap. Another employee, if the pattern held. But one he worked with more closely. One he knew well.

Caro, his admin? That was a good bet, and precisely why Eve had called in some favors and had the efficient woman under surveillance.

But she couldn't cover every member of his top-level teams in the city.

And if Yost jumped to another location, to one of the countless offices, plants, organizations Roarke had all over the planet and through the developed solar system, the potential targets were astronomical.

Couldn't compute.

Still, she tried to level the field, to connect the dots through the mountain of data Roarke had given her. The primary result was a wicked little headache. How could the man *own* so much? Why would anyone want to? And how the hell did he keep track of it all?

She pushed that aside. It wasn't the way. If Roarke himself couldn't hazard an educated guess on potential targets, how could she?

She went for coffee, using the short walk to the kitchen and back to clear her mind.

A personal vendetta. If that was the motive, why not go after the man himself? Or at least those in his inner circle?

Business. It was business. What were Roarke's most pressing projects?

She went back to his data, rubbed her throbbing temples. It looked as though he was juggling several dozen green-lighted deals even now. It was enough to make you dizzy.

Olympus. *That was his baby,* she thought. A kind of pet fantasy, and as complicated as they came. He was building a goddamn world there: hotels, casinos, homes, resorts, parks. And all of it lavish.

Homes, she thought. *Vacation and retirement homes. Villas, mansions, sleek penthouses, presidential suites. Something for the man who had, and could afford, everything.*

Right up Yost's alley.

She turned toward Roarke's office, then stopped at the doorway.

He was at his console, captain of his ship. He'd drawn his hair back so it lay on his neck in a short, gleaming black tail. His eyes were cool, cool blue, the way they were when his mind was fully occupied.

He'd taken off his dinner jacket. His shirt was loose at the collar, the sleeves rolled up. There was something, just *something* about that look that always and forever grabbed her in the gut.

She could look at him for hours, and at the end of it still marvel that he belonged to her.

Someone wants to hurt you, she thought. *I'm not going to let them.*

He lifted his head. He'd scented her, or sensed her. He always did. Their eyes locked, and for a moment stayed locked. A thousand messages passed between them in absolute silence.

"Worrying about me won't help you get your job done."

"Who says I'm worried?"

He stayed where he was; simply held out his hand.

She crossed to him, took it, gripped hard. "When I met you," she said carefully, "I didn't want you in my life. You were one big complication. Every time I looked at you, or heard your voice, or so much as thought about you, the complication got bigger."

"And now?"

"Now? You are my life." She gave his hand one last squeeze, then released. "Okay, enough mushy stuff. Olympus."

"What about it?"

"You're selling property up there. Big fancy houses, snazzy apartments, and like that."

"Marketing describes them with a bit more panache, but yes. Ah." He clicked in before she spoke. "Sylvester Yost might enjoy the advantages of a comfortable off planet home in a self-contained community."

"You could check it out. His pace of contracts in the past two years is up twelve percent. Could very well be a push for a nice, fat retirement nest. Best guess would be his Roles alias. It's not an answer but it's another link. Enough links you make a chain. Now."

She walked around the console, sat on the edge of it to face him. "You've got partners, multinational, in the Olympus thing. Investors. Anybody unhappy, annoyed because you get the big slice of the pie?"

"There are occasionally bumps, but no. The project's moving smoothly and on schedule. I took the biggest financial risk, and therefore will reap the largest profits. But the consortium's satisfied. Returns on investments are already exceeding initial projections."

She nodded. "All right. Here's how it seems to me. If

this is a business hit, the business is likely in New York. I'm thinking if it was business in, say, Australia, the hits would be in Australia. To draw you down there."

"Yes, I've considered that."

"First hit's at your hotel, when it's public knowledge you'll be on-site. Second hit is in one of your rentals, and you're in town and working minutes away. Give me a connection between Darlene French and Jonah Talbot."

"I don't have one."

"No, you do. You're just not seeing it. Neither am I." In her mind, she switched to interview mode, and Roarke to witness. "Darlene French was a maid at your hotel. You had no personal contact with her?"

"None."

"Who hired her?"

"She'd have submitted an application through the human resources department, and ultimately hired by Hilo."

"You don't supervise the hiring and firing?"

"I'd spend all my time doing so."

"But it's your hotel. Your organization."

"I have departments," he said with some impatience. "And the departments have heads. Those heads operate with the required autonomy. My organization, Lieutenant, is designed to run smoothly, on its particular internal wheels, so that—"

"Did Talbot have any tasks that involved The Palace?"

"None." Frustration slipped into his eyes. He knew what she was doing, sliding him into the witness slot so that he would answer instinctively. And she did it well. "He never even stayed there. I checked. Certainly he would have had authors who did, and certainly he'd have entertained authors or business associates there for dinner or for lunch. But that hardly makes one of your links."

"Maybe he hosted parties there. You know, professional spreads. Maybe he had one planned."

"No. He might have attended some. The publicity department at the publishing house generally arranges that sort of function. There's nothing on the slate I'm aware of. Magda's display and auction are the showcase through the month."

"Okay. Did he have anything to do with that?"

"The publishing house isn't involved in the auction. Jonah acquired, edited, and published manuscripts. The hotel and its functions are entirely separate from . . ."

She all but heard the click. "What?"

"I'm an idiot," he murmured and got to his feet. "Manuscripts. We'll publish a disc, a new biography of Magda next month. There will also be a publication detailing the auction—each piece, its history and significance. Jonah would have been involved in those projects. I think it's one of his authors who wrote the bio. He'd have edited it."

"Magda." Connections, possibilities, began to run through her brain. "She's a link. That's a solid link. Maybe you're not the target at all. Maybe she is."

"Maybe we both are. The auction."

She held up a hand, pushing off the console so she could think on her feet. "Magda Lane in residence at The Palace. Your hotel. Holding one of the biggest events of her professional life there. Not at one of her own homes, not at one of the auction houses, but your hotel. Whose idea was that?"

"Hers. At least she contacted me with it. It's a media hook," he added. "And it's working."

"How long has it been in the planning stage?"

"She contacted me over a year ago with the concept. You don't put something of this scope together quickly."

"That's a lot of time for someone who wanted to mess up one or both of you to lay things out." And Winifred Case had died in Paris eight months before. The smugglers in Cornwall, two months after that.

"Then your publishing house is putting out discs. What

else is there? Security. Who are you closest to on the security team for the hotel and auction? Think it through, I want names. Your publicity wheel, too, and . . . Jesus, what goes into this sort of thing?"

"I'll run it down by department and function."

"On her end, we have her son, her business manager, and his wife. She'd have others."

"I have those as well."

"We'll start there, do what can be done to protect those individuals." She stopped, turned back. "But the pattern is the targets work for you, so they get priority."

He was nodding, and already calling up his files on the auction.

"Roarke, what happens, to you personally, if this auction is a failure or some sort of scandal rises out of it?"

"Depends on what the failure or scandal might be. If it's a financial disaster, I lose some money."

"How much money?"

"Mmm. Conservative projections estimate the take at over five hundred million. Add sentiment and rabid fans of Magda's, the media attention, and you may easily double that. Over and above the fee for the hotel and security, I get ten percent of the gross. But I'm donating that back to her foundation, so in actuality, the money isn't an issue."

"Not to you," she murmured.

He shrugged that off. "I'll transfer these names to your unit. I intend to arrange for my own security for my people. And for Magda's."

"I've got no problem with that." Her eyes were narrowed, but she wasn't seeing the data that whizzed by on the wall screen.

"Roarke, you've got potentially a billion dollars of merchandise displayed in a public hotel. Just how much would that merchandise go for, fenced?"

He was ahead of her there. His mind had already shifted

modes, and taken him back to his past. It would be a fine, exciting heist. The take of a lifetime. "A bit less than half that."

"Five hundred million is a hell of a paycheck."

"Could be more if you hooked to particular collectors. Still, the security's solid. You've seen it yourself."

"Yeah, I've seen it myself. How would you do it?"

He ordered the data transferred to Eve's unit, went back to his own to begin the run on Olympus property. "At least one inside man in each area, preferably two. Best to have a plant on my team, and another on Magda's. You'd need all data, security codes, failsafes, timing. I wouldn't do it with less than six people. Ten would be better. I'd have a couple in the hotel, as staff or guests."

He turned to check his incoming on the three names Eve had given him earlier.

"You'd need an on-ground transfer vehicle. I'd use a hotel delivery lorry, sorry, truck. I wouldn't be greedy as I'd want the entire operation over in under thirty minutes. Twenty would be best. So I'd have earmarked the most valuable pieces. Those I had researched and already had buyers for."

He moved away, poured a brandy. "I'd have a distraction, but not in the hotel. Anything out of the ordinary in the hotel would automatically tighten security. I'd have something in one of the neighboring buildings, or in the park. A small explosion, an interesting vehicular accident, something that would draw people out, even pull in some cops. With cops outside the building going about their business, people feel safe and secure. Aye, I'd want cops about."

Jesus, she thought. *Listen to him.*

"When would you hit it?"

"Oh, the night before the auction, absolutely. All's gone well, hasn't it? What an exciting day tomorrow will be.

Everything's all buffed and polished, and already celebrities and VIPs are in the hotel. The staff's busy seeing to them, asking for autographs, discussing who's who and the like. It's prime time for it."

"Could you pull it off?"

"Could I?" He looked back at her then, his eyes wildly blue. "Circumstances being other than they are, I'd be hellbent to try. And I'd damn well do it, if my mind was set on it. Which is why I don't believe anyone else could. Because all this I've anticipated already."

"And maybe someone knows you well enough, knows your pattern well enough to have anticipated that. And so you've been distracted. What are you doing and what has your mind been on for the past several days? You're not spending the evening checking your security, going over the steps, supervising your hotel team."

"There's a point," he said quietly. "It hasn't had my full attention, but it's still solid."

"Who do you know who could pull this off, besides yourself."

"Not many. I was the best."

"Applause, applause. Who?"

"Why don't you come sit over here?" He sat himself, patted his knee. "I'm sure I'll think better that way."

"What do I look like, the bimbo secretary?"

"No, not at the moment, but that might be fun. I'll be the horny executive, cheating on his long-suffering wife. Let's hear you say: 'Oh, Mr. Montegue, I couldn't possibly!' And make it breathy."

"That concludes the comic relief portion of our program. Who?"

"Two that might have gotten close to it are dead, proving my previous point as you'll note, I'm not. There may be one or two others. I'll do some checking."

"I want names."

His eyes cooled. "I'm not a weasel, Lieutenant, even for you. I'll do the checking. If there's a chance either of the ones I'm thinking of might be involved, I'll tell you. But not before I see for myself."

She strode over to him. "Lives are on the line, so you can eject your thief's code of honor."

"I'm aware lives are on the line. There was a day all I had to my name was that code of honor, battered as it might be. I'll see to this, and give you what there is as soon as I do. For now, I can tell you that Gerade here wouldn't be able to plan out such a complex and intricate operation. He's not a thief, even a poor one. Naples, yes, he could generate the talent, and he's plenty of his own. He's a top-line smuggler with excellent connections, no honor a'tall, and a fine transpo system in the illegal export business. If you're looking for links to Yost, he's my current bet."

She bit back on impatience, reminding herself her first order of business wasn't to catch a thief, but to stop a killer.

"All right, I'll get on him."

"In the morning. You need a break. You have a headache."

"I don't have a headache." Her mouth moved to sulk. "Hardly."

In a lightning move, he kicked her left foot out from under her, snagged her by the waist, and caught her in his lap on her way down.

"I know just the thing for hardly a headache."

She tried to get an elbow into his gut, but he already had her arms pinned. Besides, he smelled fabulous. "I'm not calling you Mr. Montegue."

"You're such a spoilsport." He bit her ear. "Just for that, I don't want you in my lap."

"Fine. Then I'll just—"

The next thing she knew she was flat on her back on the floor, and under him. "Do you know how many beds are in this house?" she asked when she got her breath back.

"Not off the top of my head, but I can look it up."

"Never mind," she said, and pulled the leather tie from his hair.

chapter eighteen

"Naples, Dominic J.," Eve began when her team was assembled for the morning briefing. "Age fifty-six, married, two children. Current residence, London, England, with alternate residences in Rome, Sardinia, New L.A., East Washington, Rio, and Caspian Bay, Delta Colony."

Like her team, she studied the image on-screen of a handsome, dark-eyed man with sharp features and a carefully styled mane of deep brown hair.

"The Naples organization, of which he is CEO, deals primarily in communication systems, with the main area handling off planet work. He's known for his charitable work, particularly in the education sphere, and has strong political connections."

She paused, ordered a second image on split screen. "His son, Dominic II, is the U.S. liaison to Delta Colony and is reputed to have aspirations for a higher office. Dominic II also happens to be old friends with Michel Gerade, the son of the French ambassador."

She added the image of a man with lustrous waves of

gold hair, a full-lipped mouth, and, in her opinion, a soft chin.

"On record," she continued, "Naples is dingy, but unsoiled. There have been, in the past, some speculations, some questions, some minor investigations into activities of some of the arms of Naples Org, but nothing that stuck, or made a smear. My source, however, reports that Naples is, and has been, involved in various criminal activities. Illegals, smuggling, e-fraud, theft, extortion, and very likely murder. He's also our most solid connection to Yost."

She shifted images, ordered up a new set of triples onscreen. "These three men, Naples, Hinrick, and Gerade, met in Paris eight months ago, ostensibly to discuss plans for a multinational com system. Hinrick is a successful smuggler, and though his official record isn't quite as clean as Naples, it passes. Winifred Cates acted as interpreter for these men during their meetings. This com system never developed, and Winifred Cates was murdered. Her case remains open, and she is listed as one of Sylvester Yost's victims."

She shifted images again. "Britt and Joseph Hague, deceased. Known smugglers. They were murdered six months ago, and are listed as victims of Yost's. This has been confirmed by the recovery of two lengths of silver wire yesterday by the local authorities.

"Their bodies were found in Cornwall. Yost spent a few days in London prior to their deaths. Naples's main base is now London. These smugglers are reputed to have trespassed on the turf of a bigger, more powerful organization. It's suspected that they were hit to remove them from competition, and to make a point to others who might be tempted to infringe."

She picked up her coffee. She'd had less than three hours of sleep and needed the jolt. "Three years ago in Paris, a female entertainer was beaten, raped, garroted with a silver wire. Monique Rue," she continued as she brought the woman's face on-screen. "Twenty-five, single, mixed-race female was found in an alleyway a few blocks from the club where she worked. She had been, according to statements made by friends and coworkers, involved in an affair with Michel Gerade. She was becoming dissatisfied with mistress status. Gerade, good friend of Dominic II, clung to his diplomatic status, and issued a single statement through a representative."

Eve picked up the hard copy of the statement and read off the gist. "He and Miss Rue were friendly. He admired her talent. There had been no sexual relationship." And tossed the paper down again.

"The French cops knew that was bullshit, or whatever the French word for bullshit is, but their hands were tied. In addition, Gerade had a solid alibi as he was vacationing with his wife on the Riviera when Rue was murdered. No direct link between Yost and Gerade was established."

"Until now," Feeney muttered under his breath.

"Lastly, we have Nigel Luca, and his sheet's as long as my left leg. Weapons running primarily. Eight years ago he was beaten, raped, and found with a silver wire around his neck outside a dive in Seoul. My source reports that Luca was, at that time, employed by one Naples, Dominic J., and had likely been, as was his habit, doing a bit of skimming off the top."

"It looks like Yost is one of Naples's favorite toys," Feeney put in. "How do we get him?"

"We need a hell of a lot more before we try to extradite. This guy is well protected. I can and will pass my data onto Interpol and onto Global."

"You think they don't have some of this?" Feeney asked.

"Yeah, I think they've got some of this, and aren't sharing. I also think they haven't clicked all the links. So we will. And meanwhile, we dig. I need EDD to push for more, to find every little thread that's out there that may tie Naples to our man. My gut tells me Gerade is the weak link here, but we can't touch the greasy little bastard. Same goes for Dominic II, but the second generation here doesn't seem to be as smart, or as careful as the first. Sooner or later they'll make the right mistake. Long goal is to be ready when they do. But unless they make it on our turf, it's Interpol or Global."

"We'll set up flags in EDD. Anything comes through we'll document it, and pass it on."

"Good. All this applies to our current agenda in that it gives us a potential motive for the two killings under investigation." She brought up the chart she'd worked out the night before.

"The Palace Hotel. Darlene French. Roarke. Magda Lane. The brownstone uptown. Jonah Talbot. Roarke. Magda Lane. The victim was involved in publication projects on Lane. The merchandise currently displayed, The Palace Hotel, and about to go on the block is potentially worth upwards of one billion. Naples is a thief with a widespread com network behind him. Hinrick is a smuggler with what is reputed to be one of the best transfer and transpo organizations. Gerade just strikes me as greedy."

"It's the greedy ones you gotta watch," Feeney commented.

"Agreed. Speculation. What if the business in Paris between these three men had to do with a plan to heist the auction merchandise? Winifred sees or hears something off. She was a smart woman. She attempted to contact her friend in the FBI but was killed before that connection was made."

"Why hire Yost to kill a couple of bystanders in New York?" McNab crossed his legs. It was the first sentence he'd uttered during the briefing. Across the room, Peabody remained silent. "You do somebody on the site you plan to hit, it's going to beef up security."

"But we'd be looking for a killer. Not a thief. Shake up the staff by killing one of them in a brutal fashion, right in a guest room. Frustrate security by sliding right through them. Takes the mind and energy off the auction, puts it elsewhere. Then you hit again. Where does the investigation center? On who might have some kind of vendetta against Roarke. That was the motive we focused on. But what if it's not a vendetta. Or not that on the primary level. What if it's just profit?"

"It's got potential." Feeney pursed his lips. "But why bring Gerade into the mix? I don't see as he's got anything to offer."

Her smile was thin and sharp as she brought up her adjusted chart, one she'd finished compiling at three A.M. that morning. "Look who happens to be one of Dominic II's and Gerade's playmates. Vincent Lane, Magda's son. They've been running around together since their early twenties."

"Son of a bitch." Feeney punched the uncharacteristically silent McNab on the shoulder. "Son of a bitch."

"Yeah, I got a nice thrill out of it, too," Eve said and did her best to block out the deliberate way the young e-detective and her aide were ignoring each other. "Lane contributed to Dominic's liaison campaign, and often visits Delta Colony. Both Dominic II and Gerade invested in Lane's short-lived production company. Link by link," Eve said, "I think we've got a real chain going here. To pull off a heist of this size and complexity, you need a man on the inside. Vince Lane's as inside as they come."

"He's going to steal from his own mother." Peabody spoke now, mildly outraged. "And kill to do it?"

"He's a financial fuck-up," Eve told her. "Over the years he's put together and begun to put together dozens of schemes and projects. He's pissed away his trust fund, run through the setup costs his mother gave him, twice, for businesses. He's borrowed from her to pay off loans and I imagine a few spine-crackers, too. But for the past fourteen months, he's been a very good boy, working for Mama.

She pays him a ridiculous salary according to their financials, but he's all but dead broke. His expenses go directly to Carlton Mince, her financial advisor. I intend to talk to him, and to Lane. Carefully. I don't want Lane alerting anyone, Magda included, that I'm looking at him on this."

She stopped, coming to attention when Whitney came in. She'd already sent a full update and all data to him earlier that morning.

He glanced at the wall screen, judged where she was in her briefing, then took a seat. "Continue, Lieutenant."

"Yes, sir. Peabody and I will do a dropby on Mince and Lane at the hotel. Feeney, if you could use your connections through the IRCCA. As we've said, it's probable the other agencies already have this data on Naples. And they may have more. If they do, no matter how speculative, do what you can to convince them to reach out. McNab, see the head of the event's security at The Palace. Roarke will have already alerted him, but I want you to follow up. You're his general dogsbody until this is over. You'll be provided with complete dossiers on everyone involved in the security. Get to know and love them. I want the NYPSD and this team aware and apprised of every change, every step, every function of security at the hotel. A door guard has a butt rash, I want to know what kind. Understood?"

"Yes, sir."

Now, she drew a breath. "Commander?"

He had the faintest of smiles on his face. "Lieutenant?"

"I'd like to request that you use whatever weight you might deem appropriate with your connections in the FBI and East Washington. I want some elbow room, and Jacoby's not going to give it to me unless . . ." She trailed off before she finished the thought, which had to do with her shoving his head up his ass. ". . . without some directive. If I can have the room, and the cooperation to bring Sylvester Yost down, I'm willing to give the feds the collar."

"What! What!" Feeney was out of his chair, his face a furious red, his arms waving. "What the hell are you talking about? You don't give them dick, you hear? You've busted your balls on this, done all the work, got closer than anyone ever has to this bastard. Would've had him, too, if it wasn't for those assholes screwing us over. If you put in eight hours this week on this one case, you've put in eighty. You got circles under your eyes I could swim laps in."

"Feeney—"

"Uh-uh, shut up." He jabbed a finger at her. "You may be primary, but I still outrank you. You think I'm just going to stand back and let you pass the baton to the Feebs after you ran the damn race? Do you know what this collar could mean to you? Every agency on and off planet's been after this bastard for twenty-five years. You bring him down, you bring him in, and you're heading toward pinning on your captain's bars. And *don't* you stand there and tell me you don't want them."

"I want him more." She wasn't sure if she was touched, embarrassed, or annoyed by his outburst on her behalf, but she knew she had to clear the decks. "You got the anonymous source tip," she reminded him, keeping her eyes steady on his so he'd understand she knew where it had come from. "Without that, I wouldn't have had the Winifred angle, or at least not this soon. And without that, I wouldn't have had a tool to use on Stowe to move onto that Paris triad. Agent Stowe put in a lot of hours and grief on her investigation, too. She gave me useful data; I promised her the collar. That's the deal, Feeney. I made it, and I'll keep it."

"Well, your deal sucks. Commander—"

Whitney held up his hand. "No point in appealing to me on this one, however much I agree with you. Lieutenant Dallas heads this team. I'll give you what weight I can, Lieutenant."

"Thank you, sir. Excuse me," she said when her communicator beeped. She pulled it out, stepping aside to take the transmission.

"Jack," Feeney said in undertones. "She deserves the collar."

"At this point, we don't have a collar. Let's just see what we see. However it comes down, the department is fully aware of the work Dallas and the rest of you—"

He broke off when Eve swore.

"What the hell do you mean, you lost him? How could you lose one skinny, ugly man with a stick up his ass?"

Easily, when the skinny, ugly man also had eyes in the back of his head. Summerset had survived the Urban Wars, had worked the streets, run all kinds of cons, and though those times were past, he could still smell cop at a five-block radius.

He also knew when he was being tailed. Ditching that tail was a matter of principle, and had given him a nice warm glow of satisfaction. Though he imagined Eve had set the cops on him, possibly with Roarke's approval, that didn't mean he was obliged to comply.

He might have been out of the game, but he certainly wasn't out of shape. To assume he couldn't handle himself, defend himself, on a public street was insulting.

As it was his half-day off, he intended to stroll along Madison Avenue, do a bit of personal shopping, perhaps have a light lunch alfresco at one of his favored bistros, then if his mood held, visit a gallery before returning home and to his duties.

A civilized few hours, he thought, *that would not be disrupted by the hulking presence of the nosy and pitifully inefficient police.*

The fact that he could imagine, with some glee, Eve's fury and frustration when it was reported to her that the target had vanished, barely entered into it.

Still his thin face held a mildly smug expression as he nipped out a third-story window of a small luxury hotel, engaged the emergency escape, rode quietly down to street level, and strode purposefully to the neighboring building to take the people glide back over to Madison.

Imagine, he thought, *anyone believing a couple of clumsy-footed badges could keep up with me.*

He paused at a neighborhood market, perused the sidewalk display of fresh fruit, and finding it woefully substandard, made a mental note to order some peaches from one of Roarke's agri-domes.

There would be peach melba for dessert that evening.

Still, the grapes looked reasonably promising, and he was aware Roarke liked to support local merchants. *Perhaps a pound of the mixed green and red,* he mused, plucking one of each color from their varitoned stems.

The merchant, a small barrel of a man plugged onto two short legs, scurried out, yipping like a terrier. He was Asian, a fourth-generation grocer. His family had run that same market, in that same spot, for nearly a century.

For the past several years, he and Summerset had gone a round or two, once a week, to their mutual satisfaction.

"You eat it, brother, you buy it!"

"My good man, I am not your brother, nor do I buy pigs in pokes."

"What pig? Where do you see a pig? Two grapes." He stuck out his hand. "Twenty credits."

"Ten credits a grape?" Summerset sniffed with his long nose. "I'm amazed you can make such a statement with a straight face."

"You ate my grapes, you pay for my grapes. Twenty credits."

Enjoying himself, Summerset gave a weary sigh. "I may be persuaded to buy a pound of your mediocre grapes, for display purposes only. Consumption is out of the question. I will pay in dollars. One pound, eight dollars."

"Ha! You're trying to rob me, as usual." An event the grocer looked forward to every week. "I'll call the beat droid. One pound, twelve dollars."

"If I paid such an exorbitant amount, I would either require psychiatric treatment or I would be forced to sue you for extortion. Then your lovely wife and children would be obliged to visit you in prison. As I don't want such a responsibility, I will pay you ten dollars, and no more."

"Ten dollars for a pound of my beautiful grapes? It's a crime. But I'll take it because then you'll go away before your sour face spoils my fruit."

The grapes were bagged, the money taken, and both men turned away well satisfied.

Summerset tucked the bag in the crook of his arm, and continued his stroll.

New York, he thought, *such a city, such marvelous characters everywhere you look.* Of all the places he'd traveled, and there had been many, this American city, so full of energy and life and irritability, was by far his favorite.

As he neared the corner he watched a glide-cart operator argue with a customer. The operator's born-and-bred-in-Brooklyn accent flattened the English language like a sweaty heavyweight flattened an opponent.

A maxibus rumbled to the curb, braked with a wheeze and a belch, and disgorged a flurry of passengers. They came in all sizes and shapes, in a cacophony of languages and a hodgepodge of purposes.

And all, of course, were in a hurry to get somewhere else immediately.

He stepped back so as not to be jostled and kept mindful of his pockets. Street thieves were known to pay the bus fare for its easy plucking opportunities.

As he turned, he felt a faint prickle on the back of his neck. *Cop?* he wondered. Had they picked up his trail again? He shifted slightly, angling himself so that he could use a shop window as a dull mirror to scan the street and sidewalk behind him.

He saw nothing but the busy and the annoyed, and the small flood of tourists who enjoyed gawking at the display of wares on Madison.

But his antenna continued to quiver. Casually, he shifted his bag of grapes, slipped a hand in his pocket, and slid into the crowd.

The glide-cart vendor was still fighting with the language and his customer, passengers were still pushing their way on or off the maxibus. Out of the corner of his eye, he saw his grocer friend hyping his produce to passersby.

There was a soft whirl overhead as a traffic copter made its rounds.

He nearly relaxed, nearly told himself he'd allowed the police tag to make him edgy and foolish. Then he caught the quick flash of movement.

Instinct kicked in. He pivoted. His hand came out of his pocket, and his body was braced and set. For an instant, he was face-to-face with Sylvester Yost.

The pressure syringe skimmed over his ribs, missing its true mark as Summerset continued his pivot. His hand shot up, and the stunner in it scraped along Yost's shoulder.

As Yost's arm went dead, the syringe dropped to the sidewalk to be crushed under the feet of rushing commuters. The men were shoved hard together, held there a moment like long-lost lovers, then pushed roughly apart by the stream fighting to pour onto the bus before the doors slammed shut.

Summerset's vision blurred at the edges, tried to narrow down to a slit. He fought to clear it, to keep his balance, and would certainly have gone down if the press of bodies hadn't kept him upright.

On rubbery knees he tried to lunge forward. The faint buzzing in his ears was like an awakening nest of hornets.

His body moved too slowly, as through syrup, and his hand, still gripping the stunner, missed Yost, took down a shocked and innocent tourist from Utah, and had his terrified wife screaming for the police.

As Summerset stumbled clear, he could do nothing but watch Yost, one arm dangling uselessly, rush for the corner, and disappear.

He managed two steps in pursuit before the world went gray and he went down hard on his knees. When he was hauled to his feet, he struggled weakly.

"Sick? Are you sick?" The grocer dragged him clear, quickly stuffing the illegal stunner back in Summerset's pocket. "You need to sit down. Walk. You need to walk with me."

Through the wash of noise in his head, Summerset recognized the familiar voice. "Yes." His tongue was thick, and the words slurred like a drunk's. "Yes, thank you."

The next thing he remembered clearly was sitting in a small room crowded with crates and boxes and smelling like ripe bananas. The grocer's wife, a pretty woman with smooth golden cheeks, was holding a glass of water to his lips.

He shook his head, tried to take stock of his reaction and pinpoint the kind of tranq Yost had managed to get into him. *A small dose,* he thought, but powerful enough to cause dizziness, mild nausea, and weakening of the limbs.

"I beg your pardon," he said as clearly as he could manage. "Could I trouble you for some Wake-Up, or one of the generic brands of its kind? I require a stimulant."

"You look very ill," she said kindly. "I'll call for the MTs."

"No, no, I don't require the medical technicians. I have some training. I simply need a stimulant."

The grocer spoke softly in Korean to his wife. She sighed, passed him the water, and left the room.

"She will get you what you need." The grocer crouched so that he could study Summerset's glassy eyes. "I saw the man you fought with. You got him, but not too good. He got you better, I think."

"I dispute that." Then on an oath, Summerset was forced to lower his head between his knees.

"You got the bystander best of all. He's out flat." Amusement filtered through his voice. "The cops'll be looking for you. And you ruined my lovely grapes."

"My grapes. I paid for them."

Eve shrugged into her jacket, kicked her desk, and tried to decide if she should alert Roarke that Summerset had, as Roarke had predicted, shaken her police tag.

The hell with it, she thought. She had to get into the field. She was dumping the problem of Summerset into Roarke's lap.

Even as she stepped toward the 'link, the problem walked into her office.

"What the hell are you doing here?"

"Believe me, Lieutenant, this visit is every bit as distasteful for me as it is for you." Summerset glanced around her cramped office, skimmed his elegant gaze over her stingy window, her lumpy chair. Sniffed. "No, I see it could never be as distasteful for you."

She walked around him, shut her door with a bad-tempered slam. "You ditched my men."

"I may have to live under the same roof as a cop, but I certainly am not obliged to have them following me around on my free time." He sneered, feeling much more like himself again. "They were inept and obvious. If you were going to insult me, the least you could have done was engage adequately trained individuals."

She wasn't going to argue. She'd plucked two of the best available trackers. And both of them had already taken a lashing from the sharpest edge of her tongue. "If you're here to file a citizen's complaint, see the desk sergeant. I'm busy."

"I'm here, against my best judgment, to give a statement. I prefer discussing this with you, under the circumstances. I don't wish to trouble Roarke."

"Trouble him?" Her gut clenched. "What happened?"

He glanced at the choice of seats again, sighed, then opted to give his statement standing.

He had to give her credit. After one explosive oath, she fell silent. She listened, her eyes narrowed, flat as a shark's and just as ruthless.

When he was done giving what he felt was an admirably concise and thorough statement, she hammered him with questions over points he'd never considered.

Yes, he habitually stopped at that market, at that time, on his half-day. He most often observed the maxibus stop there as he enjoyed the rough ballet, so to speak, of passengers.

Yost had come up behind him, slightly to the left side. Yes, he himself was right-handed.

Yost had been wearing a sandy wig, a brush cut, military style, and a pearl gray overcoat. Light material, though it had been warm enough to go without a topcoat. The stunner had brushed Yost on his right shoulder, causing him to drop the syringe before the full dose could be administered.

It had, apparently, caught the bystander midchest, but he was recovering well from that and the minor scrapes and bruises received on his trip down to the sidewalk.

"Does anyone know you were carrying an illegal weapon?"

"The grocer. Otherwise, I told the beat droid Yost had the stunner, and had attempted to attack me with it and hit the unfortunate man from Utah instead. I did, however, give the man's wife my card so that all medical expenses could be sent to me. It was the least I could do."

"The least you could have done was let me and my men

do our jobs. If you hadn't ditched the tag, we might have nabbed him when he went for you."

"Perhaps," Summerset said evenly, "if you had been courteous enough to discuss your plans that involved me *with* me, rather than sneak behind my back, I might have cooperated."

"My ass."

"Quite correct, but we never explored the possibility. As it is, I managed to defend myself quite satisfactorily, made him extremely uncomfortable. It cost me some minor embarrassment and ten dollars' worth of overpriced grapes."

"You think this is a joke? Is this a fucking joke?"

His jaw tightened. "No, Lieutenant, I don't. If I found it even marginally amusing, I would not be in a police station. But I am here, voluntarily, and have given you a statement in the hopes this information may in some way assist you in your investigation."

"You can assist me in my investigation by sitting your tight ass down until I arrange for a black-and-white to take you home."

"I will not ride in a police vehicle."

"You damn well will. You're a known target. I've got enough to worry about without having you dance around the city with a bull's-eye on your butt. From this moment on, you'll do exactly what I tell you, or I'll—"

She broke off as her door opened and Roarke came in.

"Oh yeah, come right in, don't bother to knock. It's old home week."

"Eve" was all he said, brushing a hand over her arm. But his eyes were riveted to Summerset's face. "Are you all right?"

"Yes, of course." *Should have known*, Summerset thought with a vicious tug of guilt. He should have known Roarke would learn of the incident almost before it was over. "I've just given the lieutenant my statement of the events. I intended to contact you when I returned home."

"Did you?" Roarke murmured. "One of the MTs called to the scene recognized you when you checked on an injured man. He managed to pass the word up to me before you did."

"I'm sorry. I had hoped to reassure you that there was no harm done. As you can see, I was unhurt."

"Do you think I'm going to tolerate this?" Roarke spoke softly, in a tone that warned Eve the teeth of temper were ready to snap and bite.

"There's nothing to tolerate. It's done and over."

Her eyebrows went up. It was the voice of a patient father chastising a son. Her gaze cut to Roarke, saw the temper shimmer.

"All right, over and done. I've made arrangements for you to have a holiday. You have the next two weeks off. I suggest you use the chalet in Switzerland. It's one of your favorites."

"It's not convenient for me to holiday at the moment. Thank you all the same."

"Pack what you need. Your transpo will be ready in two hours."

"I'm not leaving."

"I want you out of the city, and now. If the chalet doesn't suit you, go where you like. But you will go."

"I have no intention of going anywhere."

"Fuck it. You're fired."

"Very well. I will remove my belongings and book a hotel until—"

"Oh, shut up. Both of you shut the hell up." She fisted her hands in her hair, yanked fiercely. "Just my luck, you finally say the words I've been waiting over a year to hear and I can't do my happy dance. You expect him to put his tail between his skinny legs and hide?" she demanded of Roarke. "You think when you're in the middle of this kind of mess he's just going to bop over to Switzerland and yodel, or whatever the hell they do there?"

"You of all people should understand why it's necessary to remove him from immediate danger. Yost missed. He'll be angry, his pride in his work will be damaged. He'll come in again, and harder."

"Which is why Summerset will be escorted home to that fortress we live in, and stay there, in protective custody, until I say different."

"I will not agree to such—"

"I said shut up!" She rounded on Summerset, taking one step that put her directly between both furious men. She could all but feel the bullets of heat and rage shooting out of each of them. "Do you want him sick with worry over you? Do you want him grieving if you make a mistake and something happens to you? Maybe your pride's too big for you to swallow comfortably, pal, but it's not too big for me to shove down your throat. You're both going to do what I tell you, or I'm charging you"—she drilled a finger into Summerset's chest—"with carrying a concealed. And you"—she whipped around to Roarke and gave him the same treatment—"with interfering with a police procedure. I'll toss you in a cage together and let you fight it out while I finish the damn job. But what I won't do is stand here and listen to the pair of you bicker like a couple of kids."

Roarke gripped her arm, fingers digging in like vises before he found some tattered threads of control. Saying nothing, he turned and walked out.

"Well, wasn't that fun?"

"Lieutenant."

"Shut up, just shut the hell up a minute." She stalked to her window, stared out hard. "You're the only thing he brought with him from the past that he values."

Emotion wavered over Summerset's face. Suddenly, even his bones felt weary. He lowered himself into her chair. "I'll give you my full cooperation, Lieutenant. Shall I wait here while you arrange my transportation?"

"Here's fine."

"Lieutenant," he said before she reached the door. Their eyes met. "It isn't just pride. I can't leave him. He's . . . he's mine."

"I know it." She let out a sigh. "I'll get a couple of guys in soft clothes in an unmarked to take you home. That should take some of the sting out of it." She opened the door, and turned back with a sneer to steady them both. "Next time he fires you, pal, I'm doing laps in champagne."

chapter nineteen

Eve dealt with the transportation, assigned a couple of uniforms to head over to Madison and interview shopkeepers who might have seen Yost flee the scene. Though she didn't put out much hope it would lead to anything, she ordered them to hunt up the maxibus driver for a statement.

Then she gathered up Peabody and went down to the garage.

"He'll stay put? Summerset?"

"Yeah, he'll stay put. If I doubted it, I'd lock him up. Right now, I'm more worried about . . . well, hmmm," she finished when she saw the object of her concern leaning against the side of her vehicle. "I have a feeling I'm going to need a minute here, Peabody."

"God, he looks so sexy when he's pissed. Can I watch?"

"Stand a minimum of five parking slots away, back turned." She took one step forward. "Record off," she added and heard her aide mutter, "Party pooper."

"You're loitering, ace," Eve said to Roarke. "Get moving or I'll call garage security."

"I want him out of the country." His voice was a whip, slashing clean.

"Even you can't always have what you want."

"And you're the last person I'd have expected to stand in my way on this."

"Yeah, and I'm not real thrilled about it. Summerset is now a material witness. He stays in the city, in protective custody. End of story."

"Fuck your protective custody. Your cops couldn't manage to stay on him for six blocks. Do you think I'd trust them with him now?"

"Don't you mean trust me?"

"Apparently it comes to the same."

That slash hurt, cutting deep across the belly. "You're right, it does, and I let you down. I'm sorry."

Emotion, violent and hot, sprang into his eyes. She braced for them, prepared to let him blast at her until he'd cleared out the turmoil. Instead he turned away, rested his hands on the roof of her vehicle.

"God. Would you stand there and let me slap at you? Have I gone that far over?"

"You've done it for me plenty of times. Point is, I picked the men to trail him, and they lost him. So, it's on me."

"That's bullshit."

"No, that's chain of command. Just like you figuring, because he's yours, what almost happened to him is on you. Once we both swallow that, we move to the next stage. Roarke."

She started to touch his shoulder, then stuck her hand in her pocket. "Don't ask or expect him to do what you wouldn't do yourself. I'm not happy about what happened this morning, but when it comes down to it, he handled himself. Let's give him credit for it, and get back on track."

"They would know he's important to me. What the loss of him, in that way, would do. For the money and the thrill.

Well, I've done my share of dirty deeds for the money and the thrill."

She waited a moment. "Is that an Irish thing? Deciding maybe bad stuff happens because you've been bad?"

He gave a half-laugh, turned back to her. "More a Catholic one, I suppose. It springs up at the most unexpected moments, no matter how far you stray. No, I don't think this is payment for my past. But I do think it's crept in from it, and has to be dealt with."

And deal with it he would, no matter how hurtful that might be.

"What aren't you telling me?"

"When I know for certain, I will tell you. Eve, you didn't let me down. I had no right to make you think otherwise."

"It's all right. At least I got to be there when you fired Summerset. Maybe you could wait a couple of weeks, then do it again. For real."

He smiled, trailed his fingertips over the ends of her hair. Then his gaze shifted up and over as the elevator opened. Summerset stepped out between two plainclothes cops.

Eve gave a little sigh as she watched the men lock eyes. There were things between them she would never fully understand. "But I guess right now, you'd better go talk to him and do that manly makeup deal."

"Lieutenant?"

"Yeah, what?"

"Give me a kiss."

"Why should I?"

"Because I need it."

She rolled her eyes for form, but rose onto her toes and touched her mouth to his. "They got security cams in here, so that's all you get. I've got places to go. Peabody!"

Still she waited until Roarke had crossed the garage, walked up the line of unmarked vehicles to Summerset.

"They're like family, huh?" Peabody said as she got into

the car. "Hey! That makes you sort of like Summerset's daughter-in-law."

Horror drained all color from Eve's cheeks. All she could do was press a hand to her stomach. "Jesus, I feel sick."

The Minces were staying in what the hotel called their Executive Suite, Luxury Level. This meant the room was large, airy, and separated into sitting room and bedrooms by a fancy latticed screen that bloomed with flowering vines. A corner of the sitting room was efficiently arranged into a mini-office area with a communication and data system built into a trim console so those executives fortunate enough to be able to afford the accommodations could work in style.

Mince had obviously been doing just that when Eve interrupted him. The console was humming discreetly, and there was a pot of coffee sitting on the refreshment extension.

"Oh, Lieutenant. I'd forgotten you were coming."

"I appreciate you agreeing to speak with me."

"Of course, of course, it's not a problem at all." He gave the suite a distracted look, seemed mildly surprised to find all in place. "I'm afraid I tend to bury myself in work once I begin. Poor Minnie despairs of me. I think she said she was going out to shop, or was it the beauty salon? Did you want to speak to her as well?"

"I can always arrange for that another time."

"Let me get you something. The coffee's probably fresh. I think Minnie plunked it down for me before she left."

"Thanks." She agreed because it would keep things informal, then sat on one of the pretty chairs while he fussed with cups.

"And for you, Officer?"

"If it's no trouble."

"Not at all, not at all. Such a wonderful hotel. Everything you could possibly need or want right at your fingertips. I have to admit, when Magda had the brainstorm to hold the event here, I wasn't happy. I've certainly changed my mind."

"She was set on it?"

"Ummm. She wanted the auction in New York. She had her first professional role onstage here. Though she made her true mark in film, she's never forgotten it was Broadway that gave her the first break."

"You've been together, you and Magda, a long time."

"Longer than either of us would like to remember."

"Like family," Eve said, remembering Peabody's statement.

"Oh yes, very much like family. All the ups and downs and the byways," he said as he brought over the coffee. "We've stood up for each other at weddings, held onto each other at funerals, paced the floors for each other at births. I'm godfather to her son. She's a magnificent woman. I'm honored to be her friend."

Eve said nothing while he took his seat. "Friends can be protective of friends. Sometimes too protective."

He gave her a puzzled expression. "I don't follow you."

"Does she know just how big a financial hole Vincent Lane is in this time?"

"I don't discuss the personal lives of my friends, Lieutenant. And as Magda's manager, would hardly discuss her finances or those of her son with the police."

"Even if discussing it might save her considerable grief? I'm not a reporter, Mr. Mince. I'm not here for gossip. I'm concerned with the security of your friend and her belongings."

"I hardly see what Vince's financial position has to do with security."

"You've bailed him out before, haven't you? One or the other of you. And you keep bailing him out. He sinks again. Consider this. His main meal ticket, his mother is about to give away upwards of a billion dollars. How does that sit with him?"

She caught the flicker in his gaze before he looked away. "I hardly see what—"

"Mr. Mince. I can get warrants. I can oblige you to come into Interview and ask these questions on the record. I don't want to do that, for a number of reasons. One of those reasons is my husband has a great deal of admiration and affection for your friend. I'm thinking of him, and of her, and what it could mean to both of them if there's any scandal with this auction."

"Surely you don't think Vince means to cause any trouble? He wouldn't dare."

"Does she know his current financial situation?"

Mince seemed to sink in his chair. Worry creased his forehead as he set his coffee aside. "No. I haven't told her this time. She thinks he's turned over a new leaf. She's so thrilled that he's taken such a personal interest in her foundation, in the auction . . ." He trailed off, looked back at Eve, horrified.

Then he shook his head. "But no. No. There's nothing he can do at this point to stop the event from going through. It's done, as far as the end result. All the paperwork is filed. The proceeds go to the Foundation. That's locked in. He can't stop it. It doesn't matter that he was against it initially."

"He tried to stop it?"

Mince rose, paced the room, his palms pressed together as he tried to think it through. "Yes. Yes, he argued bitterly against it. She was giving away his inheritance, his birthright. They had a terrible row over it. She'd reached the end of her rope with him, told him it was time he worked for a living, and that she would not again sail to his rescue with money to plug the holes he kept digging in his life. She said one of the benefits of the Foundation would be that she *couldn't* just pass him the money. She was setting it up that way for him, for herself, and for those who needed a helping hand."

"What happened to turn him around?"

"I don't know." He lifted his hands, spread his fingers. "He walked out on her, furious. Brought her to tears, and she doesn't shed them lightly. He was out of contact for over two weeks. None of us knew where he was. Then he came back, head bowed, full of contrition. He said she was right, of course, that he was sorry and ashamed and wanted to do everything he could to make her proud of him."

"You didn't believe him, did you?"

He opened his mouth, then let out a sigh. "Not for a minute. But she did. She adores Vince, even as she despairs of him. She was so thrilled when he asked to work on the event. And it seemed, for a time, he'd meant everything he said. Then the bills began coming in again. I had them transferred to me directly to try to spare her. I talked to him, paid them. Talked to him, paid them. Then I threatened to go to Magda. He broke down, begged me not to, promised it would be the last time."

"When was that?"

"Just before we came out East. He has been on his best behavior since, but . . ." He glanced back toward the data center. "A number of new bills have just come in today. I'm at my wit's end."

"Have any of the bills you've paid since his confrontation with his mother included transportation fees to Delta Colony or to Paris?"

Mince folded his lips into a tight line. "Both. He has friends in those places. I can't say I completely approve, though they do come from good families. There's a wildness to them, a carelessness. Vince's debts always go deeper when he's in contact with Dominic II Naples or Michel Gerade."

"Mr. Mince, can I have your permission to see the bills that came due this morning?"

"Lieutenant, I don't even share such matters with my wife. You're asking me to breach a trust."

"No, I'm asking to help you keep one." She got to her feet. "Would Vince Lane hurt his mother for financial gain?"

"Physically harm Magda? No, no, of course not. That's completely out of the question."

"There are other ways beyond the physical."

Mince's lips trembled. "Yes. Yes, there are. And yes, I'm afraid he would. He loves her. In his way, he loves her very much. But he . . . I'll bring up the data for you."

It took Eve less than thirty seconds to spot what she was looking for. "Naples Communications. One million dollars."

"Horrible," Mince said from behind her. "Vince has no need for a system of that complexity. I can't imagine what he was thinking."

"I can," Eve murmured.

"You think he'll stick to his word about not telling Magda or Lane about this?" Peabody asked as they took the elevator up to Lane's floor.

"Yeah, at least for the time being. Long enough, anyway, to give us a shot at him, and his pals."

"Screwing over his own mother. That's the lowest."

"I think murder beats that out."

They walked down the quiet hall, rang the bell beside one of the glossy double doors. Lane opened the door himself.

He was dressed casually in a spring sweater and trousers. His feet were bare, and he wore a trendy sport's wrist unit. He had a wide, perfect smile.

"Eve, how nice to see you again. Or if you're here to discuss police business, perhaps I should call you Lieutenant."

"Since I'm here to talk over some points about the auction, you decide."

He laughed, gestured her inside. "I can't tell you how glad I am that you're taking an interest. It really settles my mother's mind. Please sit, be comfortable. Liza, company!"

Lane's suite was several snazzy steps up from the Minces' suite. The living area flowed in a wide curve toward a formal dining area. Chandeliers glimmered overhead, a snow-white piano held court in a corner. A winding gold ribbon of open stairs led to a second level. And down them, brilliantly beautiful in a skinsuit as white as the piano, glided Liza.

Eve didn't think the glitters at her ears, her wrists, her neck, and her ankles were manmade. *How much did those set you back, Vinnie old pal?* she wondered.

"Hello." Liza gave a pouty little smile and fluffed her hair.

"Sorry to interrupt your day," Eve said pleasantly. "I'd hoped to confer with Vince over a few auction details. The NYPSD wants to be certain Ms. Lane's event goes smoothly."

Liza stifled a yawn. "I'll be glad when it's over. It's all anyone wants to talk about."

"It must be tedious for you."

"Well, it is. If that's all you're going to talk about, I think I'll go out and do some shopping."

"Sorry to chase you off. This shouldn't take very long," Eve said.

"Why don't I meet you?" Obviously anxious to placate, Vince moved to her, ran his hands up her arms. "Let's say twelve-thirty at Rendezvous. We'll have lunch."

"Maybe." The corners of her mouth turned up, and she trailed a finger down the middle of his chest. "You know how I love to be with you, baby doll. Don't be late."

"I won't."

She picked up a handbag from the table by the door, blew Lane kisses, and strolled out.

"All the business and security and publicity work over the past few days has been boring for her," Lane said. "She's been awfully patient."

"Yeah, a real trooper." Eve wandered to one of the three antique sofas, sat on an arm of silk. "You're very involved with the auction, and your mother's foundation. Takes up a lot of your time."

"That it does. But it's worth it."

"No problem seeing her chuck a billion dollars out the window?"

"All for a good cause," he said cheerfully. "I couldn't be more proud of her."

"Really? Even when you're flat broke and siphoning off loans for debts from her friends?" She waited a beat while his body jerked. "Wow, Vince, you're a hell of a sport."

"I don't know what you're talking about, and I find your comments in very bad taste."

"I find plots to steal from family and charity in very bad taste. I find little skunks who're too lazy to work for a living in very bad taste. But most of all, I find murder in very bad taste. Your guy missed his target this morning, by the way. You want to make sure he doesn't collect the rest of his fee on that portion of the contract."

"I want you to leave." He pointed a finger at the door in what would have been a dramatic gesture if his arm hadn't trembled. "I want you to get out. I intend to report this behavior to your superiors. I intend to consult my attorney. I intend—"

"Why don't you shut up, you miserable excuse for a humanoid. Peabody, record on."

"Yes, sir."

"Vincent Lane," Eve began, "you have the right to remain silent."

"You're arresting me?" The color that had drained from his cheeks bloomed back violently. "You think you can arrest me? You have no cause, you have no case, you have nothing on me whatsoever. Do you know who I am?"

"Yeah, I know who you are. You're scum. Now, you're going to sit down while I read you the rest of your rights and obligations. Then you're going to sit there and answer my questions. Because if you don't, I'm going to haul you downtown, into Interview. And somehow along the way, the media's going to get wind of it. By the time you're supposed to be meeting your girlfriend for lunch, it'll be all over the screen how Vince Lane has been arrested for suspicion of conspiracy to commit grand larceny, conspiracy to transfer stolen goods, and a whole bunch of other fun little conspiracies, too—topped off with the whopper. Conspiracy to commit murder."

"Murder! You're crazy. You've lost your mind. I never killed anyone. I'm calling my lawyer."

"You do that." Eve spoke mildly and stretched out her legs. "You go right on and do that. Wonder how long it'll take your friends Gerade and Naples to find out you're hiring a rep to defend you in a murder case. Wonder how long after that they'll sic Yost on you to cover their own hides. Or maybe they won't have to hire him."

She paused, studying her nails as Lane stood frozen by his 'link. "Yeah, I'm thinking he'll do this one for free. He's got his own hide to protect. You know what he does to his victims, Vinnie?" She lifted her eyes then, locked on his without an ounce of pity. "He breaks them to pieces, then he makes sure they're conscious when he rapes them. I've got a video I can show you of how he'd take on a man like you. Snap your arm like a twig, pound your face into mush so even your mother wouldn't know you. Then when you think it can't get worse, he'd butt-fuck you. And the pain of all of that is so huge, so impossible, you can't believe it's real. It's like some horrible nightmare, some personal hell that opened up and swallowed you whole. And you won't be able to get out of it, get away from it. Not until he slips that wire around your neck and pulls it tighter. And your feet hammer on the floor. You die pissing yourself."

She got up. "Come to think of it, that's just about the perfect end for you. Go ahead and call your lawyer. Let's get it started."

"No one was supposed to get hurt." Tears spurted from his eyes, spilled down his face. "It's not my fault."

"It never is with people like you." She pointed to the sofa. "Sit down, and tell me why you're not to blame."

"I needed money." He rubbed his eyes, then glugged the water Peabody had brought to him. "Mother got this insane idea to auction off her things, so many of her things, and just give it away. This damn foundation idea of hers. I'm her son." He shot her a glance that begged for pity. "Why should she give all that money to strangers when I need it?"

"So you needed to figure a way to keep it in the family."

"We argued. She said she was cutting me off. She'd said that before, but I thought this time she might have meant it. I was so angry. She's my mother," he said, looking to Eve for understanding.

"You went to see your friends."

"Needed to blow off steam. I went to see Dom. You wouldn't catch his father shoveling money to strangers like this. Dom never has to worry how he's going to pay a fucking bill. We were just talking, having a few drinks. I said something like, I should just take the stuff, sell it myself, and see how she liked it. We were just talking about how it could be done. Just talk. Then it started looking like maybe it could be done. Hundreds of millions of dollars. I'd never have to worry again. I could live the way I chose, with no one to answer to.

"I guess I got pretty drunk. I passed out, and the next

thing I know it's morning and Dom's talked to his old man. It just started rolling. We got Michel, went down to see him, and talk about it. It still seemed unreal, you know. Just like a game. But Dom's old man, he said we could do it. He knew how to set it up. We'd each take a percentage after expenses. It was business, that's all. Nobody said anything about murder. Just business."

"When did Yost come into the mix?"

"I don't know. I swear to God. We had it planned out. I was to go back, make it up with my mother, and ask to help out. Get involved in the setup so I could pass on information. That's when I found out she'd hooked up with Roarke. I didn't like that part of it. You hear things about Roarke. But Naples, he liked it a lot. Said it added spice. He brought in another partner, the German guy, and because Dom and I were tied up with other business, they met with Michel in Paris."

He licked his lips, searching Eve's face for support, for understanding. For mercy. And saw nothing but the cold, clear eyes of cop. "I think, they must . . . I don't know. They must have cooked up bringing Yost in during those meetings. All I knew then was that the German had pulled out. Naples called him a fish belly. But it left more for us, and Naples was going to arrange the transpo personally. He hired on a couple more guys. It was starting to make me nervous, all those expenses. But when I complained, it got nasty. Dom said how it was best for me to let him deal with his father direct from then on. He'd pass instructions to me. All I had to do was give them the details, the timing, pass along the security scheme, and keep my mother happy. They said they had a way to keep Roarke occupied and off my back."

He rubbed his mouth with the back of his hand. "You can see, can't you, you can see that I was in too deep to back out. You can see how it wasn't my fault. And now I'm cooperating, right? That makes a big difference."

"Oh yeah. You want to keep cooperating, Vince. You want to keep going."

"Yeah, I'll tell you everything I know. See, just a few weeks ago, Dom gets in touch. He says I have to come up with a million for a consult fee, that's my share of it. It's to go into Naples Communications, and they'll fix the books so it'll look like I've bought some swank new system. I went nuts. A fucking million. I don't have that kind to outlay. I wasn't looking at that kind of an expense. What the hell kind of consult runs a million for just my share?"

He buried his head in his hands. "And he told me. He told me about Yost, he told me about the contract, the murders. And he said there was no backing out now. We were in it all the way, so I should beg, borrow, or steal my part of the fee because once the contract was complete, Yost was going to want his money. I didn't know what to do. What was I supposed to do? She started it, cutting me out of what was mine. It's not my fault."

"Yeah, I can see how your mother's to blame for all this. You want to live, Vince? You want me to make sure Yost doesn't come hunting you? Start filling in details. Give me names."

"I don't have much." He lifted his head again. "I figured out they were leaving me out of the loop. Using me. They're the ones who should pay for all this. They're the ones you should go after."

"Oh, don't worry about that. They're going to pay."

While Eve was working to draw a more concise and thorough statement from Lane, Roarke walked into his home. He checked the security panel, noted that Mick was enjoying a dip in the pool.

He took the long way around to give himself time.

The pool house smelled of hot flowers and cool water. There was the musical sound of a fountain, spraying and tumbling, playing under the blast of the Irish rebel songs Mick had chosen to keep him company while he did laps.

Roarke walked over, chose one of the thick blue towels from the stack, and went to wait by the side of the pool.

Mick slapped a hand on the edge, shook his hair out of his eyes, and peered up at Roarke. "Ya coming in?"

"No. You're coming out."

"That I am." Mick stood up, let the water stream off him for a moment, then walked up the steps. "Christ, that's the kind of small pleasure a man could grow used to. Thanks," he added, taking the towel Roarke handed him and rubbing it briskly over his face.

There were guest robes hanging nearby. Mick selected one, bundled in. "Don't expect a man of your means and responsibilities to pop home middle of the day."

"I had an interruption this morning. You know, Mick, in all the times we've had, good and bad, all we've done together and apart, you were the last I'd have expected to come at a friend from the back."

Slowly, Mick lowered the towel. "What's your meaning?"

"Does friendship come so much cheaper these days than it did when we were lads?"

"Nothing comes cheaper these days, God knows." He looked baffled. "Come out straight with it, Roarke. You've put me in the dark."

"You want it straight?"

"Aye."

"Then here it is." He rammed his fist into Mick's face and watched his childhood friend topple backward into the pool.

Weighed down by the sopping robe, blood streaming from his mouth, Mick surfaced. There was blood in his eye as well as he lunged for the side of the pool.

But it had faded, nearly turned into a glint of humor as he hauled himself out again.

"Fuck it, you've still got a fist like a brick." He wiggled his jaw, stripped off the wet robe. "How'd you figure it out?" he began, then lifted a hand. "No, if you don't mind, I'd rather have some pants on and a whiskey in my hand when you tell me."

"All right." Roarke nodded coolly. "We'll go upstairs together." He strode toward the elevator. "Summerset's fine, by the way."

"Why wouldn't he be?" Mick asked easily, and stepped in with Roarke.

chapter twenty

Roarke waited, standing by the south window while Mick put on trousers. He kept his hands in his pockets, his eyes on the trees, and the high stone wall beyond them.

He'd used the trees, the lavish roll of lawn, the flowers, and that stone, to build a place. His place. A spot of beauty and comfort in a world that held too much pain. He'd used it, he knew, to prove to himself that the slums and miseries of Dublin were far behind him, too far behind to pant hot breath on his neck.

And so he had invited into that place, that home, a reminder of what had never really stopped chasing him. He'd invited in a friend of his childhood who had become a betrayer of his present.

"Was it only for the money, Mick? Was it only for the profit?"

"Sure it's easy for you to say that in a deriding voice, Your Highness, when you're rolling in the stuff. Of course it was for the money. Jesus, my take will top twenty-five million at a coast. And it was for the fun. Have you really forgotten how much bloody *fun* it is?"

"Have you forgotten, Mick, that however shaky the code might be, it sticks when it comes to betraying a friend?"

"Well, for God's sake, Roarke, it's not like it was *your* money I'm after putting in my pocket." Mick sighed, and buttoning his shirt walked over to fetch the decanter of whiskey. He poured two glasses, and when Roarke still didn't turn at the sound of striking glass, shrugged and sipped his own.

"All right, I admit it was a fine line, and maybe I've stomped over to the other side of it. I've a bit of envy in me for what you've managed to accumulate over the years since we parted ways."

"A fine line?" Thinking of brutal and senseless murder, Roarke did turn. "Is that what it is to you?"

"Listen." Impatient now, and a little embarrassed by it all, Mick gestured with his glass. "I was approached about the job. The actress's son started the ball rolling, and it gathered some steam. By the time it got to me, it was well-formed. The truth is, I didn't think you'd mind so much. Over the past few days I've come to see I miscalculated that end of it considerably. But I was too far into the matter to back out. Now, of course . . ." He shrugged again, casting off millions as he might a missed meal. "How the devil do you figure it? How'd you know a heist was in the works, and pin it down to me?"

"Connections, Mick." Studying his friend's face, Roarke began to do fresh calculations. "Magda's son to Naples's son, to Hinrick, to Gerade. I found it odd you never mentioned Naples as a possible when Eve asked you about the Hagues in Cornwall."

"Name sort of stuck in my throat, seeing the position I was in. As for Hinrick, he stepped out even before I was in it," Mick told him. "Pissed Naples off royal, I'm told. So you knew about the boy. Pitiful little weasel that gorgeous example of female managed to birth if you're asking me. Had every advantage all of his useless life and still whines for more. Didn't make his own, like you and me."

Mick glanced around the room. He'd enjoyed his stay, on a great many levels. But it looked like he'd be packing his bags sooner than later. "So, what do we do now? You aren't going to turn me over to your lovely wife, the cop, are you? After all, I've not done anything as yet, in actuality."

"I want Naples."

"Ah, now, Roarke, you're putting my ass in a sling there."

"And Yost."

"What in God's green earth have I to do with the likes of Sylvester Yost?"

"You're Naples's man and so is he. And he's killed two of my people so that the lot of you can get closer to the money."

"You're talking gibberish. Yost's not in this. True enough Naples might've put him on Britt and Joe, God rest them. But that's nothing to do with my dealings with the man. I've never met Yost, thank the saints. Never had truck with him. You know that's not my style."

"It hasn't been, but it's been a long time between for us, Mick. Naples set me up, and he's used two of my people like pawns. Today, Yost went for Summerset."

"Summerset?" The liquor left in Mick's glass sloshed. "You're trying to tell me Naples set Yost on Summerset? You've got to be mistaken. What purpose would there be in . . ."

His eyes never left Roarke's, but they went wide. As his color drained, he reached out blindly for the back of a chair. Levering himself around it, he sat.

"Oh Jesus. Oh Christ Jesus." Because his hands shook, he vised them around the glass, downed the rest of the whiskey. "Are you sure of this? Are you without a doubt sure of this?"

"I am." After a moment, Roarke crossed over, picked up the bottle. He brought it back and filled Mick's glass again. "He's killed two people who work for me, the second being a friend as well. It scatters the focus, draws the police—in the name of my lovely wife—off any scent there might be around the auction."

"No, no, that's why I'm here. To keep you occupied, to get close. That, and me being one of the few around who could set a workable scheme for a job like this. I was to whet your interest in a deal or two. If your cop wasn't busy on her own, I was to keep the two of you bustling around me on a personal level. Charm her, so to speak. And being right inside the house, I'd know, you see, of any changes you'd be making for the security. In addition to that, I could keep the arm on Magda's boy if he waffled. Liza has him under control, but—"

"Ah, I wondered about her. My cop has been busy on her own, hasn't she, Mick? And myself as well. If they'd succeeded with Summerset today, just how much of my attention do you think I'd have left to give to the auction?"

"I didn't know of this." Mick squared his shoulders, looked Roarke dead in the eye. "I swear that to you on my life. I would never have done this. It was a big job, an exciting one, and it gave me the added boost of finally being able to best you in something. I never could, and always wanted to. You were never like the rest of us, you know. You always had something extra. I wanted that. I'd have stolen from you, Roarke, and enjoyed it. I'd have laughed about it, bragged on it, the rest of my days. But not this. I'd never have taken part in murder."

"That was the part I couldn't get to fit."

"Naples took out Britt and Joe? There's no question of that?"

"None."

"And tried for Summerset as well." Mick nodded. "I see how it is then." He drew a long breath. "There are two men inside. One in your special security, one in the hotel. Honroe and Billick. The job's set for tomorrow. Two in the morning, precisely. At that time a maxibus and a car will have an accident at the east corner near the hotel. The bus will turn over, slide into the jewelry shop. They've hired a hell of a driver. Do you remember Kilcher?"

"I do."

"This is his son, and he's even better than his old man. There'll be a small fire, and an enormous mess. The cops, the security, even the fire department will be out there, dealing with it, handling the looters, and so forth. At the same moment, a delivery van will pull into the proper entrance of the hotel. We'll be six, and armed with tranqs. We'll take out those of your staff we must. I'll be handling your security. I've worked it to jam to give us a twelve-minute window. Couldn't widen it more than that, and that alone took me six months of hideous work.

"Your security's a marvel, and that's a fact. I'd never have made a crack in it without the men on the inside."

"That's little satisfaction at the moment."

"I suppose that's true. Still, I'm likely the only one live and kicking who could have widened that crack on you. So. Each team member has assigned goods to pluck. Every one of them must get it done and be out of the room within ten minutes. Gives them two to get back to the exit point. Anyone not there gets left behind."

He rose, set his glass aside. "I'll get my equipment and discs, so you can see how it's meant to be." He hesitated. "I should have known better than to tie myself up with the likes of Naples. I've no excuses for that mistake, and you've my word I'll do what I can to make up for it. Will you give me over to the cops then?"

Roarke met his eyes, held them. And saw all the miseries. "No."

Eve burst into the house, all but choking on her own rage. She swung toward the stairs even as Summerset slid into the hall. "Where are they?" she demanded.

"Roarke is in his private office. Lieutenant—"

"Later. Goddamn it." She pounded up the stairs, streaked

down the hall. She had a hand on her weapon when she coded herself into Roarke's private room.

He wasn't behind the console, but leaning back against it, his eyes tracking the data and diagrams on his wall screens. His unregistered equipment hummed softly.

"Where's Connelly?"

Roarke continued to study, to access. He'd nearly come to the conclusion they'd have managed to pull it off. Son of a bitch. "He isn't here."

"I need to find him, now. The bastard's part of this."

"Yes, I know."

His comment was so mild, she was two beats behind before it sank in. "You know? How long have you known?" She marched up to him, blocking his view of the screens. "What the hell kind of game are you playing here?"

"No game at all."

No, she saw that now. His voice might have been calm, but his eyes weren't. "When did you clue into him?"

"I suspected when we realized the auction items were the target. I told you there are only a few who could handle a job of this nature. He's one of them."

"And you didn't bother to tell me that."

"No, I didn't tell you because I had to be sure. Now I am."

"And you're sure because?"

"I asked him," Roarke said simply. "And he told me. I have his notes and job plans here. They might have done it," he added with a glimmer of admiration leaking through. "If everything had gone perfectly, if there'd been absolutely no mistakes, no unknowns, they might have done it."

"You asked him," Eve repeated. "Fine. Great. Where is he?"

"I don't know. I let him go."

"You—" Now she did choke. It wasn't just fury, but shock and outrage and not a little betrayal. "You just let him walk! He's a key player in my investigation, he's a fucking thief who was about to stab you in the back, and you let him go?"

"Yes. I have everything he knows about your investigation, about what was done and what's planned. It won't be much help to you regarding Yost. Mick didn't know Yost had been brought in."

"There's a lot of I-didn't-know going around. You had no right to let him go. No *right* to interfere in police business. And no goddamn sense to toss him back out on the street."

"Eve—"

"Goddamn it, Roarke, *goddamn* it. Two people are dead. Summerset might have been. I've just finished sweating Vincent Lane for two hours to get details, to get closer, and to scare him into keeping his mouth shut so the rest of the players aren't alerted. I had to get the PA to deal him down to a single charge and offer witness protection to get him to agree to fake a medical emergency. The asshole's in a posh room at the hospital, zoned out on drugs so he can't talk to anyone."

"That was clever of you. He certainly wouldn't have managed to maintain his role unless he was drugged. And since Liza is part of this, it's best he's out of her bed."

She lifted her hands, felt them clench, then whirled away before she could do something violent. "Yeah, real clever. And now you set Connelly loose. He'll spring to Naples, and they'll abort the job. Your reputation will be safe and sound. And I've lost another link to Yost."

"He won't go to Naples."

"Bullshit. He'll—"

"He won't," Roarke repeated. "If I believed that, or if I had any doubt he was out of the loop on Yost, I'd have done worse than turn him over to you. But I have none. I couldn't give him to you, Eve. I don't expect you to understand."

"Oh, that's real considerate of you. Let's hope you understand the next time we find a silver wire on a body that your skewed sense of loyalty cost someone their life."

He didn't speak, but his eyes, hot and blue, held hers for a long moment. In them she saw her lance had found its mark.

Oh yeah, she thought miserably, *I got some great aim.*

He turned back to the console. "I have all the data on the plans. I've made copies for you. Forewarned, my security will be able to handle it, but I assume you'll want to be there with your team. You'll have Naples and the rest within thirty-six hours."

And if someone died before then? he thought. *If I've cost a friend's life to save a friend?*

"If you have any questions," he began, then simply stopped. "I can't be other than what I am," he said quietly. "Whatever I've done to distance myself, I can't be other than what I am. Computer, copy all data on disc."

She waited while the computer completed the task, then took the discs from Roarke when he offered them.

"I hope to God he was worth it," she said, and left him alone.

She called her team first, requested they convene at her home office, then headed to Mick's room to toss it in hopes she'd find some clue where he'd gone.

She was ripping through the bureau when Summerset came in and froze in absolute horror.

"Lieutenant! That is a Chippendale, a valuable antique that must be treated with respect."

"A lot of things need to be treated with respect, and don't get it."

She dumped the empty drawer aside, and turned to drag the bedspread and sheets off the bed.

"Stop it! Stop it at once." He snagged the duvet, tugged. "This is antique Irish lace over silk."

"Look, ace, I'm in the mood to bash someone's face in, and yours is looking pretty good to me." She yanked, he yanked, and they snarled at each other over the tug-of-war.

She let go abruptly and had the satisfaction of watching

him stumble back three steps before coming up hard against the wall.

"When did he leave? Connelly? What did he take with him? What was his transpo?"

Summerset merely sucked air through his nose.

"Look, you know what he did, what he planned to do. Roarke would have filled you in by now." *You,* she thought with some bitterness, *but not me.* "You want him to get away with it?"

"It's not my decision."

"Hell with that. They sent Yost after you."

"Mick would not have had a part in that arrangement."

She threw up her hands, kicked the bed hard enough to make Summerset leap forward to check for damage. "What is wrong with you people? Connelly is involved up to his teeth. You had no business, Roarke had no damn right, to let him walk out of this house."

"What choice did he have?" Satisfied the antique footboard had sustained no damage, he turned to study her. "Do you understand him so little, after all?"

"Does he understand me so little," she shot back. "After all."

Summerset laid the now-wrinkled duvet on the bed. He owed her something, he thought, for the morning. "You feel he betrayed you by standing for his friend."

"A friend doesn't plot to steal from a friend."

Summerset smiled. "Mick wouldn't have thought of it that way. Neither, at the bottom of it, would Roarke. You do. You're angry, and you have a right to your anger. But it will burn off. Roarke suffers, and that will fester. Is that what you want for him?"

He stepped out of the room.

Tired, frustrated, Eve sat on the bed. The cat padded in, leaped up. He turned three tight circles, kneaded the silk and lace duvet with some enthusiasm, then curled up and stared directly into her face.

"Don't you start on me. You slept with the guy, for God's sake. What does that make you?"

She put out an all-points on Michael Connelly, though she expected he would be well into the wind. Her only hope was that word didn't spread from Mick to Naples to Yost before she closed in.

But even if the heist was aborted, she believed Yost would stick. He'd contracted for Summerset, and he wasn't the type to leave a job unfinished. It would give her time.

And if she was lucky, very lucky, she could use Yost to hook Naples. Her case would not be closed in her mind until she had them both.

"We proceed on the assumption that the hotel will be the target," she told her team. "Everything is set for it. Even if Connelly has bolted, Naples can still implement. He has all the data, and has gone to considerable expense. He'll want to make good on his investment."

"If Connelly goes to him," Feeney put in, "they may still try for it, but they'll shift strategy. They may hit sooner, or wait, come at it from another angle."

"Agreed. We put our counter-plan into place expecting adjustments, and expecting them to hit at any time."

"We'll need Roarke and his top security team," McNab commented.

"I'm aware of that. Feeney, would you discuss that level with Roarke?" She gestured to the adjoining door.

He got up, knocked, and passed through.

"Study the Connelly data until you know it backwards," Eve ordered, then went into the kitchen for coffee, and a moment alone.

Peabody slid her eyes toward McNab, away, then back again. She was getting damn sick of the silent treatment. *She* hadn't done anything. He was the one who had jumped right on some redhead. Oh yeah, she'd gotten the word on that minor orgy through the grapevine. Little prick.

"Have a good time on your date?"

"Oh yeah. It rocked."

"You bite."

"Is that an invitation?

She sniffed. "I don't go around with jerks who bounce on bimbos."

"I don't go around with jerkettes who bounce on LCs," he tossed back.

"At least an LC knows how to treat a woman."

"Sure, if you pay him enough." He crossed his legs, examined the toes of his new Airstream boots. "What's the matter, Peabody, Charles's calendar too full? You sound like a woman who isn't getting any."

"Screw you."

"Any time, Peabody. You can even have it for free."

She leaped up. So did he. "I wouldn't let you touch me again if you paid me."

"Fine. I don't have time on some stiff-assed, cornbread uniform."

"Break it up," Eve ordered. "Now!" If she wasn't mistaken, her aide was on the verge of tears. And McNab didn't look far behind. They were both giving her a bitch of a headache. "Private business on your own time, damn it. The two of you will work together through this, around this, or under this, I don't give a damn how you manage it. But when you're on my watch, you stand up and do the job. Is that clear?"

"Yes, sir." It came from both of them, at a mumble, and would have to satisfy.

"Peabody, check on Lane at the hospital, and see that the tag on Liza is still in place. I want an update on both. McNab, run a full analysis of Connelly's data. I want all possible adjustment scenarios on my desk within two hours."

"Sir, Roarke—"

"Did I give you an order, Detective, or ask for a discussion?"

"An order, Lieutenant."

"Then follow it." She marched to Roarke's door, pushed it open. Both he and Feeney were behind the console. Both looked up.

"Feeney, I've started McNab on an analysis. Will you see he gets started?"

"No problem."

She waited until the door shut after him. "I'm tired," she said, "I have a headache, and I'm pissed off at you."

"Well, that should about cover it."

"No, it doesn't. I don't have the time or the energy to waste having a sniping match with you like the one I just had the misfortune to overhear between Peabody and McNab. You were wrong to let Connelly go. But that's from where I stand. From where you stand, you did what you had to. We can't come together on that, but we need each other to finish this job. When it's finished, we'll have to deal with the fact that we're standing on opposite sides of a line. Until then, it's tabled."

She turned for the door, gave it a shove, and found it locked. "Unlock this door. Don't mess with me now."

"I'd prefer you shouted and got this done, but since it's not the anger so much that's driving you, you won't. I'll need a few moments of your time."

"I've done all the personal business I'm going to do right now."

"I hurt you. You see it as me choosing him over you. It wasn't."

"You're wrong." She turned around now, faced him across the room. "He hurt you, and you won't let me stand for you. You took it out of my hands and gave me no way to make it right."

"You'd have put him in a cage. Darling Eve, that wouldn't have made it right for me. You know some of what I was, and where I came from. But not all."

No, not all. He wasn't sure he himself knew or understood the all. But he could give her another part of it. "Your past comes to you in nightmares that try to eat you up from the inside. Mine, it lives in me. In corners of me. Do you know how many years it was before I ever went back to Ireland after I'd left? I don't. And it was some time after that before I ever stepped on a Dublin street. It wasn't until you went back with me to bury my friend that I went again to that part of Dublin that birthed me."

He looked down at his hands. "I used these, and my brain, and whatever else I could find to claw and steal and cheat my way out of that. And I left behind those who'd come through it all with me just as much as I left behind the dead bastard who'd made my life a misery. He damaged me, Eve, and might have made me what he was."

"No." She came forward then.

"Oh yes. He could have. Without the friends I made, and those pockets of escape I had with them, he would have. I was able to go my own way because there were those I could count on in the worst of times. When I took you with me to Dublin last year so I could wake and bury Jenny, I realized I'd never paid that back. I couldn't have turned him over, Eve, not even to you, and lived with it."

She hissed out a breath, swore. "I know it. I'm not calling off the all-points on him."

"I wouldn't expect it. Neither would he. I was to give you his apologies for the trouble he's caused, and his not saying his good-byes in person."

"Oh, please," she replied.

"He left something for you." He pulled a small vial out of his pocket, handed it to her.

"Dirt?"

"Soil, he claimed, dug from the Hill of Tara. That place of Irish kings long dead. Knowing Mick, it likely came out of our own gardens, but it's the thought, after all. It's for luck, he said, as you were the most regal of cops he'd ever had the pleasure of meeting."

"Regal, my ass."

"Well, as I said, it's the thought."

She jammed the vial in her pocket. "This regal cop hopes to have the pleasure of meeting him again, very soon. But meanwhile, we need our expert consultant, civilian, on this data analysis. I need to focus on Yost, and leave you compudroids to the tech work."

"Absolutely, Lieutenant." He came around the console, took her hand. "One other thing I think you'll be in the mood for."

"I don't have time for sex."

"There's always time for sex, but that wasn't what I meant. Just now. Yost, as Roles, holds the deed to beachfront property, and the house just completed on it in the Tropics Sector of Olympus."

"Son of a bitch."

"If you don't get him here, you'll get him there. He's contracted one of our own site decorators to outfit the place, and has a consult set four days from now. He's reserved a suite at the main casino hotel in three days' time. I've a line on private craft booked into the transpo station there. There's only one scheduled in from New York. I've transferred all the information to your home unit."

"I'm on it."

They separated into two teams, with McNab working with Roarke in his office on the security analysis. Eve kept Peabody with her as she outlined the best strategy for moving in on Yost. Feeney moved between the teams.

"The timing makes it clear Yost is waiting to go off planet until after the heist. Feeney, ask Roarke if Yost would be entitled to a share of the take over and above the assassin's fee, since one hooked to the other."

If he found anything odd about her consulting Roarke on that sort of criminal ethics, he didn't mention it.

"Says Yost could be entitled to a bonus based on the

take, but that would be transferred to him after the merchandise was transported and fenced."

"Okay, so why's he hanging? Probably wants to be certain it goes off smooth, and he's not required for any more work. And there's still Summerset on his slate. He'll be tuned to the media for news of the theft. I need to bring in Nadine."

They worked straight through until her team threatened to revolt without proper nourishment. Eve ate half a sandwich while working at her computer. She refused to budge until she'd read everything through one last time.

"Lieutenant, your eyes are going to bleed. Computer, save and hold data." Then Roarke swung her chair around before she could countermand his order. "It's after eight. You're exhausted, and the mind will only hold so much at a go. Send your team home and take a break."

"They can go. There are just a few more things I want to look over. Is Nadine still here?"

"No, she had to be on-air. You covered it with her, and she'll plant your story. You've covered everything twice over and more."

"Maybe. Where is everybody?"

"McNab's down in the kitchen talking Summerset out of a second dessert before he heads to the hotel. Peabody's taking a swim at my suggestion to clear her head, and Feeney's in my office working because his head's very nearly as hard as your own. There's nothing more you can do tonight."

"If there's not it's because I've overlooked it. I want to get some men up to Olympus, into the transpo station in case Yost gets by us here. I'll let Agent Stowe decide which end she wants to take when I fill her in."

"Which won't be until tomorrow, as you don't want her filled in too soon. Feeney," he called out and began to knead his wife's knotted shoulders. "Go home."

"In a minute. Dallas, we ought to alert Space Traffic Control in case Yost detours on his way to Olympus."

"We alert STC, it's one more tongue to wag," she called back. "You got any secure contacts with them?"

"I'll work on it. I used to have this . . ." He trailed off as he stepped in and saw Roarke bent over Eve, rubbing her shoulders. "Ah, well, you know, I think I'll head out now. I can give Peabody a lift."

"She's in the pool," Roarke told him, not so gently holding his wife down when she tried to rise.

"Yeah." Feeney's face brightened. "Wouldn't mind a quick dip myself."

"Go right ahead. You're going to eat," Roarke said to Eve.

"I did."

"A half-sandwich isn't sufficient." He glanced over as he heard voices. "Fine. We have company. You can have some soup while Mavis entertains you."

"I don't have time for—" She broke off, sighed. Mavis was already whirling into the room on six-inch platform slides that exploded with colored lights at every bouncing step.

"Hey, Dallas, hey, Roarke. Just ran into Feeney, and he said you were wrapped for the day."

"Not really, I still have some stuff. Why don't you play with Roarke while I finish up?" Her pleasure at the inspiration fractured when another woman, this one with twelve-inch coils shooting out of her head in screaming red, strolled in.

"Trina," Eve managed, and her stomach clutched with dread.

"We came by to give you the scoop and poop up close and personal," Mavis announced. "Trina got the line on the products and all, like you asked me. Right, Trina?"

"Right, and right down the line."

"That's great." *It's going to be okay,* Eve thought. *It's just business.* "What have you got?"

"Tell her, Trina. Oh, wine! Roarke, you are total." She

plunked her pretty butt in its crotch-shot skirt on Eve's desk and beamed at him as he handed around glasses of wine.

"Okay," Trina began. "You got your Youth supercover foundation, burnt honey tone, your mocha, same product. You can get them at any high-end department store or salon. Then you got your unisex powder, in both loose and compact. He went for Deloren there—that's mostly sold in salons and spa centers, 'cause it's too pricey for the regulars."

"How many spots in New York?"

"Oh, two, three dozen easy. He's got fine taste in enhancements. Cheek color's are Deloren, Youth and a nice rose quartz from Salina. The eye stuff—"

"Trina, I appreciate all this, but can you fine it down to whichever products you tagged that have limited distribution? Any stuff in there only sold wholesale maybe?"

"I'm getting to it." Trina curled her lips, currently painted vampire black. "Here's a guy who likes to experiment with enhancements, and isn't afraid to pay top dollar. Gotta admire that. From the looks of the video, he took the basics, and a few fancies. He keeps them all organized, so I could deduce . . ."

She held on to that word a moment, savoring it. "I could deduce he favors Youth and Natural Bliss. NB's hypoallergenic, all natural, and costs two left arms. Can't buy it over-the-counter. Can't get it unless you're a licensed consultant. Salon use only, not for resale. So this guy either has a license or a source 'cause he's got some of those salon-use-onlys in his drawer."

As did she, Trina thought smugly. "Happens I get it from Carnegy Enhancement Supplies on Second Avenue when I've got a client who can pay the fee."

She paused, sipped. "And it happens I took the trouble to call my pal there and ask her, on the quiet, about her customers for the products your guy had, or I figured were missing from the drawer. She said it was funny I should ask, 'cause she just got in an order for those exact products from one of her regulars. A big bald guy who comes in once or twice a year and picks up a supply. Pays in cash. Says he's got a salon in south Jersey."

Eve got slowly to her feet. "Did he pick up the order?"

"Nope. Coming in for it tomorrow, before noon. Told her to have it all put together as he was pressed for time. Ordered twice his usual, too."

"Roarke, get this woman some more wine."

"We did good?" Mavis asked, bouncing.

"You did fantastic. Trina, I need the name of your pal. I need her cooperation."

"Fine by me. But I got a question. How come you insult me?"

"Insult you? I was about to kiss you."

"How come you don't take care of my work? Look at you." Trina aimed a finger, tipped by a one-inch sapphire nail. "You look like something dragged under a maxibus. Skin's all tired, circles under your eyes."

"I've been working."

"What's that got to do with it? You can't take five minutes twice a day to show some respect for my work? When's the last time you used that exfoliant I gave you, or the pump lotion, or the stress repair?"

"Ah . . ."

"Bet you haven't had time to rub on the breast cream either." She turned on Roarke. "Some reason you can't slap some on your hands before you feel her up?"

"I do try," he said, throwing Eve to the wolves without a qualm. "She's a difficult woman."

"Let me see your feet," Trina demanded, rounding the desk.

Eve Dallas, who had faced death and spit in its eye, went into full retreat. "No. My feet are fine."

"Haven't used the pedia-care kit, have you?" Then Trina's eyes, with their rainbow lids and gold lashes, widened in shock. "Did you *cut* your hair?"

"No." Eve grabbed it with a protective hand, nearly stumbled over the chair.

"Don't you lie to me, girlfriend. You took the scissors to it, didn't you?"

"No. Not exactly. Hardly at all. I had to do it. It was getting in my eyes. I barely touched it. Damn it." She decided it was time to plant her feet. "It's my hair."

"It is not your hair, not once I've had my hands in it. Do I come down to your police station and strut around with a badge on my tit, or go out on the streets and hunt up bad guys so I can kick their ass? No! And this is what you do not do. You do not, ever in this lifetime or the next, mess with my work."

Trina heaved a breath. "Now, I'm going down and getting my kit so I can deal with the mess you've made of yourself."

"That's nice, really, but I don't have time for—" Eve winced as Trina fisted her hands on her hips. "That would be great. Thanks."

When Trina strode out, Eve stepped up to Mavis, gave her a hard look, and took her wine. She downed it, then scowled at her friend and her husband. "The first one who smirks eats this glass."

chapter twenty-one

She was up by six, and dove into the shower. She intended to round up her troops by eight, report to Whitney, then contact Karen Stowe.

She intended for Yost to hear the cage door clang behind him by noon.

"You're looking pleased with yourself, Lieutenant," Roarke said as he stepped under the spray behind her.

"I will be in a few hours."

"Perhaps we can make it sooner." He moved in, slid his hands up her body, over her breasts.

"Wanna play water games, hot shot?"

"I'll spot you ten points to the goal," he offered and nipped her shoulder.

"Keep your handicap." She reached around to run a hand down his flank, then felt a hard pull in her belly as his fingers slid over and tugged her nipples. "You got that gunk on your hands?"

"Trina assures me hot water only enhances the benefits. God knows you've got it hot enough."

"And I was here first, so don't even think about changing

the temp." She breathed deep, let her system relax. "I have to admit, it feels better when you put that stuff on than when she does."

"It's flavored." He turned her around, dipped his head, sucked her in. "Apricot."

"Yeah." Eve let her head fall back. "You definitely have the superior technique. Keep going."

Her blood hummed, and her mind, which had been razor-sharp on wakening, clouded. Steam billowed around them, thickening the air until her lungs clogged with it.

Then his hands were on her face, and his mouth crushed to hers.

He wanted to fill her, had to fight back the urge to take quickly and sate that need that had woken with him that morning. She was wrapped around him, her mouth open and avid. Her hips moved against his, a steady invitation.

Yes, he wanted to fill her. And instead, let her fill him.

Long, slim, sleeked with wet, she aroused him. He could live on the taste of her, the sharp heat of it. And when he used his fingertips to urge her up, to nudge her over, he swallowed that heat, and the strangled cry of pleasure that rode on it.

Every inch of her body throbbed. He could bring her that. Did bring her that, time and again. And she could feel his muscles quiver and know she brought the same to him.

Damaged, he'd said he'd been, and God knew so had she. Yet somehow they continually managed to heal each other.

There was no past when they came together.

Swamped with love, aroused beyond reason, she roped her arms around his neck. "Now, now, now!"

He drove into her, drove hard as they both seemed to need it. She cried out again, fisted her hands in the wet silk of his hair. When he lifted her hips, she hooked a leg around his waist.

And watched him. Watched him as he watched her. Tasted his breath as he tasted hers.

Slowly. Long, slow, and deep until her eyes began to swim with the pleasure of it. Endless, unspeakable pleasure that rolled inside her belly and up to the heart.

On a moan, she found his mouth with hers and poured herself into him.

And taking her, loving her, he emptied himself into her.

"Eve." It was all he said, all he thought, as he held her close under the torrent of water.

She stroked his back and hoped his heart was soothed. "Handicap, my butt."

It made him chuckle, as she'd hoped. "Next time you can spot me. Christ." He sniffed at her shoulder. "You smell fabulous."

"I ought to, with all that stuff Trina poured, rubbed, and dumped all over me last night. And a lot of help you were," she remembered, pulling back. "Where were you when she was threatening me with one of her temp tattoos?"

"Otherwise engaged. If you'd give her an hour once a month, she wouldn't be annoyed enough to ambush you." He decided it was best if he told her, rather than letting her find out on her own. "And, Eve, about the tattoo?"

"What?" She'd started out of the shower, stopped dead with a look of such horror he had to fight back a laugh. "She didn't. I'll kill her."

She raced to the mirror, and knowing Trina's favorite spot twisted around to look at her own ass. "Goddamn it! She got me. What the hell is it? A pony? Why did she paint a pony on my butt?"

"I believe, if you look closer, you'll see it's a small donkey. Or what might be referred to as a jackass."

"Oh great, oh very funny."

"I suppose we can conclude she wanted to make a point."

"I bet she didn't leave any remover around either. You tell anybody—"

"My lips are sealed. It's kind of cute, actually, the way it's kicking up its back legs."

"Shut up, Roarke. Just shut up." And to make sure of it, she slammed into the drying tube.

By nine, Eve had a tactics team placed in strategic spots on Second Avenue. They had orders to observe and report only, unless flagged. Trina's friend, who turned out to be a reasonably sensible woman, manned the main counter at the wholesale shop. Peabody, in soft clothes, replaced the scheduled clerk at another, and McNab, dressed as only he could, stood in as a customer.

Eve would have bought his cover in a heartbeat. If anyone looked less like a cop than McNab in a puce skinsuit and chartreuse knee boots, she'd like to see him.

She set up in the storeroom, watching the store on monitor with Stowe.

"Before this goes down, I want to thank you for coming through on your promise."

"Let's just get it done." Eve glanced at the long-barreled blaster holstered on Stowe's hip. "I need him alive."

"Yeah." Stowe drew the weapon, turned it to show Eve it was set on medium stun. "I thought about doing it otherwise. Thought hard about it. Imagined it." She holstered the blaster again. "But it wouldn't bring Winnie back. We'll take him breathing."

In the sales area, Peabody bore down and stepped to where McNab loitered at the end of her station. "I'm going to apologize for starting that argument yesterday. It was an inappropriate comment made at an inappropriate time."

"Yeah." He had brooded over it all night. Brooded over her. And did she have to look so pretty today? Did she have to be wearing a soft-looking dress and pink lip dye? Was she trying to kill him? "Forget it."

"If we forget it, we'll do it again. You're Feeney's man, and I'm Dallas's. That means we'll be working together a lot. Maybe we made a mistake and started doing more than working together, but there's no point in having that screw up both of us on the job."

"You figure it was a mistake. Just like that?"

His tone made her want to snipe back, but she reined herself in. "No, not really. I don't think it was a mistake, it just worked around to one." One she wished she could fix more than she'd expected. How could she have known she'd miss the skinny jerk? "I'd like to try to get past it, and go back to where we can be professional."

He'd have liked to go back, too. Back to that storeroom so that he could make it all come out different. "Okay, fine. I can chill with that."

"Good. That's good." But it didn't feel all that good. "Look maybe we could . . ." She trailed off as a customer walked in.

McNab took a moment to swear under his breath, then straightened to begin the practiced rap about a new hair reconstructive serum.

Eve checked her wrist unit. Eleven thirty-eight. The civilian clerk was holding up well. Apparently Peabody and McNab had negotiated a truce.

She hoped things were going as smoothly for Feeney and Roarke at the hotel. She pulled out her communicator to check on the status there, and it beeped in her hand.

"Dallas."

"Lieutenant, subject approaching target area, on foot. Heading south on Second Avenue, crossing on Twenty-fourth. Subject is alone, wearing a light brown overcoat, dark brown trousers."

"Positive ID?"

"That's affirmative. We have him in view, approaching Twenty-third. Should be in your target, thirty seconds."

"Stand by. Do not move in unless ordered. Peabody, McNab, you copy?"

"That's affirmative."

"All teams, keep communications open. Saddle up, Stowe," Eve said. "And let's take this bastard. I'm going out the back to circle, cut off his Second Avenue exit. Wait until he's in the shop. We'll back you up."

"I owe you." She kept an eye on the monitor, and a hand on the door.

Eve darted out the back, jogged around to the corner. She came up half a block from Yost, matched her pace to his brisk stroll.

When he reached for the shop door, she slid her hand inside her jacket.

And saw Jacoby race across the street, weapon drawn.

"FBI! Freeze!"

She didn't have time to swear. She kicked in, closed the distance, and was still three feet away when Yost whirled and met Jacoby head-on.

It was like watching a unibike plowed down by an airbus.

"Down! Police! Get down!" She mowed through pedestrians, her weapon snapping into her hand. She saw Jacoby hit the pavement, heard her communicator go wild.

With no chance for a clear shot, she ran in pursuit as Yost surged south, knocking bystanders aside, dodging his way into the street and into traffic.

"Hold fire! Hold fire!" One ill-aimed blast, and civilians would be hit.

For a big man, he moved fast, and he moved smooth. He swung west at the next corner, dragging a glide-cart over with brute strength. It tumbled into Eve's path, spilling its guts over street and sidewalk and causing its operator to shriek.

Rather than skirting it, she jumped on, took one running step over its side and, using it as a springboard, leaped.

The momentum bought her half the distance.

"Crossing to Third. Vehicular backup! Give me vehicular backup. I am in pursuit of suspect, and crossing Third at Twenty-second."

To free her hand, she jammed the communicator in her pocket, bore down, and made another leap.

She caught Yost midbody. It was like hitting a slab of re-inforced steel. She'd have sworn her bones rattled. But the tackle took him down to one knee. Before he could shove her aside and scramble up, she had her weapon pressed to the pulse in his throat.

Where it was lethal.

"Do you want to die?" she asked. "Want to die on the street like a sidewalk sleeper?"

Even as Yost raised his hands, she heard feet pounding behind her. McNab, sweat streaming down his face, chest heaving, moved into position, his weapon aimed at Yost's head.

"He's covered, Lieutenant."

"On your face, Sly. Spread them."

"There seems to be some mistake," Yost began. "My name is Giovanni—"

"On the ground." She pushed up with her weapon. "Belly down, or my finger's going to slip."

He spread himself out on the sidewalk, arms twitching as she yanked them back to cuff his wrists.

It couldn't be, was all he could think. It couldn't end for him like this, facedown on the street like a common criminal. "I want an attorney."

"Yeah, I'm real worried about your rights and obliga-tions right now." She dug in his pockets, came out with an empty pressure syringe. And a length of slim silver wire. "Well, well, look what I found."

"An attorney," he repeated in his high voice. "I insist on being treated with respect."

"Yeah?" She stood up, planted her boot on his thick neck. "You be sure to tell the guards and your fellow in-mates at Penal Station Omega you insist on respect. They don't get a lot of laughs up there. Call for a cooler, McNab. I want this guy on ice."

"Yes, sir. Dallas? Your nose is bleeding."

"Bashed it into him with the tackle." She swiped at it with the back of her hand, looked down at the bright red in disgust. "Jacoby?"

"I don't know. I had to jump over him to pursue. I think Stowe stayed back with him."

"It's her collar, McNab."

"Aw, jeez, Dallas."

"That's how it is. You're out of shape, Detective. Start spending some time in the gym so you don't pant like a dog when you run a few blocks."

She nodded as black-and-whites screamed to the curb and members of the tactical team streamed down the side-walk. "Here's your ride, Sly."

He looked up, saw her face, saw the faces of onlookers who tried to crowd in and stare. "I should have killed you first."

"Yeah, there's that hindsight thing. Hold this asshole for Special Agent Karen Stowe. He's hers. I'm Mirandizing him on her behalf." She crouched down, waited until Yost looked into her eyes.

"Winifred Cates was a friend of Agent Stowe's. I'm doing this for her. You're under arrest for assault, battery, sexual assault, and the murder by contract of various individuals whose names will be listed at the time of your booking. And that's just in this state. I'm tossing in resisting arrest, assault on a federal officer, destruction of property, and fleeing the scene of a crime. Interpol and Global will be right behind me with their party favors. You have the right, you miserable son of a bitch, to remain silent."

Eve walked back toward Second Avenue favoring her left shoulder. She'd jammed it hard against Yost's kidney area and it ached like a bad tooth. Her nose was throbbing in counterpoint and felt as if it had spread across her face and into her ears.

She'd have plunked down a hundred dollars for a bag of ice.

"Sir!" Peabody sprinted to the corner, took one look at Eve's face and winced. "Ow."

"Am I messed up?" Eve lifted hesitant fingers to her nose. Hissed.

"Just a little swollen. It'd be worse if you'd broke it. Looks like it bled really good."

"Which explains why small children ran screaming when I passed by. Where's Stowe?"

"Inside. We got the word you brought Yost down. Sir, I would have pursued as backup, but McNab ordered me to stay, and Agent Jacoby was down."

"You did right, so did McNab. What's the status on Jacoby?"

"I don't know. Stowe's in contact with the MTs. Yost caught him with a pressure syringe, heavy barbs, dead in the heart. Dallas, he went down like a tree under the ax. By the time Stowe and I got to him, his heart had stopped. We administered CPR, and the MTs' response was fast. They zapped him, got a rhythm. He was still unconscious when they took him off-scene."

"Even blind ambition and gross stupidity don't deserve a stopped heart. Stand by, Peabody. Keep this area clear. No statements to the media at this time."

Eve swung inside. Trina's helpful friend was sitting on the floor, her head back, and what looked like about ten ounces of red wine in a water glass. She gave Eve a wavery smile and kept sipping steadily.

"Are you all right? Do you need medical attention?"

She held up the glass. "This is all the medical attention I need. I'm going to drink this, go home, and sleep for eight hours."

"I'll arrange your transportation. You know it's essential

you speak to no one about what happened here this morning until you're cleared to do so."

"Yeah, you drilled me." She studied Eve's face. "I got some products that'll help with that swelling and bruising. It's great for after major face and body sculpting work. You want some free samples?"

"I'm okay. Where's Agent Stowe?"

"In the back."

"Don't go anywhere," Eve told her, then pushed through into the storeroom.

Stowe paced a line through the boxes as she talked on her pocket-link. "Keep me apprised of his status. You can reach me at this number at all times. Thanks."

"Jacoby?" Eve asked.

"In a coma." Stowe shoved the 'link in her pocket. "Critical. His heart—they may have to try to replace it. He took a direct hit. Clicked him off like a switch. I should have gone with him. He's my partner. I wanted to see you. Needed to tell you. I didn't tip Jacoby. He must have sensed something was up and tailed me. I didn't tell him about this. I didn't break faith with you."

"If I thought you had, I wouldn't have Yost on ice waiting for you to book and interview."

Stowe turned and faced Eve. "You tracked him, set up the op, and you took him down. It's your collar, Dallas."

"We made a deal. You stuck to yours, I stuck to mine. He's at Central, maximum holding. They're expecting you."

Stowe nodded. "You ever need a favor from the Bureau, it's yours."

"I'll keep it in mind. You've got to stall him on the lawyer, keep him incommunicado until after oh two hundred hours. You have a little delay getting to Central, the paperwork gets lost for his transfer to your authority."

"If I can't delay for fourteen hours, give or take, I shouldn't be working for the government. He won't tip anybody about your op. Whenever you want to interview him about your two homicides, I'll clear it. He give you that?" she asked, jerking her chin toward Eve's face.

"I got it on the tackle, bringing him down."

"You ought to put some ice on it."

"Tell me."

"It's been a pleasure." Stowe held out her hand. "Lieutenant."

"Likewise. Agent."

She ordered Peabody to find the closest 24/7 and buy some ice. In direct violation of orders, Peabody hit the closest pharmacy and brought back a cold patch with anti-inflammatories and a bottle of pain blockers.

"Where's my ice?"

"This is better than ice."

"Officer—"

"Lieutenant, if you use this patch correctly, your face will not be swollen up like a beat-up ad blimp when you check in at the hotel to recon with security. Which means, Roarke won't haul you off to the MTs or administer first aid himself. Since you particularly dislike both of these eventualities, I suggest you take what I got you and avoid this future annoyance."

"That was good, Peabody. Really good. I hate you, but it was good." Eve snatched the box, scowled at the instructions for the patch. "How the hell does this thing work?"

"I'll do it. Just hold still."

So Peabody opened the box, activated the anti-inflammatory, and affixed the patch over Eve's aching nose. The relief was considerable, and it was quick, but one look in the mirror had Eve swearing.

"I look like an idiot."

"Yes, you do," Peabody agreed, studying the result of the white strip over Eve's face. "But you looked like an idiot without it, too. Sir. Got your sun shades?"

"No, I can never keep track of them."

"Take mine." Generously, Peabody pulled hers out of her pocket, handed them over. "Better," she said when Eve slipped the dark glasses on. "A little better. Want some water to down the blocker?"

"I don't want a blocker."

"It'll give the patch a boost. Make it work faster."

Though she suspected that was a lie, Eve took the tiny blue pill, swallowed, snarled. "There. Do you think I could get back to work now, Nurse Peabody?"

"Yes, sir, I think that's the best we can do for you right now."

She stopped by the hospital first to check on Lane. He was in a gentle twilight sleep, with his condition listed as satisfactory. The cover of allergic reaction was holding. Kept quarantined, he was allowed no visitors.

Eve was informed his mother had been to the hospital twice, and had watched him through the view glass. Liza Trent had signed in once, and had stayed for under five minutes.

If any other friends or associates had come by, they'd evaded the log. Eve had come armed with a warrant and was able to access copies of the security discs for Lane's floor with only half the usual hassle.

"Michel Gerade," she said when she played the disc back in her office. He stood, frowning at Lane through the viewing glass. "Nice of him to visit his sick pal."

"He doesn't look concerned so much as pissed."

"Yeah, and he didn't bring a get-well present, did he? This confirms Gerade's presence in New York. If he participates in this attempted heist, we may link him solid to Yost. Diplomatic immunity won't cover his sorry ass on conspiracy to commit murder."

"Neither one of the Naples men showed up on disc?"

"No. I'm betting Gerade there drew the straw for errand boy. Make sure Lane is hospitalized as advertised. See here, he goes to the nurse's station, tries to pump for information. Concerned friend. Charm, charm. She bends enough to look up the chart and give him exactly what we want him to have. Severe allergic reaction resulting in seizure. Complete bed rest and mild sedation in quarantine for forty-eight hours while tested."

Eve watched Gerade walk toward the elevator. "They won't like it, but they're not going to abort a plan this long-term and complex because one of their group's in la-la land. As far as they're concerned, he'd already done his job."

She ejected the disc, filed it. "Now let's go do ours."

chapter twenty-two

It was seventeen hundred hours when Eve walked into The Palace Hotel. She used the main lobby entrance. She wanted to do a walk-through, using her own eyes and ears and instincts to map out the hotel and gauge its rhythm before she went up to base control.

The two-tier lobby was a sea of marble and mosaic, the kind of rich and regal colors and designs she'd seen on one of her trips with Roarke to Italy.

Exotic arrangements of flowers speared and spilled out of urns taller than a man. The staff was dressed in royal red or blue, depending on their function.

The guests dressed rich.

She watched a six-foot woman, wrapped in what looked like filmy scarves from neck to knee, lead a trio of tiny white dogs on a triple leash.

"Augusta."

"What?"

"Augusta," Peabody repeated in Eve's ear, nodding toward the whip-thin woman and her furballs. "This year's primo model. God, I'd kill to have legs like that. And that's

Bee-Sting over there. Lead singer for Crash and Burn. And, oh jeez, just coming off the elevator, left bank, is Mont Tyler. *Screen Queen Magazine* voted him sexiest man of the decade. It sure is fun working with you, Dallas."

"If you've finished gawking, Peabody."

"If we have time, I could gawk a little longer." And her head did swivel, seesawing back and forth, up and down as she followed Eve across the lobby.

Eve was doing some scanning herself. She measured distances to exits, to elevator banks. She spotted two of the undercovers pulling bell staff duty. She rechecked security cam positions. She looked for holes.

And as she climbed the three flights to the ballroom level, she checked out every floor between.

Security, human and droid, were on duty, flanking the entrances to the Magda Lane Display, discreetly rounding the perimeter. People queued up, wandered through to sigh and gasp over sparkling gowns, glittering jewels, the photographs, the holo-prints, the small mementos, and grand costumes.

Each display or bank of displays was ringed inside red velvet rope. That was for show. The sensor shields ringing those same displays were invisible.

Those were for security.

Auction catalogues, disc or commemorative hard copy, were on sale to those who wanted to shell out over twelve hundred dollars.

A sampling of the catalogue could be accessed on-screen in hotel guest rooms at no charge.

"They're shoes," Eve finally said, pausing by a pair of silver pumps. "Somebody else's shoes. You want to wear somebody else's shoes, you go to a recycle mart."

"But, sir, it's like buying magic."

"It's like buying somebody else's shoes," Eve corrected, and satisfied for the moment, started out.

Magda, and her entourage, stepped off the elevator.

"Eve. I'm so glad I've run into you." Magda hurried for-ward, both hands outstretched. Her waterfall of hair was scooped up at the neck. And her eyes were tired. "My son."

"Yes, I know. I'm sorry he's ill. How's he doing?"

"They tell me he'll be fine. Some silly reaction. But they're keeping him sedated and quarantined. I can't even let him know I'm there."

"Now, Magda, of course he knows." Mince patted her arm, but his gaze skipped uneasily to Eve's. "Magda's worrying herself sick over that boy," he said. And his eyes said clearly: Make it stop.

"He's being well taken care of." Eve gave Magda's hands a reassuring squeeze.

"Well, I hope . . . In any case, I'm told you were there with him when he became ill."

"Yeah, that's right. I'd dropped by to see him to go over some of the security details."

"He was fine when I left." Liza gave Eve a piercing look. "Just fine."

"He certainly seemed to be. So, he didn't complain ear-lier about being a little queasy, dizzy?"

Back to you, sweetheart, Eve thought.

"No, he was fine."

"He probably didn't want to worry you. He mentioned he'd been feeling a little off. But that was after he started to look pale and clammy and I asked him if he was okay. He got shaky fast after that, said he was sorry, but he needed to lie down. My aide suggested we call the house doctor."

"Yes, sir," Peabody confirmed. "I didn't like his color."

"He didn't want the fuss. I was about to send Peabody to get him some water, when he started to seize. We called for medical assistance. There was a rash spreading just under the neck of his sweater. They clicked on allergic reaction right off."

"Thank God you were there. I hate to think what might

have happened if he'd been alone and unable to call for help."

"You could have let me know," Liza interrupted. "I waited and waited for him at Rendezvous. I was worried sick about Vinnie."

"Sorry. Didn't think of it. At the time, he was my priority."

"Of course." And breathing a little easier, Magda smiled. "The important thing is Vince got treatment quickly." She glanced toward the ballroom. "He's going to hate missing all this, after all his hard work."

"Yeah," Eve said. "Bad break."

"Man, Dallas, you were so good." Peabody beamed as they rode the private elevator to base control. "Maybe you should have thought about becoming an actor."

"Yeah, that was a big mistake on my part. Magda's going to have to take it on the chin tomorrow when it comes out about her son. I'm sorry for that."

She stepped out of the elevator and into Roarke's conception of base control.

"Oh. Oh, Dallas," Peabody whispered, overcome by the sheer glamour of the owner's suite.

"Don't drool, Peabody, it's unattractive. And try to remember, we're here to work."

The living area was a long sweep of warm color, plush fabrics, thick rugs in gracious patterns over acres of blond wood. A gleaming copper sculpture sleeked down one wall, spilling deep blue water in a gentle arch into a small, free-form pool decked with flowers and ferns.

Tumbling from the dome ceiling was a chandelier formed of hundreds of slim globes in that same deep blue. The tone was repeated in the grand piano and the marble hearth and mantel of a cozy fireplace.

A spiral of copper led up to a second level. On its landing, pots trailed tangled vine roses.

The atmosphere was so rarefied even the presence of

cops, stacked equipment, and a half-dozen portable surveillance monitors couldn't lower it.

It was embarrassing.

When she heard a burst of laughter, Eve strode through
the luxury, rounded a curve, and stared hard at the scene in
the dining room.

The long table was loaded with food. The banquet, she
thought, had been going on for some time from the looks
of it. Plates and platters and bowls had been scavenged for
their contents. The air still hung with the scents of roasted
meat, spices, sauces, and melting chocolate.

Ranged around the scene of the crime were McNab, a
pair of uniforms—including the young and promising Officer Trueheart, whom she'd assumed would know better—
Feeney, Roarke's head of security, and the culprit himself.

"What the hell is this?"

At her voice, McNab quickly swallowed what was in his
mouth, started to choke and turn beet-red, while Feeney
pounded him helpfully on the back. The two uniforms
came to rigid attention, Roarke's man looked elsewhere.
And Roarke greeted her warmly.

"Hello, Lieutenant. Can I fix you a plate?"

"You, you—" She jabbed her finger at the uniforms. "At
your stations. McNab, you're a disgrace. Wipe that mus-
tard off your chin."

"It's cream sauce, sir."

"You." She aimed the finger at Roarke. "With me."

"Always."

He strolled out behind her, through a pretty den where
another cop was snacking on cocktail shrimp and studying
yet another monitor. Eve gave him a hard look, but kept
going until she'd reached the relative privacy of the master
bedroom suite.

Then she whirled.

"This is not a goddamn party."

"Certainly not."

"What *are* you doing, ordering up half the food in New York for my men?"

"Providing them with fuel. Most people require it at fairly regular intervals."

"A plate of sandwiches, a couple of pizzas, okay. But you've provided them with enough damn fuel to make them logy and stupid."

"Lieutenant, we have hours yet. Without an occasional break from the stress, tedium, and monotony, we'll all be logy and stupid."

He lifted her rigid chin, turned her face right and left, nodded. "Not bad," he decided, "but you'll want a blocker boost and another hit of anti-inflammatory."

"McNab," she hissed and made him laugh.

"You impressed the bloody hell out of him, taking that minor mountain down with one tackle. But did you have to use your face? I'm very fond of it."

"Apparently you've been brought up-to-date."

"Apparently. When will you get your shot at Yost?"

"I'll wait for tomorrow. He'll pay, Roarke. Between local and federal charges, covering two decades, he'll never see the light of day again. He'll get maximum, solitary, concrete cage. And he knows it."

He nodded again. "Yes, I've thought of that. And I'm content that his life from now on will be worse than death for a man of his tastes and habits."

"Okay." She drew a breath. "You may have to be satisfied with that. Taking Yost out was my priority, and I couldn't risk any delay in doing so. But removing him may screw up this op. I don't see him as directly involved. He's an assassin, not a thief, and his type wouldn't soil themselves by participating in a heist. But in the past few days, we've eliminated Lane, Yost, and Connelly from the mix. Naples isn't stupid. Even with the time and investment he's put in, he may very well abort."

"Mick won't tip him."

She wasn't going to argue that. "Whether he does or doesn't, he's out. With Naples's main security tool running for cover, a key inside man in the hospital, and his assassin on ice, it's dicey. Maybe we'll get Yost to roll on him. Maybe. We're not going to be able to offer him much in return so it'll be a matter of pressure instead of trade. We may both have to be satisfied that we've prevented a crime, and Magda's auction goes off as scheduled."

"Will you be satisfied?"

"No. I want the bastard. Giving Yost to Stowe was . . . It just was. But Naples and the rest of them would be mine. I also know that the job doesn't always give satisfaction. One way or the other, we proceed as outlined."

By midnight, she'd OD'd on coffee and had studied on monitor every inch of every public area in the hotel. With Feeney and Roarke's man she had reviewed, stage by minute stage, every variable in the security system.

When her commander came in, she rose and prepared to give him a full status report.

"A moment of your time, Lieutenant." He gestured her across the room, near the whispering waterfall. His eyes were dark and tired. "Yost self-terminated."

"Sir?"

"He was remanded to federal custody two hours ago. They were checking him into maximum holding in their facility. The clerk had a cup of coffee on his desk. The son of a bitch managed to grab it, smash it, and still cuffed, slit his own throat with a shard."

"So he got the easy way after all," she murmured. "And cost me my link to Naples."

"I'm sorry, Lieutenant."

"Yes, sir. Thank you for telling me."

"Agent Jacoby's condition is promising. His medical team believes his heart is responding to treatment. He's currently stable."

"That's good. And at least he won't be around to screw this up. If there's anything to screw up."

"I'd like to see this end with you. You remain in command." He glanced around the suite. "Looks like there's plenty of room for one more."

"Check out the dinner buffet," Eve said sourly. "We might still have egg rolls."

She stationed herself at the main bank of monitors in the living area. From there she could scan and search the target areas both interior and exterior. The night staff of the hotel went about its business, such as it was. Room service delivered or removed the occasional tray from guest rooms. A few guests returned from a night on the town while others strolled out to begin one.

Like the city, the building would never be completely quiet. Business and pleasure were twenty-four-hour activities.

She made an LC in short red satin crossing the lower lobby toward the exit. The woman looked smug and gave her little silver bag a pat. A nice fat tip, Eve assumed, then sharpened her focus as Liza passed the LC on her way in.

Liza glanced lazily around. A bit too lazily. A bit too thoroughly, Eve decided. "Feeney, take a look. I'd say our girl there has a recorder on. She's giving her pals an inside look."

"Enhance and magnify," Feeney ordered. "Sector eighteen through thirty-six." He made grunting noises as the image popped up, then ordered higher magnification on a smaller sector. Eve was treated to a very close view of Liza's cleavage.

"Now, that's beautiful."

"Jesus, Feeney."

He blinked, flushed. "I ain't talking about her, you know. The neck thing she's playing with. The dangle there's a microrecorder. State-of-the-fucking-art, too. She's probably transmitting a three-sixty right now. And full audio. The doorman breaks wind, that baby'll pick it up."

"Can you jam it?"

"Oh yeah. I could jam a transmission from the moon with the equipment Roarke brought in." He looked so delighted by the idea, Eve had to wave him off.

"Not now. Let her do the recon for them. Let them see everything nice and quiet and in order. Goddamn, Feeney, they're going for it after all." She checked her wrist unit. "Forty-five minutes to mark. Keep her monitored," she ordered, then rose to rally her troops.

At mark minus fifteen, Eve moved to the ready station, a meeting room one floor below ballroom level. Liza had already reconned the ballroom area, strolling past the target and giving her associates a shot of the secured doors and warning lights. Now she was tucked in her room, and Feeney would wait for the signal to jam. Two uniforms with a master were on hold to move into her room and take her into custody.

Eve was going to be sorry to miss it.

She fixed on her lapel recorder. "Feeney, you read."

"Gotcha."

She ran through her other team leaders, checking them on audio, and on the monitors. She checked her weapon, rolled her shoulder, and was pleased it had loosened up.

Then she scowled as Roarke slipped into the room.

"Off limits to civilians. Upstairs."

"As it's my hotel, nothing is off limits. I have clearance, from your commander. I'm in on this, Lieutenant."

She didn't doubt he could handle himself, though in his black sweater and trousers, he looked more like the type who'd do the breaking in than the type to frown on such activities.

"Are you armed?"

He glanced meaningfully at her recorder, letting her

know he was fully aware everything he said was being transmitted. "Expert consultants, civilian, aren't authorized to carry weapons."

Which meant he was carrying. Since she preferred that to him going naked into a bust, she let it pass.

"When we move, we move fast," she said to the men and women gathered in the room. "We contain quickly and completely. You have your teams. Cover each other's backs. These people will have no place to go and are likely to resist. Our intelligence indicates they'll be armed with tranqs, but we can't be sure they won't carry something more lethal. Restrain and disarm. Be aware that jamming their transmissions will also jam ours from the target area until we have it contained. Let's keep that time frame to a minimum. Lenick, get the civilian some body armor and a recorder."

At mark minus five, she was glued to the monitor, glanced up only when Roarke came up beside her. "Where's your body armor?" she asked.

"Where's yours?"

"I have the option of wearing it."

"And you opt not to because it's bulky and hampers quick movements. Let's not waste time arguing. There's Honroe, moving into position at the delivery entrance. He'll find out shortly how much I disapprove of moonlighting."

"He goes down with the rest of them, but I'll make sure you're given a minute to fire him."

"Appreciate it."

"Here's the maxibus, right on schedule. Switching op to yellow light. Be ready."

She watched the bus swerve, clip the front fender of the oncoming car. It tipped on its six side wheels, shivered, then toppled like a turtle to slide, sparks showering, into the neighboring building.

There was an impressive smashing of glass, a nice little poof of smoke. On cue, cars stopped, and people began to run toward or away from the accident. The shrill scream of the jeweler's alarm system was a muffled buzz over her audio.

On the next monitor, she watched the delivery truck glide smoothly into place at the hotel's rear, and Honroe step out of the shadows.

Like Roarke, the six figures who leaped out of the truck were dressed in black, with the addition of caps that fit snugly over heads and thin gloves that protected the hands and kept the fingers nimble.

"Mick's with them," Roarke murmured. "He's seeing it through. I didn't give him credit for it."

That's for later, Eve thought. "Seven, repeat, seven subjects, entering building from the west, delivery level."

"Wait." Eve laid a hand on his arm, gaze steady on the monitor. "There's three in the lorry," Roarke continued.

"How do you—"

"Mick's telling me. It's an old code. Three in the lorry, all with eyes and ears. Hand lasers, cop-style. One mini-launcher, heat-seeking, fully loaded."

When Mick entered the building, Roarke shifted to the next monitor. He watched as his friend went to work on the first security panel, and listened with half an ear as Eve relayed the incoming data to her teams.

"The men inside are carrying, too. More than the tranqs previously reported. Two added basic police-issue lasers. There's a woman, third back. Hand-to-hand expert. She has a blade in her right boot." Roarke glanced to Eve. "You'll use this for him."

It wasn't a question. He didn't doubt her sense of justice.

"Let's bring it down, then I'll do what I can."

"There, he's through the second level. He's better than he was."

She watched Mick jerk up his thumb, then pound with the others up the service stairs. They moved fast and orderly, telling her they'd drilled well and drilled often.

But so had she. Her mind stayed cool and focused as Mick stopped at the fire door on the ballroom level, took out a handheld unit, and telescoped it out to elbow-length. His fingers were quick and steady, and made her wonder what was in his thoughts. His unit beeped three times, and its lights glowed green.

He went through the doors first, heading for the target at a jog.

"Move out," Eve ordered. "Feeney, prepare to jam on my signal."

"Copy that." His voice spoke in her ear. "They're at the doors, working on outer security. Second from the rear's antsy. He's sweating. Hey, Dallas, I got an ID on him. Looks like Gerade wanted to be in on the kill."

"Beautiful."

"And they're through. E-guy's adjusting his jammer. It's flipping through levels, backtracking. He's keying in another code manually. Must've gotten it from one of the inside men. He's got a thirty-percent clearance."

Eve stepped onto ballroom level, held up her hand. From the other direction, her secondary team leader mirrored her move. At her nod, they moved forward. Fast.

"Jam it!" she ordered and swung through the door. "Police! Hands in the air. Up!" she shouted, then sent out a warning blast that nipped the toes of the woman's boots as she reached down.

Return fire whizzed past her ear. Even as she pivoted, she saw one of the figures in black jerk back from the stun shot out by one of her team.

Someone shoved over a huge glass display. It boomed and shattered like cannon fire. Through the shouts and scrambles for cover or escape, she saw Mick send Roarke a sunny grin.

Then she was too busy to be amused or baffled as the woman in black hurled a two-foot vase at her head, and followed the toss with a screaming leap.

Eve had a half-second to decide. The undoubted satisfaction of a good, bloody hand-to-hand, or . . . With some regret she fired her weapon and dropped her opponent into an unconscious heap.

"Too bad," Roarke commented. "I would have enjoyed watching that."

He turned toward Mick and, since there was little left to do, slipped the weapon he wasn't supposed to have back into his pocket. "I'd like a look at that jammer of yours."

"Well now, I have a feeling it'll be going into police custody. A terrible waste." Mick glanced about as his former associates were rounded up. In a slick move, he palmed the jammer to Roarke, then stepped away, raising his hands cooperatively in the air.

There would be times, countless times later, when Roarke would look back and remember that moment. How he'd stood there, amused, exhilarated. And unguarded.

He'd remember the laughter in Mick's eyes, and how it had switched over, in a flash, to alarm.

He'd turned, rounded on the balls of his feet, one hand digging out the weapon. Fast. Christ, he'd always been fast.

But this time, this one time, not fast enough.

Gerade had the knife at waist level, the blade a hard glint in the brilliant lights. His eyes were wild, mad, terrified. Roarke heard Eve shout, saw the stream from her weapon hit. Even that, too late.

At the same instant Mick leaped in front of him, and took the knife in the belly.

"Well, hell." Mick sent Roarke a bemused look as he went down.

"Ah, no." Roarke was on his knees, pressing a hand to the wound. Kill blood, deep and dark, gushed through his fingers.

"Little fucker," Mick managed through hideous waves of pain. "I never gave him the guts for it. Never knew he was carrying. How bad he get me?"

"Not so bad."

"Damn, you used to be handier with a lie."

"I need an ambulance, surgical MTs." Eve rushed over, took stock, and continued to shout into her communicator. "I've got a man down. Knife wound to the belly. Get me medical assistance in here."

Then she stripped off her shirt without a thought, and tossed it to Roarke so he could staunch the wound.

"Now, that was a pretty thing to do." Mick's face had already gone from white to gray. "Am I forgiven then, Eve darling?"

"Stay quiet." She crouched down to check his pulse. "Help's on the way."

"I owed him that, you know." Mick shifted his eyes to Roarke. "I owed you that, though I didn't expect to pay so dear. Christ, doesn't anybody have any fucking drugs for a man?" He fumbled out, gripped Roarke's hand desperately. "Hold onto me, won't you? There's a lad."

"You'll be all right." Roarke squeezed as if he could make it so by will alone. "You'll come round."

"You know I'm done." A trickle of blood bubbled through his lips. "You got my signals, didn't you?"

"Yes, I got them."

"Just like old times. Do you remember . . ." He moaned, had to fight for a breath. "When we took the mayor's house in London, cleaning out his parlor while he was upstairs ramming it to his mistress while his wife was visiting her sister in Bath?"

He couldn't stop the blood. Couldn't hold back the stream of it. He could smell death creeping close, and could only pray Mick could not. "I remember you snuck up the stairs and took videos of it with his own bloody camera. And later we sold them back to him, and fenced the camera as well."

"Aye, aye, those were good times. Happiest of my life. Jesus, what a flaming shame it is that my mother, bless her black heart, should be right after all. At least I got the knife in my belly in a fine hotel and not a second-rate pub."

"Quiet, Mick, the MTs are coming."

"Oh, screw 'em." He sighed hugely, and for one moment his eyes were clear as crystal. "Will you light a candle for me in St. Pat's?"

Roarke's throat wanted to close, his mind to reject. But he nodded. "Aye."

"That's something then. Roarke, you were ever a true friend to me. It's happy I am for you that you found that one thing. See that you keep hold of it. *Slan*."

And turning his face to the side, he was gone.

"Ah, God." Helpless sorrow flooded over him, into him. He could do nothing but rock, his bloody hand clinging to Mick's while the sorrow drowned him. His eyes were stark, naked with it when they lifted to Eve's.

While the business of law went on around them, she rose, signaled her men and the MTs who rushed into the room back. And went to her husband. Kneeling with him, she put her arms around him, drew him in.

Roarke laid his head on his wife's breast, and grieved.

He was alone with his thoughts when dawn broke. From the window of his bedroom, he watched day tremble into life and whisk away the dark, layer by thin layer.

He'd hoped for rage, had searched for it. But he hadn't found it.

He didn't turn when Eve came in, but the worst of the ache eased because she was home.

"You've put in a long day, Lieutenant."

"So have you." She'd worried, all through the hours

she'd had to leave him to himself. She opened her mouth, shut it again. No, she couldn't offer the empty, standard line and tell him she was sorry for his loss. Not to Roarke, not for this.

"Michel Gerade has been charged with murder, first degree. He can scream diplomatic immunity until he chokes. It won't save him."

When Roarke didn't respond, she dragged a hand through her hair, tugged at her borrowed shirt. "I can break him," she continued. "He'll roll on the Napleses. He'd roll on his first-born if he thought it would help him."

"Naples is under, and he'll go deep and stay there." He turned now. "Did you think I wouldn't have checked already for myself? We've lost him. This time, at least, we've lost him and his bastard of a son. They're as out of reach as Yost is—burning in hell."

She lifted her hands. "I'm sorry."

"For what?" He crossed to her now and, in the soft half-light, cupped her face in his hands. "For what?" he repeated, kissing her cheeks, her brow. "For doing everything that could be done, and more than that? For, at the last, giving my friend, who was none of yours, the very shirt off your back? For being there for me when I needed you most?"

"You're wrong. Anyone who saves your life is a friend of mine. He helped us so that we went into that op fully prepared. And when we get Naples and his bastard of a son, he'll have had a part in that, too. You were right about him. There was no taste for bloodshed in him. And in the end, he stood up for you."

"He'd have said that wasn't so much of a thing altogether. I'll want to take him back to Ireland, and bury him among friends."

"Then we will. He was a hero, and the NYPSD is issuing him a posthumous citation that says so."

Roarke stared at her, took one step back. Then to Eve's

utter shock, threw back his head and roared with laughter. Deep, rich, from-the-belly laughter. "Oh Jesus, if he wasn't dead already, that would kill him for certain. A citation from the fucking cops as his epitaph."

"I happen to be a fucking cop," she reminded him between her teeth.

"No offense, no offense, my gorgeous and darling lieutenant." He plucked her off her feet, swung her around. And knowing just how Mick would have enjoyed it all, Roarke felt the worst of the weight of grief lift. "He'll have a great laugh over it, wherever he might be."

She could have said it wasn't a joke, but an honor. One of the highest and most serious it was in her power to arrange. But she was so relieved to see the glow back in Roarke's eyes, she shrugged. "Well, ha-ha. Now put me down. I want to catch some sleep before I go back in. With this auction coming off as planned tomorrow night, it's going to be another long one."

"Let's sleep later. We're young yet."

He gave her a last spin. They would, he thought, start the day with a celebration of life, not a mourning of death.

Capturing her mouth with his, he stepped onto the wide platform and tumbled her onto the bed.